Reading *Isobel's Song* was pure fun. Author Daryl Lott weaves a fictional tale of Isobel and Kelvin throughout revolutionary Texas. As friends of Sam Houston, they are often at the most important events from traveling to Texas through the battle of San Jacinto. While it is historical fiction, you want to believe that someone like Isabel was around—especially at San Jacinto. This is a fun read—I highly recommend it!

— DR. EDDIE WELLER, PROFESSOR OF HISTORY,
PASADENA, TEXAS

Absorbing tale of early Texas seen through the eyes of young Isobel as she encounters major historical figures. Depicts the plight and betrayal of the American Indian tribes with devastating honesty during the Jacksonian era. A descriptive and truthful account of an exceptional time on the American frontier with noble and base characters on a life journey together. A touching origin prologue as she meets Davy Crockett in Tennessee as a young child forms a solid base.

— PATRICIA GARRETT, UNIVERSITY RESEARCH
LIBRARIAN (RET), HOUSTON, TEXAS

Isobel's Song is more than a good novel it's a journey that allows the reader to accompany the characters on their travels and experiences during the early Jacksonian period of American history. It's a journey to the Texas frontier from her sister state of Tennessee. The writer has woven a wonderful tapestry of American and Texas history together but has also infused them with the Christian faith that governs the lives and thinking of the main characters. It's a wonderful blend of fact, fiction and faith. The book draws you into the sights, sounds, and smells of that era. All your senses will be engaged. I think it's a wonderful read.

— REV. DOYLE DAVIS, BAPTIST PASTOR, HOUSTON, TEXAS

ISOBEL'S SONG

GRACE AND MERCY IN THE FIGHT FOR TEXAS

FAITH & FIDDLE SERIES
BOOK ONE

DARYL LOTT

The below two maps from *Texian Iliad A Military History of the Texas Revolution* by Stephen L. Hardin, University of Texas Press, 1994. Hardback Edition. Used by permission.

Map "Campaign of 1836"

Map "Battle of San Jacinto"

ISBN: 979-8-9993790-1-6 (paperback)
ISBN: 979-8-9993790-2-3 (hardback)
ISBN: 979-8-9993790-09 (ebook)
ISBN: 979-8-9993790-3-0 (audiobook)

Cover design and interior formatting by *Hannah Linder Designs*

For Becky
And Our Children and Grandchildren
(All Texans)
From the Following Texas Counties
Harris
Galveston
Hamilton
Cherokee
Bexar

INTRODUCTION

Some people enter our lives quietly, their purpose not immediately clear. In this story, you may meet a few such souls—characters who seem minor, one-dimensional, or cast in a certain light that doesn't tell their full story. They may appear for a moment and seem to vanish. Their situations may frustrate you. You may wonder why they're here at all.

But the road ahead is longer than a single book.

This story, like life, is not always tidy. Some threads won't tie off neatly by the final page. Some hearts won't be healed in time for the last chapter. But grace is patient. Growth takes root in silence. And sometimes the smallest seed becomes the mightiest branch.

You may also find situations that reach beyond the natural, where Heaven brushes the Earth. In quiet places, a melody might stir that no one else hears. In storms, a presence may stand unseen, guiding the way. These glimpses are not fantasy, but reflections of a deeper truth: God is near, even when He seems hidden. His calling can come like a whisper or like a song.

Though this book is part of a longer journey, rest assured, it offers a full and satisfying ending. You won't be left with a cliffhanger. What needs to be resolved will be, and what continues will do so with purpose.

So, if a character seems like a dead end, hold on. Their arc may just be beginning. Across these books, you'll find that no path is too crooked, no heart too far gone, and no melody too faint to be redeemed.

Welcome to the journey.

I opened my eyes, and the before sunlit room was now wrapped in outer darkness. Instantly I felt a shock running through all my frame; nothing was to be seen, and nothing was to be heard; but a supernatural hand seemed placed in mine. My arm hung over the counterpane, and the nameless, unimaginable, silent form or phantom, to which the hand belonged, seemed closely seated by my bedside. For what seemed ages piled on ages, I lay there, frozen with the most awful fears, not daring to drag away my hand; yet thinking that if I could but stir in one single inch, the horrid spell would be broken. I knew not how this consciousness at last glided away from me; but waking in the morning, I shudderingly remembered it all, and for days and weeks and months afterwards I lost myself in confounding attempts to explain the mystery. Nay, to this very hour, I often puzzle myself with it.

— MOBY-DICK, *CHAPTER IV*, HERMAN MELVILLE

PROLOGUE

September 13, 1813
Winchester, Tennessee

The rough fabric of Anne's skirt tugged hard against her waist as Isobel clung to it, her tiny feet dragging over the soggy ground. Every step sent a cold, sticky splash up her legs, but she barely noticed. The haze pressed in, heavy and stifling, and settled on her like damp heat. Around them, the unforgiving, bitter edge of the frontier erupted into havoc. Grating voices barked commands, curses sliced through the breeze like arrows, and she heard the distant wail of someone in despair.

She held Isobel's small hand tighter, and she wasn't sure if the tremor she felt rose from her daughter's fingers or her own. Step by step, she forced her focus forward. She wouldn't look back. Her daughter's wide eyes roved over the pandemonium, her young mind struggling to make sense of the harsh, unrelenting noise. Fear drummed a frantic beat in her breast, but she couldn't let it show. Not now. An anxious stare burned into her, silently pleading for some kind of comfort, some sign everything would be safe and well.

Forcing her lips into a smile that didn't quite reach her eyes, she gave the little girl's hand a gentle squeeze. "It's alright, darlin'. We're fine. Won't be long now." The lie tasted sour in her mouth as she fought to smooth the worry on her face. A prickling sensation crept over her skin and wrapped itself around her like a shawl.

Lachlan walked beside them, silent and strained. He scanned the mob expecting trouble at any moment. Anne could sense it too. Everything teetered on the brink.

"Call to arms!" The command tore through the town square and rippled out, heavy and electric.

"Fort Mims massacre! They done murdered us!" A man hollered, his face angry-red .

"Come on now, sign the roster! We need every fightin' man we can get!" A third man, parchment in hand, waved it high, as folks began to gather 'round, the gravity of his proclamation sinking into Anne's bones.

"What're ye plannin' on doin', Lachlan?" She reached down in fear and gathered little Isobel from the muddy trail. The child was too young to understand, but Anne could feel the tremble in her daughter's diminutive frame. She reckoned it reflected the storm building in her own heart.

"I'm aimin' to do my duty, woman." His speech was firm, unyielding, like a line drawn in the dirt. His eyes didn't meet hers though, fixed instead on the throng like he was already half-gone. "Just like our fathers did before me, there's no two ways about it."

She clutched Isobel tighter, feeling the fervor of her little body against her chest. She searched his face, desperate for a flicker of hesitation, a motive for him to stay. "Don't forget ye got a wee daughter right here."

Lachlan hardened. "She's the very reason I'm signin' up. Ye think I wanna see her scalp, or yours, danglin' on some wampum belt? That ain't happenin'."

Anne's stomach twisted. "William's one of your kin. Does he know anythin'?"

He shook his head. "He might be a Creek chief, but it don't mean I heard a lick of news from him."

The multitude swelled around them, tightening like a knot and pulling everyone closer together. Isobel spun and squirmed, slipping out of her mother's grip. Her elfin feet hit a slick, muddy puddle, and she splashed dirty water as she bounded away. Anne's heart hammered as she pressed through the swarm, chasing daughter through the chaos.

She detected a glint of Isobel's small figure weaving through the maelstrom. The little girl ducked under swinging arms and slipped through a forest of buckskin-clad legs, her miniature form almost invisible in the frenzy. She caught fleeting glimpses of the bright dress flashing against the darker colors of backwoods garb. Each flash spurred her forward, but no matter how fast she pushed herself, Isobel remained beyond her grasp, barely out of reach.

Anne spotted a rough-hewn table, where a large roster book lay open, its pages dancing in the wind, and a quill and ink rested nearby. Relief surged through her as she whispered a quick prayer of thanks. The book would draw the little girl as surely as a magnet pulls iron. Every evening, she read to her from their family Bible, the stories spinning a comforting ritual of worship and love.

Isobel looked back and spotted the table, interest flashing in her eyes just as Anne suspected it would. She dashed to the table and snatched up the quill pen with a fierce grip. The movement drew a collective gasp from the crowd, their chatter fading into stunned silence as they surveyed the small girl. She focused on the pen, curling her fingers around it with determination.

Anne strained against the mass, but the crowd held firm, unmoving. Her heart raced as she saw Isobel raise the plume, poised to write. Before the tip touched the paper, a tall man stepped forward, sweeping her into his arms. She dangled in his grasp, quill still clenched in her fist, her eyes wide with surprise and single-mindedness.

"Well now, I reckon you might be a bit young for signin' up, little missy." A grin tugged at the corners of his mouth as he hoisted her up. "Ain't seen too many soldiers in petticoats and bare feet, have we?" He chuckled, the sound rumbling deep in his chest, as he gently pried the pen from her teensy fingers. "But you sure got more spunk than a lot of grown men 'round here, I'll give ya that."

Isobel stared into the man's eyes, her lips shifting into a bright smile that looked to ease his formidable features. Before she could say a word, Anne reached them and held out her hands, swiftly gathering the youngster into her arms. "Thank ya kindly for grabbin' her, sir," Anne said with relief. "She has her own mind, this one."

"I reckon she does, ma'am. I got a couple of young'uns at home with my wife. They'll get away from ya. That's fer sure."

"Are you signin' up and leavin' your family here?" Something soft stirred in her as she looked at him.

Lachlan stood next to her, catching up after being stopped by another local as Anne had pursued their daughter.

"Yes, ma'am. I told my Polly I had to sign up if I didn't want her scalp strung up on a lodge wall. She weren't none too happy 'bout it, but we gotta do what we can to keep our homes safe from the redcoats and Indians."

"Aye, sir. It's what I said to my wife not a minute ago," Lachlan said.

"We got this wee lass here who's learnin' more with every step she takes." Anne glanced down at Isobel, her eyes shimmering with pride. "She's mindful, sharp, and as headstrong as a mule."

The tall man bent his knees, lowering himself until his eyes were level with Isobel's. His rough hands rested on his thighs, and his steely expression waned as he met her wide, curious look. "I see it in her eyes." He mellowed as he studied her. "She's got a sense for what's goin' on, don't she? Picks up on trouble. Does she know her name?"

Lachlan touched the brim of his hat. "Why don't ya ask her yourself?"

The man looked back to the child, a sunniness crossing his weathered face. "What's your name, lass?"

"Isobel," she said clearly, despite her small size. "You?"

"Well now, it's good to know ya, Isobel." He straightened with an easy chuckle. "I'm David."

"Lachlan MacIntosh," her father replied, extending his hand as David stood. "This is my wife, Anne."

"David Crockett." He shook their hands warmly. "It's a right pleasure to meet you folks. Looks like we'll be shoulder to shoulder on the battlefield."

"Sure seems that way," Lachlan agreed. "I reckon it's General Jackson we'll be teamin' up with."

"I hope so, but it'll likely be General John Coffee." Crockett bowed to Anne. "I wish my Polly was here to greet ya, ma'am. I'll make sure to tell her about you and leave her some notes on how to find your place while we're gone. You never know, ya might need a hand with somethin'."

"That's mighty kind of ya, David. Isobel and I manage most days, but knowin' we've got someone to reach out to is a real blessin'."

Anne's pulse quickened as she whirled toward the sound of a new voice. A man towered over the swarm, his voice crashing through the square like a storm. The words hit like lightning—*massacre, bloody redcoats*—echoing through the low murmur around them. She froze, dread seeping through her core. Her daughter couldn't hear this. Not now, not ever.

A glance at her daughter, though, stopped her cold. She was ready to whisk her away from the wicked speech, but Isobel wasn't scared. She stood rooted, fixed on the words as if they were pieces of a puzzle she was desperate to solve. Confusion furrowed her brow, but the look on her face wasn't fear. It was *interest*.

Panic rose in Anne's chest. She had to get her daughter out of there, away from the poison dripping from the man's mouth. She spun back, searching for a reassuring look from Lachlan, but there he stood, engrossed in idle talk with David, half his attention on the speaker and the rest lost in the onlookers' hum.

Before she could act, a tug on her hand yanked her focus down to the ground. She blinked, looking into Isobel's bright eyes. Something flickered there, an excitement Anne hadn't seen before. It reminded her of the way she had looked when David crouched to her girl's eye-level earlier and spoke to her like she was an equal. A person, not a child.

A knot twisted hard in her stomach. This wasn't about what the man was saying, it was about the one listening, the one she'd have to comfort when the dust settled and Daddy was gone. Her daughter saw and heard everything, her little face a mess of questions and fears she wasn't old enough to say out loud.

Anne eased herself down and brushed her hand across the little one's brow, unraveling the faint lines of trouble and coaxing calm over the gathered skin. "It's all right, Isobel," she said softly, trying to sound steady, like she believed every word herself. "Don't you worry none. Daddy and David, they're gonna look out for each other. We can rest easy knowin' David's keepin' an eye out for Daddy, makin' sure he's all right."

Isobel's gaze bounced between her father and the tall, unshakeable man beside him. Then she turned to her mother, eyes wide, lips trembling. Now the fear that had been absent moments before rose in her child's eyes. Anne's heart clenched. She knew that look—the weight of waiting, the ache of not knowing. "They gotta go and fight for us, honey," she murmured, giving that small hand a gentle squeeze. "But don't you fret. They'll be back before too long. Ain't nothin' gonna keep them away from us. They'll come home as soon as they can, safe and snug."

Anne's pledge appeared to settle her for a moment, but then David, always watchful, caught the worry still flickering in her eyes. Without a word, he bent down and held out his hands, inviting the child into a hug. Her girl smiled just a little and rushed into the tall man's embrace.. The sight loosened something in Anne's chest. He met Isobel's eyes with a tender look, speaking in a low and grounded voice. "Now don't you go botherin' yourself, Isobel. We ain't gonna be gone too long, I promise."

Her wide eyes searched his face, fingers clutching his shirt, her small figure pressed close as she took in the uneasy scene around them. After a moment, he gently loosened her grip and lowered her to the ground.

David reached for the fiddle case strapped to his back, the gesture bringing a flash of expectant delight to her eyes. "How 'bout a mountain tune?" He tilted his head.

A giggle burst from her daughter. Isobel gave his hand a firm squeeze and her earlier dread seemed to melt away.

David tucked the fiddle under his chin, fingers dancing on the strings with a practiced grace. As the bow met the strings, bright, playful notes leapt into the wind, weaving through the assembly, cutting through the gloom like the first golden rays after a storm. The music pulled everyone in, softening troubled faces, and soon hands clapped, feet tapped, and some folks even started to dance.

Anne's heart swelled as Isobel's little hand clasped her daddy's and she hopped along to the music as though there wasn't a danger in the world.

When the tune finally ended, David knelt, catching the lass's gaze with a friendly look. "How 'bout a big ole Tennessee squeeze that'll last 'til we meet again."

Anne considered the moment as her daughter wrapped her arms around him, squeezing as if her life depended on it. Then she sensed the faintest thread of hope, praying it'd be enough to bring them all back home.

April 30, 1865
Galveston, Texas

THE MEMORY of the long-ago day stayed with Isobel, woven into the fabric of her thoughts, resurfacing in quiet moments and unexpected times. Sometimes, as she sat by the sea, with the waves lapping at the shore and the vastness of the ocean extending beyond the distant horizon, her mind drifted back to that prophetic time. The image of the crowded square, the frightened faces, and the sound of David's kind words and music lingered like a shadow on her heart.

In such tender interludes, she would find herself tracing the worn edges of the family Bible, the leather supple under her touch from years of handling. Her fingers invariably tarried on the *Deaths* page where the names of her mother and father were inscribed. Among the whispers of God's faithfulness, she found Mama and Daddy waiting.

At other times, her steps would lead her to the Alamo, where she'd stand in silence, eyes distant, recalling absent friends. Quiet moments and reflections brought the past rushing back, memories flickering like candle flames in a draft, filling her mind and quietly tinting her thoughts with the blood-red hues of communion and devotion.

CHAPTER ONE

August 11, 1823
Rutledge, Tennessee

The hill behind the barn rose like a promise, and Isobel climbed it barefoot, her toes gripping the damp morning earth as if the whole ridge might lift her into Heaven. Mist clung low to the grass and brushed her shins, a melody, soft and faraway, called her higher. She didn't know where it came from. Maybe it lived in her heart like Jesus. She only knew it meant *go*.

Beside her, Lyddie ran with a brilliance clear as the sky, skirt hitched in one hand and a clutch of wild violets in the other. Her braid bounced with each step, and her laughter came out in bursts, catching on the breeze like a mockingbird's trill. She didn't ask where they were going. She never did. If Isobel ran, Lyddie ran too.

At the top of the hill, they flopped down in the clover and stared up at the sky like it might answer back. Lyddie made crowns from the flowers while Isobel picked shapes from the clouds. They traded stories about animals they'd never seen and places they'd never been. They wove dreams into the hush between their words. When Lyddie leaned close to whisper a secret, Isobel welcomed it like a cool breeze, something too sweet to keep and too strong to forget.

When the sun climbed higher and its heat settled deep into the grass, Lyddie turned her face toward the house. Her brightness faded like it always did when the shadows shifted. "I gotta get back or Miss Eunice'll send for me." She said it plain, like it didn't hurt. Like it was normal. Isobel sat up, dirt smudging her elbow, and looked hard at her friend. "She ain't your mama. Why does she get to tell you what to do?" The question hung there, heavier than the heat. Lyddie didn't answer right away. She only shrugged and started gathering her violets again, like the answer had always been too old for either of them to carry.

Isobel followed her down the hill, slower now, she kicked at tufts of grass with her bare feet. She noted the way Lyddie held herself straighter when they got near the fence line, the way her eyes stopped wandering, and her say-so tucked itself away. The same Lyddie who raced the wind and made up songs was suddenly quieter, smaller. It stirred something hot in Isobel's chest.

"Mama says y'all belong to the Grangers." The words tasted wrong as she said them, like gravel in her mouth. "But that can't be right. People can't belong to people."

Lyddie kept walking, eyes on the ground. "It don't matter what folks say is right," she said. "It just is."

Isobel frowned and looked back at the hilltop, she wished they were still up there with the sky and the clouds and the crowns. "But if I say you're my friend, not a slave, then you ain't. Right?"

Lyddie glanced over and her lips tugged up only partway. "You can say it all you want. I like it when you do. But it don't change nothin' for Miss Eunice. She still sends for me. And I still come."

They stopped at the rail fence where the woods began to thin. Isobel reached for Lyddie's hand and gripped it tight, like maybe friendship could make a shield. "Someday I'll fix it. I don't know how or when or what to do, but I'll fix it. I promise."

Lyddie's eyes shimmered but didn't spill. "You're a dreamer, Isobel MacIntosh."

Isobel set her chin like her daddy's when he went out to hunt. "Somebody's got to be."

At the fork where the path split, one trail curved toward the MacIntosh cabin and the other dipped down to the Granger quarters. Here, the girls slowed. They stood a moment, neither wanting to cross into what came next. Lyddie tucked the violet crown into Isobel's hair, gentle as a prayer, then turned without a word and started down her side of the path. Isobel balled her fists tight at her sides, then turned the other way toward the log cabin where supper would be waiting and no one would ask where she'd been.

The cabin door creaked as Isobel stepped inside and left dusty prints on the worn plank floor. The smell of cornbread and stew wafted through the room, but her appetite had vanished somewhere on the trail. Her mama stood at the hearth, stirring the pot with a wooden spoon, while her daddy sat near the window, whittling a peg for the fence rail.

Isobel didn't sit. She didn't even take off her crown of violets. "Why does Lyddie have to go back?" The question was sharp with something she didn't yet know was called grief. "Why do the Grangers get to keep her like she's a mule or a milk cow?"

Anne's hand stilled on the spoon. Lachlan set down his knife and turned toward her, brows drawn low. For a beat, the cabin suffered a profound quiet.

"Because folks have chosen to believe a lie," Anne said. "They say it's the law, but that doesn't make it right."

"But she's a person," Isobel said. She stepped closer and the heat rose to her cheeks. "She's my friend. She runs and sings and laughs just like I do. How can anybody look at her and not see that?"

Lachlan leaned forward in his chair, elbows on his knees. "Aye, lass. You're right to ask. Some hearts harden to the truth when it costs them comfort. Slavery brings coin and power. And too many would rather hold onto both than admit they're wrong."

Anne knelt and brushed a curl back from Isobel's brow. "We hate it too, Belle. We always have. But the world's slow to change, especially when it's steeped in sin."

Isobel clenched her hands until they hurt. "Then I don't want to be like the world."

"You don't have to be, honey," Anne said. "You be like the Lord who came to set the captives free."

A silence settled between them, broken only by the soft bubble of the stew. Isobel's eyes burned, not from smoke, but from something deeper. She turned toward the fire and whispered, "One day, I'll make it right. I'll find a way. I'm a child of the King and so is Lyddie."

Anne placed a steady hand on her shoulder. "Hold that promise close, Belle. Don't ever let the world talk you out of it."

CHAPTER TWO

April 10, 1825
Rutledge, Tennessee

The boy on horseback rode beside her father with the easy seat of someone raised in a saddle. His back was straight, his boots dusty, and there was a book tucked beneath one arm like it belonged there. Isobel had seen plenty of boys in Rutledge, but none who carried pages with his powder, and none whose eyes scanned the hills like they were hunting for stories. She didn't know his name yet, but her breath caught the way it sometimes did when the fiddle started up in church and the world hushed for something holy.

The creak of saddle leather and the muffled clip of hooves on packed dirt carried up the lane ahead of them. Isobel dropped the hoe and wiped her hands on her apron, stepping out from the bean rows. The sun hovered low as it angled across the ridgeline and cast gold on her father's shoulders and the stranger beside him.

Her father called out before she could speak. "Isobel, this here is Kelvin MacDonald, son of Callum MacDonald from Williams Mill.

He'll be stayin' with us a few days as he conducts some business for his father."

Kelvin. The name sounded crisp, like a page turned fresh and clean.

She curtsied without thinking, only half-aware of the dirt clinging to her dress. "Welcome to Rutledge, Mister MacDonald."

"Kelvin's fine," he said and dismounted. He didn't wear a hat, and his hair, light brown and sun streaked, clung a little to his forehead. He was lean but not slight, with a frame that seemed made for running, climbing, and chasing whatever caught his curiosity.

He assessed her with the faintest twinkle, not cocky, not shy, but something in between. "I heard you folks had a fine garden."

"We do," she said, though the sound came out like it belonged to someone else. "If you like beans and blisters."

That earned a chuckle, low and easy. "Better than scrawny cabbage and half a ration of sassafras tea."

Her father led the horses toward the small corral, waving over his shoulder. "Go on and show him where to wash up, Belle. I'll see to the animals."

She turned toward the cabin, heart thudding harder than it should. Kelvin walked beside her in silence for a time, then glanced down at the dirt under her fingernails. "You work the rows yourself?"

"All of us do. Mama, too, though not so much these days. Her legs won't let her kneel long."

He thought for a moment. "You ever read *Robinson Crusoe?*"

Her steps slowed. "No."

"You'd like it. Survival, solitude, making a life with your own hands. There's a part where Crusoe builds a fence using only drift-wood and stubbornness."

Her dimples glowed despite herself. "Sounds like Daddy. He built this place with nothin' but a hatchet, a mule, and heart full of hope."

They reached the wash basin, and Kelvin dipped his hands into the water, scrubbing off the trail dust. She handed him the towel, and he dried his arms with care. She saw him pause at a pale scar on his forearm.

"What happened there?"

"Burned it when I was little. Tried to move a boilin' kettle while my mama was out of the kitchen. Thought I could do everything grown men do. Turns out, water disagreed."

He said it with a grin, but the story lodged itself in her mind. Not many boys talked that way. Most bragged or brawled. Kelvin noticed things. Carried stories like they were treasures.

At supper, he bowed his head when her father invited him to ask the blessing for the food. His prayer was plain and true, not showy like the ones traveling preachers gave when they came through Rutledge. When he lifted his head, he reached for the bowl of stew but paused when he saw Isobel observing his movements.

"Do you read every night?" she asked.

"Almost. I carry a few books with me. Want to see?"

After the meal, while Mama cleaned up and Daddy went back out to mend a fence post, Kelvin opened his satchel and spread his library on the roughhewn table. One book had a cracked leather spine, another looked hand stitched, and the third was a printed newspaper of some kind.

"This one's Addison's *Spectator*," he said, tapping the first. "That one's Plutarch. This other's from Benjamin Lundy. It's called the *Genius of Universal Emancipation*, a paper about liberty."

"Plutarch?" she repeated. "That's a name?"

"Roman historian. Talks about lives of ancient leaders. Bravery, treachery, wisdom. The kind of things that either hold a republic together or tear it apart."

She sat down before she realized it, her elbows propped up like a child listening at the knees of a grown-up. "You've read them all?"

"Some more than once."

"Do you remember it all?"

He looked at her, speaking more quietly. "Not all the words. But the meanin' sticks. What a man stands for. What makes him change. What makes him fall."

She traced the edge of the *Genius of Emancipation*. "Do you believe liberty's worth fightin' for?"

"I do," he said with no hesitation. "Even when it costs something dear."

His words settled heavy in her chest, and for a long while, she didn't speak. She watched the candlelight dance on the pages of Plutarch and thought about what liberty meant for folks like Lyddie. Thought about what it might mean for herself.

Later, when Mama asked her to fetch the night pails and check the latch on the smokehouse, she stepped outside to a sky flung wide with stars. Kelvin followed her without being asked, leaning against the doorframe while she worked.

"Doesn't seem right to sit still on a night like this," he murmured.

She glanced over. "You restless?"

"No. Just aware."

She tilted her head. "Of what?"

He looked past her, toward the dark ridges beyond the trees. "That we're small, but not powerless."

She didn't know what to say to that. Only that it stirred something in her—a quiet awareness that this boy was not passing through her life like a visitor. Something had shifted. Perhaps it was the way he read books like they mattered. She liked the way he looked at the world like it was half puzzle, half promise.

She stepped closer to him. "You reckon you'll work at the mill like your father?"

Kelvin shrugged. "Don't know yet. I might. I think God calls different folks in different ways."

Then he added. "Maybe through another person."

She blinked. "What?"

He cocked his head. "You've got that look folks get when the future taps 'em on the shoulder."

Isobel sensed the blood rise in her cheeks. She turned back to the smokehouse and finished latching the door, her fingers suddenly clumsy.

As they walked back to the cabin, neither spoke again. Something unspoken had taken root. Not love, not yet. But something that had the makings of it.

That night, long after the cabin had gone quiet and Daddy's snore settled into its steady rhythm, Isobel lay still beneath the sheet, wide-eyed. She could still feel the hush between them, that silent thread stretched taut from the smokehouse door to the cabin porch. It hadn't broken. It lingered. Not a word had been spoken, but something had passed between them all the same. It hummed low in her chest, like a plucked string waiting to be answered.

The cot creaked when she shifted, the sheet pulled high under her chin though the summer night was mild. Moonlight filtered through the curtains in pale bands, laying quiet over the plank floor. From the hearth came the faint crackle of cooling embers. Nothing moved. Nothing stirred. Still, sleep would not come.

Kelvin was just down the hall on a straw mat beside the stove, close enough that she could hear if he turned in his sleep. She wondered if he lay awake too. Wondered if boys thought the same kind of thoughts as girls did when the night pressed in.

She folded her hands over her stomach, the way she did when praying, but no words rose up. Only a tangle of feelings she didn't have names for. Not yet.

He had talked like grown men talked, but not with pride or swagger. It was like he already carried something heavy and close to hold it still. She thought of the scar on his arm and the story he'd told. Of liberty costing something dear. Of him inspecting the ridgeline like he expected more than trees.

There was a steadiness in him she'd never seen in a boy before. Not in the boys who showed off during harvest or elbowed one another when girls walked past. Kelvin had a mind that moved faster than his feet and a way of seeing that left her both curious and a little breathless.

She closed her eyes and tried to picture the pages he'd shown her. Plutarch, Addison, and Lundy. Those names appeared far off, like cities she might never reach, but the way he spoke made her think she could. She just might walk into those words one day, wearing boots scuffed with foreign soil and hands rough from freedom's journey.

17

It could be that was what she wanted. Not *just* the boy, but the world his words opened.

The floor creaked once, faintly, and then fell still again.

She let the gasp go she hadn't realized she was holding.

Lord, I don't know what this is yet, but if he's meant to be part of my story, let me be worthy of it.

Outside, an owl hooted once, then again, as if echoing the thought.

Isobel turned on her side and tucked her hands beneath her cheek. The bedding smelled of woodsmoke and lavender. She didn't know what the morning would bring, but tonight she had seen something new in the world.

And it had a name.

Kelvin.

CHAPTER THREE

December 13, 1828
First Presbyterian Church
Rev. T. H. Nelson, Pastor
620 State Street
Knoxville, Tennessee

The winter light slanted through the high windows of the church, softened by the frost that clung to the glass. A hush had settled over the pews, the kind of silence that wasn't empty but waiting. Isobel stood just beyond the sanctuary doors, one gloved hand resting on her father's arm, the other curled tight around a small bunch of dried lavender and winterberry. She could hear his breathing, shallow and measured, beside her.

The wooden floor creaked underfoot as the pianist found the first chord. Her heart kept time with it. Not quick, but steady like Kelvin's accent when he first spoke her name. Steady like the way he had stood graveside last winter, his coat damp with snow, his jaw set against the cold and the grief of burying both of his parents in the same week.

She had stood beside him then. She stood now.

The atmosphere inside the church held a scent of pine and old wood polish, mingled with the faintest trace of coal smoke. Somewhere behind the altar, Reverend Nelson could be heard murmuring final words with Kelvin, likely calming the boy who had become a man far too soon.

Lachlan shifted beside her, and she glanced up. His mouth was tight with pain, but he carried on. "I can do this, Belle," he whispered. "Let's not keep your young man waitin'."

She pressed her cheek lightly to his shoulder. "We'll take it slow."

He chuckled. "That's the only speed I got left."

She let the corner of her lips lift, though tears pricked the edges of her vision. Anne sat in the front pew, hands clasped and trembling in her lap, with a neighbor woman beside her if she needed help to rise. Isobel's mother wore her best shawl and a bonnet trimmed in faded ribbon, but it was her eyes, tired but hopeful, that Isobel would carry in her heart as she walked.

The doors opened. The music swelled. With her daddy's arm linked in hers and the past behind her, Isobel stepped forward.

Each step rushed ahead and still dragged behind, too quick and too slow all at once.

The aisle stretched longer than she remembered. Polished wooden pews lined either side, filled with familiar faces from Rutledge and beyond. Neighbors and friends who had watched her grow from barefoot in the garden to this moment wrapped in lace and quiet resolve. A hush rippled through them as she passed, like the rustle of wind before a storm, reverent and full of knowing.

One face was missing.

Isobel had searched for it more than once in the crowd, though she knew better. Lyddie would not be sitting among the guests with flowers in her hair or tears in her eyes. She was gone. Sold south the year before to a cotton plantation down the Mississippi, destination unknown.

No letter had come, and none could. Lyddie could not read, could not write, and Isobel had no name for the man who bought her. Only the sick knowledge that someone had.

The loss pressed against her joy like a bruise under lace. She carried it quietly, like a stone in her pocket, cold and aching.

Lyddie should have been here. Laughing. Singing. Holding her hand as they once dreamed they would.

She would have been the one sitting beside the mother of the bride. Her place was empty.

She kept her eyes forward, though she caught glimpses as she moved. She saw hands folded over hymnals, a child perched on a lap, a woman dabbing her eyes with the edge of her glove. Anne's gaze met hers from the front pew. Isobel saw everything in it. Pride. Worry. Longing. Love so fierce it nearly swept Isobel from the aisle.

Beside her, Lachlan leaned heavier with each step, but his hand stayed firm on her arm. She could feel the tremble in his body, the way his knee faltered now and then, but he didn't pause. Didn't ask for help. His boots struck the planks in rhythm with hers, the same way they had sounded when she was small and he'd carried her on his shoulders down this very aisle after special Easter and Christmas services.

She glanced up at him, catching the hard line of his jaw, the sweat at his temple despite the cold.

"Almost there, Daddy," she whispered.

He gritted his teeth. "I'll see you to him, Belle. That was the promise."

At the far end of the aisle stood Kelvin.

He beamed, but not fully. The look in his eyes calmed her. There was something in the way he held himself, shoulders square, hands folded, suit pressed though worn, that reminded her of oak trees in winter. Stripped back but rooted deep. He lost his parents and their mill but still he stood. Still, he waited for her with a heart that hadn't closed in on itself.

The last few steps came slower. Lachlan's breath grew ragged, but he tightened his grip as if it were his lifeline. When they reached the front, he stopped, shoulders lifting one last time.

"Thank you, Daddy."

"She's everything to me and I give her to you," he said softly, but loud enough for Kelvin to hear.

Kelvin stepped forward and took her hand.

Lachlan released her fingers into Kelvin's and then reached for the edge of the pew. The neighbor woman moved quickly to steady him as he lowered himself beside Anne. His lips moved, possibly in prayer, maybe in farewell.

Isobel didn't look back.

Kelvin's hand was tender in hers. He didn't squeeze, didn't tremble, just held her, the way he always had.

Before Reverend Nelson spoke a word, before any vow had been spoken, she already knew.

This was covenant. Not just between her and Kelvin, but with God, who had brought them together into this quiet, holy moment.

Reverend Nelson's speech rose behind the pulpit, low and clear, the way a river sounds when it moves beneath a sheet of ice. She heard the words but didn't need them. The promises had already been carved deep into her spirit, long before this day, long before the lavender bouquet had been tied with ribbon or her father had straightened his collar to walk her forward.

She looked at Kelvin, his eyes fixed on hers. No fear. No flinching. Only a solemn kind of peace like he already knew how sacred it was to bind one life to another in the holy love of the Savior.

A year ago, they had stood side by side at two graves, his mother's and his father's, dug barely a week apart. Williams Mill had gone quiet then, the church bells muffled by snow, grief, and smallpox. His mother had died first, slipping into fever before help could arrive. His father had followed her days later, too worn from tending her to fight the illness off himself.

Kelvin hadn't wept at the service. Not once. But later, under a sycamore tree near the mill creek, she'd seen him sink to the ground, hands clenched in dead grass, the sound he made more like breaking than crying. She had sat beside him in the cold until the moon came up and the creek froze over.

He lost everything he had known. Except her.

Now here he was, standing in a pressed shirt and worn boots, speaking vows with a lilt that did not shake. Promising not just to love her, but to keep walking, even when the way turned steep. Promising to honor, to lead, to shelter, and to provide.

When it came time for her to speak, she found her oratory waiting.

"I do," she said, and the words carried more weight than she'd ever known two syllables could hold. I do take him with my whole heart. I do hold fast to what God has given.

Her hands didn't tremble, though her heart did.

The room was still as Reverend Nelson lifted his hands in blessing. He asked God to bind what had been joined and to seal it with grace that would not fail. Isobel heard the words and let them sink deep. She thought of her father's labored panting, her mother's trembling legs, the empty spaces at Kelvin's table, and her friend sold down the river. She thought of how love didn't shield you from sorrow, but it stood with you in it.

Reverend Nelson's preaching gentled as he went on. "Let us never forget the love of Jesus Christ, who gave Himself for us, that we might be made whole. It is His love that teaches us how to love one another and His grace that carries us when our strength gives out. There is no truer bond, no firmer hope, than the salvation found in Him alone."

When the blessing ended, Kelvin leaned forward and kissed her, not quick, not long, but with a quiet reverence that made her knees weak and her soul certain.

The quiet church erupted in noisy celebration, but it did not touch the hush in her spirit.

She was no longer Isobel MacIntosh.

She was Isobel MacDonald.

She was not afraid.

The sky had turned to pearl by the time they slipped out the back door of the church. Snow threatened, though none had yet fallen, and the chill bit at her cheeks. Inside, the guests lingered, voices rising over the clatter of dishes and the scent of cider, but Kelvin had taken her hand and drawn her away before anyone could stop them.

They didn't speak, not at first. He led her toward the edge of the churchyard, past the old stone wall where ivy still clung in patches. Beyond it, the fields sloped down toward the river, where winter wheat lay sleeping under the frost.

He stopped beneath a walnut tree, its branches stark against the clouded sky. His hand stayed in hers, heartfelt and sure, his thumb brushing slowly over her knuckles.

"You all right?" he asked.

Her throat was tight. "I'm more than all right."

He turned toward her then, fully, the way he always did when he meant for his words to matter.

"You sure this is the life you want?" He asked quietly, but not uncertain. "It won't always be a balmy church and a borrowed suit. You know that."

"I do." *That's the second time I said that today.* She lifted her chin. "And I want it more than anything."

He searched her face for a moment, like he was committing something to memory, then gave a half-bright look that reached his eyes.

"I don't have land yet or a trade that pays right. I've got some books and grit and what's left of my good coat. That's what I brought to the altar."

"You brought yourself," she said. "That's all I ever asked for."

She stepped closer and rested her hands on his chest, just above where his heartbeat echoed steady and strong. She could sense it through the wool of his coat. A quiet drum that had kept time through loss and through loneliness. That sound alone made her want to weep.

"I've known you broken," she whispered. "And I've known you brave. I've seen you carry grief that would buckle many men, and you never once laid it on my shoulders. You stood when you could have fallen. You listened when you could have shut the world out. And you loved me through it."

His eyes glinted, and he looked away for a second, as if the weight of her words needed room to settle.

"Some men carry power like a banner," she said. "Others chase it with noise and crowds. We may walk among them someday. I want you to know not one of them could ever hold my heart the way you do."

He surveyed her again and, in that moment, the whole world stilled.

"I don't need a hero," she said. "I married a man I love and admire. That's the rarest kind."

He swallowed hard, then pulled her into him. Not tight, not hurried, just close enough to fold her into the quiet strength he carried without ever speaking of it.

She closed her eyes against his shoulder and let herself take it all in. Her husband. Her light. Her love. Her one true vow.

Whatever lay ahead, whatever darkness or fire or call God placed on their path, she would walk it beside him.

She would *never* stop thanking her God for the precious gift of this man.

CHAPTER FOUR

December 24, 1831
The Hermitage
Nashville, Tennessee

The late afternoon sun stretched low, casting its golden glow across the slow-moving Cumberland. Sam Houston squinted as the light glinted off the water, the reflection stirring memories he hadn't called for. He saw himself as a boy again, roaming the woods of Tennessee, the trees and streams his first teachers. His mother's voice mixed with the wisdom of his Cherokee companions, roots that held fast to this land even now. Yet the horizon tugged at him, its distant clamor as persistent as the river's flow.

Amber leaves floated downstream like scattered souls, rudderless and adrift. He shifted his stance, the wooden deck creaking beneath his feet. The call of the West jerked harder, its pull so strong he could almost touch it in his core. But the mountains of Tennessee clung to him like invisible threads, binding him in ways he both welcomed and resented.

The steamboat's whistle shrieked, slicing through his reverie. Sam blinked, pulled back to the present. The hum of activity onboard returned, commands rising, boots clattering upon the planks. He sighed, rolling his shoulders against the winter wind as the bustling waterfront of Nashville faded behind him. Ahead the pier came into view, a familiar dock lined with familiar faces.

Alfred and Betty stood at the forefront, unmistakable amongst the gathering crowd. Their presence brought a small smile to Sam's lips. He waved to them, then glanced at Black Coat, standing silent at his side. The Cherokee chief scanned the riverbank, his expression unreadable but charged. He was looking for Jackson, or at least the promise of what Jackson could deliver.

"Looks like we're home," Sam said.

Black Coat fixed his dark eyes on the figures ahead. "You think the Great Father will hear us?" Sam caught the bitterness underneath his friend's question.

"He's not here." He jerked his chin toward the mansion. "We'll meet him in Washington City. This is just his family."

Black Coat frowned. "He does not live in his home?"

He shook his head. "He governs from Washington. But his family will offer hospitality."

A raven soared above the riverbank, drawing Black Coat's observation. He pointed upward. "*Colonneh*," he murmured.

Sam followed his gesture. "Raven," he translated. "It's a good sign."

The steamboat bumped the dock, and the deckhand shouted "Make fast the starboard line!" A young boy caught the rope with deft hands and tied it to the bollard. Sam watched him weave through the bustling workers, marveling at the seamless dance between the deckhands and dockhands. A grin tugged at his lips.

Alfred spotted him. "We see ya, General. Come ashore, sir."

He clapped Black Coat on the shoulder. "Let's go."

They stepped onto the gangplank, navigating through the crowded pier. The atmosphere was thick with the mingling scents of coal smoke, river mud, and freshly unloaded cargo. Men barked orders, crates clattered across wooden planks, and laughter rippled from groups of laborers.

Betty greeted him first, her embrace warm in the cold. "My goodness, General, you look better than the last time we saw ya."

"I *am* better," he replied. "Betty, Alfred, meet my friend Black Coat."

Alfred extended his hand, his grip firm and welcoming. "Nice to meet ya, sir."

Black Coat gave a squeeze of the hand, his regard steady. "I am Black Coat of the Cherokee nation. It is with pleasure I meet friends of the Raven."

She raised an eyebrow. "The Raven?"

He chuckled. "It's what the Cherokee call me."

Alfred glanced up. "Plenty of ravens 'round here. Ain't that right, Betty?"

She muttered, "They get in my garden."

Sam laughed, the tension easing. But as his view fell on the mansion in the distance, his brow furrowed. Something was off. The building looked unfamiliar, its silhouette transformed. "The Hermitage looks... different."

Alfred said, "Got remodeled while you were out west. Big changes."

Sam shook his head. "I'd never have recognized it."

They started up the trail, Alfred leading the way. The cotton fields stretched out beside them, bare and quiet under the winter sky. Black Coat paused, crouching to scoop up a handful of soil. He turned it over in his palm, studying it closely.

"Your land is rich," he said softly. "Our land is dry. Our women carry water from the river to our gardens."

Sam stopped beside him, resting a hand on his shoulder. "The president will hear your message, old friend. We wrote it on the petition."

Black Coat shook his head, letting the soil slip through his fingers. "Words cannot carry the heaviness of the sorrow."

They reached the family graveyard as the last of the sunlight faded.

Sam knelt before Rachel Jackson's stone, the marker catching his eye. He read the words inscribed there aloud, though no louder than a whisper. "A being so gentle and virtuous, slander might wound but could not dishonor..." His throat tightened as the reality of her absence settled over him. "Rest in peace, Auntie Rachel."

Black Coat scanned the burying ground. "This is a peaceful place."

"The president told me I can rest here when my time comes," said Alfred. "He say there ain't no such thing as black and white in heaven."

Black Coat looked into Alfred's eyes. "Is there red?"

"I reckon not. The president say ain't no colors at all in heaven. We all the same there."

Black Coat brushed something from his glistening eye. "Are tears there?"

"When Miz Rachel passed, the president read from his big, black Bible. He said Jesus was gonna wipe away all dem tears ever one done cried."

As they turned back toward the house, Sam noticed Black Coat lingering near the graves. The Cherokee chief stood still, his scan sweeping the rows of markers. Here, among the dead, distinctions of skin color and tribe seemed to fade. He wondered if his friend saw something deeper in this place.

Sam nearly tripped. "Alfred, I don't have my walkin' stick with me."

"If ya need a walkin' stick, we got plenty of saplin's and limbs around here." Alfred gestured to a hickory grove. "I see you got a big knife on your belt."

"It is big, ain't it?" He fingered the knife's pommel. "I got the coat and knife as gifts back in the territory before we left."

Alfred surveyed the scene. "See anything ya like, General?"

"Yes, sir." Sam spied a hickory sapling standing tall and straight. He drew the knife from his belt and cut the young tree, shaping it into a sturdy walking cane.

When they reached the mansion, Sarah Jackson greeted them at the door. Her sharp yet tender eyes swept over the group. "Welcome to the Hermitage, General. Merry Christmas."

Sam tipped his hat. "Thank you, Sarah. I'd like you to meet Black Coat, a Cherokee chieftain."

Sarah extended her hand. "I welcome you here, Chief Black Coat. The president's home is open to you."

Black Coat bowed. "It is an honor to represent my people in the Great Father's home."

Inside, Alfred led them to Sam's room, where a pile of letters and newspapers waited on a desk. Sam settled into a chair, breaking the seal on a letter from Jackson. He scanned the words, and his grip tightened. By the time he reached the end, his fist slammed onto the desktop, the letter crumpled in his hand.

Black Coat straightened, his expression calm but alert. "*Colonneh?*"

Sam shoved the letter aside, grabbing a newspaper. His eyes locked on the article Jackson had marked. The words ignited a fire in his breast, and he shot to his feet, the chair clattering behind him. "Some Ohio fool named Stanbery called me a fraud. Said I stole money meant for the Cherokee."

Black Coat's reply was steady. "I have seen no such money, *Colonneh.*"

Sam paced the room, his anger spilling over. He picked up his new cane. "I'll see the man in Washington. I'll challenge him to a duel and end this slander."

Black Coat's look followed him. "Words are powerful. They bring anger. They bring tears. They bring death."

From the doorway, Sarah cut through the tension. "But they also bring love. Especially at Christmas."

Sam froze, the meaning of her words sinking in. He exhaled slowly, his grip on the cane loosening. "I'm sorry for my outburst," he said, but his gaze remained fixed on the cane.

CHAPTER FIVE

March 1, 1832
Rutledge, Tennessee

It had been a year since they buried her parents on the ridge behind the cabin, side by side beneath the hickories. The old log home stood quiet now, shutters drawn, hearth cold. Their neighbors had been kind, but kindness couldn't fill an empty table. With Mama and Daddy gone, there was nothing left in Tennessee to hold them. What once was home was now only a memory, and it was time to turn toward whatever waited beyond the horizon.

"I'm ready." Isobel shut the cabin door, hearing the creak of hinges for the final time. She tightened her buckskin jacket, resisting the north wind that whipped her hair into her face. The cold stung her skin, but there was no turning back now.

Kelvin stood waiting, his contemplation soft as he studied her. "If you're ready, I'm ready." He pulled her close, his lips hot against hers, a momentary shield from the chill.

Pulling back, she flashed him a spark of mischief. "We should write 'G-T-T' on the door." She rummaged in her coat pocket for a piece of chalk, always handy for leaving messages.

"G-T-T?" His brow lifted.

"Gone To Texas, Kel." She beamed, the thought of their journey brightening her mood.

He chuckled, the sound taking out the chill between them. "I love ya, but we gotta go to Maryland first."

Her shoulders slumped. "I know. But Texas better be waitin' for us when we're done."

"It will be." He tilted her chin up. "One day, we'll be glad we listened to our postmaster and saw the lawyer. If we're ever separated, this'll make sure we can handle things."

She swallowed her frustration, forcing a smirk. "You're right, Kel. I know it. And I'm grateful for the postmaster's advice. It's only... I detest delays."

Kelvin brushed a stray hair from her face. "We'll get there, Belle. It's all part of the journey. At least the road to Maryland's decent. We'll make it in a week."

She exhaled, letting his steady presence calm the storm within her. "I hate walkin' the wrong way first."

"That's what I love about you," he teased, steering her toward the barn.

Inside, Isobel reached for the brush near the door and strode to Sally, their faithful mule. She swept the bristles across Sally's coat with ease, her movements tender and deliberate.

Kelvin secured the pack saddle, the buckles clicking as he fastened them. Every strap, every knot was precise. Their provisions were meager; only enough to last the miles eastward. Everything else had been sold or left in the postmaster's care for forwarding.

"Good girl, Sally." She stroked the mule's neck. Sally nuzzled her in return.

Kelvin kissed the back of Isobel's head, his voice low. "You're makin' it harder on yourself. We gotta sell her in Maryland."

She whirled, her eyes narrowing. "Not to just anyone. I'll see they're decent first."

He smirked, dipping his head in mock solemnity. "Should we ask for character references?"

"You can laugh, but I mean it. Too many folks don't see the difference between animals and property." Her tone lowered. "Or worse... people."

Kelvin's expression sobered. "You're thinkin' of Lyddie."

Her memory recalled things sharp and bitter. "The auction blocks. People in chains get no say about who buys 'em." Her words wavered, but she kept brushing.

He sighed. "That's why we're going to Texas. No slavery there."

"For now," she said. "Texas is in the cotton latitudes. King Cotton's claws stretch far and deep."

He set the brush aside and framed her face with his hands. "We'll fight him, Belle. It's a war for liberty. It's a war worth fightin'. And we won't be alone."

Her hands rose to cover his, their touch grounding her. "Not by ourselves, no. With God's help, He'll give us somebody to fight alongside of. We'll be more than conquerors."

She kissed him, the promise of his love steadying her. They weren't heading to Texas for entirely their own benefit. They were building a future, a place where they'd work the land, serve their neighbors, and stand against the wrongs they couldn't abide. Together, they'd face every trial, finding strength in their shared purpose. Texas wasn't merely a destination. It was their calling.

CHAPTER SIX

April 13, 1832
Mrs. Queen's Boarding House
1100 Pennsylvania Avenue
Washington, D.C.

The evening had a bite to it, cool enough to remind Sam of the Tennessee mountains. The tap of his cane on cobblestones balanced him as he walked beside Senator Alexander Buckner and Representative John Blair. The three of them walked in the waning light.

"The Indian Removal Act gnaws at me somethin' fierce," Sam drawled, stepping across a hole. "As much as I love and respect Andrew Jackson, I wish this tribulation wasn't heaped on the Cherokee."

Blair gave a low hum of agreement. "You ain't the only one feels that way. Lots of folks in the mountains remember livin' alongside 'em, seein' the good in their ways."

Sam's grip tightened around his Hermitage hickory walking stick. "Crockett and me, we fought the Indians plenty, but we didn't want 'em all run off like this."

Buckner chimed in, his remarks measured. "Jackson swears it's for their own good. Says the settlers would overrun 'em otherwise, maybe even wipe 'em out."

Sam exhaled, his jaw tightening. "He gave me his oath. Promised the Indian Territory would be theirs for good, no white man meddlin' there. I believed him. Still do."

The conversation shifted, Blair pulling a folded newspaper from his coat. The headline screamed accusations, the word "fraud" glaring back at Sam like a personal insult. Stanbery's name was there, of course. Always stirring up trouble, always dragging him into it.

"What's Stanbery got against you anyway?" Blair held up the paper.

Sam hardened. "He hates Jackson, and he despises anyone loyal to him. The man don't care about the Indians. He just wants to see us ruined, and I'd say the sentiment's mutual."

As they neared Mrs. Queen's Boarding House, Sam glimpsed a figure stepping out into the fading light. That gait, that posture. It could only be Stanbery. His pulse quickened, anger igniting like dry tinder. "Well, I'll be! If it ain't the devil himself."

Buckner spoke slowly, his expression wary. "Better think twice. This isn't the place for a fight."

Sam stopped in his tracks. "He insulted the president and me. I called him out, and he ignored me. There's no honor in that."

Blair raised a placating hand. "He's a congressman. You start somethin' now, you'll only make trouble for yourself."

But his grip on the stick tightened, his knuckles whitening. "Trouble's already here." He strode forward, closing the gap between him and Stanbery. The words burst from him before he could stop them. "You sorry rascal!"

The hickory cane cracked against Stanbery's shoulder with a force that reverberated up Sam's arm. Months of frustration and simmering rage found their outlet in each strike. Stanbery stumbled, eyes wide with shock, but he didn't relent. The man had to answer, and if he wouldn't do it with pistols, then he'd do it with bruises.

The glint of steel stopped him cold. Stanbery's hand trembled as he leveled a pistol at Sam's chest. For a moment, time stood still. The world narrowed to the barrel of that gun, the faint click of the hammer as it fell.

Nothing. The pistol misfired.

Stanbery's wild-eyed desperation only fueled Sam's anger. He delivered one final blow, sending the man sprawling. He didn't look back at his companions. The fight was done.

Buckner caught up first, his observation was thick with unbelief. "I've seen some things in my time, but that... Lord Almighty."

Blair's face was pale. "He's hurt bad. We should do somethin'."

Sam turned on his heel, his answer cutting through the cool night. "Leave him. He's lucky to be breathin'. He fired a gun at me. I'd say he got off easy."

Blair sighed. "The man's a sitting member of Congress. This won't end here."

"No, it won't," Buckner added. "He'll bring charges. You know that, don't you?"

Sam stopped walking, his arm smarting, the essence of their words settling on his shoulders. "Let him. I called him out fair and square. If he'd answered like a man, we wouldn't be here."

"You can bet there'll be a warrant for your arrest in the next day or two." Blair pulled a business card from a pocket portfolio. "Better be ready."

A tightness crept into Sam's chest, his pulse quickening as unease flickered beneath his calm exterior. He clenched his jaw and muttered, "I don't care." The edge in his declaration betrayed the cracks forming under the surface.

"Take this card, my friend." He handed it over. "This lawyer knows Washington City better than any other. He's gotten folks out of some real tight spots. I'll cover the cost."

Sam reached for the card and read the name, the content of it sinking in. "Thank you, John." He hesitated for a moment, then lowered his head, his resolve fading. "I'll go see him."

CHAPTER SEVEN

April 16, 1832
Court Street Law Office
Frederick, Maryland

The rhythm of Saracen's hooves was steady beneath Sam, comforting him as the countryside rolled by. He patted the stallion's neck. "Good boy, Saracen. We've got important law business today."

The air appeared cleaner and freer, far from the bustle of Washington and the steam-powered tumult of the trains. Sam shook his head at the thought of Jackson's enthusiasm for riding the iron beast. The president claimed it was progress, but he trusted the solid strength of the mighty horse under him over the clatter of the train car. Out here, on the open road, the world was limitless.

As Frederick's streets came into view, he guided Saracen over the cobblestones, stopping to ask a passerby for directions. Following the man's advice, he soon spotted the building. It was a modest, white-brick structure with two doors and a weathered sign hanging above the left door. *Key Law Office.*

"This must be the place, boy." Sam dismounted, tying the horse to the hitching post. The stallion dipped his head to drink from the trough as he unloosed a feedbag from the saddle horn, spreading oats on the ground. Saracen scooped them up with a greedy tongue. He grabbed his hickory cane, its polished surface gleaming in the sunlight, and made his way up the creaking porch steps.

Inside, the law office was simple but orderly. A man sat at a desk buried under papers. At the sound of boots thumping on the wooden floor, the lawyer looked up, his sharp eyes assessing the newcomer. A glimmer of recognition passed over his face.

Rising from his seat, the lawyer circled around the elegant desk and extended a hand in greeting. Sam sensed anticipation as their eyes met for the first time, bridging the divide between client and counsel. "Francis Scott Key, General."

"Sam Houston, Counselor."

Key gestured to a worn wooden chair in front of the desk. "Please, General. Sit."

He eased into the seat, letting the cane rest on his knee. Key settled back into his own chair, tapping his fingers on the top of the desk.

"Word travels fast about a man like you, General," Key said. "I suppose you're here because of Stanbery's charges against you."

Sam said, "That's right. The man called me a fraud, smeared my name in Congress, and ignored my challenge to a duel. I reckon he thought that'd be the end of it."

Key tilted his head. "Instead, you found him and…"

"It was a chance meeting," Sam interrupted, leaning forward. "Didn't go lookin' for him, but when I saw him, I asked his name to be sure. When he confirmed it, I demanded he show proof of his lies." His fingers curled tighter around the cane. "He refused."

"And the cane?" Key's inspection shifted to the polished stick resting on the chair.

Sam picked it up, holding it with a quiet reverence. "This here's special. Hickory, cut from the Hermitage. A gift from President Jackson's family and staff."

Key raised an eyebrow. "You used it to strike Stanberry?"

Sam's jaw tightened. "He insulted my honor and refused to answer me like a man. I did what any man of honor would've done."

Key sighed, leaning back in his chair. He tapped a quill-pen on a blank sheet of paper. "General, you understand the consequences of this. Stanbery's a sitting member of Congress. The House will act, and they won't take this lightly."

His lips pressed into a thin line. "Let 'em act. I won't apologize for defendin' my name, or the president's.

Key began jotting down notes, his pen scratching across the paper. "You've had a storied career, General. Governor of Tennessee, hero of Horseshoe Bend. Now you're here, embroiled in this mess. What brought you back East after all these years?"

Sam exhaled, his stare drifting to the window. "A lot's happened since Nashville." He paused, the ghost of the memory pressing against him. "My wife left me. Said she didn't want to be my wife no more. Reckon she loved her childhood home more than she ever loved me. It broke somethin' in me, Counselor. Fell into the bottle, lost my way."

Key's pen stilled as he looked up, studying Sam's face.

"I went back to the Cherokee," he continued, quieter now. "Chief Ooleteka took me in when I was a boy, after my father passed. He called me 'The Raven.' When I couldn't stay in Tennessee no more, I went west to the Arkansas territory to be with them again."

Key looked up from his notes. "You've lived a life most couldn't imagine."

"I've lived, alright," Sam said, his reply edged with bitterness. "But wherever I go, gossip and slander follow. Now this Ohio congressman thinks he can add to it. He's wrong."

Key set his pen down, folding his hands over the desk. "You understand the stakes here, don't you? This isn't about your reputation. The House may bring formal charges. There's talk of incarceration."

Sam met Key's glare, his expression hard. "Let 'em. I've fought bigger battles than this."

A knock at the door interrupted them. Key rose, moving to answer it. "I'm sorry, General. My apprentice is in Washington filing a writ and will not return for a day or two."

Sam sat back in his chair, gripping the cane. "No need to apologize. I recall my apprentice days as an attorney's assistant. Learned a lot workin' in the courthouse."

The faint creak of the door broke the stillness as Key opened it, revealing a young woman, her face framed by loose blonde strands and a calm, studious expression. Beside her stood a young man, his posture protective. Sam noted the quiet connection between them as they seemed to stand as one.

Key greeted them with his usual formality. "Good afternoon. I am Counselor Key. I don't recall another appointment for the day, but how may I help you?"

The young man offered his hand, and Key took it. "Kelvin MacDonald, sir, and this is my wife, Isobel." He carried the steady hum of someone accustomed to earning his place. From his pocket, he pulled a folded paper. "I got a letter of introduction from the post-master of Rutledge, Tennessee. We haven't set up an appointment yet."

Key unfolded the note, scanning it. "This is a thoughtful introduction, Mr. MacDonald. My assistant will be available tomorrow to arrange our services. I'm occupied with a client." He motioned toward Sam.

Sam rose from his chair, planting his cane on the floor. "Mr. and Mrs. MacDonald, I reckon. I heard you mention Rutledge, Tennessee, which I know well. I'm Sam Houston, the former governor of our fine state."

The couple froze, their wide-eyed expressions almost comical. Kelvin recovered first, bowing his head. "General Houston, we owe you an apology. Truth is, we've never seen you before. We've heard your name plenty, but only what folks say or what the papers print."

Sam chuckled, the sound breaking the tension. "No need to apologize. It's a pleasure to meet people from back home." He extended his hand, clasping Kelvin's in a firm shake.

Isobel's excitement shone through her tentative look, though her hands remained clasped in front of her. Sam could see her effort to restrain her enthusiasm.

Kelvin straightened, glancing at his wife. "This is an honor, General. We're lucky to have met you."

Sam gestured toward Key. "If y'all have time to wait, Mr. Key might be able to help you once we're finished here."

Key replied, "Certainly, I can accommodate your friends, General."

"We don't want to impose," Isobel said, her response earnest. "We'd be grateful but don't want to be a bother."

"Allow me to show you to our parlor. You can rest while I complete my business with the general." Key ushered the couple through a door that led to the right side of the building.

THE PARLOR SMELLED of faint wood smoke, the fireplace adding heat to the modest room. Isobel traced a finger over the sturdy table's edge, its surface well-worn from years of use. Across from her, Kelvin shifted in a high-backed chair, his buckskin jacket creaking with the motion. The crackle of the fire mixed with the muffled sounds from the adjoining room, setting her nerves on edge.

"Didn't think we'd see Mr. Key today," she murmured, leaning closer to Kelvin.

"Neither did I." He ran a hand over his sleeve. "We only came to see his assistant, remember? I was ready to leave the letter in the mail slot if no one answered." He laughed softly. "Can you believe it? First Mr. Key, now General Houston."

Isobel smoothed her dress over her knees. "If I'd known, I would've worn somethin' nicer. They probably think we're mountain trash."

He shrugged. "They didn't seem bothered. Besides, it's plain to see we're from Tennessee. No mistakin' it."

She chuckled, motioning toward the chairs. "These look like they could've come straight from a cabin along Richland Creek."

He chuckled, but Isobel raised a hand, glancing toward the door. "Hush, now. We don't want to be sent out for makin' a ruckus."

The sound of raised voices drifted through the wall. She straightened in her chair, her ears straining. A single word stopped her cold. "Kel, did you hear that?" she asked, her eyes alight with excitement.

"What now?" He glanced around as if expecting trouble.

"They said 'Texas,' undeniably clear." She quickened, but he shook his head.

"I wasn't listenin' in. Not my way to eavesdrop." His words carried a hint of reproach, but she waved it off.

"Don't be so proud of yourself." She leaned closer. "You can't help it if your hearin' ain't what it used to be."

Kelvin sighed. "Guns blastin' in my ears as a boy didn't do me any favors." A faint snicker softened his words.

Isobel's mind raced. "Kel, I reckon the general's plannin' to head to Texas once his legal troubles are done. If we play our cards right, we could join him."

He leaned forward, his eyes narrowing with interest. "That *is* a stroke of luck. You really think he'd let us tag along?"

"Not luck," she whispered fiercely. "Providence, the hand of the Lord. We'll ask him outright." Isobel listened with her full attention. "I can't make out what's bein' said, but I think the meetin's gettin' over."

"What are ya gonna do?"

When the room quieted and the sound of pacing began, she opened the door between the two rooms. "Gentlemen, excuse me for buttin' in. Might I ask if General Houston intends to go to Texas once his legal business is settled?"

Kelvin stepped into the room. "We hope this ain't too forward, but Texas is why we've come to Mr. Key's office today. We hate to stick our noses into your private affairs. If you're headin' there, General, we'd like to join you."

Sam leaned back, his expression shifting from surprise to a slow, considerate approval. "I am, once this mess is settled. But I gotta warn you. Texas is not for the faint of heart."

Kelvin squared his shoulders. "We know the risks, General, and we're ready."

Sam studied them for a moment. "You can find me at Brown's Indian Queen Hotel in Washington City. We can make plans there."

"Thank you, General," Isobel said. "Tennessee's our home but we believe our future lies west." As she spoke, a wistful smile played on her lips, her thoughts weaving through memories and the promise of new beginnings. She believed, deep down, Almighty Providence was guiding her path.

Sam tipped his hat. "I hope to see y'all in Washington. Good day, ma'am."

She observed as he made his way out of the office, his admiration falling upon the stallion tethered to the hitching rail. With a gentle hand, he offered the beautiful animal more grain. The imposing horse plunged his nose into Sam's hand, the crunch of oats unrestrained and rough. Isobel stood still as the stallion devoured each morsel with the passion of something wild and untamed.

CHAPTER EIGHT

April 24, 1832
Opening Day of Trial
The United States House of Representatives
Washington, D.C.

T hey almost hadn't come.

General Houston had pressed two gallery tickets into Isobel's hand himself, with a grin and a wink. "You ought to see how the House of Representatives handles a frontier man in buckskins. Y'all come. This may be the last circus you see before you light out for Texas."

Counselor Key had echoed the invitation. "You'll both want to hear history being made."

They stayed in Washington City, hoping to be included on General Houston's trip to Texas. That was if he could keep himself out of prison.

Now, Isobel sat poised in the upper gallery of the United States Capitol, her gloved hands folded neatly in her lap. The hush below hummed with anticipation. She had never seen such a room—marble columns rising like sentinels, polished desks in rows, lawmakers rustling papers and clearing throats as though the weight of a nation didn't hang in the air. But it did. She felt it pressing on her sternum.

Kelvin leaned in close, his whisper warm at her ear. "Look at the general. He's got the nerve of a man walkin' straight into a gale."

Isobel followed his gaze downward. Sam stood at the center of it all—defiant, unmistakably himself. He wore his fringed buckskin coat like a banner, a deliberate affront to the silk cravats and starched collars around him. Whispers flicked like moths through the chamber, murmurs about dignity and respect and proper attire.

Sam didn't blink.

Counselor Francis Scott Key bent toward him, voice low, jaw tight with the tension of a seasoned lawyer trying to preserve decorum. Isobel couldn't hear the words, but the posture told the story.

Then Sam spoke words clear enough they rose through the open air to the gallery above. "The people deserve to hear from me, not just my lawyer. This is who I am, Counselor, buckskins and all."

Key gave a reluctant nod and turned to the Speaker.

"Mr. Speaker, my client will take charge of his own defense, with your approval."

Speaker Andrew Stephens rapped the gavel once. "I so allow."

Mutters rippled through the chamber as Sam stepped forward, his boots striking the floor with deliberate purpose. Isobel sat transfixed. He appeared unwavering, determined, and larger than life.

"I call William Stanbery to the stand," Sam declared.

Stanbery appeared, reluctant but composed, his features pale beneath a sheen of perspiration. He took the oath and sat with rigid dignity, eyes darting toward Sam, then away. Isobel wondered about this man and looked forward to hearing his side of the affair.

"Mr. Stanbery," Sam began, voice steady as stone, "you've alleged fraud on this floor, claiming President Jackson and I conspired against the United States. I ask you plainly; do you have any evidence of this claim?"

"Objection!" the prosecutor barked, rising abruptly. "This is irrelevant. Mr. Stanbery is not the one on trial."

James K. Polk, seated among the representatives, called out, "I demand an answer!"

Speaker Stevens raised a hand for calm. "The House will vote on the objection."

The room filled with hushed mutters, hands rising. After a tense pause, the result was clear. The objection failed.

All eyes turned to Stanbery.

Isobel held her breath.

Stanbery's face went pale under the magnifying glass of the moment. He shifted uncomfortably. "It was no part of my intention to impute fraud to General Houston."

A polite way to walk backward, Isobel thought. He could not unspeak the words, but neither could he prove them. The moment seemed to drain the heat from the chamber, if only for an instant.

"I now call Senator Buckner," Sam said, already turning toward the lawmaker making his way to the witness stand.

Buckner stood tall, dignified, his every movement measured with political care. He took his oath and met the gaze of the House.

"Senator," Sam said, "did you witness my encounter with Mr. Stanbery?"

"Yes, sir."

"And what do you recall?"

Isobel noticed Buckner's eyes flash toward the gallery. A brief glance. Perhaps he had spotted her. She stiffened, aware of her own visibility. She tightened her grip on Kelvin's arm, her heart pounding.

"We were discussing your opposition to the Indian Removal Act," Buckner began. "And Mr. Stanbery's accusations. You expressed anger —said he had lied."

"Did I voice that aloud?"

"You did."

"What exactly did I say?"

"You said, 'That man lies about me and about the president.'"

Sam nodded. "And then?"

"Then, as if summoned by thought, he appeared before us. You addressed him directly."

"Then what happened, Senator Buckner?"

Buckner recounted the incident for the House. The legislators listened, mouths silent, pens poised.

Isobel found her gaze drifting downward to two physical elements that etched themselves into her memory: Sam's buckskin coat and the hickory cane he had used to strike Stanbery. The symbols of the man. One frontier born, the other frontier forged. They had made him beloved in Tennessee but dangerous in Washington City.

By the time the session adjourned for the evening, the trial had taken on the tempo of theatre, a slow drumbeat of drama and consequence. Isobel gathered her sweater, but her thoughts remained entangled in what she had witnessed.

Sam had not come to Washington to blend in. He had come to bear witness, to stand his ground. And whatever the verdict, he had made his case clear to the watching world.

As the chamber emptied, Isobel whispered to Kelvin, "I think he's already won."

Kelvin nodded. "The law might say one thing. But the people will remember today."

April 24, 1832 (Evening)
The White House

THE DOORKNOB TURNED with a weight that felt too familiar. Sam stepped into the president's office, the White House quieter than usual in the late hour. Dusty light pooled near the shuttered windows, and behind the desk, Andrew Jackson stood like a statue carved from grit and endurance.

Without looking up, Jackson tossed a coin purse onto the table.

"Get yourself a proper suit. See my tailor. This evening."

The leather pouch landed with a soft jangle. Sam stared at it a moment before stepping closer.

Jackson's voice was gruff, but it didn't carry the heat of anger. More like weariness. The kind of weariness that came from shouldering a nation and fending off enemies in every direction—political and otherwise. And the weariness of grief. Rachel. Always Rachel.

"You're makin' my life harder than it needs to be," the older man muttered.

Sam squared his shoulders. "These are the only clothes I have with me, sir. I meant no disrespect."

"I know you didn't," Jackson said, his tone softening just enough. "And I appreciate your efforts with Stanbery. You handled yourself like an honorable man. That's more than I can say for half the House."

Jackson sat, fingers briefly kneading his chest—the old dueling wound, deep and ragged from a bullet never removed.

"But listen to me," Jackson went on. "You and I, we carry more than our own reputations. When you wear those buckskins in front of the whole House of Representatives, it doesn't just reflect on you—it reflects on me. On this office. On the whole idea that men like us from the frontier belong here at all."

Sam's pride bristled, but he nodded. The buckskins were a stunt, but they were also his life, his skin, his people. But Jackson wasn't wrong either.

"I understand, Mr. President," he said quietly. "I appreciate the coins. I'll get a suit."

Jackson studied him for a long moment, the edge of judgment fading into something like kinship. "Just make sure it fits, Sam. You're about to step onto a bigger stage than Tennessee. Don't let northern presses write your story for you before you even pick up the pen."

Sam closed his hand around the coin purse. "No, sir. I understand. I apologize."

April 25, 1832
The United States House of Representatives

THE NEXT MORNING, Isobel's heart lifted the moment Sam entered the chamber.

Gone were the buckskins. In their place stood a man transformed —his broad shoulders wrapped in a fine black coat, a crisp linen shirt at his collar, and polished boots striking the floor with purpose. The suit fit well, almost too well, as if the cloth hadn't yet earned the shape of him. But the pride in his bearing hadn't changed. If anything, it gleamed sharper.

He made his way toward Counselor Key, who turned from the desk and gave him a once-over, eyebrows raised.

"Counselor," he said loud enough for Isobel to hear, "I'll take the lead after your opening statement."

Key crossed his arms, his voice firm. "I never advise clients to act as their own counsel, but I'll bow to your wishes. Are you sure you're capable?"

"Don't worry, Mr. Key. This is mine to carry."

Key studied him a beat longer, then sighed and stepped aside.

After a brief opening from the lawyer, Sam rose once more, his words echoing across the chamber, steady as a stone dropped in deep water.

"Mr. Speaker," he began, "arraigned for the first time in my life on a charge of violating the laws of my country, I feel all that embarrassment which my peculiar situation is calculated to inspire."

A stillness settled over the House.

"I am a man of broken fortune and blasted reputation. I seek no sympathies, nor need; the thorns which I have reaped are of the tree I planted; they have torn me, and I bleed."

Isobel sat motionless, her hands trembling. His words landed hard, each one heavy with consequence. Around her, debate began to stir— voices rising, tempers shifting—but she hardly noticed.

Her gaze remained fixed on him. For better or worse, Sam had made his stand. *This is my general. Now and forevermore.*

CHAPTER NINE

May 7, 1832
Washington, D.C.

The spring breezes of Washington City whispered across the Potomac, tousling Isobel's unadorned hair. She didn't mind. The river sparkled under the slant of sunlight, and the dirt path beneath her shoes felt just muddy enough to remind her they hadn't been swallowed whole by the grandeur of Washington City.

She walked beside Kelvin, her fingers laced with his. For once, there was no rush. No crates to move. No secrets to guard. Just fresh air and the faint promise of wildflowers blooming at the river's edge.

"You think General Washington really tossed a dollar across this river?" she asked, squinting across the water.

"Doubt it. Just a tale to make folks love him more."

She grinned. "I wonder if he coulda foreseen this trial? General Houston knockin' a man flat probably wouldn't sit right with him."

Kelvin squeezed her hand as they stepped around a muddy spot. "Well, they were both known for fightin' their own way."

A patch of wildflowers caught Isobel's eye, their colors vivid against the green. "Let's pick some of these," she said, kneeling to select a handful.

"Sure thing. You want one for your dress?"

"No. I got a notion."

"For the courtroom?"

"Mm-hmm. Just wait."

He gathered more blooms, and Isobel tied them into a bouquet with a ribbon from her bag. Not tidy. Not delicate. But bright and full of meaning.

At the capitol steps, she plucked one stem from the bundle and tucked it into the buttonhole of the doorman's coat.

"Good mornin'. Hope you have a good day, sir."

He beamed. "Why thank ye kindly, ma'am. Gonna be busy in there today."

Inside, the hush felt familiar now. The columns didn't look quite so tall. She and Kelvin found their usual seats in the gallery and leaned in as the chamber filled below.

Sam entered moments later, walking with Counselor Key. The transformation was striking every time. Now he wore that fine black suit like he'd been born to it. But beneath the polished exterior, Isobel still saw the man they'd come to know over dinners in the hotel lobby, those long evenings trading stories over bowls of stew and borrowed whiskey. Sam had laughed with them and confided in them.

Now, as Sam scanned the gallery and spotted them, he gave the smallest nod. Not showy. Just enough.

Kelvin leaned close. "He's ready to finish all this up."

The Speaker called the chamber to order, and Sam rose to his feet. The hush that followed felt deeper than before, heavy with expectation. His closing remarks were not just a defense—they were a reckoning.

From her lap, Isobel lifted the bouquet.

Kelvin saw the movement at his side.

With a quick flick of her wrist, the wildflowers tumbled from her fingers and spiraled through the open air. The colors fluttered like banners as they fell toward Sam's feet.

Applause filled the chamber as the bouquet berthed itself on the chamber's floor like a wreath proffered to the Caesars of old.

Isobel's unmistakable Tennessee accent echoed through the room. "I had rather be Sam Houston in a dungeon than Stanbery on a throne!"

Sam kept his scrutiny fixed below, but Isobel knew the flower stunt was working. She hoped he would stick with them all the way to Texas.

A ripple passed through the room. Heads turned. Smiles broke across more than a few faces.

The flowers and vocal encouragement seemed perfectly timed. Sam knelt to pick up the arrangement. He maintained his focus on the floor, clearly wanting the attention on him.

Then, with a commanding presence, he began.

"So long as that proud emblem shall wave in the Hall of American legislators," he said, gesturing toward the flag, "so long shall it cast its sacred protection over the personal rights of every American citizen."

His voice deepened, and with it came the full gravity of the moment.

"So long as that flag shall bear aloft its glittering stars, so long I trust, shall the rights of American citizens be preserved."

He didn't raise his voice.

He didn't need to.

The stillness that followed was broken only by scattered murmurs. Then a wave of noise, some in admiration, some in protest. Applause met objection. The Speaker of the House banged his gavel and barked for order, but the chamber swelled with the chaos of a body stirred to life.

Isobel sat still in it all, her hands folded again. But her mind was full.

This wasn't just a moment of victory or defiance. It was a line drawn. Sam Houston had made himself known—not by hiding who he was, but by naming it plain. He had taken the law's blows and answered with something that sounded like grace.

She whispered under her breath, so quiet Kelvin almost didn't hear it.

"This is my general. Now and forevermore."

The trial was finished. The verdict would come later but for Isobel, the matter was settled.

May 14, 1832
The United States House of Representatives

THE HOUSE TOOK days to reach its decision.

On the final morning, the gallery filled early. Tension bristled in the chamber, but no one spoke above a whisper. Isobel sat beside Kelvin, her gloved fingers resting on the rail. Sam stood below them in silence, head high, hands folded behind his back.

The Speaker of the House rose with deliberate weight, gavel in hand.

"General Samuel Houston," he intoned, "this body finds you guilty of Contempt of Congress."

A pause, the kind that dares interruption.

"Your punishment is a formal reprimand from the Chair. I so execute your reprimand now. This is over."

The words struck the floor like iron dropped on wood—official, public, inescapable. And yet, somehow, it wasn't defeat. Not in Sam's eyes.

He didn't flinch. He gave no apology. Only a slight dip of his head, accepting the reprimand with the calm of a man who'd already counted the cost.

When the chamber emptied, he found them waiting in the corridor outside.

"I sure do appreciate y'all's support from the gallery," he said, offering his hand to Kelvin and then to Isobel.

Isobel shook her head. "No need for thanks, General. Our talk back in Mr. Key's office wasn't idle blathering, sir."

He seemed to understand she meant more than just moral support. This was loyalty rooted in calling.

Her thoughts galloped like wild horses on the vast prairie. She could feel the pattern forming now—thread by thread. Whatever had brought them to Washington City, it hadn't been chance. This whole journey bore the marks of something larger than herself. A tapestry she couldn't yet see in full, but whose Maker she trusted.

Isobel believed friendships, rare and sacred, were God's answer to her prayers for guidance and assistance.

Sam's eyes glimmered with determination. "Meet me tonight at Brown's Hotel. We'll plan our next move. This ain't a path for the faint-hearted."

The substance of his words settled over her, steady and real.

There would be danger ahead. No question.

But she knew, with quiet certainty, they wouldn't walk it alone.

CHAPTER TEN

May 14, 1832
Brown's Indian Queen Hotel
Pennsylvania Avenue
Washington, D.C.

The sight of Brown's Hotel made Isobel pause. The elegant facade stood in stark contrast to the mud-slicked streets and clamor of the federal district. Lifting her skirts, she stepped carefully, avoiding only the worst of the muck. "Can you believe it? I've never seen anything like it," she said in awe.

Kelvin chuckled, following behind her. "Wait 'til we get inside. They say it's real fancy. Might make up for all the sludge we've been dealin' with."

She grimaced, inspecting her grimy shoes. "These are ruined for sure."

He swept her off her feet, carrying her toward the hotel's entrance. "Just part of my duties. A little dirt won't stop us, and the general's not expectin' us to arrive spotless."

She gave him a playful glare but softened as she looked back at the hotel. "It's somethin' else though. Makes me wonder what type of place we're steppin' into and what kind of adventure we're startin'."

He met her eyes. "Whatever it is, we're with the general. From Tennessee to Texas, we're in this together. I've been prayin' on your thought about the Lord guidin' our steps. I reckon it might be true."

Inside, the lobby buzzed with energy. The room was thick with the aroma of expensive liquors and the hum of conversation. Men hoisted glasses and offered toasts to General Houston.

Kelvin leaned closer, gesturing toward the bar. "Imagine the deals struck in this place. I bet more than a few men woke up regrettin' some of 'em."

Isobel's attention drifted to the crowd. She spotted Sam surrounded by a small group, his presence commanding despite the informal gathering.

When the hum quieted, Sam stepped forward. "I appreciate your support, friends. I've had my share of trials, but I'm not one to let hard times keep me down. I've defended the right of every citizen to question those in power. I aim to show what one man can do with the resources of this great country. You'll hear of my journey in the papers soon enough, but as for my destination, that'll remain my secret for now."

The crowd erupted in cheers, some shouting "Huzzah!" She winced at the noise, glancing toward the door as if expecting someone from the White House to come investigate the commotion.

Sam elevated his hands to quiet the room. "Thank you again for your support. Remember, our nation needs us all to stand behind President Jackson. Now, I must bid you a good evening. I've got an expedition to prepare for."

As the throng began to disperse, Sam's eyes found Isobel and Kelvin. He motioned at them, a subtle gesture to follow him upstairs. Without hesitation, they made their way to his private room on the fourth floor.

Inside, Sam poured everyone a drink and motioned for them to sit. "It's good to have you here. When I raised my Hermitage hickory against Stanbery, I didn't expect events to turn out like this. President

Jackson's stood by me through it all, and I owe him more than I can say. I've been thinkin' about Texas. The kernels of all that's possible have taken root in my imagination, and they're growin' with each beat of my heart."

Kelvin leaned back, his expression thoughtful. "I don't think we can imagine the seeds of possibility. For with God, all things are possible."

Sam's eyes sparkled. "They are. I hope y'all are ready to see it through with me."

Isobel squeezed Kelvin's hand. "General, you won't find me shirkin' any task. But I'll tell you, these fancy clothes are about the poorest thing I've ever worn." She peeked at Kelvin. "If I can climb four flights of stairs in this contraption, I reckon I can handle Texas."

Sam laughed, raising his glass. "That's the spirit. Practical or not, I can see you've got the grit we'll need out there."

Kelvin took her hand, pressing a kiss to her fingers. "I knew that from the start, General. She's tougher than most men I know."

Isobel's cheeks flushed, but she held her head high. "Thank you kindly, both of you. But grit or not, I'd be glad for you to call us by our given names. Since you're our general, we'll call you that, if it suits you."

Sam said, "So, the first order of business is settled. Now, on to the next." He shifted his eyes back and forth between them, a hint of curiosity in his expression. "Either of you ever set foot in New York City?"

CHAPTER ELEVEN

June 3, 1832
Fulton Street & East River
Brooklyn, New York

The coach jolted to a stop, the horses stamping as if relieved the journey had ended. Isobel clutched her skirt, eager to escape the cramped space. The long days on the road had left her stiff, coated in dust, and aching for fresh air. She glanced out the window, taking in Brooklyn's streets. The buildings loomed taller than anything she'd seen before, their brick facades bustling with life.

"Finally here," Kelvin said, stretching as much as the small cabin allowed.

Sam adjusted his coat but didn't respond. Isobel caught the tightness of his jaw, the ever-present reminder of his battlefield wound. It flared often, though he seldom spoke of it.

The driver climbed down and came to the door. "Brooklyn." He opened the door with a quick flourish.

Isobel hesitated, glancing at the driver's outstretched hand. Propriety dictated she accept the assistance, but her instincts screamed to leap out and plant her feet firmly on the cobblestone street. With a quiet sigh, she took his hand and stepped down, Kelvin and Sam following.

"Much obliged," Kelvin said.

"Name's MacGavin," the man replied, adjusting his hat. "Drive this route most days. You folks heading into the city?"

Kelvin's eyes lit up. "MacGavin? That's a Scottish name."

"Aye, sir. My people hail from the Highlands."

Isobel's heart leaped at the connection. "We're the MacDonalds, originally of Scotland too. Though our families crossed the sea after Culloden."

"Same as mine, Mrs. MacDonald," MacGavin said. "My grandfather fought at Culloden before fleeing to America."

Kelvin chuckled, clapping MacGavin on the shoulder. "If every man who claims to have fought there in truth did, the British wouldn't have stood a chance."

MacGavin joined in the laughter, his weathered face softening. "Ain't it the truth, sir."

Isobel glanced at Sam, whose polite face betrayed a heavier, quieter hurt. War was no jest for him. She had seen it in his eyes before. He had memories too heavy to share. The Creek War and his time as a rejected husband had left scars deeper than the visible wounds he carried.

Kelvin, ever perceptive, shifted the conversation. "Mr. MacGavin, meet General Sam Houston of Tennessee. He's been our governor, our congressman, and is now our good friend."

MacGavin's eyes widened. "*The* General Sam Houston? It's an honor, sir."

Sam tipped his hat. "Pleasure's mine, Mr. MacGavin. Did your father serve in the Creek War? Seems to me I remember a MacGavin or two there."

MacGavin replied, "He did, sir. Now he works as a caretaker at West Point. The cadets love to hear the accounts of a man who fought Indians and crossed swords with the redcoats."

He extended his hand to MacGavin. "Send him my regards. The stories of the old soldiers keep the past alive, and the young men should hear them."

"I'll be sure to tell him, General."

He reached into his pocket, pulling out a gold coin. "For your fine service, Mr. MacGavin."

MacGavin's hands trembled as he accepted the coin. "Thank you, General. My wife will be grateful for this kindness. Such coins are rare in our household."

"You earned it," he said. "Now, how do we get across the river?"

"There's a steam ferry down the street," MacGavin replied. "It'll take you across in ten minutes or less. I'd be happy to drive you there."

Kelvin said, "That'd be much appreciated."

As they climbed back into the cabin, Isobel read the sign aloud. "Fulton Street. Is it named after Robert Fulton?"

MacGavin replied, "You're right, ma'am. His steam engine powers the ferry. You'll see the ingenuity of it for yourself soon."

The coach lurched forward, wheels creaking over the cobblestones. She leaned toward the window, catching glimpses of the towering skyline and bustling docks. Her heart swelled at the view. This wasn't a mere city. It was a testament to the boundless ambition of a new nation.

Kelvin broke the silence. "Although I don't like it, I'd like to see more of this place someday."

Sam said, "It's a sight, all right. A man could build something lasting here… or lose himself trying."

Isobel turned her thoughts back to the driver. She imagined the confident ease with which he handled the reins. She envied that freedom, that mastery of the world outside the constraints of society. Her hands curled into fists, the urge to burst free surging within her again.

Soon, they reached the landing. MacGavin helped them down, his wide smile revealing his pride in the city. "Safe travels. And General, it's been an honor."

Sam touched his hat one last time. "Likewise, Mr. MacGavin. 'Til we meet again."

Isobel watched the boat approach from Manhattan. The wind tugged at her hair, the river stretching out. It was more than a crossing; it was a step toward something vast and unknown. For the first time in days, the shackles of the journey seemed to loosen, replaced by the promise of what lay ahead.

CHAPTER TWELVE

June 3, 1832
The Steamboat *Nassau*
East River, Between Brooklyn and Manhattan
New York, New York

The Tennesseans waved goodbye to MacGavin as his coach rattled away from the Brooklyn ferry landing. Kelvin lingered at the water's edge, his gaze fixed on the sprawling skyline ahead. "We've always avoided New York City, General."

Isobel folded her arms. "The place ain't for us. Never has been." She eyed the distant city as if its sickness could reach across the river. "Stories of yellow fever and cholera have been comin' outta there for years. We kept to the mountains, to the clean air where death don't ride on the breeze."

Kelvin's fingers tightened around his suitcase handle. "You won't get no argument from me."

Sam concurred. "We all agree."

The ferry deck shuddered beneath Kelvin's boots as he stepped aboard, the atmosphere thick with the smell of coal and water. Merchants and dock workers shuffled past, their chatter blending with the rumble of the steam engine. She followed close behind, her bag tucked under her arm, eyes wide taking in the scene. "Never seen so many people in one place."

Kelvin grunted, his attention drawn to the towering smokestacks exhaling clouds of black exhaust. The ferry's whistle blared, cutting through the noise. Isobel jumped, a startled giggle escaping her. "Lord, I wasn't ready."

He chuckled and wrapped an arm around her waist. "Well, we're awake now."

They leaned against the railing, the river's turbulent waters stretching before them. Manhattan's waterfront loomed closer, quick with color and motion. Hawkers called out their wares, carts laden with goods rattled down the docks, and ships rocked on the tide like restless giants. The city was alive, its pulse beating in time with the ferry's iron heart.

"It's like nothing else," Isobel murmured. "The life of it all."

Kelvin noted the dockworkers as they hauled crates and barrels. "Didn't figure we'd ever see this when we signed up with the general. The world's bigger than I thought. Guess we'll go as far as the road takes us."

"Only God knows how far that'll be," she said, her inspection drifting to the water. "Jonah tried to outrun God, didn't he?"

He smirked. "Forgot God's everywhere. Hard fact to overlook."

"Sure is. If God didn't rule in Texas, I wouldn't set foot there." She wrinkled her nose as debris floated by. "I wouldn't eat fish from this water."

Kelvin chuckled. "I'll pass on that meal."

Sam joined them at the railing. "Fishermen must cast their lines upstream. The sanitation here leaves a lot to be desired."

"No Tennessee brook trout here," she said.

They all laughed. Sam handled the rail, his expression thoughtful. "Washington crossed this river in the Revolution under the cover of darkness. He ordered silence from every man, and not one dared make a sound. Got the army outta New York to fight another day."

She imagined the quiet crossing, the fate of the nation balanced on the dark waters. "Someday there'll be a bridge here. These ferries will be a thing of the past."

Kelvin gave a low whistle. "A bridge? Hard to picture it."

Sam chuckled. "Who knows what marvels the future holds."

The sun caught the water, scattering light across the river's surface. Isobel squinted, mesmerized by the bustling docks ahead. Ships unloaded goods from the Atlantic's opposite shore, the workers' shouts carrying over the water. "Kel, look there. They're speaking an Irish brogue."

Sam said, "The Irish are everywhere in this city. Half the stevedores are Irish."

She considered the laborers, their movements precise and rhythmic, each crate and barrel handled with care. "Makes you wonder what stories those crates hold. What secrets crossed the sea."

Kelvin shrugged. "Maybe the same tales our mamas told us, wrapped in different paper."

She said, "Could be. This place has its own magic, though. Can you feel it?"

Sam softened. "Magic or desperation. They come here to escape tyranny, to make somethin' of themselves."

"My folks left Scotland for Charleston for the same reason." Isobel scanned the crowded docks, the teeming masses moving with purpose. The sheer number of people, their cries rising in a medley of languages, made her chest tighten.

"This city is the heartbeat of business in America," Sam said. "It's why we're here."

"What exactly is our business, General?" She shielded her eyes from the sunlight.

"We're here to secure funding for our journey to Texas. Land speculation is hot right now, and we aim to be in it. The land is distributed through empresarios to settlers."

Kelvin frowned. "I've heard of Stephen F. Austin."

Sam said, "His father started the colonization but died before he could see it through. Stephen took up the work. The laws keep changin' though. Mexico's unstable, and every new government tweaks the settlement rules. Austin's patient, maybe too patient."

"But Americans can't settle there now, can they?" she asked.

He sighed. "Technically, no. But the laws are barely enforced. Folks come in under the laws the settlements were founded."

Isobel straightened. "Slavery is not legal there."

Sam shook his head. "No. Landowners skirt the law by using indentured servitude instead of outright slavery."

Her face hardened. "I despise slavery. It degrades everyone involved. Kelvin and I agreed we'd never own another person."

Kelvin added, "We want you to know where we stand, General. If there's ever a vote, I'll always vote against it. We believe free labor is not only the right thing to do, it's more efficient."

Sam dipped his chin. "I appreciate your honesty. I've owned slaves before, but I see where the country's headed. Slavery's the great divide that could tear us apart."

Isobel said, "The world's changin'. England's already lookin' to its colonies for cotton. They won't need us forever."

Sam studied her, a flicker of respect in his eyes. "You've got a sharp mind. You might be right."

"We have an understanding, General." Her words were smooth, but her eyes clouded as they drifted beyond him. The steam ferry *Nassau* insulated her from the world outside. Yet, her thoughts raced to the vast expanse of cotton fields she had seen stretching endlessly across the South. Fields that seemed to consume the sun itself.

She swallowed, her heart heavy with the unspoken. Could their agreement, so fragile and tentative, hold up when laid bare under the harsh, unyielding light wielded by King Cotton on a sea of white?

Her view flickered back to the general, but her mind remained far away, tangled in the relentless stretch of land where every stalk of cotton told a different story than the one spoken on the *Nassau*. Was she, like Jonah fleeing on the sea, trying to outrun something that could not be escaped? Was Texas a great fish prepared to swallow her? Was Texas the end of the line? She didn't know.

CHAPTER THIRTEEN

June 3, 1832
South Street Seaport District
Manhattan Island, New York

I sobel followed Sam across the busy dock, her steps uncertain. She gripped her dress and surveyed the bustling scene. Kelvin stayed close, silent, but the shared yoke of their unease was almost tangible. Manhattan was unlike anything she'd experienced before, and following Sam seemed her only anchor.

The hired carriage stood near the ferry landing on Manhattan's cobblestone streets. Beyond it, towering ships filled the harbor. Isobel took them in. Their tall masts stretched skyward, crisscrossed with lines and furled sails. The breeze carried the sharp tang of salt and coal mingling with the rhythmic creak of wood and the splash of waves against hulls.

"I didn't expect to get wet." She brushed a faint spray from her cheek. Her eyes fixed on one ship, *Henri IV.* A shout rang out from the rigging high above. The language, edgy and unfamiliar, startled her. It might have been French. Isobel strained to understand, but the sailor's words blended into a strange melody of hollers below and the cadenced movements of the crew.

High on the mast, another man wrestled with a canvas sail. His quick hands worked with confidence, but the height made Isobel's stomach lurch. She imagined the ship tossed on the open seas, its crew clinging to spars and ropes in a storm. The thought sent goose-bumps prickling her arms.

"Isobel," Sam said, grounding her. He stood beside the open door, his look shifting to Kelvin. "Give her a hand."

Kelvin's touch steadied her as she stepped up, his hand sure. Settling into her seat, she exhaled slowly. The harbor outside was alive with movement and noise. Ships swayed, dockworkers shouted, and carts rattled over uneven stones. Inside, it was silent, the sudden stillness heavy. Kelvin sat beside her, his eyes forward, while Sam took his place facing them.

Kelvin broke the silence. "This day will stay with me, General. The sights I've seen today stand apart in my mind."

Isobel's stare drifted out the window. "It's like stepping into a story you'd only ever heard about."

"In our time together, we've seen wonders folks back home couldn't imagine," Sam said. "The fruits of it all will be for our children. That's my hope." He looked out toward the driver. "Number One Broadway."

"Is that the address of the land company?" Isobel asked, curious about its importance.

"No," he replied. "It's where we'll stay the night. I sent word ahead to the land office. Our meeting's tomorrow. Tonight, we rest so we're ready to meet these northern businessmen on their home ground."

Relief washed over Isobel. "I'm glad to hear it. I worried I'd be expected to meet them dressed like a pirate and smelling of horses."

Kelvin chuckled. "The general always looks after us."

"Nonsense," Sam replied. "An army that doesn't rest before battle risks defeat. Tomorrow we'll need sharp minds. These northern men know how to separate folks from their money. I've seen it firsthand."

As the carriage rolled into the financial district, the bustling streets shifted to rows of noble buildings. The wheels clattered over stones, the noise mingling with distant vendor calls and the pulsing hammers of metalworkers. Sam pointed out a building as they passed Wall Street. "See the one with the columns?"

Isobel and Kelvin glanced at the building. "Yes," they said together.

"It looks like a Greek temple." Isobel tilted her head. "Right, Kel?"

Kelvin shrugged. "Never seen one in person. Just drawings."

"It's Federal Hall," he explained. "President Washington took his first oath of office there. Back then, New York was the capital."

"Washington stood there?" Her question carried awe as her mind lingered on the building.

Sam replied, "The federal government moved to Philadelphia later, but this place is full of history."

She let the significance settle in her mind. The world outside was loud and chaotic, yet inside, the quiet carried an emphasis of its own. Her thoughts wandered to her childhood, to simpler times when her mother's kitchen smelled of fresh bread and herbs, her father's words smooth in the background. Those moments had been magical in their smallness, untouched by the complexity of places like this.

The carriage clanked to a halt. Isobel blinked, pulled back to the present as Sam stepped out. Number One Broadway stood before them. It was a four-story building, modest yet dignified. Its brick facade caught the soft afternoon light, the carved double doors framed by delicate stained glass which scattered colors on the stone steps.

"It reminds me of Brown's Hotel." Isobel traced the details with her eyes. "Smaller, but there's something inviting about it."

Kelvin joined her. "It's grounded. I like it."

Sam gestured toward the understated sign above the door. "*Washington HQRS*. During the Revolution, this was Washington's headquarters. The hotel's owner built onto the original structure."

"History is at our feet," Isobel said, stepping onto the cobblestones. The thought of walking where Washington once stood sent a shiver through her. She paused, letting the significance of the moment settle before following the men inside.

The dining room was quiet, the clink of silverware the solitary sound as they ate. The weariness of the day hung over them. Words unnecessary. Isobel glanced at Kelvin, his tired face matching her own. "Good stew," he mumbled.

She agreed. "It is."

When the plates were cleared, they made their way to their room. As night fell, Isobel stood by the window, gazing out at the transformed city. Lights twinkled like stars, reflecting off the water as ships swayed gently in the harbor.

"Isn't it something?" she whispered.

"It surely is. The city's alive, even now."

Her breath fogged the glass. "It's so different from home. There's a kind of magic here."

Kelvin leaned against the wall. "It's like anything could happen in a place like this."

The city's pulse slowed, its buzz fading into the distance. Isobel turned from the window, her body heavy with exhaustion. "We should rest. Tomorrow will be another adventure."

Kelvin pushed off the wall and stretched his arms. "Yeah, but I can't imagine tomorrow could top today."

With one last glance at the glowing cityscape, they climbed into bed, the mattress soft beneath them, the sheets cool against their skin. By degrees, her contemplations slowed, her body sinking deeper into the coziness of the bed.

"Kel," she whispered into the dark.

"Yeah?" He was quiet and already half asleep.

"Do you think we'll ever come back here? To New York?"

He sighed. "Maybe." The word was thick with the pull of sleep. "Maybe someday."

Isobel's lips curved though no one else saw. Her eyes fluttered shut as sleep overtook her. Wrapped in the stillness of the night, she drifted off, the hum of the city below lulling her into a deep, peaceful slumber.

CHAPTER FOURTEEN

June 4, 1832
Washington Hotel
No. 1 Broadway, Lower Manhattan
New York, New York

The first shimmer of dawn crept over the horizon, slipping through the curtains like a secret whispered in the dark. Soft, golden light spilled across Isobel's hair, giving it a glow as she stirred, the last traces of sleep still tangled in her mind. She awakened, blinking away the remnants of dreams that clung to her like the rising mist of the river below.

With Kelvin still lost in slumber, she slid from the bed. She moved with the quiet elegance of the alley cat she saw darting onto the street as she reached the window.

Leaning against the window frame, Isobel observed the endless rows of tenements stretching toward the horizon. Her heart ached for the women, already awake to stoke stoves, stir pots, and coax children out of bed. They bucked up through lives pressed thin by poverty, a life she knew, if not for the gifts of God, could've been hers.

She whispered a soft prayer. "Lord, thank you for keepin' us from that path, from the kind of life no soul deserves."

The city was still waking up, the sun's rays beginning to stretch across its rooftops, when she heard Kelvin stir behind her. He sat up on the side of the bed, rubbing sleep from his eyes. "You're fair as the mornin' sun, lass."

She unfolded her arms and tousled his hair. "Thank you. I was but gazin' at the buildings of this city holdin' so many souls in their distress."

"Aye, 'tis a stark contrast, us nestled in this plush room while others dwell in cramped quarters where dawn's light scarce finds its way." He shook his head.

A sharp rap shattered the quiet. Without hesitation, he crossed the room and swung the door open.

Before him stood a chambermaid, her skin a rich, dusky brown that seemed to make her smoky uniform blend into the shadows behind her. In one hand, she balanced a kettle, the steam rising in gentle curls, filling the doorway with its heat.

"Mornin', sir. I've brought ya some hot water fer yer shavin' bowl. You want me to pour it now?"

"I'll take it from you. Have you lugged this all the way up to the fourth floor yourself?"

"Sho' have, sir. Ain't nobody got to help me with my work."

"My husband can take the pot now, Miss."

"No, ma'am." The maid shook her head. "If the boss man found out a white man took my kettle, I'd be in a bad way."

"What's your name, Miss?" she asked.

"Swanee. Jus' like the river."

"Are you a free woman, Swanee?"

"Yes, ma'am. I was born free up in Albany. Others of my family are down south livin' in bondage. But I work fo' wages in the hotel."

Swanee poured the steaming water into the basin, the splash of it filling the room with a faint hiss as it began to rise.

Isobel checked out her small purse. It was hardly anything but as she opened it, the sight of a single dime caught her eye. "Swanee, it ain't much, but here."

"Thank you, ma'am. When I get mo' money, I'm gonna be buyin' my uncle's freedom. He's in Virginia workin' on a tobacky plantation. Dey done tol' me when I get eight hunnert dollars I can get him."

Isobel embraced Swanee and told her she and her kin would be in her prayers. "We appreciate you, Swanee."

Swanee gathered her kettle. "Always happy to help, ma'am." Then, she was gone.

"I still don't understand how people can own other people. It violates everything our Republic stands for."

"She gave you the answer, Belle. Eight hundred dollars."

"I reckon we can't do much about it now. But we must do something sometime down the line."

"Giving her a dime counts as something. It might not seem like much, but if a lot of folks pitched in, it'd add up. We need to focus on this morning's business with the general."

"Aye, I know we have business, but helping folks like Swanee weighs heavy on my heart."

Kelvin pulled her into his arms. "I know, and I'm proud of you." He kissed her and set her free. "Let's get cleaned up and meet the general."

Tension coiled in her heart. She thought of the single dime. *It's all I can do for now.* Their little group was more than a social gathering, she knew that much. It was about something bigger.

"We keep on," she said. "We just keep on."

Upon seeing them, Sam said, "Our driver from yesterday told me walking to the offices today would be the better choice if the weather was agreeable."

"Good advice, General. I'd like a good walk this morning." Isobel patted her empty belly. "Right after we eat. I'm so hungry my stomach's growlin' like a bear."

"The hotel's breakfast service can't be too bad." Sam lifted his head. "I smell bacon."

"Let's get to it, General." Kelvin looked for the dining room.

As they stepped into the room, Swanee greeted them. When she saw Isobel, her eyes twinkled.

"General Houston, this young woman is Swanee. She is responsible for drawing hot water, cleaning rooms, and serving breakfast."

Swanee dipped her head. "Good mornin', sir. I'll be tellin' everyone I served the famous General Houston."

Sam chuckled. "The pleasure's mine. You've already impressed Mrs. MacDonald, and that's not easy."

Swanee replied, "Thank you, sir. I'll be gone to fetch coffee and eggs."

"Don't forget the bacon," called Kelvin.

As she disappeared into the kitchen, Isobel turned to Kelvin. "It's the little things."

Kelvin added, "And we keep doin' 'em, one step at a time."

CHAPTER FIFTEEN

June 5, 1832
Galveston Bay and Texas Land Company
No. 63 Cedar Street, Lower Manhattan
New York, New York

I sobel stretched her arms as the sun warmed her face. "I could kiss the fella who gave you the tip to walk this morning. This weather is divine compared to the South in summer."

Sam looked her in the eye. "The driver knew what he was talkin' about. A stroll like this clears the head and keeps big ears out of our business."

"Do you think I'll have a part to play at this meeting, General?" Doubt tinged Isobel's countenance.

"You'll have the most important role," Sam replied. "The unschooled Tennessee wife. Let them think you're just along for the ride. Meanwhile, you'll be watchin', listenin', and catchin' what they think they're hidin'. Can I count on you?"

A sly look spread across her face, "Oh, I reckon I can manage. I've played the role plenty."

Kelvin chuckled, kissing her cheek. "She's outwitted many a man with the ruse."

The trio walked in step, their boots striking the cobblestones with purpose. As they turned onto Cedar Street, Isobel's eyes locked on a scene that made her stomach churn. Workers with hunched shoulders shoveled piles of waste into carts, their faces slack with exhaustion. The stench hit her like a wave, and she gagged, pulling a handkerchief to her nose.

"Are they doin' what I think they're doin'?" she asked.

Sam answered, "Night soil men. They gather manure and sell it as fertilizer. Hard work, but it pays decent."

She grimaced. "City life has its wonders, don't it?"

Kelvin smiled, though his face betrayed his discomfort. "Wonders, indeed. Let's pick up the pace."

The smell faded as they approached Number 63, a modest brick building with a carved wooden sign. Sam gestured toward the door. "Here we are. Time to go to work."

Kelvin pushed the door open, holding it for Isobel and Sam. Inside, the office smelled of ink and wood polish. A man in a black coat looked up from behind a wide desk, his pen pausing mid-stroke. His gray eyes sharpened as he assessed the newcomers, then softened as recognition dawned.

"General Houston," he said, standing and extending a hand. "Anthony Dey. I've heard much about you."

Sam took his hand with a firm grip. "Mr. Dey, this is my associate, Mr. MacDonald, and his wife, Isobel. We're here to discuss your Texas ventures."

Dey gestured to the chairs before returning to his seat. "You've come to the right place. The Galveston Bay and Texas Land Company represents prominent empresarios, including Lorenzo de Zavala and David Burnet. We facilitate grant transactions for settlers looking to make a new start."

Sam leaned forward, his glare steady. "I understand the Mexican government has tightened immigration laws. How does your company navigate such matters?"

Dey replied, "Indeed, the laws are stricter, but the border is poorly enforced. Many settlers cross undeterred. Any investment there is a high-risk endeavor. It's not for the faint of heart."

Kelvin arched a brow. "And the scrips you sell? What's their purpose?"

"They signify association with us," he explained. "While not essential for claims, they carry priority with empresarios, signaling reliable backing."

Kelvin tilted his head. "So, they're more a suggestion than a requirement?"

"Precisely," he replied. "A practical tool in an unpredictable system."

Sam exchanged a glance with Kelvin, then turned back to Dey. "We've come seeking sponsorship. My name carries value on the frontier. I'd like to offer my endorsement of your enterprise in exchange for support."

His expression grew contemplative. "General, your reputation precedes you. Although the company cannot sponsor new ventures due to current jeopardies, I am willing to back you personally. I can provide funds and scrips for your journey with the understanding that you'll keep me informed of developments in Texas. The hazards there are higher than anything I've ever seen."

"Sir, if I could interrupt ya for a minute." Kelvin leaned in, closing the distance to sharpen his point. "You're right 'bout the big risk we're takin' with this plan. Failure's a real possibility. But I gotta say, if we fail in Texas, there's a way out. Thirty years before we declared independence, my grandfather and Isobel's fought side by side at Culloden. The consequence of the battle still lingers in our family lore, a thread of history tyin' us to a blood-soaked field far from here. Despite their bravery and fightin' spirit, they lost. Their way out was a ship. They got themselves outta Scotland and made it to America. America will always be here to take in the strays and losers like our grandfathers."

Sam's eyes glinted with a rare flicker of admiration. "Well said,

Kelvin." His remark carried more intensity than the simple words, it was a subtle acknowledgement that Kelvin had nailed it.

Kelvin brushed a hot tear from his cheek.

"The MacDonalds may not know of this, but the Houston clan in Scotland is a 'sept' or branch of the MacDonald line. My ancestor was Sir Hugh of Padvinan. My father considered Sir Hugh the progenitor of the Houston clan. He lived in the century following the Norman Conquest."

Kelvin's mouth fell open, shock flickering across his face and replacing any hint of a tear. Isobel snapped her eyes from the window, her expression tightening. Dey, however, remained unfazed as if he'd been expecting this all along.

"My American forebear was a Dutch naval officer," he revealed. "He was one of many Dutch settlers in New York, and we here in America owe much to him. There is a city street here bearing his name. If I have an accurate understanding of young Mr. MacDonald, America will always be our fallback point. She will never fail us."

"America will ever be our anchor, sir. The union is now and forevermore the spine around which our new organism will grow. Her people will provide her with heart and courage. The star of Texas will one day grace our 'Star Spangled Banner' as my lawyer loves to frame it."

Dey handed Sam a paper entitled, *Memo of Understanding*.

"This appears to be agreeable and in order," he said. "We would prefer to examine it a bit closer before signing it. We saw a park nearby, and since it is such a lovely day, we'll study our duties and obligations and return in a short time to affix the signature."

"As you wish, General. This is more than a business transaction to me. It manifests something I cannot place into words. Please take the time you need to study the instrument and sign it with confidence."

The trio left the offices, strolling a few blocks until they reached a small park. They settled onto the available benches, preparing to review the agreement. Sam and Kelvin, having already read it, handed the paper to Isobel, eager for her input. Surrounded by a compact forest, they all shared a sense of relief being outdoors. She finished reading the single page, her opinion forming in mere moments.

"I reckon there's nothing sinister in this contract, General. I can see the cause in investin' in shares of the Galveston Bay Company."

Back at the office, Dey explained the company's interest in Texas. Convinced of his integrity, Sam added his signature next to Dey's.

The trio returned to the lawn and rested in the little wooded plot. The melodic chirping of songbirds and the outlying clip-clop of horses on nearby roads provided a peaceful backdrop, allowing each of them to slip into their own reasonings.

Sam's observations drifted away from the grounds, his eyes distant. Isobel sensed his mind may be wandering back to the White House, imagining the moment he would advise the president of their situation.

Kelvin seemed at ease, soaking in the tranquility. He closed his eyes, savoring the birdsong and absence of people vying for his attention. Isobel, having spent countless hours watching her husband in moments like these, understood his inspirations as he connected with nature.

Amid the serene silence, a question pierced the stillness.

"The Houston clan is a sept of the MacDonalds?" she asked, stirring from the brief respite in the woods.

"Isn't every clan a sept of the MacDonalds?" Sam guffawed.

"Is the story true, General?" Kelvin's expression was earnest.

"Have I ever lied before?"

"No, sir,"

"Then you may accept the story as truthful. My father passed it to me as a lad, and I have no reason to believe he concocted such a tale."

"I come from the MacIntosh clan." Isobel placed her hands on her hips.

"Aye, she does." He kissed her cheek.

"As in William MacIntosh?"

"Yes, sir. The Creek chief was my kin."

"Did your father fight in the Creek War?"

"Sure did. Fought alongside Mr. Crockett. I was too young to have clear memories, but I heard the stories Daddy told later."

"A lot of good men and women were lost in the fight." Sam bowed his head.

Kelvin lifted his right hand with reverence and placed it in Sam's right hand as he would any other man of Scottish heritage. Isobel sensed the almost imperceptible change and stepped in to observe the special moment. As masculine hands clasped, she positioned both of hers on theirs, thus forming a triumvirate of certainty with which to navigate an uncertain future. The trio made a deathless three-stranded bond, not with contracts or blood-stained palms, but with a wordless pledge of their lives, their fortunes, and their sacred honor to a trinity of souls with the beloved name of *Texas* engraved on each of their hearts.

CHAPTER SIXTEEN

June 11, 1832
The White House
1600 Pennsylvania Avenue
Washington, D.C.

"The president will see you now, General Houston." The attendant's announcement was calm and deliberate. His white suit gleamed in the dim hallway, every line ironed to precision. Sam gave a wave, acknowledging the man's composure as much as his words. Without a glance back, the attendant led the way.

Sam followed, each step on the polished floor heavier than the one before it, as if the force of the moment pressed through his boots. The atmosphere tightened as he neared the Oval Office, the significance of this meeting coursing through him.

Inside, Andrew Jackson stood behind the desk, eyes sharp and probing. "What do you have for me, Sam?"

"I've been investigating this *Galveston Bay and Texas Land Company*. They're positioning themselves as key players in Texas settlement. Beyond Austin's colony, they seem to have the broadest reach."

Jackson leaned forward, his brow creasing. "How?"

"The empresarios hold massive tracts, granted under Mexican law. They swear loyalty to Mexico and its church, but the government's faith in them is dwindling. They've lost control over illegal immigration. The flow won't stop."

Jackson's lips pressed into a thin line. He rubbed his forehead, exhaling before responding. "Attorney General Butler is working to buy Texas from Mexico. If these settlers keep pushing boundaries, it'll undermine those talks. You see, don't you?"

"I suppose it's true, sir, but I must remind you the negotiations have drug on with no progress. I don't know anyone who takes them seriously. It's one thing to be patient, but it's quite another to be strung along on a fool's errand."

Jackson shot to his feet, fury ripping through him. His jaw clenched tight, eyes blazing as the words hung in the charged air between them. Sam could see he'd struck a nerve, hit the tender spot where he aimed. But he wasn't one to lose control for long. The president forced himself back into his seat and regained his grip on the moment.

Sam didn't flinch. The president needed to hear it and understand whatever good faith had existed in the negotiations was long gone, snuffed out months ago. He wasn't backing down, not on this.

"You may be right," conceded Jackson, "but these people pouring into Texas do not grasp what the word *revolution* means. It's another word for blood. You know what it means."

Sam met his stare, unyielding. "I know it better than most. Texas will rise. The settlers are cut from the same cloth as those who broke free from the British. They won't endure what's happening."

The president gave him a shadowed look. "If revolution comes, the United States cannot intervene. Mexican sovereignty must be respected. If you find yourself in trouble, you'll be on your own. Do you understand?"

"I do, sir. I expect no rescue. But I must see Texas firsthand, to gauge the situation."

Jackson's expression softened, a flicker of camaraderie. "If you're going, I require intelligence. I need to know if they are negotiating in bad faith as you suspect. I hanker for knowledge about these Comanche Indians I've heard about. They're the reason Mexico opened the land to settlement in the first place. If we can get ahead of this, we may save lives. Will you serve me in this?"

Sam's jaw tightened. "I'd hoped to serve you. I'll assess immigration, Mexican negotiations, and the Indians. Sending you updates will be my highest priority. I should inform you I'll be traveling with a young couple from Tennessee. They've been indispensable since the Stanbery trial."

"You trust them?"

"With my life. And the life of Texas."

Jackson tapped the desk. "Take this." He opened a drawer, retrieving a pouch. Coins and crisp bills emerged, their rustle breaking the silence as he counted a thousand dollars. "An amiable loan, Sam. Use it wisely. This mission is delicate. I need clarity about Mexico's intentions and the Comanche. The Indians may pose a bigger threat than the Mexican army."

Sam accepted the funds, gratitude mingled with resolve. "I'll see it done. You should know Mexico is weak. Its laws are toothless, its army disorganized and poorly staffed."

Jackson tilted his head. "You're hoping for a quick, decisive outcome?"

"Hope isn't a strategy," Sam replied. "Texas's size is its greatest defense. Guerrilla tactics will win, not battles over fixed positions."

The president sighed. "We'll see. But remember, unpredictability rules once the first shot is fired. Don't underestimate your enemy. European-trained officers are formidable enemies."

Sam held firm. "True. But Texas isn't Europe. Its wild expanse is no ally of traditional armies. We'll fight smart."

Jackson stood, extending his hand. "Old friend, I await your reports." He looked Sam in the eye. "Please don't start a war."

Sam clasped his hand, a rare moment passing between them. "You have my word, sir."

CHAPTER SEVENTEEN

June 12, 1832
Brown's Indian Queen Hotel
Pennsylvania Avenue
Washington, D.C.

The familiar room welcomed them, a pocket of quiet away from the bustling city. Isobel set her satchel by the bed and sank into the chair near the window. She snuck a look at Sam, whose steady presence filled the space.

"What's next, General?" Kelvin asked, breaking the silence.

Sam removed his hat and placed it on the table. "Tomorrow, we're off to the attorney general's office for passports."

"Passports?" She raised an eyebrow. "Aren't those for leavin' the country?"

"We won't be in the Union the whole time," he replied. "Indian Territory and Mexico are places where passports are needed."

Kelvin cocked his head. "When do we start?"

Sam rubbed his chin. "Reckon we'll be in Nashville soon. We'll take a coach to Wheeling, Virginia, and then board a steamboat to

Nashville. I always stop in Tennessee on my way to and from the Indian Territory."

"I see," she said. "How'd your meetin' with President Jackson fare?"

"It went fine. We're under orders for a presidential mission."

"Did you let the president know we're part of this mission?" Kelvin asked.

"Yes. I made sure y'all are accounted for in every detail." Concern lined Sam's eyes. "Get some rest and be ready for a journey that could stretch to six months. I'll take my supper elsewhere. Got some details to iron out."

"Good evenin', General." Confidence bloomed in Isobel. She followed Kelvin to the door, glancing back as Sam busied himself with papers on the desk. The burden of immense responsibility hung on his shoulders.

The door clicked shut behind them, and their footsteps echoed in the quiet hallway. Isobel's pulse quickened. She heard a melody, faint and distant. She'd never heard the tune before. She swiped a hand across her brow, the humidity sticking to her skin.

"You alright?" He placed the back of his hand on her forehead.

"Wonderin' about that tune." She looked into his eyes. "You hear it?"

He shook his head. "No."

She couldn't explain it, not in full, but deep inside she knew. She wasn't walking down a hallway, she was stepping onto history's grand stage, her path already woven into something far greater than she could see.

"You sure you're alright?" He squeezed her hand.

"I'm thinkin'." Her notions drifted to the soft light pooling at the end of the hall. "It's big, Kel. Like we're steppin' into somethin' bigger than us."

Kelvin placed a reassuring hand on her shoulder. "We'll manage. One step at a time."

CHAPTER EIGHTEEN

June 13, 1832
Office of the Attorney General
Washington, D.C.

The clink of silverware and the robust scent of coffee filled the room as Sam leaned over the breakfast table, his face sharp. "Here's the plan." These moments provided their marching orders. "We'll take the carriage to the attorney general's office. Passports will take most of the morning. Once that's done, the coach is yours for the day. I'll spend the afternoon riding Saracen and handling errands." He paused, a faint smirk breaking the bounds of his seriousness. "The president keeps my boy stabled. Says he won't let him get too fat."

Kelvin said, "Saracen's a fine horse, General. Glad he's in good hands. I reckon he's part of the future we're headin' toward."

"Yes, he is," Sam replied. "He's carried me through plenty and still has miles left. When the time is right, I'll fetch him myself or send someone I trust."

Isobel tilted her head. "He's stayin' in Washington City?"

"A horse slows you down on a trip like this. Makes it harder in ways you'd never think. He's better off here for now." Sam possessed the solidity of experience, though the thought unsettled her.

The coach rolled up to Brown's, its wheels crunching over the gravel drive. The driver tipped his hat as he opened the door. Isobel, Sam, and Kelvin stepped inside, the polished wood and rich upholstery enveloping them.

The city passed in a blur of smoky facades and clattering hooves. She let her ideas drift, wondering what the future held for the capital and for her. She had little time to ponder before the carriage stopped in front of an imposing stone building.

Attorney General Butler stood in the doorway, his broad frame commanding attention. "Good morning, sir." His expression softened when his eyes fell on Sam. "The president told me you need passports for your mission. Follow me."

"Thank you," Sam replied. "He made it clear we're to gather intelligence without interfering with your legal efforts. I'm pleased to introduce Kelvin MacDonald and his wife, Isobel, who are accompanying me."

Butler shook their hands. "A pleasure to meet you both. Any friends of the president and General Houston are welcome here."

Inside, a large table awaited, laden with forms, quills, and ink. Isobel hesitated when she noticed a measuring tape fixed to the wall. "What's it for?"

"You'll see." Sam motioned her to focus on the paperwork.

She set to filling in the blanks:

Name: Mrs. Isobel MacDonald
Age: 20 years
Height:

Her pen hovered over the blank space until realization struck. The tape on the wall. She rose, motioning for Kelvin to help. Once they determined her height, she returned to her seat.

Height: 5 feet, 3 inches
Hair color: Blonde
Complexion: Fair
Eye color: Blue

She checked out Sam's form, noting with surprise he stood at over six feet, two inches. She found Kelvin was five feet, nine inches. Most men around the hollers were shorter than Kel.

When they finished, she gathered the forms and handed them to Butler's assistant, who directed them to an elegant parlor. Rich cocoa-colored furniture and velvet chairs filled the room. She sank into one, running her fingers across the mahogany table's smooth surface. The idea of sitting where dignitaries once discussed the nation's future was surreal.

Her thoughts drifted to her parents. They'd instilled a love of learning in her, teaching her to read, write, and use critical thinking skills. Books, often communal and worn, had been treasures in the holler. Her father insisted she marry a man who valued knowledge as much as she did, which led her to Kelvin. Their connection wasn't romantic alone. They shared ideals and dreams.

The assistant reappeared. "Mr. Butler was called away, but he signed your passports. If you'd sign these copies, we'll have everything ready shortly."

Isobel's frustration bubbled up as she peered at yet another stack of papers. Her fingers twitched with the urge to crumple them. "More copies?" she muttered.

Sam didn't look up, his pen scratching across the paper. "It's necessary. Lawyers, speculators, and officials have their ways."

She folded her arms, leaning back in her chair. "How do you handle it? All this writin' and signin'? It's endless."

He looked at her, his expression patient. "Government's a slow beast. Patience, ma'am. Things never move as fast as you want."

"Patience ain't my strong suit," she admitted. The denseness of the unfamiliar processes and responsibilities settled over her like a too-heavy cloak.

DARYL LOTT

Kelvin placed a hand on hers. "You'll get there. Watch and learn. You're not alone."

She took his hand, her frustration tempered but not gone. She relied on them, grateful for their steadying presence. There was so much to absorb, so much she didn't know. Yet, she resolved to find the solution.

The clerk returned sooner than expected, handing over their completed passports. "Good luck to you all. Your mission is urgent. I pray for your success."

Sam tipped his head. "Thank you, sir. Luck and prayers will both be welcome."

As they stepped outside, the sunlight hit Isobel's face, toasty and bright. She touched the passport's cover, the embossed design pressing into her fingertips. *The United States of America.* Her grip tightened on the document. *This is real.* The weight bored into her heavier than it should, as though it carried all the burdens and tribulations of the odyssey ahead. Isobel recognized the pull of the West striving with the invisible tether of her mountain roots. The struggle between her past and the promise of new beginnings occupied a new battlefield in her heart.

Kelvin broke through her thoughts. "You ready?"

"Ready as I'll ever be."

CHAPTER NINETEEN

July 1, 1832 (morning)
The Steamboat *Heliopolis*
Confluence of the Ohio and Cumberland Rivers
Smithland, Kentucky

The steady rhythm of the steamboat's engine pulsed through Isobel's body as she leaned against the rail. The Ohio River stretched before her, its currents carrying driftwood and branches that danced on the water like fleeting memories. The *Heliopolis* chugged forward, a hulking twin-hulled vessel with the power to clear the waterway of dangers hidden beneath its placid surface.

Kelvin stood beside her, bright with curiosity. "This boat's a marvel. It's not just a transport – it clears the river. Snags, tree trunks, debris. Captain Shreve's invention saves lives and cleans out trade routes."

"Practical and clever," Isobel murmured, her eyes tracing the snagging apparatus. "Men dream big when the stakes are high."

Sam joined them, resting his forearms on the railing. "This whole country's built on big dreams. Steam engines, railroads, bridges.

Congress argues about them all, but none of it happens without sacrifice."

Isobel's deliberations shifted to the crew. It was a mix of white laborers and Negro slaves working in grueling unison to feed the hungry snagging machine. She swallowed hard. "Plenty of sacrifice here," she said. "Not all of it chosen."

A new mouth broke into their conversation. "Am I addressing General Samuel Houston of Tennessee?"

Sam pivoted, his sharp eye meeting that of a slender man in a tailored coat. "Yes, sir. And you are?"

"Alexis de Tocqueville, at your service," the man said with a graceful bow. "Permit me to commend your nation's ingenuity. This vessel is remarkable."

Kelvin stepped forward, extending a hand. "Kelvin MacDonald, sir. And this is my lovely wife, Isobel."

He turned his attention to her, bowing low as he kissed her hand. "Madame MacDonald, your beauty is surpassed only by the grace with which you carry it."

Isobel held her composure steady. "Thank you, sir. Though my husband's flattery rivals your own."

The Frenchman chuckled. "A happy meeting. I find myself intrigued by your country. Its vastness, its contradictions. May I pose a question, General?"

Sam opened a palm. "Ask away."

"*Merci, Générale.* Our people consider the native inhabitants of this continent fascinating. I know of your personal relations with the Indians and am curious to hear about them from someone who has intimate knowledge of their customs. Have the Indians a religion?"

De Tocqueville leaned toward Sam as he explained. "Some of them have no belief in the immortality of the soul. But generally, the Indians believe in a god who punishes or rewards the deeds of this life in the other world."

"Have they any form of worship?"

"The Osages, who live on the frontier of Mexico, pray every morning to the rising sun. The Creeks have no worship. It is only in times of great calamity, or before undertaking some great enterprise, that they devote themselves to some public manifestations of worship."

"What sort of government have the Indians?"

"Generally, a patriarchal government. Birth makes the chiefs. Among the tribes with European contact, they are elected."

"What is the status of women among the Indians?"

Isobel leaned in a bit, her ears straining to catch every word of the response.

"Complete servitude. The women have to do all the unpleasant tasks and live in great degradation."

She was not surprised. No society she knew of treated women as equals to men. Her own upbringing, which granted her more autonomy and education than most, was a rare exception.

"Are the Indians intelligent?"

"I believe that both Indians and black people are as intelligent as white people. Freedom begets intelligence. Slavery does not. The Indian is born free. He makes use of this freedom from his first steps in life. Surrounded by dangers, pressed by necessities, and unable to count on anyone, his mind must be ever active to find means to ward off troubles and to maintain his existence. The necessity imposed on the Indian gives his intelligence a degree of development and ingenuity, which are often wonderful."

"And the black man has no recourse to exercise his intelligence?" asked de Tocqueville.

"The first notions of existence that he receives make him understand that he is the property of another, that care for his own future is no concern of his, and that the power of thought is for him a useless gift of Providence."

Isobel's fury boiled over, prompting her to stride down the deck, away from the two men. Staying would have led to an embarrassing outburst.

A Negro man on the snagging platform admired the river, and she deliberated whether he, too, sought solace. Nearby, a white laborer also enjoyed the view during a brief break. She approached them to express her gratitude for their difficult work. "I appreciate y'all's effort. I see how tough it is, but anyone travelin' in safety owes y'all a debt."

"Thank you, ma'am." The white man shouted up to her.

The Negro man remained silent, his view fixed on the water. She wondered if he was not permitted to speak to a white woman or if he was unaccustomed to people acknowledging his labor.

"I mean to show my appreciation to both of you. You're hard-workin' folks who may not get many thanks from passengers."

"We thank you, ma'am," the white man replied. "Me and Pompey work together every day, savin' each other from danger more times than I can count. He don't talk to no white lady. It ain't his way, but any kindness shown us is a thing we ponder at night."

As the light of day faded into the evening, a chorus of frogs and crickets began their nighttime song. A wave of calm washed over her, reminding her of childhood, when she learned nocturnal species were the most abundant in the forests and rivers. The familiar symphony, whether in Tennessee, Washington City, or here in Kentucky, always brought her comfort.

A tap on the shoulder jolted her back to the present.

"Where are you, Girl?" Kelvin wrapped his arms around her. "I've been callin' you and got no response."

"I'm sorry," she replied. "The general and Mr. de Tocqueville got my mind racin' against its will in a fitful rage. I've been trying to calm myself down, so I don't embarrass us."

"It must have been outrageous, whatever it was."

"It's the same old issue. White men makin' the rules and customs. Everyone else must comply or be in chains or an outcast. For over two hundred years, slavery has divided our country. And women? We're treated like domesticated animals in the household." Her blood pressure rose again.

Kelvin dipped his head. "I know we're goin' to Texas to chase our dreams, but I fear the same old conditions will shape the settlements there. Since it's the two of us, our impact is limited."

Isobel turned to face her husband and wrapped her arms around his neck. "I understand, Kel. But I can't shake this feelin'. Remember the preacher teachin' us about Gideon? He was the least of his family, but an angel appeared to him and told him God was going to use him to save Israel. We have to do somethin', but I don't know what we can do now."

Kelvin took her hand. "Something might come up in the future. Gideon and all those other men and women we studied in the Bible had one quality in their favor. They were obedient. The smartest thing we can do now is bide our time and be patient." He kissed her cheek. "If the time ever comes when an angel or the Lord gives you a task, you can count on me to back ya up."

"Have you ever seen an angel, Kel?"

"Sure. I'm lookin' at one right now."

Isobel loved him. She appreciated his little joke, but her mind churned with convictions about the choices available to persecuted Indians, even after forced resettlement, compared to the lack of choices for Negroes due to their status. The injustice gnawed at her. Seeking an outlet, she remembered the paper and pencil she'd packed to jot down her observations. "I need to process my thoughts on paper. If you'll excuse me."

Kelvin kissed her and released her to her passions.

Later, in the dim light of their cabin, Isobel put her thoughts to paper. The verses spilled out, raw and urgent, a poem for those silenced:

Of chains and choices,
they are ours to make.
Of chains and choices,
they are ours to take...

CHAPTER TWENTY

July 1, 1832 (evening)
The Steamboat *Heliopolis*
Confluence of the Ohio and Cumberland Rivers
Smithland, Kentucky

Isobel glanced at the worn scrap of paper balanced on her knees. She worked her fingers around the edges of the page as if the words could somehow escape. It wasn't much of a poem, just something she scribbled when the oppressiveness of the world got too heavy.

The idea hadn't been hers; it came from her lawyer. Francis Scott Key, his words still sharp in her memory, had described the bloody night in vivid detail. He'd stood helpless as British warships blasted Fort McHenry to pieces. He'd been powerless, his frustration boiling beneath his skin, until he did the only thing he could. He wrote. His reaction is what stuck with her. Not the flag or the glory, but the act of writing when there was nothing else to do.

Unlike Key's stirring words, meant for a nation, Isobel's sentiments were destined for no one. No eyes but her own would ever see what spilled out on the paper, and that was fine with her. Her poem was a call to action addressed to herself.

The grip of King Cotton tightened on everyone. The coarse fibers of her dress scraped against her skin and the endless toil of workers on the snagging platform troubled her. Laborers, slave and free, bent under the sun and hauled debris to clear the way for steamboats. Every bale loaded downstream carried the grievousness of human suffering, feeding a system too vast to topple – yet.

The country, bound by this machinery of greed, moved as if hypnotized. She tucked the poem away and stepped on the deck, her thoughts simmering. The *Heliopolis's* twin hulls plowed through the dark waters as the crew toiled under the glow of a full moon. The snagging boom lurched, lifting logs and trash from the river, clearing paths for commerce. It was ingenious, though she wondered if anything could clear the hazards choking the soul of the nation.

"Evenin', Isobel." Sam's familiar drawl broke through her musings.

She turned to face him. "Good evenin'. Did you enjoy your chat with Mr. de Tocqueville?" In many ways, she saw her general as a reflection of the conflicting interests that plagued America and its people. He was a kind and intelligent man. He was a war hero whose wound still caused him great pain. He stood for the rights of the Indians, whom he revered as the guardians of the natural world. Serving under the president for the greater good of everyone, he held the Union above all else. And yet, he also owned slaves. Isobel couldn't comprehend it, but in him, she saw the embodiment of an age, an era consisting of a complex tapestry of ideals and contradictions. The complexities of individuals and the vastness of the country defied categorization into *good* and *bad*.

"I did. It's important to share our perspective with men like him. The South draws curious eyes from all over, tryin' to make sense of us."

"General, I hope you don't mind I was listenin' in on your talk." She paused for a reaction, but his countenance remained calm.

"Not at all."

"The questions Mr. de Tocqueville asked are the same ones most people would have, includin' me."

Sam leaned on the rail. "I figured as much. I know your curiosity comes from a good place, not one to catch me in a bind."

"Thank you. But the contradictions gnaw at me. We're a nation built on the idea all men are created equal, yet we hold millions in bondage. How do we reconcile those?"

"I can't debate your point." He surveyed the riverbank. "It sure is hypocritical when folks who love liberty and call themselves patriots own slaves. It's plain to see why many from afar see it as hollow, 'cause that's what it is."

"Isn't it possible to give everyone on our continent their freedom?" She looked at him as if she were a schoolgirl again.

"Recall the Haitian Servile Insurrection?" He answered her query with a question.

Isobel's mind drifted back to the harrowing episode. She recalled how the Negro population had risen in rebellion against the masters. In their quest for liberation, their revolution spiraled into a bloodbath, claiming the lives of countless slaveholders, including children. It was a tragic event, one nobody wanted to see repeated. "I remember it."

"White men here fear the same outcome. Liberty unleashed without preparation led to chaos and ruin there. The slaves got their freedom, but no tools to build a future. The results were misery."

"But isn't education the answer?" She grew insistent. "Teach them, give them the tools."

"Who will? And at what cost? The South's power lies in slavery. It's not the labor alone, it's the Three-Fifths Rule, which gives political clout to the slave holder and not the slave."

She clenched the railing, frustration burning. "I see white and black men working together on this boat. They depend on each other. There's the proof we can work side by side."

Sam's head swayed in silent disagreement. "Maybe. But this is an exception. It's a dangerous pursuit. Necessity breeds cooperation."

"And yet, you admit intelligence isn't tied to race. How can we justify denying freedom to people equal to us in mind and spirit?"

Sam's jaw tightened. "The system's wrong. I don't deny it. But change won't come easy. Slavery is wealth, power, and survival for many. It's not a mere moral matter. It's an economic issue."

"It's reprehensible on every level," she shot back. She turned away, tears stinging her eyes. She wiped them and willed herself to stay composed.

"I hope slavery ends for the betterment of the nation and for all mankind." Sam could not argue against her basic contention. "We aren't there yet. I see clear as day bondage can't withstand the opposition arrayed on it from all over the globe. I long for the day we change to free labor. I don't know how it happens. The white men of the South will never give up their positions without a fight."

"I agree." Isobel stumbled back a couple of steps. Her vision blurred as the world tilted. Her hand shot out, fingers curled around the cold metal rail. She gripped it tight, knuckles pale, as the dizziness threatened to pull her under. She heard something.

The faint strains of something familiar tickled her ears. Was it... fiddle music? Her eyes flicked across the deck, scanning the boat. The steady hum of the riverboat filled her ears, but nothing stirred. She turned toward the riverbank, squinting at the dense wall of trees swaying in the breeze. Still, no sign of life. No more than the low murmur of the water and the distant spectral sound of strings carried on the wind.

Sam gave her a reassuring pat on the shoulder. "Are you alright?"

She shrugged. "Do you hear music, General? Maybe a fiddle?"

He paused and listened. "No. Nothin' but the boiler and engine hummin'. I think ya got yerself a little too worked up. Happens to me sometimes."

"As Mr. Stanbery found out." Isobel's pulse calmed.

"No music involved there, unless ya count me strummin' his head." Sam grinned.

"If you weren't an honorable man, Kel and I wouldn't be here. I'm prayin' and hopin' Texas will be different from other places in the cotton latitudes. The mixture of peoples there requires it. There's Indians, Negroes, Mexicans, pirates, Jews, pagans, Christians, thieves, robbers, soldiers, sailors, scholars, Germans, Irish, men of letters, illiterate buffoons, and now us. Kelvin, you, and I will venture into the melee. We gotta take the lesson of the snagging platform. It's an ingenious but simple design manned by varied people working together for the common good of all who take passage on the vessel."

"I can't argue with your facts. So, we enter the fray. Texas is an explosive mixture of all the people you named, with the smell of revolution hangin' in the air like gunpowder." Sam raised an imaginary glass in a toast and exclaimed, "To the *Heliopolis* and to Texas."

CHAPTER TWENTY-ONE

July 10, 1832
Allen House Slave Quarters
Allendale Plantation
Clarksville, Tennessee

The oars sliced through the sluggish waters of the Cumberland, each stroke a steady rhythm against Sam's pounding thoughts. Borrowing the skiff from a *Heliopolis* crewman had been easy enough but returning it before the riverboat shoved off may have been an impossible promise to keep. The little boat nudged the muddy bank, and he tied it off to a low branch with a taut pull. His boots slid on the slick earth as he climbed out, his pulse quickening with every unsteady step. The familiar shape of the slave quarters loomed ahead. One chance, one last look at her – his Liza.

Dilsey stood on the porch, her broom sweeping dust between the floorboards. Her movements carried a rhythm, a flow he hadn't realized he missed.

"Dilsey!" He called, his shout breaking the stillness.

She froze, gripping the broom as her head snapped toward the sound. "Who's there?" She trembled.

"It's me," he said, stepping from the shadows of the trees.

"Marse Sam!" She let the broom fall and clutched her chest. "Lord, have mercy, you scared me."

"I'm sorry. I didn't mean to. Thought you'd know my voice."

She squinted, wiping her hands on her apron. "Ain't nobody expectin' you here. They all say you gone for good."

Sam lifted a brow. "I almost didn't come back. This is my last visit. I need a favor."

"A favor from me? What kind of favor?"

He reached into his vest pocket and held up a silver dollar. "Go to the Big House. Bring Liza here. Don't tell her I'm waitin'. Please bring her."

"Miss Liza don't ever come to these parts. What makes you think she'll listen to me?"

"You've got a way with her, Dilsey. Please. I need to see her one more time. I'll hide in your cabin."

She glanced at the coin, then back at him. She sighed, picked up her broom, and leaned it against the porch rail. "I'll do my best, Marse Sam. Coffee's on the stove if you're waitin'." She hurried down the trail, her steps quick and certain.

He stepped into the cabin, greeted by the thick scent of fresh coffee and wood smoke. The space was tidy, almost too perfect, each corner reflecting her meticulous care. He poured himself a cup, the beverage grounding him as he sank onto a chair by the window.

The memories came unbidden. Liza's laughter echoing through Allendale's halls. Her eyes shining in the candlelight. Eleven weeks of marriage. A union so brief, yet it was etched into his soul like a scar. He rubbed a hand over his face, wishing he could forget but knowing he never would.

Dilsey words outside snapped him from his thoughts. "Miss Liza, you gotta hear them river birds sing today."

Through the window, he watched the two women approach. Dilsey pointed toward the trees, her arm sweeping wide. Liza hesitated, her steps slow and uncertain.

"They sound so sweet, Miss Liza. Like they know your troubles and want to lift 'em away."

Liza's lips curved into a faint smile, her eyes softening as she listened. The birdsong swirled around them, cloaking the clearing in a mystical melody.

He clenched the windowsill. She looked as she had the day they wed, her hair catching the dim light, her posture graceful. He longed to call out to her, but he stayed silent, hidden behind the wooden frame.

Liza spoke softly. "The river don't care, does it? It keeps movin', carryin' life along with it. Birds, fish, people. None of it matters to the river, it flows along with no worries."

Her words wrapped around him like a bittersweet song. He closed his eyes, holding the moment tight.

As the women turned back toward the Big House, he set a twenty-dollar gold piece beside the empty coffee cup. It was the least he could do for Dilsey. She had always been a better companion to Liza than he ever was. He slipped out of the cabin and down to the riverbank.

The water moved steady and sure, like time itself. Sam stared at its surface, the reflection of the trees trembling with each ripple. He'd come to say goodbye, and now, he had. Forever.

CHAPTER TWENTY-TWO

July 11, 1832
The Hermitage
Nashville, Tennessee

The *Heliopolis* glided to a stop, her hull scraping against the dock's weathered planks. The river's scent filled Isobel's lungs, heavy and earthy. She stepped off the gangway as it hit the dock with a dull thud. The boards beneath her boots shifted, adding to the unease of unfamiliar ground. Kelvin followed close behind, while Sam leapt down with an effortless ease revealing his comfort in any setting.

A tall, broad-shouldered man waited at the pier's edge. His drawl greeted them like an old friend. "Welcome to the Hermitage." Alfred's handshake was firm, his smile genuine.

"I'm Isobel MacDonald." She clasped his hand. "And this is my husband, Kelvin."

Sam stepped forward, extending his hand "These two are with me, Alfred."

"Pleasure's mine. Welcome home, General." Alfred's respect for Sam shone through every word.

They followed Alfred up a narrow path winding through the trees, the sun dappling the ground in golden patches. He pointed out a spot with reverence. "There's where General Houston found the perfect hickory saplin' for his cane."

"We've heard about the cane." Isobel shot Sam a grin.

A few paces ahead, something dark caught her eye near the roots of a poplar. She paused and stooped to pick it up.

Alfred glanced back. "That's a raven feather, sure enough." He shook his head. "Can't imagine why anyone'd want it."

Isobel turned it over in her fingers, the glossy black sheen catching the light. "It's beautiful," she said quietly, though that wasn't the only reason she tucked it away.

Alfred gave her a puzzled look but didn't press.

He led them to the mansion's heavy oak door. It creaked open, revealing the cool interior of the entry hall. "Guests have arrived."

Two women rose from their chairs. Betty embraced Sam, while Sarah's reserved look lingered on the young couple.

"Sarah, Betty, these are Isobel and Kelvin," he said, beaming.

Sarah said, "Welcome. I'm Sarah Jackson. My husband is visiting his father in Washington City." Her words carried no affection, but Isobel refused to let it deter her.

"It's a pleasure to meet you, ma'am," she said with a respectful dip of her head. "We were hopin' to walk around the grounds a bit, if you don't mind."

Her expression softened. "Of course. The lawns and gardens are lovely this time of year."

Sam caught up with them as they stepped outside. The sun bathed their faces as he pointed toward a grove of trees. "The little burying ground's that way. Rachel's laid to rest there."

"We'll pay our respects." Her stare followed the path.

He tipped his hat before turning back to the mansion. "See y'all later."

The land stretched wide and tranquil, the plantation's rhythm undisturbed by its absent master. Inside, Sam settled into a leather chair in Jackson's study, the smell of old books and polished wood enveloping him. He sat undisturbed in the quiet room as sunlight gleamed off the columns outside.

The creak of footsteps drew his attention. The couple entered, their expressions a mix of awe and curiosity.

"What did y'all think of the place?" He looked up with a keen expression.

"Everything feels... intentional." Isobel traced the spine of a book with her fingers. "Like every detail was made to fit with perfection."

Kelvin added, "This study's somethin' else. A man could get mighty comfortable here."

Sam poured three servings of Tennessee whiskey, the liquid splashing in each vessel. As they raised their drinks, Isobel led the toast. "To our absent host, the President of the United States. May he long enjoy good health and prosperity."

"Hear, hear." The men lifted their glasses.

As they drank, Sarah appeared in the doorway. "The president always says you're his favorite guest, General." Her eyes softened. "Since Mother Rachel passed, I've tried to keep things runnin' smooth. I thank the Lord for Betty and Alfred. They help me when I struggle."

Sam said, "You're a fine host. Auntie Rachel would agree."

Her expression changed. "That means a lot. Mrs. MacDonald, I envy your travels. Our home is charming, but I imagine your adventures outshine it."

"On the contrary, Mrs. Jackson." Isobel dipped her head to honor their hostess. "I've never seen a manor so beautiful. It must be quite a challenge to run such a place while its master is off leadin' our country."

"Yes, we've got over a thousand acres in cultivation. I fear my husband isn't meetin' his father's expectations with the upkeep of the plantation while he's off in Washington. I'm tellin' you this 'cause General Houston's like kin to us, and our family has no secrets from him. As trusted friends of his and the president's, I want y'all to call me Sarah."

"Thank you, Sarah." Isobel's eyes twinkled. "General Houston is leadin' our party out west to add another jewel to the crown of America. We've got a lot of work ahead, but the reward is worth every bit of it. Please, call me Isobel as my friends do."

"It near slipped my mind." Sarah's cheeks burned red with embarrassment. "A mail pouch came a few days ago from Washington with some letters for General Houston. I'll fetch it right away. I'm sure it's important for your mission."

Sam rubbed his chin as she dashed out to retrieve the mail. He reached for the bottle of whiskey, the liquid catching the light as he poured himself another glass. Isobel could tell their raised eyebrows and exchanged glances bothered Sam.

"This is the first time we've had to relax since we started west. I'm gonna make the most of it." He brought the glass to his lips and emptied it once more.

"Don't mind us, General." They settled into other chairs in the study. "You're in friendly company." He tipped the decanter again.

"General, may I ask you a question?" Isobel shifted in her chair.

"Yes."

"She said there are over one thousand acres under cultivation. Do you know how many slaves the Hermitage requires?"

Kelvin's view drifted to the doorway as Sarah reappeared, a leather bag clutched in her hands.

"I can answer her," Sarah interjected, handing the pouch to Sam. "The Hermitage needs about a hundred and fifty workers to keep runnin'. My husband finds the whole administration part tedious and complicated. I reckon it's why his father called him to the White House."

"I often wonder if free labor would be more efficient and easier to manage, with each worker earnin' wages. I believe free labor is superior to slave labor in every way."

"I don't know." Sarah looked about for a seat. "Do you mind if I sit? I don't want to break in on a private conversation."

Isobel motioned for Sarah to sit by her. "We'd be delighted if you'd join us."

"I think of the Nat Turner Rebellion over in Virginia a couple of years back. All it did was lead to the deaths of over fifty white folks, some of 'em children. When I see a small army of over one hundred people with hoes and shovels out there every day, I can't help but think of those uprisings. The servants here are treated better than most others. On one hand, the Hermitage is a safe place for them, but on the other, I know everyone yearns for liberty."

"I can speak for your father-in-law on this." Sam sipped from his glass. "The preservation of the Union is his highest priority. If it means endin' slavery, then so be it. I agree with him with my whole heart, but right now, folks aren't ready to face it head-on. The whole U.S. economy rests on the backs of those millions of field hands. Like you said, 'everyone yearns for liberty.' I don't know the answer to our national problem. The pitch and roll of ethical issues create a storm-tossed sea that's hard to navigate."

"It's the question of the day." Kelvin lifted his hand and pointed to the ceiling. "But nobody's got any good answers."

"I'm afraid you're right, Mr. MacDonald." Sarah shook her head.

"I wish it weren't so, but when sides can't be reconciled, war with its bloodshed and death becomes the only solution." Isobel bowed her head as if the bloody episode had already occurred.

"I hope there is something less fraught in the mail pouch." He reached in and retrieved an envelope.

He unfolded the letter addressed to him, the paper crackling as he smoothed it out. He scanned the neat handwriting of President Jackson's message, taking in the mention of James Prentiss, a member of the Galveston Bay and Texas Land Company. The words outlined the next steps in his quest to secure backers for his endeavors in Texas. He looked up at the MacDonalds. "Don't y'all get too comfortable here with Mrs. Jackson's hospitality."

"Really, General." Sarah's brow furrowed, and her lips pressed into a tight line as she pulled her arms close, locking them across her chest. "Betty's busy in the summer kitchen right now fixin' a feast to celebrate your visit. She takes great pride in servin' Hermitage guests and runs her kitchen like magic. Please, don't go spoilin' the day by talkin' about leavin' before dinner."

"Alright." He patted her hand. "I'd never go against the hostess' wishes when it comes to food and hospitality."

Sarah said, "It's settled. No talk of leavin' before supper."

IN THE BACK PARLOR, the dining table buzzed with the anticipation of residents and guests, all eager for the meal Betty prepared. Isobel watched her move among the staff, ensuring they served dinner in flawless style. No one was disappointed.

Betty's eyes flashed as she cleared the plates. "Y'all might want to leave a little room." Her warning carried a hint of mischief. "The best is yet to come. Georgia peaches are in season, and our master loves peach pie. When ya eat your pie tonight, think of him."

Sarah said, "My father-in-law isn't the only one in the Hermitage who loves Betty's pie. When the peach harvest is good, we buy enough for slave and free to put 'em up in preserves. This year the peaches are plentiful, and Betty meets the steamers to take delivery. She's a wonderful cook and kitchen manager."

"Thank you so much, Betty." A dash of color splashed on Isobel's cheeks.

Kelvin shared his approval between final bites of his pie. "It was delicious."

Sam leaned back in his chair, patting his stomach with a satisfied sigh. He raised his hand. "Brandy, please."

As the diners finished their meals, Aaron, the after-dinner table attendant, stepped forward, moving with a skillful grace. He filled each snifter enough to cover the bottom.

With a familiar sparkle in his eye, Sam raised his glass high. The room quieted in anticipation, everyone turning their attention to him, knowing he would deliver the evening's toast. "To the Hermitage, her family, and her staff. May they ever be the congenial hosts to wayward misfits such as myself and my companions."

"Hear! Hear!" The diners toasted the Hermitage with glasses held high.

"General, you've got your hostess's permission to share what's important in your latest post from Washington." She inhaled deeply. "I'm sure our absent and unseen master is thinkin' about the good of the republic when he's movin' his pieces across the continent like a chessboard."

"Well said, Sarah." He glanced around the table. "Y'all remember our next stop on this journey. The president told me we need to head to Cincinnati. We can find further support for our mission there."

Isobel leaned closer to Kelvin and whispered, "Cincinnati? Aren't we headin' backwards, away from Texas?"

He shrugged. "I suppose river travel takes many switches to and fro to go from one point to another."

Sarah raised another toast. "To Cincinnati on the Great Ohio. Fare thee well, General."

CHAPTER TWENTY-THREE

July 21, 1832 (Morning)
The Orleans Coffee House
Steamboat Landing, Ohio River
Cincinnati, Ohio

The aroma of coffee curled around Isobel as she stepped into the cafe. Her boots tapped on the wooden floor, muffled by the hum of conversation. She glimpsed Kelvin's face as it lit up.

Kelvin's grin spread wide as he inhaled. "Solid ground feels good underfoot. And fresh coffee smells even better."

She stretched, her hands pressing against her lower back. "You've got a point, but I'll take the steamboat over a stagecoach any day." Her attempt to ease the persistent ache from days of travel fell short. She sighed, her study wandering over the bustling room.

"Sure, boats are smoother." Kelvin shook his head. "Those boilers make me nervous. I've heard stories. Folks blown sky-high in an instant. They're a marvel, but they need work before I trust 'em completely."

Her fingers brushed the rim of a table as she steadied herself. The distant hiss of a steam engine outside made her chest tighten. She cast it aside. "I'll pray we never see such a disaster," she said, looking at Sam. Steamboats had been the sole option on this journey, no use dwelling on their dangers now.

A man in a tailored suit approached and extended a hand. "General Houston, I'm James Prentiss. It's an honor to meet you. I represent the Galveston Bay and Texas Land Company."

Sam grasped the man's hand. "Well, Mr. Prentiss, I reckon you're why we're here. Got news about the operation?"

"Indeed, sir. We've got eager investors lined up, though they're cautious, given the rumors about rebellion in Texas. How about we discuss it over a drink?" He gestured toward a table by the window.

Sam followed him. "Sounds good. Let me introduce my associates. This is Kelvin MacDonald and his wife, Isobel. Anything you've got to say to me, you can say with them present."

Prentiss tipped his head in greeting. "A pleasure, Mr. and Mrs. MacDonald."

Settling into a chair, she admired the scene outside. The landing bustled with life. Steamboats unloaded cargo as the deckhands' calls rose and fell in a steady rhythm. "This spot's lively." She peeked at Prentiss. "Good coffee, good company, and a view worth taking in."

Prentiss said, "Glad you think so, ma'am. Coffee for everyone? General, I expect something a bit stronger for yourself." He signaled a porter, adding bourbon for Sam.

As the drinks arrived, Prentiss wasted no time. His remarks dropped low, urgency evident in every word. "The investors are committed because of your reputation, but they're nervous. The whispers of rebellion are gettin' louder. They fear a revolution could ruin everything and leave us all empty-handed."

Isobel's stomach churned. The gravity of his words hung heavy, though he hadn't said it outright. *The Republic of Texas.* She looked at Kelvin, his dark eyes fixed on his coffee. He exhaled.

Sam leaned back, cradling his glass. His look turned to the docks, as if seeking answers beyond the horizon. "I don't blame folks for being skittish. The Mexican government's unstable, shifting like sand.

Stephen Austin's doing his best, swearing loyalty to Mexico and its laws, but those laws don't hold much weight these days. Investing in Texas is a gamble, no doubt about it. Most folks'd tell you it's a bad bet. That's not a lie. Still, the payoff could be worth the risk."

Kelvin muttered, "It's a huge gamble, all right. But aren't all things nowadays?"

Isobel's vexation simmered beneath the surface. Her impressions swirled, a tangled mess of hope and hesitation, like leaves caught in the wind before they settle on the ground. "It's like tryin' to read tea leaves in the dark." Her stare drifted out to the landing where the sunlight pooled across the people gathered there. Their voices brought back the faint echoes of her mother's teachings and infused her with the quiet strength of lessons learned long ago.

She pictured Mama sitting with the Bible open on her lap, the pages rustling with each careful turn, filling their old cabin with love. The names of the people in those stories floated back to her now. They were familiar, like old friends. She remembered the way she spoke of them, as if they were giants, not because of their certainty, but because of their trust. Through the centuries, they had stood at the limits of the unknown, faces turned toward a veiled future. The pause before the fall. The breath before the leap. Yet, they walked forward. Mama called it faith. She called it obedience. "We'll sort it out. The more we learn, the clearer it'll get. I pray every night askin' the Lord to light my path." The words lingered, full of promise, but her chest tightened, the pressure building as if something inside her was bracing for what came next. She knew she was right. Her God *would* light the way. Yet as the ancient faith of her mothers settled in her heart, uncertainty gnawed at the edges, refusing to loosen its hold.

Sam's eyes softened as he looked upon her. "That's why she's here." He gestured to her. "She sees ahead, connecting hopes and dreams like numbers in a ledger."

Isobel's head dropped. "And blood." She whispered it.

Sam agreed. "That's the real risk. Tell your investors this: backing Texas isn't like the joint-stock ventures they're used to. It's a cause. Would they have bet on Washington and Adams during the Revolution? The smart money was on King George, but the patriots won. That's the kind of stakes we're talkin' about."

Prentiss hesitated. "Are you sayin' you plan to lead a revolution, General?"

Sam straightened. "Don't put words in my mouth. I'm sayin' I'm heading to Texas in peace. Too many have forgotten the horrors of war."

Isobel clenched her hands in her lap. "I hope we can avoid bloodshed."

Prentiss seemed to relax, tipping his glass. "Whatever happens, my partners and I are with you."

Sam curled his lips. "Appreciate it."

The tension eased as bourbon flowed. Joking and light conversation returned, though her thoughts lingered on the future. Prentiss reached into his coat and pulled out glossy paper. "I've tickets for the theater. They're putting on a special matinee. Shall I pick y'all up later?"

Isobel's pulse quickened. She'd read scripts before but had never seen a full performance. The thought of sitting in a grand hall, enjoying a play unfold, flooded her with a mix of excitement and wonder.

Kelvin nudged her, pulling her from her thoughts. "Sounds like a good plan."

Now, standing on the frontier of something new, she could almost see the curtain rising around her. Anticipation sparked in the stillness as the world transformed into a stage and time itself waited for its next cue. Every moment was part of a tale still unfolding. Her heart pulsed faster as a question lingered. What kind of play was she in? The laughter, conflict, and silences all hinted at the answer. Was this a comedy, history, … or tragedy?

CHAPTER TWENTY-FOUR

July 21, 1832 (Early Afternoon)
New Cincinnati Theater
Third Street, between Sycamore and Broad
Cincinnati, Ohio

The carriage creaked to a halt in front of the inn as shafts of golden light stretched across the cobblestone road. Isobel stepped down, her shoes brushing the gravel, and caught sight of Prentiss waving from the hotel doorway. He motioned them forward with an eager hand.

Inside the coach, Prentiss' energy filled the cramped space, his knee bouncing in rhythm with the uneven ride. "You'll never guess." He leaned over, eyes gleaming. "I spoke with the manager. They're expectin' us. The whole town's buzzin' about the New Cincinnati Theater. It's only been open since the Fourth of July, and tonight, we've got a special guest." He winked at Sam, his excitement clear.

She listened, half her attention caught by the world outside. The bustling port city unfolded through the window. Steamboats were tied along the riverbank, their decks alive with workers hauling cotton bales and crates of goods. The atmosphere held the tang of industry, tinged with the faint sweetness of molasses wafting from the warehouses. She thought of the women in northern mills she'd heard about, toiling under the oppressive eyes of overseers. Their lives revealed a different kind of bondage, no less stifling than the servitude she despised. Liberty, she mused, was a fragile gift too often misunderstood. Her resolve to spread its true meaning tightened within her soul like a shield.

The carriage jolted to a stop in front of a building. Prentiss peered out, his face alight with anticipation. "Here we are." The grand facade of the theater loomed ahead, its clean lines and polished stone standing amid the city's energetic chaos.

As they stepped onto the gravel path, Isobel's scrutiny flitted across the gathering crowd. Conversations hummed, punctuated by the occasional burst of laughter, but there was something else. A fleeting undercurrent lingered beneath the surface. She couldn't name it. Her fingers brushed her collar as unease rippled through her. The glances, brief but weighted, lingered long enough to set her nerves on edge. Did their southern dress make them stand out? Or was it something more?

At the box office, Prentiss handed their tickets to an usher. Before they could move toward their seats, a man in a crisp coat approached. "General Houston?"

Sam's eyes lit with recognition. "James Caldwell! I'll be! What brings you here?"

"This theater's mine," he replied with pride. "We opened on Independence Day."

"Bravo." He shook his hand. "Last time I saw you was New Orleans, wasn't it?"

"Still have the theater there, but this city's booming. I knew I had to set up shop."

Sam introduced the group, and Caldwell offered a brief welcome as they moved inside. The usher led them to a modest box with a clear view of the stage. She took in the space, appreciating its charm but noting its lack of grandeur compared to New York's theaters.

Before long, a commotion stirred in the crowd below. Isobel's chest tightened as the noise grew. Words cut through the hum like barbs.

"Out with him!"

"Away with the scoundrel!"

Her pulse quickened. The accusatory shouts were aimed at someone in their group – at Sam. Her throat went dry as Caldwell rushed onto the stage, his hands raised for calm. The patrons' wrath turned toward him, their jeers drowning out his pleas.

"General," she whispered, her hands trembling. "What's happening?"

Sam stood, his presence commanding though the room buzzed with hostility. "Ladies and gentlemen." Sam spoke steady and strong. "You're mistaken." His words carried over the din like cannon fire, silencing the crowd for a heartbeat. "I've shed blood alongside Ohioans in the Indian Wars, and I've come to your city as a guest. Let us enjoy this fine theater and show respect to those who've worked hard to bring us entertainment tonight."

For a moment, the throng faltered, but the shouts reignited, louder than before. "He's an assailant of female purity!" The accusation struck like a bullet, and Isobel's stomach dropped. His failed marriage to Liza was the subject of such rumors and innuendoes.

Actors took the stage, struggling to steady their song as they tried to soothe the mob, but the effort unraveled. The assembly's rage spilled over, forcing the performance to a ragged end. Disappointment hung thick as theatergoers shuffled out, their murmurs fading into the night.

Outside, her thoughts swirled. "Mr. Prentiss," she began, "did the manager know who was coming?"

Prentiss gave a knowing look. "I made it clear. Figured he'd handle it smarter."

She turned to Sam, her brow furrowed. "General, isn't your buddy, Stanbery, from Ohio?"

Sam's jaw tightened, his eyes darkening. "Shoulda never spared him." He carried the depth of a regret too bitter to name. Isobel knew not to pry further. Some wounds weren't meant for her questions.

Kelvin clapped him on the shoulder. "We've got friends here. A handful of loudmouths don't speak for everyone. We'll need to keep it in mind."

Prentiss said, "You said it. This city's gonna be a cornerstone of America's future. I can't help but believe Texas is a part of Cincinnati's destiny. We'll ride this out."

Sam dropped his shoulders as if the severity of the afternoon was catching up to him. He looked at Prentiss and Isobel, his face softening for a moment. "I reckon you're right. I'll come 'round to your thinkin' after a spell." He calmed, but there was a hint of something darker under the surface. "Best I spend some time in quiet reflection in my room."

Prentiss and Kelvin exchanged glances, and Isobel's lips twitched, her eyes telling a different story. *Quiet reflection* is what he called it, but she knew better. Kentucky bourbon and Tennessee whiskey. His version of thinking things over had a way of burning as it went down.

CHAPTER TWENTY-FIVE

July 21, 1832 (Afternoon)
Hoffman Trading Co.
Water Street and Elm Street
Cincinnati, Ohio

The city unfolded like a restless dream, alive with commerce and voices mingling with the cadenced sounds of life. Isobel and Kelvin moved through the bustling streets, the energy of Cincinnati pulling them in. Ahead, the docks sprawled along the river, a labyrinth of iron and wood where steamboats swayed against the current. It wasn't New York's polished expanse, but it had its own rugged charm, untamed and full of promise.

She squinted at the line of vessels, their hulls packed with goods promising fortunes and secrets. Cotton bales, stacked high like the bones of the land's wealth, dominated the landscape, but both knew the riches didn't end there. The warehouses stood like giants, their bellies swollen with whatever treasures or troubles the river had brought in. From across the water, the state of Kentucky loomed like a distant country.

Kelvin broke through her thoughts. "They know how to pack it tight. You see how the offices and storage are all mashed together?"

Isobel eyed the four-story buildings rising like sentinels over the docks. "It's clever. Ain't wastin' a speck of land. It's like the hotels in New York, how every corner gets put to use."

His curiosity got the better of him. He stopped outside one of the warehouses, his hand brushing the rough wood of the door. "Think we could take a look, see what they're doin' here?"

She smirked. "You think they'll roll out a welcome mat for strangers?"

Kelvin knocked on the door. "One way to find out."

A gruff answer came from within. "Come in."

They exchanged a glance before stepping inside. The room smelled of dust and sweat, the atmosphere heavy with the grit of labor. Behind a sturdy wooden desk sat a man who looked to be in his late twenties, though his weathered face suggested years of hard work. His rolled-up sleeves revealed strong, calloused arms, and his cap and gloves lay discarded on a table, hinting he'd been working outside moments prior.

They greeted him. "Afternoon, sir. I'm Kelvin MacDonald, and this here's my wife, Isobel. We're passin' through on a layover 'til Monday. Seen our share of warehouses in New York and Baltimore, and we were curious how things run here. Would you mind us takin' a look around?"

The man exhaled, rubbing his temples as though the burden of the day pressed harder than usual. "Most days I'd say yes, but today's been rough. Steamboat came in late yesterday and threw everything off. Saturdays ought to be for my wife and kids, not cleanin' up messes." He sighed, his frustration clear.

Isobel stepped forward. "We didn't mean to add to your troubles. If it's not a good time, we'll get outta your way."

The man's eyes softened. "Ain't no trouble, ma'am. Been a day where everythin' piles up at once."

Kelvin leaned on the desk. "What if we helped? Two pairs of hands might get things sorted quicker."

Isobel added, "And we'd get to see how circumstances work. Feels fair, doesn't it?"

The man hesitated, then said, "Name's Josef Hoffman. I own this place. I got help durin' the week, but I give my men Saturdays and Sundays off. Guess I bit off more than I can chew."

Kelvin shook his hand. "Well, Josef, reckon you're not alone today."

Hoffman chuckled, then turned to her with a raised brow. "You ever handle a ledger, ma'am?"

Isobel met his look with a playful glint. "Sir, I've wrestled more than a few ledgers into shape back home. I'd be happy to take a look while you and Kelvin sort things out in the warehouse."

He studied her for a moment. "All right, but don't go messin' it up worse than it already is." His words held more trust than doubt.

Isobel hunched over the ledger, the steady scratch of her pencil the solitary sound in the quiet office. Her mind whirred as she moved through the columns, working sums and differences, her brow creased in concentration. Page after page, she chased down the numbers, her intuition telling her something was off, but it hadn't shown itself yet.

Her fingers tapped on the frame of the desk as she paused to think, eyes skimming back over the entries. There it was. A small, almost imperceptible misstep, a figure entered twice, hidden deep in the flow of numbers. She leaned her head, lips curving as satisfaction set in. The solution. With a few quick marks, she corrected the balance, smoothing out the mess and giving Hoffman relief.

She leaned back in her chair, the heftiness of the task easing as she closed the ledger with a soft thud. As she finished, the familiar sound of boots thudding against the wooden floorboards reached her ears. They were heading back, their low chuckles drawing nearer.

When the men returned, taking off their gloves, she looked up with satisfaction. "Got it all squared away." She stood up to greet them.

Hoffman wiped his brow. "You found the problem?"

She handed him the book. "Payroll got entered twice back in May. It was throwin' everything off."

He studied the page and let out a whistle. "I'll be. You fixed it. Been staring at these numbers for weeks."

"Needed a fresh pair of eyes," she said. "You're tryin' to do too much at once, Josef. Might be time to hire a foreman or an accountant."

Hoffman chuckled. "You sound like my wife. She's been tellin' me the same thing."

Kelvin clapped him on the shoulder. "Listen to her. She's got the right idea."

Hoffman said, "Guess I will. Appreciate what you all did today. Don't hesitate to come back if you need anything while you're in town." He handed his card to her. "You can write me at this address."

Isobel shook his hand. "Much obliged, Josef. We'll be sure to wave goodbye as we pass by on Monday."

Exiting the office, the couple strolled along the waterfront. The wharf appeared quieter than the bustling scene of earlier. As they rounded a corner, they turned their view away from the water toward the cityscape. The vista spread out before them as the fading sunlight illuminated the surrounding hillsides with a golden hue.

"This city is a sight to behold, Kel. Fits right in with the hills and the river. No wonder it's growin' like a wildfire." She tilted her head. "Look at those spires. They don't rightly belong with the rest of this place. Somethin' about 'em. Like they been standin' here longer than the rest ever dared to."

Kelvin, still brushing dust from his sleeves, followed her look. "Ain't they pretty? Those are the churches. A wide array, I suppose. They stick out, don't they?"

She stared. "Like they're reachin' for a higher station. Amidst all this noise and chaos, they stand so still. Reminds me of the old churches back in Tennessee, like they're rooted in a deeper reality."

He chuckled. "Maybe they are. Folks build tall and proud when they got the Lord to believe in."

She bowed. Her considerations lingered on the spires. There was a quietness to them calling to her, like a whisper beneath the city's roar. "Oh, Kel, do you reckon we could attend services tomorrow? It's been a spell since we were in worship, and who knows when we'll get another chance."

"A splendid idea. But with all those steeples 'round here, where should we go?"

She bowed her head. "Like all those seeking the Lord, we'll follow His guidance in the morning."

CHAPTER TWENTY-SIX

July 22, 1832
Second Presbyterian Church
Dr. Lyman Beecher, Pastor
Fourth Street and Vine
Cincinnati, Ohio

The sun peeked through the thin curtains, bathing the inn's unpretentious room in a gentle glow. Isobel stirred first, blinking away the remnants of sleep. Beside her, Kelvin shifted, their silent rhythm an unspoken language. No words passed between them as they dressed, their motions fluid, almost rehearsed, as though morning routines were the one constant in a world that demanded too much.

The hallway lay quiet, steeped in Sunday morning stillness, with only the faint whisper of Isobel's steps for company. The scent of fresh bread and coffee greeted them in the kitchen, mingling with a rare comfort she hadn't known in days. He poured two mugs, and she broke the bread into small pieces, her sentiments lingering on the empty chair at the table's head.

"He's still meditating, I reckon," he muttered, sipping his coffee.

"I worry about him at times, Kel."

He took a piece of bread. "I know."

Her grip tightened around her cup. "Yesterday...they weren't criticizin' his politics alone. It was personal, like they were diggin' into his wounds on purpose."

His jaw strained. "They knew where to aim. Sam's marriage. They knew it was a wound they could tear open and pour salt in."

"Like they did to President Jackson," she said, barely above a whisper. "They went after him through Rachel. Knew how much he loved her. I'm grateful for having had the honor of paying my respects to her at the Hermitage. It's cruel. They find the tender places and strike."

They ate in silence, the melancholy of unspoken thoughts pressing down. Isobel broke the quiet. "We oughtta pray for him today. This mission ain't no ordinary one. I don't know why, but somethin' tells me the general's at the heart of it."

He looked out the window and pointed. "There's a steeple with a clock in the tower, Belle. Reckon it's tellin' me it's time to sing and worship."

Hand in hand, the couple left the inn and strolled through the sunlit streets, Kel's boots echoing on the cobblestones. Approaching the church entrance, they read a weathered sign, "2nd Presbyterian Church, All Welcome."

At the door, a young woman greeted them. "Are you visitors?"

Isobel glanced at him. "Well, it looks like we stick out, Husband."

He tipped his hat. "Yes, ma'am. We're passin' through."

"I'm Harriet. My father's the pastor. Let me show you in." She gestured them toward the pews. "I hope you'll make yourselves at home."

Isobel said, "Well, Harriet, I'm Isobel and this here is my husband, Kelvin. Like he said, we're strangers in these parts. Our people were Presbyterians from Scotland, so there's a bit of Scottish Protestant in us, but truth be told," she paused, a smirk growing on her face, "it was the clock up on the tower that caught our eye and pulled us in."

Harriet's expression softened, a thoughtful look crossing her face. "Clocks and towers," she repeated, almost musing. "It's amazing, isn't it? How the Lord uses everything in His creation, no matter how small or unexpected, to guide us where we need to be."

Isobel exchanged a quick glance with him, a spark of under-standing passing between them. "Ain't it the truth," she said. "Harriet, would you mind showin' us to our seats?"

"Of course. We'll sit together for worship."

The moment the pastor's deep baritone resonated through the sanctuary, the mood shifted. "Let us pray," he called, his words calm but commanding. Isobel bowed her head alongside Kelvin, her heart heavy with pleas for Sam, for their journey, and for clarity. She imag-ined the solidarity of the congregation joining her.

The soft murmur of prayers ebbed away, and the preacher's words filled the quiet again, steady and sure. He spoke of the community's needs, of a nation divided, of families in need of healing. Each word appeared to weave through the room, touching hearts in ways only the faithful could experience. Isobel listened, her contemplations drifting from the pastor's words to her own private fears and desires, ones too intimate to say aloud.

The sermon painted pictures of Cincinnati's transformation from a humble river settlement to something greater, something almost sacred in its potential. "A beacon on a hill." He lifted his observation across the pews. "Much like Jerusalem of old."

Isobel flicked her stare up to meet his, entangled in the vision he spun. She squeezed Kelvin's hand, appreciating the strength in his grip. The future, it seemed, held both hope and uncertainty. Yet for this moment, they were anchored here, in this church, surrounded by prayers whispering of dreams as fragile as their own.

A faint melody drifted through the sanctuary, teasing her ears. *That fiddle.* She jolted. It was the same haunting strain she'd heard aboard the *Heliopolis*. The tune lingered for an instant before it faded, its absence pressing into the silence. She strained to catch it again, but the music was gone, as elusive as the player who conjured it.

Dr. Beecher gestured to the heavens above. "God, who seeth the end from the beginning, hath prepared the West to be mighty." They leaned forward, captivated by his words, sharing the belief their efforts were part of Providence's divine plan. "Look now at the history of our fathers and behold what God hath wrought, a powerful nation in full enjoyment of civil and religious liberty, where all the energies of men find scope and excitement on purpose to show the world by experiment of what man is capable."

After the service, Harriet approached them and invited the couple to Sunday dinner with her family. They accepted and walked with her to the church's parsonage.

IN THE COZY PARLOR, Dr. Beecher introduced himself and his large family to the newcomers. Kelvin extended his hand to the pastor. "We sure do appreciate Harriet's invite, sir."

Beecher grasped his outstretched hand. "Thank you. Harriet's taken to the area more so than I have."

Isobel leaned in, her Southern drawl lilting. "Pastor, I have a question 'bout your sermon. You said we all enjoy civil and religious liberty, but in the South, where we're from, it's not true."

"You look like a bright couple to me. I know you're from the South so you may see things in a different light. Many Americans do not agree with slavery. I suppose the majority do not, especially when one considers the preferences of the millions of Americans in bondage now. The question is not, 'Should we free the slaves?', the issue is, 'How do we free the slaves without destroying our entire economy and social system?'"

Kelvin asked, "So, you believe in a gradual emancipation?"

"Yes. We must give these people their freedom in a responsible manner that allows them to learn skills and achieve literacy. To place them at the mercy of a cruel world would be inhumane."

"Father, I am not sure you are aware of a shopping trip I made across the river," said Harriet. "I witnessed a slave auction."

Isobel's heart clenched as Harriet recounted the scene. "There was a mother." She paused. "There was a child." Her words cracked. "She screamed, 'My baby, my baby!'"

Isobel's hand enveloped Harriet's, a lifeline in a raging storm. "It changes you, don't it?"

Harriet's lips quivered, her eyes meeting Isobel's with a pleading, haunted look. "Father, people fear abolitionists, but if they saw what I saw, they'd have to show mercy."

Isobel's expression softened, but there was no dismissing the horror in her eyes. "Nothing prepares you for such a sight."

Kelvin's mouth tightened into a thin line. "The West is sprawlin' out. Texas is next in play, and it's where me and Isobel are headed. But we ain't blind. We know Texas ain't gonna be free soil, not with it sittin' smack in the middle of cotton country."

The room fell quiet for a beat, the direness of his words settling like dust on the floor. The tenderness of the dining room wrapped around Isobel like her favorite quilt. Her bones buzzed, a small, fleeting moment of peace in a world of apprehension. Across the table, Harriet caught her eye, offering a soft, knowing expression that cut through the noise.

Isobel's heart swelled with gratitude as the meal drew to a close. She stood and brushed the creases from her dress, but her mind reflected on the conversations left hanging, unfinished.

Harriet asked, "Isobel, why don't we step outside for a bit? I think Father's got Kelvin in good company for now."

Isobel blinked, caught off guard by the offer. She was grateful for the escape. She glanced toward Kelvin, already deep in conversation with Dr. Beecher. They looked like they were having a delightful time. "Sure thing." She followed Harriet to the door.

Harriet closed the door behind them. "Sometimes I think these moments are a gift. A little pause before the world catches up with us again."

Isobel looked at her. Harriet had a way of cutting to the heart of things without even trying. "A pause. I wish the pauses lasted a little longer. Thank ya kindly for invitin' us to dinner. It's mighty refreshin' to chat with another woman. My two traveling companions are hopeless at times."

Harriet said, "My father and I don't always agree, but I inherited most of his viewpoints. I wanted to speak with you about what I saw at the slave auction. I'll never see slavery the same way. I think most people see nameless dark people toiling away in a cotton field as their image of slavery. People here work hard in the fields as well and find it difficult to be sympathetic to others working as field hands. What I saw changed me. I don't know how to address it as a young woman."

Isobel replied, "I reckon I understand where you're comin' from. I'm a southern girl myself, born and raised down there, but I can't figure out why slavery's got such a hold on our folks." She shook her head. "We've made some good friends here in Cincinnati, and I'm hopin' we can keep in touch in the months and years to come."

"You may always reach me through my father in the Presbyterian Church or any of the Christian societies he founded. His assignments are irregular, so don't be discouraged if we move from Ohio. I will value any letter you send to me."

Isobel embraced her. "I reckon we're like sisters now. I've never had a sister. You're my first."

Harriet beamed. "I'm grateful you see it that way."

Isobel creased her forehead. "Can I ask you about the fiddle music in church?"

"What fiddle music?"

Isobel cocked her head. "You don't have a fiddler in church?"

"No, but I think Father might like the idea. I'll ask him."

Isobel scratched her head.

"Are you alright?" Harriet patted her arm.

"I think so. I keep hearin' a fiddle tune."

Harriet shook her head. "I hate it when I get a melody stuck in my head. Sometimes it won't leave."

Curiosity flickered in Isobel's eyes. Her lips parted a bit, as if she were on the verge of asking a question, but she held back. The question she was processing made no sense. "I suppose."

As they stepped back into the house, the faint strains of the fiddler's tune still echoed in her mind, a haunting melody clinging to her reflections. The ambience of the room enveloped them once more, the smell of wood smoke and fresh-baked bread mingling around them.

Kelvin turned to Beecher. "We thank you for invitin' us into your home."

Beecher's eyes were kind but tired, the lines of age showing in his face. "You both are welcome anytime. Come back when you can."

The afternoon's joviality lingered in Isobel's thoughts as the door closed behind them. She tucked her arm through Kelvin's as they moved down the porch onto the street. The golden light of the late afternoon cast its hues on the cobblestones.

They walked in silence for a moment, the flow of the Ohio in the distance guiding their steps. Isobel's mind wandered back over the last few days.

Kelvin interrupted her thoughts. "It's been somethin', hasn't it? Seein' how they run things here, the way folks treat their workers, the way business is done. It's not what I expected."

Isobel fixed her eyes on the horizon where the banks of the Ohio meet the sky. "It's opened my eyes in ways I didn't think it would. There's lots of good here, *real* good. Makes you wonder, don't it? How we can see the same things so different, North and South."

He looked down at her. "It does."

Isobel's steps slowed. "Did you hear the fiddle music in church?"

He leaned his head back as though the act would allow him to recall things better. "You mean like on the *Heliopolis*? No, but my hearin' ain't near as good as yours. What did Harriet want to talk to you about?"

Her mind drifted back to the conversation with Harriet. "We're sisters now."

He took her hand. "That's real nice. The Northern folks strike me as hard-workin' and God-fearin'. If they have a fault, it's like Josef's. They try to do more than one thing at a time. But I tell ya this. If it comes down to a fight, I wouldn't want to tangle with 'em."

Isobel lifted her brow. "You think it'll come to war?"

His features darkened. "I pray it don't. But their industry. Their numbers. Their machines. They're miles ahead of us. Their wealth ain't measured by people in chains. It's real wealth, invested back into their factories. If our country don't heal this divide, those are the folks we'll be facin', and it won't be pretty."

As they reached the Ohio, the delicate refrain of the fiddle returned, haunting and beautiful. Isobel paused and scanned the horizon, but the source of the melody remained hidden.

He touched her arm. "Belle? You alright?"

She squeezed his hand, though the music still echoed in her mind. "I'm fine. Let's keep walkin'."

They continued along the riverbank, their hands clasped together, the Ohio's gentle current carrying the fading strains of a fiddle downstream, a melody she alone could hear.

CHAPTER TWENTY-SEVEN

September 3, 1832
Cantonment Gibson
Confluence of Arkansas and Neosho Rivers
Indian Territory, United States

Isobel gritted her teeth as she stepped out of the stagecoach, her ankles screaming in protest as her boots hit the uneven ground. Every move was a sharp reminder of how far they had traveled and how much farther they still had to go. She gathered her dress, the thick fabric snagging on shoulder-high shrubs that clawed at her legs and refused to let go. Each step was a battle, her feet aching as she broke free. "Did we lose the trail again?" Her query was edged with a weariness she couldn't hide.

The driver swung a leg over the side of his seat, his boots scraping the worn wood as he dismounted with a grunt. He plucked a fraying handkerchief from his pocket, mopping his brow as he surveyed the thicket choking the route ahead. "Yes, ma'am. This time of year, the brush swallows up any road or path."

Without a word, Kelvin and Sam set to work, shirts discarded, and gloves pulled tight. They hefted their axes, a practiced process between them. Blades met thick branches with sharp cracks, each swipe shoving the vegetation back little by little.

Isobel watched her husband following the arc of his arms as he worked. Sweat glistened on his sun-darkened skin, and she couldn't look away from the flex of his muscles, each swing of the ax a testament to his strength. Her throat tightened, not from exhaustion but from something else. "Be careful, Kel," she called out, softer now. "We can't afford an accident out here."

He glanced back, his look steady and calm as he drove the blade into the wood again.

She turned her eyes to Sam, noting that the years showed in his face but not in his build. Despite some stray gray hairs and lines etched deep around his eyes, his muscles flexed and strained with a vigor rivaling Kelvin's. She ladled water from the coach's little barrel and filled cups for the men. She walked toward them, but her steps slowed as she reached Sam. Her focus landed on a jagged scar slashing across his right shoulder, the skin puckered and worn. The sight disturbed her. "Does it hurt?"

Setting his ax aside, he accepted the cup, taking an ample drink. "Don't worry 'bout me. I can keep up with any man."

Isobel's chest tightened, a dull ache swelling as she took in the silent stories etched into his flesh. "Creek arrow?"

A shadow of the old pain flickered in his eyes. He set the cup down.

She poured the cool liquid onto a cloth and wiped his face with gentle strokes, then turned to her husband. She traced the tired lines of Kelvin's face with her eyes. "Y'all look exhausted. Not sure how much longer we can keep this up."

The teamster accepted the water with grateful hands. "We don't have far to go, ma'am."

Isobel studied her filthy trail dress, the fabric stiff and dark with dirt, layers of it marking the days they'd been on this leg of the journey. "Six weeks. Didn't figure the steamers and coaches would lose their ways to overgrown banks and trails."

The coachman let out a dry chuckle. "That part ain't in the ads, is it?" He raised the cup to his lips, eyes gleaming with weary humor.

Sam picked up his ax, eyeing the dense thicket ahead. "Could be easier to walk the rest of the way."

The driver shrugged, casting a look over the mess of limbs littering their so-called road. "Would be. Ticket's good for all the way, but, well, you see what it looks like."

Sam turned to the driver with a calculating look. "Wanna help us rig a travois?"

Together, they went to work, cutting sturdy branches and lashing them together until a travois took shape. Their bags loaded and secured, the men shouldered the poles, moving forward with steady steps, while Isobel took the lead, clearing brush with determined swipes of her hatchet. Limb by limb, she kept the pathway open.

As they trudged the last stretch and Cantonment Gibson came into view, Isobel's heart stilled. She had conjured images of powerful stone and log walls, grand and imposing, something displaying the awesome power of the United States Army. Instead, before her stood a crude assembly of tents, the rain-soaked canvas sagging, and rough wooden shacks dotting the riverside. Isobel pressed her lips together, willing the buildings to be sturdy, but the weathered and rotten boards offered her little assurance.

She turned to Kelvin, and whispered, "This is it? This is the fort we've come all this way for?"

Kelvin peered ahead. "Reckon it is. It may not be much, but it's what we got."

Sam looked back at her. "Well, we didn't come this far for the scenery, did we?"

Isobel let out a long, tired sigh, scanning the camp again. No, it wasn't what she'd dreamed, but they'd made it. "General, I can't take another step in this dress." She scrunched her nose. "I know I stink to the four winds, and y'all don't smell like daisies yourselves."

Kelvin glanced at her, his brows lifted in amusement. "The river?"

She gave a peaceable shrug. "Better than nothin'."

Sam peered up and down the bank, a cautious look in his eye.

"Alright, but let's be quick about it. You two go first, and I'll make myself scarce."

The cool water tugged at Isobel's skin as she waded in, her dirty clothes bundled over one arm. She was determined to have something fresh to wear once it dried. She kept her eyes down, relieved to be washing away layers of trail dirt and sweat, the river's current doing its best to cleanse days of grime from her complexion. Kelvin's chuckles rippled out as he dunked under, then came up shaking his hair like a dog. She joined in, the relief of it all settling over her like a balm.

After they'd redressed, Kelvin hollered for Sam, who returned and bathed. They all looked, if not fresh, at least more human.

Sam slid his hat back on, an amused look spreading across his face. "Well, now, that was a good idea. Sure saved us from runnin' any poor soul out of the fort the minute we set foot there."

Isobel shook her head, exasperation and merriment mingling. "Don't y'all ever think about what you look and smell like before meetin' someone?"

They shrugged, answering in their usual easy way.

She waved her hand dismissively. "What is this place anyway? I can't make heads or tails of it."

Sam gestured to the settlement with a sweep of his hand. "This here's the western frontier of the United States." His reply was steady as if it were a lesson. "Government put up this camp 'bout eight years back tryin' to keep peace among the Osage and the Cherokee."

Kelvin shot him a sidelong glance, brow raised. "So, are the Indians at war?"

He shook his head. "Don't fret yourself. We're on Cherokee land now. The Creek are up north, sittin' between the Osage and Cherokee. Far as I'm concerned, we're as safe here as anywhere."

Isobel eyed the rough layout of the place. "This fort don't look mighty."

Sam let out a laugh. "Well, you can see the government ain't exactly pourin' money into the Indian Territory. This station was supposed to be temporary. Everywhere we've been, folks are hollerin' for federal funds to fix up roads, build bridges, and get steamers runnin'. Captain Shreve's snag boats'll push the need more, clearin' up rivers for more traffic."

Kelvin glanced over to her. "I reckon she's tryin' to say this place looks downright primitive, after Nashville or Cincinnati."

Sam said, "Primitive or not, this is the most civilized spot we're liable to see 'til we hit a city again. For now, we gotta report to the commander and show our passports. They'll have a mail pouch, if either of y'all got any words to send back. I have to post messages to Washington and the Hermitage."

She glanced at Kelvin. "Josef and Harriet."

"Yep," he said.

THE THREE OF them strode across the grassy stretch that served as the camp's plaza. Isobel squished the wet ground under her feet. She turned to her husband. "You ever known a camp built on the *low* side of anything?"

He shook his head. "It's like they want to get sick."

Sam's mouth twisted as he looked at the scene. "They oughtta get out of this marshy terrain."

They reached the main structure and stepped through the doorway. The place was stifling, the front door stretched wide open, reaching for any stray breeze that might roll off the river.

Sam spotted a familiar face, Commissioner Henry Ellsworth, a presidential appointee, all prim and proper, and one of the men tasked to enforce the Removal Act. "I'm glad to see you made the trip out here, Mr. Ellsworth."

He pivoted at the sound of his name, his face shifting from surprise to politeness. "General Houston. What an opportune encounter. I'm here on behalf of President Jackson, mind you, looking over conditions in the Indian Territory."

"Our president's got me on a similar job." Sam looked him in the eye. "Mine deals with the Comanche, south of here."

Isobel looked at Sam with a curious expression. He turned back to Ellsworth. "Apologies for the lack of introductions. Let me present my friends, Mr. Kelvin MacDonald and his wife, Isobel. The president authorized their place on this mission and knows full well he's fortunate to have them on board."

Ellsworth gave a polite look before gesturing toward the men standing nearby. "As chance would have it, these three gentlemen here fell in with me on the Ohio. Fine travel companions."

The first stepped forward. "Charles LaTrobe, of His Majesty's Royal Commission on the West Indies. I am delighted to meet each of you. General, your fame has preceded you." He displayed a crisp bow.

Sam sized up the second man, who carried himself like an officer. The stranger gave a bow and spoke in a thick European accent. "Count Albert-Alexandre de Portales of the *Confoederation Helvetica*."

Sam exchanged glances with Isobel and Kelvin, their faces awash in confusion. The count's face brightened. Isobel sensed he knew they were clueless.

"Switzerland." The count let the familiar name settle in.

Isobel's eyes were bright with curiosity. "I've heard there are mountains west of here as stunning as your Alps."

Portales placed a hand over his heart and offered a compliment. "I have not seen them as of yet, Madam MacDonald, but they could not be a match for your beauty."

A flush crept up her cheeks. "Thank you, Count. I must say, European gentlemen are unmatched in courtesy." She turned her attention to the last unfamiliar face in the group. "And, sir, you leave us wonderin' about your own name and story."

The man bowed from the waist. "These men were my companions during a recent tour of Europe." His eyes twinkled with a tenderness that set him apart. "They were gracious guides. Now, I'm fortunate enough to repay a small portion of their kindness. I am Washington Irving, from New York."

Isobel's eyes sparkled with a mix of awe and curiosity. "Are you the author of *The Sketch-Book of Geoffrey Crayon?*"

A glimmer of amusement shown from Irving's face. "You flatter me, Mrs. MacDonald. Yes, I am the same man as the author." He chuckled. "I write in hopes of capturing tales worth sharing. My friends here took me through Madrid, where I found stories of the Spanish Conquest and their daring exploits on our continent."

Her expression shifted from admiration to something almost child-like, a small shiver running through her. "Well, I'll look forward to those tales, but the story about the Headless Horseman kept me awake for a few nights."

Kelvin put his arm around Isobel. "I can attest to it, sir."

Irving smiled, humor radiating in his countenance. "Then I've done my job well, haven't I?"

A thoughtful look crossed Sam's face. "The yarn 'bout the fella who took a nap and woke up years later got me good. I thought it was kinda silly at first, but the more I sat with it, the more it seemed to speak to some things I've been through myself. There's truth hidden in it, I'd say."

Irving's eyes softened with appreciation. "Thank you, General. That's about the highest compliment a writer could desire." A hint of satisfaction laced his gratitude. "To know you saw those truths is why I travel from the archives of Madrid to the American frontier, seeking tales. Fiction reveals the heart of issues better than anything else." His admiration shifted in Isobel's direction. "And with the printing press, it's my hope more voices, men's and women's, will tell the stories America needs."

A federal official's request squeaked out like the creak of old hinges. "Next case please." He sat behind a worn desk, eyes lifting to meet anyone coming forward. They moved up, passports in hand. Sam's fingers tensed as he held his out.

The official took the passport. "All the Tribes of Indians, whether in amity with the United States, or as yet not allied to them by Treaties, to permit safely and freely to pass through their respective territories

General Samuel Houston, a Citizen of the United States, and in case of need to give him all lawful aid and protection."

The man rose from his chair and leaned in. "You are the said 'General Samuel Houston' I presume. I'm William Archer."

Sam met the man's stare. "He and I are one and the same."

Archer handed the passport back. "It is a pleasure to meet you in person. I've heard you pass through here on a regular basis, but I haven't had the chance to encounter you until now. Welcome to Cantonment Gibson," he said formally. "Please, let me know if your party needs any assistance. Mr. Ellsworth's group has already received my offer of support, and we're here, ready to help with the missions President Jackson's given each of you."

Sam clasped the man's hand. "Thank you, Mr. Archer."

Isobel paced forward, passport held out, a subtle but unmistakable gleam in her eyes.

He glanced over her credentials, reading out loud the familiar words, identical to Sam's but carrying her own name. "Thank you, Mrs. MacDonald. Welcome to the Indian Territory of the United States of America."

She accepted the document back, her lips curving with satisfaction.

Kelvin walked up and handed over his own passport without a word or any sign of expectation. Archer took it, gave it a quick once-over, then passed it back. "Thank you, sir. Have a safe trip and a successful mission."

AS THEY STEPPED out of the office, the three Tennesseans and the four explorers blinked against the midday sun. They made their way down the short path to the riverbank, boots mashing mud in the damp earth.

Irving's eyes sparkled as he fixed them on Sam. "General, I'm gathering material for my next writing project. I'd be honored to speak with you and tap into your frontier experiences."

An easy expression crossed Sam's face. "At your service, sir. Some folks don't mind hearin' my opinions on certain matters." He raised his volume. "Gentlemen, it's time we headed to my home. You're all welcome to join us at Wigwam Neosho."

The Ellsworth Party declined the invitation with the polite regret of travelers who had their own course set. Irving assured him he'd be around the area for the season and looked forward to meeting again in the days to come.

After parting ways, Sam's group gathered their things, casting their eyes to the hills rising above the fort where they'd make camp. His home, a wigwam nestled to the northwest, was close enough to reach tonight, but walking there was a stretch after a day on their feet and swinging axes and hatchets.

Isobel glanced at the horizon. "General, how far is your place from here?"

"About three miles. It's an easy walk."

She looked down at her worn boots and aching feet. "I hope you don't think less of me, but we can't go that far on foot now, can we?"

Sam replied, "I know Indians who can run twenty-five or thirty miles at a time. They don't depend on horses for gettin' around."

She huffed. "Well, I can promise you I'm not runnin', sir. Especially in this damp dress."

Sam shrugged. Isobel expected a snicker which didn't come. "Don't you worry. We'll get horses and proper clothing at my place. My wife's got what we need."

"*Wife?*" Isobel and Kelvin sang out together, their eyes widening as they stared at him in astonishment.

CHAPTER TWENTY-EIGHT

September 4, 1832
Wigwam Neosho
Arkansas (ArKANsas) River
Indian Territory, United States

Isobel scratched her head, shooting Sam a sideways glance. "I'm havin' a hard time understandin' your marital status, General."

His laughed rolled out, deep and slow, like far-off thunder. "Can't blame you there. It's a tangled web, courtesy of my dual citizenship. American and Cherokee." His mirth faded as he glanced at the water. "Back home, my marriage to Eliza Allen isn't dissolved by legal paperwork, but we both know it's over. I left her and Tennessee behind."

Isobel exchanged a look with Kelvin, who nodded silently. They'd heard parts of this story before, but this hinted at something deeper. There was something tied to this land and its people.

"And here? Your Cherokee life?" Isobel pressed.

His face softened, his answer quieter. "Chief Ooleteka, John Jolly to white folks, took me in as his own when I was sixteen. His niece, Tlahina, became my wife. Some might call her Diana Rogers." A flicker of pride lit his face. "She's the heart of this place. She keeps our trading post runnin'."

Isobel caught the change in his expression when he spoke of her, his posture settling into something almost sacred. She could tell Tlahina was more than a spouse; she was his anchor here.

He chuckled. "She's getting us ready for this expedition. You'll see soon enough."

Isobel tilted her head. "I need a ledger to keep track of your marriages, General."

Kelvin smirked. "What's missin' is her bein' half-Scottish."

Sam guffawed, deep and full. "Funny you should say it. Her daddy was a Scotsman! Makes it a proper Tennessee match." His laughter echoed, rolling over the river like a shared joke with the land itself.

The creak of a door drew Isobel's attention. A tall woman emerged, her dark hair flowing past her shoulders. Practical yet graceful, she moved like she belonged to the earth and sky. Her calm inspection swept over the group before her face broke into good humor.

"Welcome home. It's good to see you alive and well." She noticed Isobel and Kelvin. "And you've brought friends. Welcome to Wigwam Neosho."

Isobel replied, "Thank you, Mrs. Houston. It's a pleasure to meet you."

"It's Tlahina, please," she said, her eyes crinkling.

"I'm Isobel MacDonald, and this is my husband, Kelvin."

Tlahina answered, "I imagine Colonneh will tell me your stories soon enough."

"Colonneh?" Isobel repeated, trying to catch the unfamiliar name.

"Means Raven," Sam explained. "Chief Ooleteka gave it to me."

Isobel glanced at her. "She's beautiful," she whispered, not intending for anyone to hear her. "I mean tall and strong. Like she's made for this life."

Tlahina said, "Thank you. You're lovely yourself."

Kelvin leaned back. "Seems we both married above our stations."

Sam wiped his forehead. "We sure did."

She led them inside, the wigwam a blend of function and charm.

The central hearth heated the space, and shelves displayed goods from distant travelers. Isobel's fingers brushed a beaded pouch as she wondered about its journey. Kelvin inspected a cast-iron skillet, giving it his silent approval.

"This is no fancy shop like in Nashville," Isobel said with admiration. "But it's remarkable."

Sam said, "Out here, the wares need to serve a purpose. Her skill in gathering supplies is worth more than any city merchant."

Tlahina moved toward the fire. "Rest a while. I'll fix supper."

Isobel hesitated, watching her work. Guilt pricked at her. She wasn't raised to let others labor as she sat idle. Sam caught her reluctance and leaned in. "Custom here is to treat guests like family. Respect means letting her take care of you tonight."

She dipped her head. "Yes, sir."

Sam added, "Tomorrow, I reckon she'll set you on tasks."

As the scent of roasting squash and venison filled the room, Kelvin drifted closer to Tlahina. "Comanches come through often?"

"They do." She stirred a pot. "They trade things for iron pots. A skillet like this one can fetch a lot of hand-made leather goods."

Isobel perked up. "What about crops? You have the three sisters?"

Tlahina replied, "Corn, beans, and squash. Same as Tennessee, but the rains aren't as kind here. When it's too dry, we haul water from the river."

Kelvin shook his head. "That's a heavy load."

Sam grew firm. "The Cherokee bear their burdens with a strength most men can't imagine. They adapt, they survive."

She watched Tlahina, her movements precise as she worked. The crackling fire painted her in soft hues, a matron in tune with her essence. Isobel inhaled in the rich aroma, her thoughts drifting to the mountains and hollers. Her mother's words floated back, along with the bittersweet ache of loss. She looked over to Kelvin, who savored the squash with quiet satisfaction.

"This is wonderful," he said. "Tastes like home."

Tlahina said, "If you're from Tennessee, a Cherokee likely taught someone how to do it."

He dipped his head. "Could be. Makes sense."

Tlahina focused on Isobel. "Want to help with the fry bread?"

Isobel's face lit up. "I thought you'd never ask."

LATER, Sam led Kelvin to the stables. The place carried the scent of hay and leather. The horses stirred as they approached, their curious eyes following the men.

"Tlahina keeps them in when Comanches roam in the area," he explained. "She's careful."

Kelvin said, "She's thought of everything."

Sam gestured to the animals. "These are our mounts and mules. They'll carry the essentials. No wagons out here. Just rivers and trails."

Kelvin ran a hand over a mule's back. "They're strong. Good stock."

Sam said, "Tlahina has an eye for what's needed. She knew we'd need the best for this journey."

AS THEY RETURNED to the wigwam, the women were setting out the fry bread, its golden edges glistening with honey.

Sam clapped a hand on Kelvin's shoulder. "Get ready. You'll be eating this plenty once she learns the recipe."

Isobel handed Kelvin a plate. "I'm not sure I'll match Tlahina's skill, but I'll give it my all."

He beamed, taking a bite. "You always do."

CHAPTER TWENTY-NINE

November 30, 1832
Wigwam Neosho
Arkansas River
Indian Territory, United States

I sobel lingered in the shadows by the door, watching Washington Irving's silhouette lean into the pale light spilling through the wigwam's opening. His presence brought a strange comfort, a steady beat in their uncertain times. Most days, he came filling the space with jokes and parables destined for his pages.

A sharp chill lingered, as if winter had decided to stay. He spoke with Tlahina. Isobel stepped forward, careful not to disturb the exchange. "Good morning, Mr. Irving."

He spun, his expression brightening with the easy curiosity that kept him on the verge of discovery. "Ah, Isobel! And what stories do you carry today?"

Her lips curved despite the chill settling on her skin. "Stories, is it? Are ya fit for lore as feral as the wind outside."

He lifted the steaming mug. "Wild winds and wilder tales. It's why I'm here."

Isobel glanced toward the back of the wigwam, where Sam would be standing after he came in. Irving never pushed him too hard. He let words flow, catching them like falling leaves, ready to weave them into something timeless.

Isobel rubbed her hands together. "Mr. Irving, can I ask ya a question?"

He replied, "Yes, anything."

She looked into his eyes. "Is Sleepy Hollow a real place?"

He answered, "It is. It's in New York."

She reflected for a moment. "Where we'll be goin' ain't on no charts. We gotta make our way through the woods and across rivers."

Irving looked at his feet, then back to her. "Have you ever heard of Rokovoko?"

She shook her head.

He rubbed one palm with his thumb. "I have a friend who says Rokovoko isn't down on any map; true places never are."

She scrunched her eyebrows together and noticed Tlahina listening to them. "What does it mean?"

He tugged at his ear. "What do you think he means?"

Isobel shrugged. "Maybe he's sayin' the real truth of a place is made up of what we learn for ourselves. It's what we hold dear in our hearts. That's never gonna be on any map."

Irving shook his head with deliberate care. "You astound me." He went round to Tlahina. "You amaze me as well. Both of you are far beyond clever. You're staking truth out here on the prairie." He chuckled. "There's a tale there somewhere."

Tlahina gestured toward the back door leading to the corral. "Colonneh's out there with the horses. Says he and Kelvin'll be in before long."

Irving's eyes lit with a familiar spark of excitement. He set his mug down. "Guess I'm in for quite the morning."

Isobel caught the fondness in his observation as it returned to her. Something about this untamed land brought him alive, like the stories around every bend were crafted just for him. She tucked a strand of hair behind her ear.

"Have you finished preparing for your journey?" His curiosity was unmistakable.

"We're hoping to wrap up today," she replied. "After months of work, and we'll leave at daybreak. If all goes to plan, we should reach Fort Towson by tomorrow night."

"You'll do well," Irving said. "General Houston is a capable leader, whether guiding three or three hundred."

Her chest swelled with pride. "He says preparation's the same, no matter the size. But I feel safe with him and Kelvin leading us. They've become close these past months. And thank you for taking Kelvin on those hunting trips. He's learned a lot in your company."

His face softened. "Kelvin's a sharp young man. I've learned a thing or two from him as well."

She hesitated before asking, "You've seen the Spanish archives, haven't you? Do you think Spain's content to let Mexico go its own way?"

He swirled the last sip of coffee in his cup, his expression thoughtful. "They don't have much choice. They're stretched thin with dwindling resources. They've lost almost all their holdings in the Americas, aside from Cuba and Puerto Rico."

Her curiosity deepened. "You're more interested in Spain than most Americans."

"Spain's mark is everywhere." His eyes drifted toward a window. "The language, the faith. The Catholic Church still shapes Mexico. All immigrants must convert. To understand Mexico, you need to grasp Spain's legacy."

Tlahina, quiet until now, joined the conversation. "Does Spain still trade with her former colonies?"

Irving answered, the spark of knowledge returning. "Oh yes. Europe still craves the New World's resources. Cotton, sugarcane, and coffee." He lifted his cup. "The world's more connected than ever."

The back door creaked open, and in stepped Kelvin and Sam, cheeks flushed from the cold outside. Kelvin's words carried a note of finality that tugged at her heart. "We're almost ready to leave."

Irving raised his mug in a gentle salute. "Isobel tells me you expect to reach Fort Towson by tomorrow. I wish you good luck, truly."

A glint of humor sparkled in Sam's eyes. "We'll need a fair amount of luck, but as they say, the more we prepare, the luckier we get." His mirth was infectious, and soon everyone joined in.

As the merriment faded, Tlahina announced, "Friends, I have something to share." She looked toward Sam, and he gave a subtle acknowledgement.

Tlahina straightened, gathering herself. "I desire all the best for you. Some of you will start new lives, meeting friends you've yet to know. Please recall this friendship as fondly as I do." She continued. "Colonneh and I have decided to *split the blanket*, as my people call it. We made the decision with my chief's guidance."

Silence settled over them, heavy with the truth Tlahina had shared and the ache it carried.

"Although we've split our blanket," she continued, "we still bear hope for one another's success."

Isobel reached out, her hand finding Tlahina's in a loving squeeze. Tlahina met her eye, giving a look that spoke of courage Isobel hoped she could carry on her own journey.

Sam stood before them. "We are getting what Americans call a divorce. Each of us needs to go farther down our own trail. She's been preparing for this since I went to Washington. Made sure all our supplies and horses were ready for the mission. And I've signed over any claim I had on the Wigwam Neosho. My hope is she'll continue to prosper. Her people will always be my people."

The silence thickened, words either too heavy or too light. Isobel glanced at Kelvin and Irving, both at a loss, unsure how to respond.

Tlahina broke the tension. "Don't look so sad, my friends. Today is for celebrating our friendship. I want to give each of you a token of my affection."

Isobel's heart swelled, struck by Tlahina's strength and generosity, a reminder of courage and grace in the face of change.

She called Kelvin forward and handed him a small wooden box with his initials carved on top. Inside, a brass compass rested, its needle suspended over a detailed rose. "May you never lose your way, my friend."

He stared, speechless. "Thank you, Tlahina. It's beautiful."

She swung to the famous author, handing him a book. "Mr. Irving, having you here these past few months has been like attending a university. This ignited my imagination. It recalls your short stories about monsters and supernatural naps, but this one is different. The previous owner told me the author's mother was a champion for women's rights in the last century."

He accepted the volume, "*Frankenstein* by Mary Wollstonecraft Shelley." Recognition flashed in his eyes. "I'm astonished such a work found its way to the American prairie. I look forward to discussing it with you. Thank you, Tlahina."

She looked at Sam. "Colonneh, will you accept this gesture of my love? When you first came to our village, you took no note of me. I was but ten years old. You carried two things with you: a book and a rifle. This writing is special. I discovered it after you left for Washington. The elements damaged the cover, so I tanned deerskin for a new one. I hope you remember our friendship when you read it."

Sam's eyes glistened, staring at the familiar title, *The Iliad* by Homer. He'd believed it gone, yet here it was, renewed by her care. "I thought I'd lost this. My dreams and passions are tied to this book. Every time I open it, I'll think of you."

Isobel's eyes filled with emotion as Tlahina turned to her, lifting a large rolled-up bundle. With care, she unfastened its ties and revealed a dark buckskin blanket, thick, and durable.

"For my fellow frontierswoman," she said, placing the blanket on the table. "Comanche women use their blankets to protect their belongings on the trail."

As she unrolled it, Isobel gasped at what lay within. A stunning collection of clothing and gear. At the top was a golden-brown blouse, fringed with foot-long deerskin strands and silver crosses. Below it, she saw a pair of matching trousers and knee-high buffalo hide moccasins.

"Comanche matrons crafted these. They were made for me, but my height proved too much. Their design allows you to ride astride in any weather, keeping you protected and dignified. Your presence has been a gift. I hope these clothes carry our friendship with you."

Isobel's words failed her. She clung to Tlahina, tears streaming down her face. When she found her voice again, it wavered but carried firm conviction. "I've never seen anything more resplendent than this. Please thank those who made my gift. I'll do my best to honor their skill and generosity."

Kelvin and Sam sat in silence. Irving, marveling at the craftsmanship, said, "I assure you, no European queen is adorned in anything as fine. Young Isabella of Spain owns no treasure like this. American Indian women spin gold from hides, as New York ladies look to London and Paris for their finery. Nothing there compares to the beauty of what's made here."

Kelvin added, "It's so true, Mr. Irving."

Tlahina took Isobel's hand. "Would you mind helping me with the meal? Colonneh asked me for fry bread in our last supper together."

Isobel answered, "I'm still in awe, but I'd be honored to help."

THE WOMEN SET to work in the kitchen and the men ventured outside to prepare for tomorrow. Sam and Kelvin checked each horse and mule, making sure hooves were sound and spare horseshoes, nails, and tools were packed for any emergencies. The mules, munching oats, were fitted with pack saddles ready to carry supplies. Clothes, flour, cured pork, coffee, dried fruit, and gunpowder.

Sam gestured to a bag. "I trust this powder. It's from DuPont."

Kelvin said, "I've heard of DuPont. They say it's the best."

He dipped his head. "Gives us an edge. Mexican troops still use charcoal in their flintlocks."

Kelvin frowned. "I don't know. My father could fire three rounds a minute with his Brown Bess. It takes me that long to load one shot with a rifle. But at least it's accurate."

Sam agreed. "Riflemen need muskets for cover. We also have Cherokee bows and tomahawks. Faster than muskets. Our flintlock pistols stay holstered on the saddle."

Kelvin glanced at the corral. "The horses look ready for the open trail. Tlahina has three beauties here."

Sam crossed his arms. "She's got a gift for choosing horses and running this place. Wigwam Neosho is hers in full now. She built it, and she'll keep it thriving."

He admired his compass. "She knows what people need. That's how you run a business."

Sam tied a loose strap on one of the mules. "Isobel has the same gift. Providence put her in my path. Whatever good comes our way, it all started in Mr. Key's office."

Kelvin let out the soft hum of agreement.

A whiff of hot food drifted their way and Sam said, "I smell squash and fry bread."

Kelvin sniffed. "So do I."

CHAPTER THIRTY

December 1 & 2, 1832
Fort Towson, Indian Territory
North Bank of the Red River
International Boundary:
Coahuila y Tejas, Estados Unidos Mexicanos,
and the United States of America

Isobel shifted on the hard, wooden chair, watching Sam who was hunched over the table, his quill scratching against paper. Candlelight cast flickering shadows over the charts and letters sprawled before him. His voice, low and steady, broke the silence. "I wrote Mr. Ellsworth a fine letter. Told him the Comanche retreated to their winter hunting grounds near San Antonio de *Béxar*."

Kelvin studied a hand-drawn map, his brow furrowed. "And when spring comes?"

Sam tapped the envelope. "This cover buys us time and freedom. By the time anyone checks, I'll have what I need." He formed a daring face. "Tlahina said they moved south days ago. It's the truth."

Isobel leaned forward. "What if the Mexicans send someone to verify? You're supposed to be the one checkin' on *them*."

He met her glare, confidence brimming. "Then I'll know if they're honest or only stringin' us along."

MORNING SUNLIGHT SPILLED through the narrow window, splashing against Isobel's face. She layered herself in Comanche-crafted deerskin, her breath rising in pale clouds against the cold. Excitement buzzed through her veins. This was the day they'd been preparing for.

Stepping outside, she saw Sam already dressed in his worn buck-skin pants and weathered red shirt beneath a hunting frock. His boots gleamed with brass eagle spurs, and his low-crowned hat presented the ambience of command.

Sam asked, "Ready to set out?"

"More than ready." She adjusted the colorful breastplate. Her husband gave her a quick wink as he buckled his own belt, a hint of her own thrill mirrored in his eyes.

Kelvin said, "Let's get on with it."

She chuckled, eyeing his boots with their rough, rusty spurs. They were nothing like Sam's polished ones, but they fit him fine. It was his tricorn hat that held her thoughts. His mother insisted he take it on his father's death, saying it had brought him luck in war. He tapped the brim now. "Keeps the rain off."

Isobel knew better. His daddy's spirit was right there, tucked in each of the three corners. And now Kelvin had added his own touch. He put an eagle feather on one side, and their clan badge on the other, carrying a piece of the past and future in one glance.

She watched him adjust the hand-me-down hat, fingers brushing the worn MacDonald crest fixed to it. The brooch, the arm clutching a cross, and the words *Per Mare Per Terras* held his true pride. "By Sea By Land," he murmured, eyes distant. "Same as Grandda and Da wore."

Isobel reflected on the moment. "They'd be proud. Not every man rides with his family's battles pinned to his hat."

His mouth lifted. "I reckon they'd want us to keep that spirit, even out here."

She tipped her head back, her mind drifted upward, her soul pulling her to memories of those who had gone before. A mighty presence encompassed her, unseen yet undeniable. Her lips parted, a whisper on the fringe of reverence. "We're surrounded by such a great cloud of witnesses," she murmured, her spirit thick with both weight and wonder. Her hand rested over her heart, the devotion of those who'd paved the way filling her chest. "We gotta keep the faith movin' on down the line. They did it for us." She paused, as the promise settled in her soul. "Now it's our turn. We gotta do our part."

Kelvin raised his hand. "Amen, sister."

Isobel glanced down at her own attire, Tlahina's gift. The golden-brown deerskin blouse and pants, ivory and blue breastplate, and red otter sash all held the touch of her friendship. She neither had a hat, nor wanted one. She moved a stray strand of hair behind her ear, and in doing so, revealed a raven feather woven into her hair, fastened Cherokee-style with sinew and bone. It dangled, waiting for the breeze to lift it into the sky.

Kelvin's gaze lingered on it. "You're still carryin' that thing?"

She nodded once. "Tlahina showed me how to keep it from fallin' apart. Cedar shavings, a pinch of lavender. Said it would hold its spirit that way."

He tilted his head. "What's it mean to you?"

Isobel ran a finger along the edge of the feather, its black gloss deep as nightfall. "It's more than just somethin' I found at the Hermitage. It's a mark now. MacDonald, MacIntosh...and Raven." She met his eyes. "We carry that name for him, too—for the general. For what he gave up, what he took on. We're Raven Clan now, whether the old blood says it or not."

Kelvin reached out and tapped the feather gently, like he might a badge of rank. "Lets people know who we run with."

She dipped her chin. "Exactly."

He gave her a look of quiet approval. "Feels right, don't it?"

"It does. Tlahina thought of everything," she said, fingers grazing her soft boots.

They mounted up. Her saddle fit snug, the Cherokee blanket's bright colors and beads flashing beneath her.

Kelvin inspected her. "Lookin' like you were born to ride, Belle."

She adjusted her red belt. "And you with the tricorn. You're a family legacy all on your own."

With that, they rode out, her heart lifting, ready for the journey and the history they carried with them and were destined to make.

When they received their horses, they agreed to wait several weeks before naming them, allowing time for the animals' true personalities to emerge. The connection between Isobel and her mustang was almost telepathic, as if the mare understood her thoughts and aspirations. The horse desired to fulfill Isobel's vision for the future, earning the name *Dream*.

Kelvin named his sorrel *Skipper*. The quarter horse, spirited yet calm, reminded him of his father's old stallion by the same name. "He's got a mind of his own," he said, "but we're workin' it out."

Sam's mount, a light brown buckskin with a dark mane, exuded a proud, fiery spirit. The horse often reared, flashing his strength, and Sam admired his boldness. "*Apollo*," he said. "A name fittin' his flair."

Kelvin tethered the three pack animals, each one fitted with wooden saddles loaded up with packs and supplies. Nearby, their own saddlebags held smaller essentials within easy reach.

As they departed Fort Towson, heading south toward the Red River, silence settled over them. Isobel suspected the men were lost in private thoughts as she was.

When the murky line of the Red appeared, Sam raised a hand, signaling a halt.

"You've been more than companions and colleagues. I need to share a warnin'. The territory across the water is full of perils that could cost you your lives. There's disease with no doctors, there're outlaws with no lawmen, there're hostile Indians with no friendly forts, there're natural disasters with no Christian aid. It's a perilous place where dangers and predicaments will shape our new destinies."

Kelvin stood tall in his saddle. "Like the Israelites of old, we know there're giants in the land, but it flows with milk and honey."

Isobel patted Dream, looking at Sam. "We know the risks. It's in our blood, as it's in yours, General. From the Scottish Highlands, over the ocean, to the Blue Ridge, Great Smokies, and across the countless rivers of America, our blood drives us to places our children will treasure and uphold. You'll hear no bawlin' or grumblin'."

As they neared the river, the horses slowed. The muddy bank lay ahead, the water's glistening surface catching the morning sun. Isobel stroked Dream's neck. She looked at Kelvin, sharing the silent satisfaction in this simple, needed pause.

Sam shifted his weight. "Kelvin, you familiar with your Roman history?"

He gave an answer. "I reckon I am, General. This here reminds me of a certain moment."

Sam leaned in. "What moment?"

A glint appeared in Kelvin's eye. "When Caesar led his Thirteenth Legion across the Rubicon. He knew there was no turnin' back."

A sudden sound of splashing pulled their attention back to the water. Isobel looked at them over her shoulder as she charged into the muddy river, her pony cutting through the shallow current with ease.

Kelvin's eyes widened. "Guess Roman legions aren't on her mind."

Isobel and her Dream were already traversing the river at an unwavering speed. The mustang moved as if spurred on by a spirit shared only between horse and rider. Dream's golden mane caught the morning sun, reflecting beams and blending them into Isobel's own bright hair. The raven feather flew as if it had wings. She rode with fierce energy, her sapphire eyes set on the far shore.

Nearing the opposite bank, Isobel released the reins, trusting Dream to find their way. She lifted her arms, stretching them out wide as the wind enveloped her. The tail wind and the oncoming rush of virginal air teased her sleeves as the breeze played at the deerskin fringes in a way the Comanches foretold in their design. She gulped breath untouched by memory, and Dream's bespattered hooves met a foreign soil that, until now, had dwelt only in her imagination.

Dream halted on the shore, holding her head high as she snorted the unfamiliar atmosphere. Isobel continued extending her arms letting the cool breeze, now heated by raw emotion, blow through her golden locks and Dream's flaxen mane. She bowed her head with outstretched arms and thanked God she was in Texas at long last.

The men witnessed the sight. In mutual silence, they watched the young woman and the mustang fly over their *American Rubicon*. There would be no more days of anticipating this moment. It was here, and Isobel seized it like no other.

Apollo raced through the water with his rider spurring him on ever faster. The pack mules were not as enthusiastic as the other members of the party, but Kelvin and Sam were soon beside Isobel.

Sam surveyed Isobel and Dream. "I'll remember that vision for the rest of my life."

Isobel brought her arms down, patting Dream with both hands. "Have you gentlemen concluded your lesson from Rome's history so soon?"

Sam pressed a hand to his heart. "Even Julius Caesar with all his pageantry couldn't have matched your arrival here. Aren't you going to welcome your friends to Texas?"

Isobel flipped her tresses back and the north breeze caught them taking them out of her face. Her eyes blazed with a raging, vivid blue, as striking as fields of bluebonnets in full spring bloom, alive and intense, pulling in everything around them. An energy of resoluteness emanated from her fair skin like the aurora of the far north. A smile, brimming with promise, twinkled on her face.

"Welcome to Texas, my husband and my general!"

Map of the Republic of Texas and Indian Territory

CHAPTER THIRTY-ONE

December 2, 1832
South of the Red River
Jonesboro, *Coahuila y Tejas*

The three riders entered Jonesboro beneath a sky the color of ash, their pack mules trudging under bulging loads. Isobel inspected the settlement, a rough scattering of cabins and sagging tents, as though the land itself hadn't yet decided if this place should be a town. Claims here were as unstable as the shifting sandbars of the nearby river.

Sam reined in his horse with a decisive tug, his eyes on a sturdy log cabin ahead. "We'll stop here. Might be able to get some news on the trail south."

Boots hit the ground with a dull thud as the group dismounted, the uneasy silence of the village settling over them like a damp blanket. Isobel adjusted her clothes, dust swirling around her as she strode toward the cabin. The door creaked open before she could knock, and a woman emerged, her brown work dress as plain as her guarded expression.

"Name's Mrs. Gordon," the woman said, her introduction fixed. "Who might you be?"

Isobel stepped forward, polite but firm. "Isobel MacDonald, and this is my husband, Kelvin. The gentleman with us is General Houston." Each name carried the merit of their purpose and the miles behind them. "We're from Tennessee, headed to Nacogdoches."

The woman's sharp eyes softened. "Well, I can offer a meal, though things are lean. Kindness in return wouldn't go amiss."

Sam tipped his hat. "We'll make sure to repay your trouble."

Mrs. Gordon's look lingered on Isobel, curious yet cautious. "Y'all come on in. That's a Comanche outfit you're wearin'. Smart choice for travel. Got somethin' to keep it dry in the rain?"

Isobel answered, "Yes. We've all got ponchos in our saddlebags. We try to be prepared."

Kelvin cleared his throat. "You got any news about the course south, ma'am?"

She crossed her arms, her words shifting toward him. "Rugged road, but it's passable. Folks say Comanches have been settin' up near the river. They ain't caused problems, but it could change."

Isobel's jaw tightened, the comments knotting inside her frame. Trouble with the Comanche was the last thing they needed.

Mrs. Gordon gestured to the distant horizon. "Nacogdoches is 'bout 180 miles. You'll cross creeks and the Sabine River. Southeast of here, there's a ferry run by an old Choctaw if the water's high. If not, you can ride across. Beyond there, it's a lonely stretch with few cabins. Don't fret if it feels empty. It is."

Isobel traced each landmark in her mind, forming a mental map from the woman's words.

Sam asked, "What land is this on?"

Her back straightened, her chin lifting. "This here's David Burnet's grant. My husband applied for official ownership, but we ain't heard back yet."

"It's helpful, ma'am," he said. "When I reach Nacogdoches, I'll look into your claim and pass along any news."

The relief in her face was subtle but unmistakable. "Are you Governor Houston of Tennessee?"

"I was."

She extended her hand. "Thank you, General. My husband's out huntin'. He'll be sorry he missed you." She handed Isobel a basket. "Mrs. MacDonald, could you visit the chicken coop?"

Isobel stepped outside, the cold biting through her doeskin dress. At the coop, she gathered eggs, her hands stiff from the chill. Her respect for Mrs. Gordon deepened as she looked at the small, fortified cage. Every scrap of value here needed defending from prowling animals or desperate men.

Back inside, the scent of frying rabbit wrapped around her like the comfort of a shawl. As Isobel stirred batter, Mrs. Gordon's words carried a quiet ache. "My husband prefers potatoes, but we won't have any 'til summer."

Isobel followed her view to the dormant patch of earth outside. "Maybe by then, you'll have more than enough."

Kelvin tethered the horses to a picket line. His movements were deliberate as he removed the packs, if only for a little while. She caught herself watching him, his calm strength a grounding force in the harshness of the frontier.

When they sat down to eat, Mrs. Gordon served the rabbit with pride, its crispy skin gleaming. Isobel savored the earthy richness, expressing her appreciation.

"Rabbit's a mainstay," Mrs. Gordon said, her remarks lighter now. "Fills the pot when there's nothin' else."

Kelvin chuckled. "Been huntin' rabbits since I was a wee lad."

She gave her approval. "Good thing, Mr. MacDonald. Rabbits are plentiful on the route. Won't waste powder or shot snarin' 'em."

As the meal wound down, the conversation turned toward Texas. Mrs. Gordon turned serious. "Folks pass through here talkin' about Texas. Some lookin' for a fresh start, others runnin' from somethin'. Two kinds of settlers, near as I can tell. Austin's people try to work with the Mexicans. Others think they're wastin' their time."

Sam leaned in. "What do *you* think?"

159

She let out a sigh as she gathered her thoughts. "I think the patience Austin's shown has gotta run dry, General. He's a good man and a square dealer, if there ever was one. The Mexicans might've thrown away their best chance for peace by pushin' him. There's always gonna be young hotheads itchin' for a scrap. Reckon they missed out on the American Revolution, and now they're lookin' to start one of their own."

Isobel's hands trembled. "I pray we find a way to settle things without bloodshed. Those hotheads don't know what war costs."

Mrs. Gordon looked around the room. "The Mexicans keep givin' 'em cause to revolt. If you plan to stay in Texas, remember what I'm sayin', you'll have to fight. Don't know when, but I don't think this peace'll last more than two or three years."

The room fell quiet, the fire's crackle filling the space. Sam broke the silence. "People like you and your husband give me hope for Texas. Level-headed, and resourceful. We'll need folks like you if this land's to stand."

Mrs. Gordon replied, "Obliged, General. I wish you success on your journey."

As they prepared to leave, Sam pressed a small pouch of coins into Mrs. Gordon's hand. "For your kindness," he said.

Isobel had barely settled herself in the saddle when Mrs. Gordon stepped forward, putting a cloth sack into her hands. "Tuck this into your saddlebag, dear." She left no room for refusal.

Her fingers clinched the bag, its weight heavier with the care Mrs. Gordon had poured into it. A quick peek inside revealed corn fritters. Their comforting aroma drifted from the cloth sack. Her heart swelled at the thoughtful gift, ensuring they'd stay fed through the day without stopping to cook.

The trace offered no shelter—just the sting in her lungs and the bite in the wind. She tightened her grip on the reins, Kelvin riding close beside her. Sam's directions carried over the clip-clop of hooves. "The Sabine's seventy-five miles off. We'll cross it in two days."

They set off southward. Their passage wound through stretches of bare trees and rocky ground, its path worn but clear enough for Kelvin to keep his new compass tucked away for now.

Sam shifted in his saddle, squinting at the way ahead. "Figure we got time for 'bout ten more miles today 'fore we halt. Horses and mules can handle it."

She patted the cloth sack. "We won't have to stop for cookin' neither. She packed a bag of corn fritters to hold us over."

Kelvin gave a low chuckle. "She sure is a kind lady."

Sam's expression grew reflective. "Kind, yeah, but there's more to her than kindness. She's the sort you can trust. Got a good head on her shoulders. And her feelin's 'bout the situation match up with mine. It squares with what President Jackson's hearin' too. If she's right, we got two camps here. One pushin' for peace, the other itchin' for war. Even patient ol' Stephen Austin's 'bout at his breakin' point. The Mexicans, they're playin' him in some kinda stallin' game, just draggin' things out."

Kelvin rubbed his chin and turned to Sam. "Is this what Mr. Dey was worried about back in New York City?"

Sam replied, "Reckon so. Can tell y'all now Jackson's tryin' for a peaceful buyout of the territory. He's hopin' to settle it without blood-shed, but he thinks the Mexicans are stringin' him along. Can't quite get a read on what they're plannin'."

Isobel leaned forward, eyes steady on him. "What's it tellin' ya, General? You got a potential enemy sittin' on some serious military might, playin' games. They mess with Stephen Austin, a longtime ally, then don't straight-talk with the President of the United States in negotiations. As a general, reckon it means somethin'?"

His face hardened. "Sure does. Armies stall when they ain't ready to throw down. It's a tactic, and it don't bode well."

A chill crept over her, colder than the wind slipping through her deerskin dress. The tension in his words hung heavy with what was left unsaid. Out here, war wasn't some distant threat, it was knockin' right at their doorstep.

Kelvin's ideas broke through the quiet, low and discerning. "Might come down to us tippin' the scales one way or 'nother. Three people can add enough weight to a cause so it prevails."

Sam glanced over, a glint of respect in his eyes. "Could well be. While others drag their feet, we best keep movin'."

They'd pressed on through the full ten miles. With weariness settling in, they stopped and made camp. Kelvin cleared a patch of ground before he built a neat fire pit and stacked wood under an iron grate. The flames flickered to life, casting an amber glow over the campsite and three tired faces. Isobel was grateful for the sight of a simple fire and Mrs. Gordon's corn fritters. There were enough to stretch them again for breakfast.

Sam insisted, "Coffee with the fritters first thing tomorrow. Gotta keep our wits sharp." His study fell on Kelvin's foresight with approval. The coffee pot sat on top of their gear, ready to go.

Kelvin moved in silence, as he unsaddled the horses, then he and Sam unloaded the packs from the mules. Their movements almost synchronized as they worked together to clear the terrain of any rocks and sticks to make it fit for sleep. Isobel extended and smoothed a canvas tarp across the ground before she layered it with her worn woolen covering. She rolled her coat into a pillow, then unrolled her new Comanche cover and spread it over the top.

After she kicked off her boots and folded her deerskins under the blanket to keep them dry, she crawled into her makeshift bed, savoring the bulk of the covers around her. With a soft smile, she glanced up at Kelvin. "There's room for you too."

He nestled beside her, close enough to feel his contentment, and she relaxed, letting the fire's hiss lull her into a sense of peace.

Nearby, Sam spread out his Cherokee bedroll with a practiced hand, the years of wilderness living evident in his every move.

"Good night, General," she murmured, her sentiment softened by the firelight.

Sam's eyes twinkled in the dim glow. "Good night, MacDonalds. Can't think of a better way to spend our first night in Texas. Hopin' our luck holds for what's to come. I'll take first watch."

His words sank deep, a stable reassurance that made the night a little less dark, and whole lot safer.

Kelvin settled beside her, his breathing soft and steady, the ease with which he drifted off a quiet marvel to her.

Above them, the stars scattered across the sky like tiny lanterns. The night crisp, she nestled closer to the solid presence of his body beside her. The closeness grounded her amidst the vastness around them. In the stillness, the worries that whispered at her all day melted, replaced by a sense of wonder.

How was she so fortunate as to have this man by her side? She traced a finger over his hand, a quiet reminder of her presence, as her eyes drifted closed. His steadfastness and the rhythm of his heart eased her into a peace she rarely knew on the trail. Out here, with his hand touching hers, he was more than strength and unwavering resolve; he was home.

CHAPTER THIRTY-TWO

December 6, 1832 (Morning)
"The Redlands"
Coahuila y Tejas

Rays of sunlight broke through the thick pine canopy, casting shifting patches of light on the forest floor. Isobel squinted, making out the path ahead. "General, I can't see my way through here," she murmured, her warning swallowed up by the dense woodlands.

Sam grunted, swinging his hatchet to clear a stubborn branch blocking their way. "This is the thickest woods I've ever seen."

Kelvin tugged on the reins, struggling to keep the mules steady. "Do you think we lost the trail?"

Sam shook his head and pointed to a faint blaze mark carved into a pine trunk. "Nah, we're still on it."

Kelvin had to dismount to adjust the pack saddles, and Isobel found herself in the lead. Her stomach tightened as Dream took a hesitant step forward. Behind her, she heard the men working to secure the loads.

"Careful, Belle," Kelvin called over his shoulder, tightening a strap. "Ain't no tellin' what's lurkin' in these woods."

As Sam cinched down another tether, he cast a quick, wary glance back at her. "Isobel, don't forget to look up." His eyes flickered to the limbs overhead, shadowed and thick with pine needles. "Panthers and bobcats like to settle up there. That's where they'll come from, silent as the night."

An icy tingle ran along her back as the warning echoed in her mind. Panthers and bobcats waiting in the branches, watching. She tilted her head back and squinted at the narrow shaft of sunshine piercing through a hole in the tree canopy. Up there, where daylight failed to reach, shadows clung solid, like something hidden and hungry. She steadied herself with the thought Kelvin had his new compass. Without it, this forest could swallow them whole.

Dream jolted to a stop, snapping her focus back to the trail. Her heart kicked as her eyes landed on a man, so close that his stare sliced through her like a blade.

A mounted Indian brave. His eyes bore into hers, unwavering, a grimace carved into his lips. In one hand, he grasped Dream's bridle, his fingers steady and unyielding. In the other, a tomahawk raised head high, silent and menacing. Isobel's mind scrambled for something, *anything*, to do.

Footsteps thudded behind her. *Kelvin.* She thrust an arm out in the universal signal to stop, never breaking eye contact with the Indian. Her heart thundered, but she held his scrutiny, locked in strained silence, the world around them shrinking to the space between her own eyes and his.

Sam moved closer, positioning his body with precision, keeping her steady presence between himself and Kelvin. His command was calm, low. "Nobody move."

Isobel didn't dare shift as Sam locked eyes with the brave. She followed his movement in the taut and tense woods as he spoke a few strong words in Cherokee. The language flowed soft from his lips, a gentle offering in a standoff that came across as sharp as the deadly tomahawk.

The warrior's eyes flickered. He gave a small incline of his head, then responded in a tongue both foreign and fluid to her ears. She clenched her fists, unsure how to cross the invisible line that kept her apart from the delicate exchange unfolding before her.

After a beat, Sam's face moved into positive territory. "He's Comanche." He glanced at her with a trace of reassurance. "Told him we're lookin' to pass through peaceful-like, said it in Cherokee. I think he understands enough of it."

He pivoted back to the warrior, adding, *"Osiyo."* He gave her a quick look. "It's a Cherokee greeting."

The warrior's face softened a shade as he lowered his weapon and gestured to himself. *"Numunuu,"* he said. *"Peta Nocona."* He pointed the tomahawk at her, murmuring something else, as he glanced at her dress with a look she couldn't quite decipher.

Sam turned back to her, a trace of amusement across his face. "Name's Peta Nocona. Thanks to Tlahina, I picked up a bit of tradin' post Comanche. He thinks his mother made the clothes you're wearin'."

Nocona released the bridle, his dark eyes steady on Isobel. *"Numunuu."*

Her eyes darted to Sam, brows lifted. "What's he sayin'?"

"Numunuu," he clarified, "it's what the Comanches call themselves. He's introducin' himself to you and Kelvin."

Understanding dawned, and she turned back to Nocona and lifted her hand toward his chest. *"Numunuu. Peta Nocona."* She pointed to herself, then to her husband. "Isobel, Kelvin."

Nocona's eyes flicked to her outfit and boots, his face revealing a look of recognition.

She smoothed the deerskin, breaking her tension. "Gift from Tlahina," she explained, "Cherokee trader at Wigwam Neosho."

Nocona raised his hand, lifting it high, mimicking the height of someone tall.

She gave a brief lift of the chin, her grin widening. "Yes, that's her."

His face softened in a flash of understanding, and he spoke again. "*Tsaaku mia.*"

As Nocona turned his horse to ride north, Sam lifted his hand in a casual wave. His words carried relief as he watched the Comanche fade into the trees. "*Tsaaku mia.* Means farewell, go in a good way."

December 6, 1832 (Early Afternoon)
Nacogdoches, *Coahuila y Tejas*

THE TRAIL STRETCHED INTO A CLEARING, and a settlement sprawled ahead, its ramshackle buildings scattered like cards tossed haphazard on a table. Dust swirled in the midday light as Isobel squinted at the rough edges of a village.

"This here's Nacogdoches." Sam's words carried relief. "We've got friends here. Let's see if we can track 'em down."

Kelvin's eyes widened. "Biggest place we've seen since Cincinnati." His awe tugged a chuckle from Isobel.

"It's a funny name, General." Curiosity crossed her face. "Sounds like the town over in Louisiana."

Sam's lips curved into a grin, a bit of amusement beneath his weather-hardened features. "Indians have stories about it."

She leaned in, drawn to the tale she was certain he would tell.

"Tlahina once relayed a story about the two towns." Sam's stare was distant, as if seeing it play out. "An old Caddo chief, dyin' and wise, called his twin sons, Natchitoches and Nacogdoches, to his side. Told 'em to walk three days, one to the risin' sun, the other to the settin' sun, and settle there."

She pictured the Caddo chief, frail but determined, and his sons setting out to carve villages into the wilderness. "I don't reckon I know how to say the names right," she admitted.

Sam explained, "The Louisiana town's NAK-a-tish. This one's NA-ka-DO-ches."

Kelvin chuckled. "The Caddos sure knew their way through these woods."

"They did," he agreed. "The Spaniards thought so too. They called the Caddos friends using their word *taysha*. Spaniards pronounced it *tejas*, and we Anglos turned it into *texas*."

"Texas means friends?" she asked.

Sam chuckled. "In three languages."

Kelvin scratched his head. "Maybe we oughtta pick up some Spanish, General."

His chuckle echoed. "Either that or Caddo."

Isobel's amusement grew. "I'd like to learn Spanish soon. It's gotta be the language of law and business."

Sam's expression shifted, his face serious now. "You're right. Learnin' Spanish ain't optional if you plan to succeed in Texas."

As they rode into town, a two-story building caught Isobel's eye. Stone and brick, unheard of luxuries in these parts, formed its sturdy walls. The broad porches on each level gave it a quiet confidence, a stark contrast to the modest log homes around it. This place had been built to endure throughout generations.

The roadways bustled with wagons groaning under heavy loads, riders tipping hats, and townsfolk moving about their business. Their dusty pack mules blended right in. She scanned the unfamiliar streets, hungry for their stories.

Sam pulled her from her musings. "I think they fought a big battle here this summer."

Her back straightened. "What kind of battle?"

His expression hardened. "I'll tell you what I *think* happened, but I got the information second hand at Fort Gibson. How much truth there is to it, I can't say."

"Please go on," Isobel urged the general.

Sam leaned forward. "Y'all know there's a civil war brewin' in Mexico," he began. "On one side, you got the *Centralistas* with Presidente Bustamonte. They want Mexico City callin' the shots, which is why they made those April 6, 1830, laws bannin' Anglos, favorin' Mexicans in land grants, and puttin' slavery in it although it's already outlawed. Then, there's the *Federalistas*, led by General Santa Anna. They want the states to hold the power, stickin' to the Constitution of '24. They're all for Anglo immigration and lettin' states manage property."

Isobel narrowed her eyes, trying to piece it together. "So, this *Santa Anna* is on our side in this civil war?"

Sam replied, "Yep, and he's winnin' it, too. The Mexican officer here in Nacogdoches was a *Centralista*. Tried to disarm the Texian militia after some scrap down in Anahuac."

Kelvin straightened in the saddle. "What happened next?"

"An old friend of mine took the militia here to confront him. The officer refused to support Santa Anna, and another fight broke out with door to door fightin'. I heard the Texians killed about fifty cavalry troopers. It was a big dust up."

A shiver run through her at the image of fifty men lying dead. "When did this happen, General?"

"This last August," he replied. "Four months back."

She examined his face, her mind racing. "The fellas who led the militia here to face off with the officer are friends of yours?"

"One's a lawyer, Travis. Don't know him in person," he said. "But the other, that'd be Bowie."

Her eyes widened. "The knife fighter?"

"That's him," he confirmed. "He's a frontier character, got his hands in a lot of pies. Good man to have if a fight breaks out."

Kelvin gave a low chuckle. "Looks like the lawyer and your friend Bowie keep the pot stirred 'round here."

Sam said, "Folks are hopin' Santa Anna'll settle things down, maybe bring us closer to peace."

Isobel's heart softened. "I sure hope so."

CHAPTER THIRTY-THREE

December 6, 1832 (Late Afternoon)
Sterne Residence
Nacogdoches, *Coahuila y Tejas*

The road narrowed, bordered by scattered buildings, when Isobel spotted it – a house tucked behind a white picket fence, flanked by chimneys on both sides, she pointed. "General, could the house ahead be the one?"

Sam squinted. "It is. Sharp eye."

They dismounted, leaving the animals tethered outside the gate as Sam pushed it open with a creak. He strode across the neat yard, his boots crunching the gravel path leading to the porch. Isobel stayed back with Kelvin while Sam knocked on the door. She hoped this was the residence of his Tennessee friend, Adolphus Sterne.

The door swung open, and a petite woman with kind eyes and confident face stepped out, her eyes widening as she recognized him. "General Sam, well, I declare! What a surprise. Welcome to Nacogdoches and our home."

He tipped his hat. "Eva, it's good to see you. We've ridden hard from Fort Gibson and need a place to rest. Hope I'm not presumin' too much."

Eva said, "Nonsense. You're always appreciated here." Her eyes shifted past him, landing on the young couple with curiosity.

"These are my friends." He waved them forward. "Kelvin MacDonald and his wife, Isobel. They're agents on a mission from President Jackson, same as me."

They approached, nerves humming as Eva extended a hand. "Pleased to meet y'all, Mr. and Mrs. MacDonald."

"Oh, please call us Isobel and Kelvin," she said.

"Sure will. It's Eva." She opened the door. "Come in. You must be tired from the road. Let's sit and share some tea."

Inside the cozy parlor, the scent of tea mingled with wood smoke. Isobel took in the delicate details. A glint of sunlight beaming through the lace curtains danced on embroidered cushions and the polished table. Eva poured hot refreshment, her movements effortless as if welcoming guests was second nature.

"Is Adolphus at home?" Sam settled into a chair.

"Not at the moment," she replied. "He's in town on business but should return soon. Around here, we call him Adolfo."

"Adolfo?" She raised an eyebrow. "He's taken up a Spanish name?"

She chuckled. "He has. It smooths dealing with Mexican officials. We converted to Catholicism, as the law requires. It wasn't too hard for me, but for my husband, a German Jew, it was a bit more of an adjustment. Still, he does what's needed to keep the peace."

Kelvin shook his head in sympathy. "It's no small thing, converting to another religion."

Eva sighed. "It's been the law ever since Austin brought the first families here. But many new settlers don't understand the American Bill of Rights doesn't follow them into Mexico."

A pang of respect and sadness pricked Isobel. "But still, it must be tough for Adolfo. We read in our Bibles 'bout the Hebrews facin' endless persecution. Just 'cause somethin's been that way don't mean it's right now. I'm lookin' forward to meetin' him."

Sam chuckled. "He's a remarkable man. Cultured, sharp-witted, and a real linguist. This town's lucky to have him."

"What does he do here?" Isobel asked.

"He's the *alcalde*," she replied. "It's what they call the mayor."

Impressed, Isobel said, "Sounds like his hands are full. I wish we had time to ask him for some Spanish lessons."

Eva said, "He speaks four languages: German, French, English, and Spanish. He might enjoy teaching, but his duties keep him busy."

Sam leaned back. "No time for lessons on this trip. We need to speak to him about the latest scrap here and rest our animals in advance of heading to San Felipe."

Before she could ask more, the front door burst open with a bang, and she jumped. A man strode in, his polished boots thudding against the floorboards. Clean-shaven, with a tailored suit and an unbuttoned collar, he exuded both confidence and practicality. As he removed his hat, he beamed at Sam.

"My old friend! You've kept me waiting long enough." His greeting was genuine, with a hint of mischief. Spotting the pot, he observed, "My wife's treating you well, I see."

Eva asked, "Would you like some tea?"

"Please." His focus shifted to the MacDonalds.

"These are my companions." Sam introduced them.

Kelvin offered his hand. "Honored, sir."

Adolfo shook it, then turned to Isobel. "And this charming lady?"

She introduced herself. "I'm Isobel. It's a pleasure to meet you."

Adolfo replied, "The pleasure's mine. Welcome to Nacogdoches."

Sam furrowed his brow, his expression serious. "What's the situation here? Things appear to have changed since summer."

Adolfo's face darkened. "Yes, the tension's been rising ever since the Fredonian Rebellion of '25 and the cursed April 1830 laws. The Mexicans have been tightening their grip."

Sam said, "I remember you were jailed for your role in the rebellion."

Adolfo turned somber. "Locked up in the big stone building you passed on your way in. If not for my Masonic connections, I might still

172

be there. General Meir y Teran's report to Mexico City warned them *Tejas* would be lost if they didn't assert control. That's when they passed those laws." He paused. "The recent skirmish killed fifty *solda-dos*. It's escalating."

Isobel leaned forward, her eyes sharp. "General, if Mexicans killed fifty American troops inside our borders, what would President Jackson do?"

The room fell silent, the question hanging. He rubbed his chin and responded. "There'd be a reckonin'. Swift and sure. But the situation's different. Mexico's got a civil war brewin'."

"How many Mexican troops are left in East Texas?" Kelvin asked.

"None," Adolfo replied.

Sam's eyes brightened. "So, we can meet and organize without interference?"

"Yes, but it won't stay like this forever. Now's the time to act."

Sam leaned forward, a spark of determination in his eyes. "We'll ride to San Felipe and talk to Austin. I wanna to know what's on his mind. Splittin' up *Coahuila y Tejas* into separate states sounds like the first step of self-government."

"Texas is part of another Mexican state?" Kelvin frowned.

Sam wiped his brow. "You notice the flag flyin' by the old stone house?"

"Sure did. Green, white, 'n red," he replied.

"Vertical stripes, green, white, 'n red," Sam clarified, glancing at Isobel. "Did you catch what was on the middle white stripe?"

She thought back and answered, "Two gold stars."

"Spot on," Sterne said. "Those stars are the heart of the matter."

Eva, quiet until now, inclined forward, her eyes shining with intensity. "Two stars for *Coahuila* and *Tejas*. Two stars, two states. But what we want is one, *lone* star, not two."

Determination hardened in Sam's expression as he agreed. "If Santa Anna wins the election, we can ask for *Tejas* to be its own state."

Isobel's heart pounded. "Will it prevent war, General?"

He met her eyes, uncertainty shadowing his features. "I hope so."

The conversation shifted, but the seriousness of their words lingered. As the evening wore on, the comfort of the Sterne household wrapped around them. They shared stories, merriment softened the tension, and the parlor buzzed with life.

Isobel rose from her seat to check on Kelvin, who had left the party an hour before. Looking outside, she watched Kelvin tend to the animals, his hands moved with care as he brushed their coats and checked their hooves. Nearby, Sam and Adolfo slipped into the study, their voices low as they discussed the skirmish and plans for Texas. Before the door latched, she heard him ask Adolfo about Mrs. Gordon's land claim.

"Would you like to assist me, Isobel?" Eva asked. "We can sort out the provisions while the servants wash and mend your clothes."

"Of course. We appreciate your help so much." Isobel remembered their postmaster still held most of their luggage. "Would you care if I sent your address to my postmaster in Tennessee? I'd like for him to ship our trunks here."

"Please do," Eva replied. "We'll hold any mail or packages for you."

"Thank you so much." Her attention turned back to the maids working hard. Grateful for the attendants' help, she attempted to express her appreciation in French. "*Merci.*"

"*Je t'en prie.*" They gave Isobel an appreciative look.

"Eva, if you don't mind me askin', what's the status of your staff?" She glanced over at the housekeepers moving through the room.

Eva didn't flinch. "They're house maids from New Orleans. We've been together for a long time."

"Are they free?" she pressed.

"They're indentured servants. Slavery's not legal in Mexico," Eva replied.

Isobel reflected for a moment. "Mama told me some of our kin came to America under indentured servitude. It's how many of us got here, but indentured sounds a lot like bein' a slave, don't it?"

Eva sighed, a shade of unease in it. "I suppose you're right. I haven't pondered it much."

A familiar frustration stirred within Isobel. "We've spent time up North, in Ohio and New York. The issue of slavery keeps the pot stirred. I worry it'll drive America into a civil war, one bigger than this strife in Mexico."

Eva's face softened, a glimmer of shared worry in her eyes. "I dread the same. We'd pay our workers wages if it was our choice. But the way things are, others aren't of the same mind."

Isobel responded with a mix of hope and resignation. "Even if Texas breaks from Mexico, I fear the United States might not take us in as a slave state."

"Maybe you can bring it up to Mr. Austin when you reach San Felipe," Eva suggested.

Isobel's lips twisted into a weary grimace. "I reckon they'll tell me it ain't their top concern, like our Founding Fathers did back in '76."

Eva reached over and rested her hand on Isobel's. "If you get a chance, push 'em to face it. Sortin' it now could save everybody a heap of trouble down the road."

"Especially the Negroes," Isobel murmured, her heart heavy with the distress of it.

CHAPTER THIRTY-FOUR

December 13, 1832 (Morning)
"The Old Three Hundred"
Stephen F. Austin's Colony
San Felipe de Austin, *Coahuila y Tejas*

They rhythmic clop of hooves on hard-packed dirt echoed through the stillness, a steady cadence to the wild, endless landscape stretching in every direction. Isobel tightened her grip on the reins, as the worn leather pressed against her calloused palms. The sharp chill of the morning nipped at her cheeks, her breath curling into faint clouds before vanishing into the thickening fog. This land, untamed and unapologetic, had a way of stealing her breath and stoking her determination all at once.

"Mosquitos in winter," Kelvin muttered from ahead, his perspective carrying a note of wonder mixed with irritation. "Never thought I'd see the day."

She nudged Dream forward. Her mare's snorts came in soft puffs, matching the mist swirling around them like restless spirits.

"Takes a real freeze to kill 'em off," Sam's explanation cut through the quiet, steady and sure as always. "Haven't seen ice in these parts yet."

"Tennessee's already blanketed in snow," she chimed in, her words carrying a kindness that defied the chill. "Back home, folks are haulin' wagons over creeks with frozen slush in 'em. Maybe a few mosquitos are a fair trade – though I can't imagine what this place is like in the summer."

Kelvin chuckled low. "Like sittin' in an oven, I reckon."

Sam turned, the closest thing to satisfaction flickering across his face. "You'll see soon enough."

The trail dipped, the scrub oaks thinning to reveal the hint of a river in the distance. Isobel inhaled, catching the faint scent of damp earth and moss, which promised a stream nearby. Dream shifted beneath her, hooves crunching against the loose rocks scattered along the ridge.

"This looks like a Tennessee holler." Kelvin was light, but his words were laced with weariness.

"River's close." Sam scanned the horizon with the sharp perception of a man who read the land like a map.

As they descended the slope, the view opened, revealing a ribbon of water cutting through the trees below. Isobel's chest tightened, relief and awe warring within her. "At last," she murmured.

The trail vanished into the brush, forcing them to navigate by instinct and whatever traces of a path they could find. Kelvin muttered, frustration etched into his features.

"I see it!" Isobel called with triumph. "The ferry!"

Ahead, a flat-bottomed raft sat tethered to a bank, weathered but sturdy. Sam urged his horse forward. Solace coursed through her as they went down to the river, the faint acrid scent of wood smoke mixing with the smell of mud.

The ferryman, a wiry man with a battered hat, waved them down. "Howdy! Lookin' to cross?"

"Yes, we are." Sam waved his hand. "Is this San Felipe?"

"Sure is." The ferryman replied. "Been runnin' this ferry since before Austin brought his first settlers. Name's John McFarland."

Isobel caught Sam's look as he dismounted. "Appears we can't go anywhere without findin' Scotsmen," he teased.

Kelvin laughed, the sound carrying across the water. "We Scots know a good opportunity when we see one."

The ferryman gestured for them to lead their animals onto the craft. "Four bits American for three riders and their stock." He secured the rope as the raft shifted under their weight.

She handed Dream's reins to Kelvin and turned to McFarland. "I'm Isobel MacDonald. This is my husband, Kelvin, and our friend, General Houston."

MacFarland's appearance sharpened at Sam's name, recognition flashing in his eyes. "General Houston? Didn't expect a man of your reputation today."

Sam offered his hand. "Reputation or not, we appreciate the ride."

The boat creaked as it slid across the water, the current pulling at the ropes. Dark ripples swirled below, a mix of fascination and unease knotting her stomach. The river was both a barrier and a promise. Isobel was at the threshold of the unknown.

"Welcome to San Felipe," he said as the flatboat bumped the opposite bank. "Y'all lookin' to settle?"

Sam disembarked first, his boots scuffing the deck. "We're here to speak with Stephen Austin."

McFarland tipped his hat, his curiosity clear but unspoken. "Peyton's Tavern's on the west side of the plaza. Good place to get your bearings."

"Thank you." Isobel followed as the men led their stock onto the shore.

The town unfolded before them in modest strokes. Rough-hewn buildings clustered around a central square, their log walls blending into the surrounding trees. Smoke curled from chimneys, the stillness stirred by the quiet rhythm of a village carving itself out of the wilderness.

"This place has promise," Kelvin said, with cautious optimism.

Isobel surveyed the streets. It wasn't home, not yet, but there was a spirit here. She couldn't quite solve the puzzle.

As they approached the plaza, a boy with sun-darkened skin stepped forward. "*¡Buenos días, señores!*"

"Good mornin'," Isobel replied. She hoped he spoke English and might help them. "We're lookin' for Peyton's Tavern. Can you point us the way?"

The lad gestured for them to follow. "*Sígueme.*"

She glanced at Kelvin, who gave an agreeing look, and they fell in step behind their guide. The scent of roasting meat and spiced corn drifted through the settlement, teasing her senses. Children darted between buildings, their cheering ringing out like bright notes against the town's earthy sounds.

Their escort led them to a sturdy building on the plaza's edge, its wooden sign swinging in the breeze. She quickened her pace until she was beside him. "My name is Isobel," she said, weaving her words with gestures, her hand to her chest, her name drawn out with care. She pointed toward him, eyebrows raised in question. "What's your name?"

The youth's teeth flashed white. "*Me llamo, Miguel Mancha,*" he said with a small, theatrical bow.

"Pleasure to meet ya, Miguel," Isobel said. She turned and pointed to Kelvin, who was adjusting the reins of a mule. "This here's my husband, Kelvin." With a motion toward Sam, she added, "And he's General Houston."

Miguel's expression softened into something almost reverent. "*Placer conocerte,*" he said, bowing again, his scan sweeping over the men. His deference wasn't lost on her. She thought it odd to see Sam viewed as a towering force in a foreign land.

Miguel straightened and gestured forward, his hand moving in an invitation to continue. She followed, a quiet satisfaction settling in her spirit. They were strangers in a strange land, but in the boy's easy demeanor and gracious words, she found the smallest strand of connection. The attachment was a small thing, but it anchored her, a fiber of familiarity stretching across the vast unknown.

The faint strains of music floated on the cool breeze, teasing at the edges of her awareness. Isobel paused, tilting her head, struggling to catch it again. *Yes, there it was.* The fiddle tune, its notes weaving through the hum of the town like a filament of golden light. It was the same melody she'd heard before. It beckoned her, drawing her forward with an insistence she couldn't ignore.

She closed her eyes as she walked, letting the harmony fill the empty spaces within her, and replacing them with a quiet fullness she hadn't realized she'd been seeking. Her heart swelled with something she hadn't expected. The fear of never finding her place loosened its grip and let Providence slip through. Her footsteps quickened, as though the melody had taken hold of her, urging her forward. A thought rose unbidden, soft but certain. *You belong here, if you'll let yourself.*

CHAPTER THIRTY-FIVE

December 13, 1832 (Midday)
"The Old Three Hundred"
Stephen F. Austin's Colony
San Felipe de Austin, *Coahuila y Tejas*

T he log cabin loomed ahead, its twin chimneys like sentinels guarding the sprawling front porch. Isobel took in its sturdy frame, its dark timbers weathered by years of sun and storm and marveled at how different it was from the dogtrot cabins she knew back in the Smokies. No breezeway split its center. This place was whole, self-contained, and somehow grander for it. A *tavern* McFarland had called it, meant for travelers and locals alike, nestled right in the heart of Commerce Plaza.

As they dismounted, the scent of fresh-cut timber and the faint tang of smoke wrapped around them. Isobel's fingers brushed the course reins before tying her mare to the front rail alongside their mules. Miguel strode ahead with that unshakable confidence of his, as if he owned the place.

She hesitated on the first porch step, the sturdy planks beneath her boots creaking. The glow spilling from the windows promised rest, though her nerves prickled at the thought of stepping into a room full of strangers.

Miguel paused at the door, casting a glance over his shoulder, his face unreadable. "Come on." The words a low rumble meant for her alone.

Isobel straightened her shoulders, willing her uncertainty to stay hidden. She followed him through wide doors, her heartbeat quickening as the tavern's noise and hum of life enveloped her. *You belong here, if you'll let yourself.*

"*Señora* Peyton, *tengo nuevos amigos aquí,*" Miguel said.

"*Gracias,* Miguel." She handed him a piece of cornbread. Isobel noted the way his shoulders relaxed, this was an obvious ritual between them. A bit of cornbread and a splash of buttermilk in exchange for new faces at her door. Simple, clever.

"Welcome to the San Felipe Inn," she said, her words carrying with ease over the drone of conversation. "Or as some folks call it, Peyton's Tavern. My husband, Jonathan, and I own the place. I'm Angelina Peyton. Looks like you've already met my friend, Miguel." She gestured toward him with a fond expression that said she knew exactly how persuasive he could be.

Isobel adjusted her stance, fingers brushing against her skirt as she stepped forward. She steadied herself, unwilling to falter in the unfamiliar surroundings. "Yes, ma'am. He was right friendly and helped us since we got off the ferry."

Isobel's words earned a pleasant expression from Angelina, her piercing eyes scanning her with what she hoped was approval.

She squared her shoulders, drawing confidence from the memory of her mother's admonition. *Speak plain, speak honest, and folks will listen.* "I'm Isobel MacDonald," she continued, glancing toward Kelvin as he doffed his hat. "And these here gentlemen are my husband, Kelvin, and our good friend, General Samuel Houston of Tennessee."

The last name lingered for a moment, sparking whispers among the patrons nearby. She sensed the weight of their curiosity, but she kept her chin high, set on not allowing the attention to rattle her.

"General Houston. My word," Angelina said with a mingling of surprise and delight. Her observation went over their small party before landing on the towering man at Isobel's side. "There's been talk 'round town you might make your way to Texas. It's a right pleasure havin' you and your friends here."

He inclined his head in that easy way of his, the faintest shadow of something tugging at the corner of his lips. "Thank you, Mrs. Peyton. Do you have quarters for us?"

"Yes, sir, General, we surely do." There was a spark of something in Angelina's eye Isobel couldn't place. "Had some land speculators passin' through from New Orleans a few days back. They left this mornin' headin' to *Bexár*, so we got two rooms open."

"Thank you," Sam said.

She leaned against the counter, wiping her hands on her apron. "Now, I gotta warn ya, our accommodations ain't as fancy as them inns and hotels you're used to in Nashville or Washington City. Usually, bachelor men just put out bed rolls on the floor." She paused, a playful smirk creeping onto her face. "But I wouldn't dream of puttin' you there, General."

Isobel glanced at Sam, who chuckled low in his throat, his shoulders relaxing as he met the innkeeper's good-natured jab. "We sure do appreciate your hospitality. We've been on the trail from Nacogdoches and figured we'd come here to meet with Mr. Austin."

The name Stephen F. Austin stirred something in Isobel. She'd heard the tales of his leadership and patience, his dreams of building a state in this unbroken land.

"He ain't here now." Angelina shifted to something more matter of fact. "He's out and about with surveyors, markin' out property lines and mappin' the settlement."

"He's a cartographer?" Sam asked with interest and authority.

"Sure is." She beamed, her reply tinged with pride, like she was bragging on kin. "His maps are the finest 'round these parts. He's off with Seth Ingram and Horatio Chriesman right now, surveyin' plots on the Brazos and Colorado Rivers."

Isobel listened in, imagining the men trudging through dense brush, compasses in hand, chains clinking as they measured leagues of uncharted land.

Angelina continued, her words painting a vivid picture. "Takes 'em days and weeks to cover each league. They're over four thousand acres apiece, y'know. They wait for this cooler weather 'cause it's easier to shoot their lines and compass through them dormant trees."

Sam's deep reply broke through her thoughts. "Well, Mrs. Peyton, I reckon we aren't certain how long we'll be stayin'. Hopin' to catch Mr. Austin while we're here."

She gave an experienced reply. "Y'all in the right place, General," she assured him, her hands settling on her hips. "Everybody in San Felipe comes through my tavern sooner or later. This here village might as well be the capital of Texas."

Isobel couldn't help but glance around the establishment, taking in a medley of settlers, traders, and wanderers crowding the space. The hum of conversation and the scrape of chairs against the wooden floor gave the inn a lively pulse, a reminder this wasn't just a stop on their journey, it was the heart of something bigger.

Kelvin stepped up. "Is there a place in town for our horses and mules?" he asked. Isobel caught the strain of weariness carried by the long journey.

Angelina didn't miss a beat as she wiped down the counter. "Sure is. José Leal runs a livery stable on the east side. Y'all walked right by it comin' off the landin'. Miguel can show you the way back to José's barn."

Kelvin moved toward the door and said, "I'll go to the stables." Miguel followed him out, the two marching to the barn.

Inside, Isobel and Sam gravitated to a sturdy table near the corner of the room. The rich, buttery scent of fresh cornbread filled the air, tugging their attention to the hot skillet. He pulled out a chair for her, and she sat, smoothing her dress as she glanced around the room. The whisper of comfortable conversations surrounded them.

Angelina appeared moments later, a plate of cornbread in her hands, the golden crust gleaming in the lamplight. Isobel murmured her thanks, the heat of the bread a welcome comfort against her palms as she broke off a piece. The wetness of cornmeal mixed with butter filled her mouth, easing the stress in her shoulders.

At that moment, the door creaked open, and a man stepped inside, his appearance sharp enough to slice through the room's homespun charm. His suit, crisp and tailored, stood in stark contrast to the rough spun clothing of the other patrons. Isobel's fingers paused on the rim of her buttermilk glass, her eyes narrowing as she studied him. He didn't look like someone passing through. No, this man appeared driven by purpose.

"Howdy, Buck." Angelina greeted.

The man, broad shouldered, with a confident, easy swagger, touched the brim of his hat as he made his way closer. His boots clicked against the wood floor. "Hey, Angelina. Looks like you got some visitors." His gaze shifted towards Isobel. His eyes lingered just a second too long, measuring her up. Then politeness erupted from his mouth. "May I present myself to you, ma'am? I'm William B. Travis, attorney at law. But folks 'round here call me *Buck*."

His manners were impeccable, but something in his confidence made her stiffen. She answered, "Pleased to meet you, Mr. Travis. I'm Isobel MacDonald. My husband, Kelvin, and I are travelin' with General Houston of Tennessee." She motioned toward Sam.

Buck's expression shifted in an instant, broadening with genuine excitement. "My Lord!" He nearly stumbled over his words. "It's a pleasure to meet both of y'all. General Houston's here at last." He sounded as if he'd been anticipating this moment for ages, like Sam's presence was a turning point in his world.

Before she could gauge Sam's reaction, he stood up, his imposing figure quieting the room like a gust of wind snuffing out a candle. He crossed his arms, his demeanor unyielding, his words deliberate. "Don't think you should read too much into my bein' here, Travis. I figure the colony can find its way to self-governance without stirrin' up trouble."

Sam's warning, rough like macadam grit, carried weight. Buck's expression faltered, but his eyes flickered with something indecipher-able, a fusion of respect and calculation. Isobel sat in silence, taking it all in. This man, Buck, with his polished manner and keen interest, was clearly a player in whatever game was unfolding here. And Sam, ever the stoic, was already drawing his line in the sand.

The conversation deepened and shrank the room as it thickened with friction and the weight of unspoken stakes. Isobel sat near the corner, her fingers tightening around her coat.

Travis leaned in, his language carrying the kind of conviction that could ignite a crowd. "You sure do sound like our esteemed empre-sario, General." He straightened, squaring his shoulders like he was bracing for the pushback. "Stephen Austin keeps tryin' to smooth things over with Mexico City, makin' gestures towards loyalty at every turn. He'll tell ya he's sworn allegiance legally and in spirit. Me, on the other hand, I ain't taken no such oath, and neither have many others who came here after the Laws of April 1830."

His words carried a sharp defiance, one that prickled under Isobel's skin. She couldn't help but study him, the hard set of his jaw, the fire in his eyes. This was a man who didn't flinch from confronta-tion. She turned to Sam, waiting for his response, knowing it would come slow and deliberate, like the first rumble of thunder before a storm.

"You're still young, Travis," Sam said with a weary patience. He didn't chase the lure, didn't take the bait. "Got a lot to learn 'bout war and what it does to a country. Peace, well, it's always the better option long as it holds."

Isobel exhaled, not realizing she'd been holding her breath. Sam's calm steadiness was like a lifeline in the room, but she caught the flicker in Travis's eyes, admiration, maybe, but also frustration. He wasn't backing down.

Travis's delivery was softer now but no less determined. "General, I got nothin' but respect for ya and yer thoughts. Yer service, it speaks volumes. But this Mexican government? It's double dealin' at best and downright deceitful at worst. Incompetent bunch, run by fools and thieves." His eyes burned with the pressure of his conviction, sweeping the room as if daring anyone to disagree. "Texians, you'll see soon enough, will have to spill blood to carve out our independence."

Isobel's stomach turned at the resolve in him. *Blood.* She didn't doubt he believed it. She didn't doubt he was the first to spill it. The room turned colder now, the space between them heavier. She glanced at Sam, his expression obscure, his silence more telling than any response could have been. She knew Buck's opinion of the Mexican government was an answer to one of President Jackson's questions. The words drifted between them like smoke, thick and choking, as if the future had already begun to burn its way forward, soaked with sacrifice and fire.

Sam stroked his chin. His answer, when it came, was calm but firm, like the rumble of a distant storm. "You might be onto somethin' there, Travis. In fact, I reckon you're right. But it's the duty of us all to seek peace first."

The words settled over the room, carving a space in her heart. She hesitated for a beat, but the anxiety curling within her ribs wouldn't stay silent. She gathered herself and spoke clearly, though laced with unease. "Mr. Travis, *Buck*, we're new to Texas. Spent a spell in Nacogdoches, heard 'bout your doin's there. Both sides done shed blood already. Appears to me, bein' fresh to this, things could spiral quick-like without warnin'. Am I seein' this right?"

All eyes turned to her, and she resisted the urge to shrink back. Travis shifted, his expression softened just enough to let a flicker of respect slip through.

Travis looked her in the eye. "You ain't wrong, Mrs. MacDonald." He was stable, almost resigned. "Every day more Americans come into the colony like y'all did. The new laws aren't too forgivin' about it. Mexico's clingin' to Texas with a desperate grip, stoppin' folks from comin' in and takin' their land." His words dipped lower, heavier with the weight of what came next. "Only way we keep things calm is pack up and head back to America. Anythin' Austin does to please Mexico City ain't gonna bear fruit in the long run. I'm not hankerin' for a war, but it *will* come when the Mexicans find a strong leader who can rally their army."

Isobel's pulse quickened. The sureness in his outlook was chilling, as though he'd already seen the war before it arrived.

"Apologies," Travis added, tilting his head. "If I'm more of a pessimist than y'all."

Isobel's throat tightened. She glanced toward Sam, his face unfathomable, then back to Travis. His words weren't just an observation, they were a warning, stark and unyielding. The shift was unmistakable, every word heavier, every risk more immediate. If there was a future here, it was a sharp-edged one. Travis had already drawn blood.

Isobel continued, "Buck, I don't mean to knock your opinion. I agree with General Houston. You're most likely right. But I fear a Mexican army would spill a lot of blood in a revolt. Those who'd fall in such a mess deserve every shot at peace we can muster."

The scrutiny of the room shifted toward her, and Travis's sharp eyes dwelt on her. For a moment, she wondered if she'd overstepped, but then his expression softened.

"Isobel, take heart in knowin' we don't decide wars based on one man's say-so," Travis continued. "Even if I wanted to, I couldn't drag the colony into war. They call me a *hot-head* and a *rabble-rouser*, and maybe they're right, but I reckon cooler heads should steer the ship." He paused, his lips curling into a faint, self-aware smirk. "I'm young, but I ain't foolish. The Mexican government's fixin' to back us into a corner, scrappin' them contracts and agreements like they mean nothin'." His throat tightened on the last words, the anger there quiet but unmistakable. It wasn't just defiance, it was frustration with a system that seemed rigged to collapse. He leaned forward, his words low and deliberate. "Ever seen a lion with nowhere to go?" His words filled the space, charged, a quiet warning. "It don't lie down and wait. It bares its teeth. It fights."

Isobel swallowed hard, grappling with his meaning, the force of what he was saying falling like stones on her chest.

Before she could respond, Sam's calm, steady way broke the tension. "Mind joinin' us for some of Angelina's cornbread, Buck?"

Travis's eyes lightened, the hint of promise softening his features. "Thank ya kindly, General. It'd be my honor to share a table with ya."

The pressure in the room ebbed, but the undercurrent of unspoken worry lingered. These men, their words heavy with consequence, weren't just producing an afternoon's discussion; they were molding the future of a land Isobel couldn't yet understand. And for better or worse, she realized, she and Kelvin were now part of it.

CHAPTER THIRTY-SIX

December 13, 1832 (Late Afternoon)
"The Old Three Hundred"
Stephen F. Austin's Colony
San Felipe de Austin, *Coahuila y Tejas*

Angelina's door creaked open, and Isobel's head turned instinctively toward the sound. A man filled the doorway, his frame broad enough to block out the daylight behind him. Sandy-haired and rugged, he carried himself like he owned every room he walked into, his boots landing heavy on the wooden floor. The atmosphere tightened, thickening with the weight of his presence, and Sam straightened, as if bracing for impact.

"Is that my old friend Sam Houston sittin' at your table, Angelina?" the man boomed, his question rolling through the room like a thunderclap.

She wiped her hands on her apron, then gestured toward Sam. "Sure is. He's lookin' for Stephen Austin."

Sam's face lit with recognition, as the man strode further into the room. "Howdy, Jim. It's been a coon's age since I seen ya. Last time mighta been Arkansas. Hard to say."

"Or New Orleans." The man's words hinted at both friendship and mischief. "It coulda been either one. Good to see ya. Now that you're here, we can get down to business."

Sam turned to Isobel. "This is my old friend, Jim Bowie."

Isobel's heart thumped. Bowie wasn't just another man in a room. He was a force. Back in Tennessee, his name was spoken with near reverence, woven into whispered tales of knives and pirates that made her blood run cold. She examined Travis, who leaned back in his chair, the tension in his posture betraying his attempt at calm.

Travis shook his head. "Don't go stirrin' the pot, Bowie. He warned me not to make a fuss 'bout him bein' here."

He turned his face to Travis, his face turning sly, almost challenging. "Ain't but one reason he'd come. He's fixin' to wrest Texas away from Mexico and bring us into America. I know him, and I know Jackson."

The walls pressed closer, the strength of Bowie's words hanging like a storm cloud. Isobel's throat tightened as her eyes darted between Sam and Bowie. The camaraderie connecting the two men was undeniable, but so was the unspoken danger lurking beneath their words.

Isobel caught the flicker of annoyance in Angelina's eyes as she folded her arms and leveled a pointed look at the men. "Gentlemen, please. These folks ain't settled in, and you're houndin' 'em like a bird dog chasin' quail."

Bowie found an empty chair. "Fair enough. I'll give 'em a day."

"Buck, you got your dominoes?" Angelina shifted the mood with an ease Isobel couldn't help but admire.

"They're at the office," Travis said with an undercurrent of defiance.

"Why don't ya fetch 'em?" Angelina asked like she was corralling rowdy boys. "Y'all can jaw 'bout politics over a friendly game."

Travis tipped his hat and rose to his feet. "I'll be back in no time." He made his way toward the door as Kelvin stepped inside, his timing impeccable as always.

Kelvin halted in the doorway as he came face-to-face with Travis. "Beg pardon, sir."

Travis's sharp eyes flicked over him before a faint smile touched his lips. "William B. Travis, attorney at law. If your wife's at the table, you must be Kelvin." His manner was smooth and practiced.

Kelvin squared his shoulders and carried a weight Isobel recognized all too well. "Yes, proud to say she's my wife." He didn't waver as he added, "And if you're the same lawyer Travis who conjured trouble up and down East Texas, reckon I've heard plenty to already know you."

Isobel's stomach knotted as the words hung between them. For a moment, she braced for Travis's response, unsure if he'd meet Kelvin's challenge head-on. Instead, his grin widened, his confidence undented. "My friends call me *Buck*. I'll be back in a shake with my dominoes, and we'll have ourselves a game." He stepped past Kelvin and out the door.

Kelvin's expression softened just enough to reassure her, but Isobel's mind lingered on Travis's retreating figure. Whatever game he intended to play, she suspected it wasn't just with dominoes.

Kelvin approached the table, his eyes taking in its generous size. It was sturdy, meant for holding more than meals, plates, drinks, and, judging by the buzz of the room, a good round of dominoes. As he drew nearer, his attention snagged on the stranger sitting there, then to the imposing knife hanging from the man's belt. The blade was impossible to ignore.

The man stood, the chair creaking as he pushed it back. He gestured toward an empty seat. "Jim Bowie, sir. At yer service."

Kelvin accepted the gesture with a polite tilt of his head. "Pleasure's mine. I'm Kelvin MacDonald."

As they settled into their seats, Travis reappeared with the dominoes in hand. Angelina brought out another round of hot cornbread. Isobel and Kelvin shared a glass of buttermilk. Travis, noticing Angelina nearby, inquired about sweet milk, which she fetched.

Angelina didn't bother asking Bowie what he wanted to drink. "General, you want the same drink as your knife-slingin' friend?"

Sam chuckled and shifted in his chair. "Yes, ma'am. Me and him, we see eye to eye on such matters."

Travis placed a bag on the table and pulled it open with a practiced hand. He emptied the sack and began shuffling the little blocks across the smooth tavern table. Isobel's fingers brushed against the wood, feeling the years worn into it. Grooves, scratches, and countless stories were etched into its surface. What had once been rough-hewn was now polished to a smooth, time-worn veneer by countless hands.

Isobel turned her curiosity to the dominoes, their sleek surfaces catching the light. She leaned forward. "These are beautiful, Buck."

Travis kept shuffling them in circles. "Most are black, but a skilled hand carved these white ones from bone. Can't say what kind of bone 'cause the fella who traded 'em didn't know neither. This little village, it's got potential to be somethin' big one day, but for now, land grants and tradin' settle most debts. Money ain't exactly flowin' around."

"It's why Texians hold their property rights so dear," Bowie said, his statement landed with the authority of someone who believed it as law.

Isobel probed, "Does it include slaves, Mr. Bowie?"

Bowie's expression didn't flicker, his reply just as measured as before. "All property, Isobel. Even dominoes."

His seriousness sent a chill through her, the bluntness of his remarks brushing against her sense of unease. Her fingers toyed with the rim of her glass as she bent forward, trying to shift the conversation's weight. "Basic block game?"

"How 'bout *Mexican* block?" Travis interjected, quick and mischievous, like he'd been waiting for this moment.

"What's that game?" she asked, catching the exchange of glances between the men. The slight furrow in Sam's brow and Bowie's faint smirk told her she wasn't the only one in the dark.

Travis leaned back in his chair. "It's where I, as the owner of the dominoes, change the rules as we play, tryin' to win no matter what."

The room erupted in a laughter that rolled off the tavern's weathered walls. Bowie's and Sam's mirth drew radiance from Isobel. Kelvin, usually so composed, smirked as he shook his head.

Travis let the merriment carry for a moment before he rested his elbows on the table and spread his hands in mock confusion. "Why y'all laughin'?"

CHAPTER THIRTY-SEVEN

December 24, 1832
The Peyton Tavern
San Felipe de Austin, *Coahuila y Tejas*

T he door burst open, letting in the sting of winter. Travis
strode in, waving a stack of papers like a triumphant herald.
Isobel's heart jumped at the sight, though she kept her face
composed. Her hands tightened on the pewter mug of cider before
her, still holding the heat from the hearth.

"Merry Christmas, General," he declared. "Looks like Mr. Austin,
albeit unseen, got you the land grant you were after."

Sam's chair scraped against the floor. "It's the best Christmas
present I ever got."

Travis chuckled and turned to the others gathered around the
table. "The MacDonalds also got their league from our *empresario*."

Her mind raced. *Our league.* The consequence of it settled over her
like a mantle. "Buck, did you see where the grants are?"

He leaned forward with the kind of energy suggesting he'd studied
every line of those papers with a lawyer's keen eye. "Near the headwa-
ters of Karankawa Bay. Anglos ain't allowed to own land within

twenty-six miles of the coast. Mexican born settlers get the prime coastal properties. But these plots? Close enough to have Gulf access by rivers and creeks."

A faint smile formed on Sam's lips and grew into something more. "I reckon we got a lot of Tennessee horse tradin' in our future, Isobel."

She tried to suppress a nervous giggle. *Horse tradin' indeed.* The enormity of it pressed down on her. "It's overwhelmin' to think Kelvin and I own 4,446 acres of Texas."

She glanced down into the dark swirl of her cider, the realization sinking deep. Expanses of wild, untamed land capable of either shaping their future or swallowing them whole. The papers on the table seemed almost unreal. She knew now why people would fight to their deaths, rather than have their holdings taken away from them.

Travis broke the silence. "I hate to be the bearer of bad tidings on Christmas Eve, Isobel, but you got a mere 4,428. Mr. Austin and his surveyors adjusted their measurements for a league, and you lost eighteen acres."

Isobel shook her head. *Eighteen acres.* They never had as much property in Tennessee. Now, it could be tossed away by adjusting the survey chains.

Kelvin said, "Buck, thank you for bringin' us the delightful news. As someone from Alabama, you know how sizable an open area of forty-four hundred acres is."

Travis said, "I know nobody could secure such a title anywhere in the United States."

Angelina spoke up. "Ain't it any wonder folks back home all got *Texas Fever.*"

Travis, ever curious, shifted his attention to her. "Where's your husband this evenin', Angelina?"

She wiped her hands on her skirt. "He went over to Farmer's Hotel to be of use with their Christmas bakin'. They expect to be busy tomorrow. They offered him space in their ovens in exchange for his help."

The domesticity of it all... The thought of bread rising in hot ovens as the Lord blessed her own world beyond measure made Isobel's jaw tighten. Her fingers brushed against her cheeks, damp with tears she hadn't realized were falling. She pressed her lips together, swallowing the lump in her throat. "I promised the general he wouldn't see me bawlin', but it's gettin' harder to keep my promise."

Her eyes burned, betraying her vow to remain strong.

Sam placed his hand on her arm. "I think we're all overwhelmed. As much as we tried to prepare for this day, it was only a misty dream until we achieved it."

The door swung open with a draft, sharp and cold against her skin. Bowie strode in, his presence commanding as ever. "Merry Christmas."

"Merry Christmas, Jim," Angelina replied. "Are ya gonna see your young bride on Christmas?"

His expression softened, a rare glimpse of vulnerability in the hardened frontiersman. "I hope to see Ursula when I get to *Béxar*. I'm leavin' in the mornin'."

"How far is it?" Sam asked.

"It's about 150 miles, but the road ain't bad."

Isobel's focus lingered on Bowie for a moment before shifting to the files scattered on the table. *Dreams achieved or struggles burdened with bloody sacrifices?* She likely wouldn't know the answer until the dust of this new life settled. If it ever did. The comfortable haze of smoke in the tavern wrapped around her like a cocoon, though her restless thoughts churned beneath the surface.

Sam's cadence cut through her contemplations, calm and commanding. "If you don't mind, will you escort us to San Antonio?"

"Sure. It's always safer in numbers. We can make good time if we take horses and leave the mules here." Bowie leaned back. "Let's have a toddy. Angelina, can you serve us some Christmas cheer?"

"I sure can." She moved and set to work. "Maybe Buck can bring his dominoes out for a holiday game."

Travis patted the leather satchel slung on his chair. "I got 'em with me."

Angelina glided across the room, filling glasses with a grace Isobel admired. Her easy way cast a comforting glow over the gathering.

Sam rose to his feet, glass held high, his eyes gleaming with a rare, unguarded happiness. The others followed suit, their glasses catching the light of the fire. "To our first Christmas together in Texas. May it be the first of many among good friends and good times."

The words hit Isobel straight in the chest. Kelvin squeezed her hand, grounding her, but it wasn't enough to stop the tide. Her vision blurred as tears welled until they spilled over, hot against her cheeks. She couldn't hold them back. Not on Christmas. Not after everything. She faltered, the sound soft but sufficient to draw every eye in the room.

Kelvin tightened his grip around her hand, his own eyes glistening with unshed tears. The rawness of the moment overwhelmed her, and before she could apologize, Sam was already on his feet, his steps slow and deliberate. Without hesitation, he put his hand on her shoulder, a steady anchor in the storm.

The sway of the comfort broke something within her. The weeping came unrestrained, the sobs rising unbidden and echoing across the room. Bowie's hand rested on her other shoulder while Travis stood close by, their silence louder than any words could be. It wasn't sympathy; it was solidarity, a shared understanding of the struggle they all knew was coming.

Angelina murmured a benediction, its sound flowing through the room like a prayer. "God bless Texas."

CHAPTER THIRTY-EIGHT

December 31, 1832
The Veramendi Palace
130 Soledad Street
San Antonio de *Béxar, Coahuila y Tejas*

T he wind bit through Isobel's coat as she huddled into its collar, trying to keep the chill off her cheeks. Cold and relentless, it seeped past every layer she wore. She stroked Dream's neck, her fingers brushing the soft hide beneath the mare's mane. The rhythmic clip-clop of hooves followed her everywhere, a steady heartbeat in the wilderness. The faint whiff of leather and the sounds of the trail settled her nerves like an old lullaby.

Ahead, the men rode like statues, their frocks pulled tight against the breeze. Kelvin's broad shoulders hunched as his free hand gripped the reins, while Sam and Jim mirrored his stance with coats buttoned high, faces shadowed by the brims of their hats.

She brushed the hair out of her face. "We've been ridin' south, but it don't feel a lick warmer."

Kelvin glanced back, the palm of his glove creaking as he flicked his reins. "Dry air causes it. Makes it cut deeper than it ought to."

Isobel frowned at the answer but said nothing, her inklings drifting to the landscape. The sun had long dipped behind the horizon, and the growing darkness softened the jagged edges of the land. *Béxar* loomed in the night, its silhouette half-formed, the town's fringes blending into the dark.

Jim lifted an arm, pointing ahead through the shadows. He had a quiet authority about him, which made it clear when they needed further direction. "Here's the turn. Palace ain't far from here."

Isobel tilted her head, the word catching in her ears. "Palace?"

A low chuckle rumbled from Jim's chest as he shifted in his saddle. "It's the word some folks use. Not much more'n a big house, though. *Hacienda*'s another name for it."

"Hmm." She let the term drift in the space, turning it over. *Palace.* The notion of such a word was as distant and foreign as mild weather had been on this southbound journey. She kept her eyes forward, wondering what kind of place they were riding into.

"Here we are." He spoke into the dry South Texas night, light and nearly flippant as if what lay ahead wasn't worth a moment of awe.

Here we are. She scanned him, but his eyes were fixed on the adobe structure ahead, his hand sweeping toward it with an ambience of accomplished ease. Her chest tightened. The double doors towered above them, larger than anything she'd ever imagined, let alone seen. A palace, he'd called it, but it looked more like a fortress. It stood weathered and imposing, while radiating a sense of permanence she found both thrilling and intimidating.

Isobel slid from her horse, her legs shaky, though she prayed no one noticed. The riders fell into line, boots crunching against the gravel and dirt as they followed Jim toward the entry. Each step made her feel smaller, the heights of the men and the vastness of the doors in sharp contrast to her own slight body.

Jim's instruction came again. "This way." His hand rested on the wood as if he could coax it open with sheer confidence. Failing the coaxing method, he knocked on the door.

A servant opened it with a consummate bow, and Isobel stepped into the cool, shaded expanse of the Veramendi Palace. A tremor ran through her at the sight of the grand hall, a world away from the dust and cold outside. Her boots landed harder on the polished floor, the clack of footsteps swallowed by the vast space. There, standing at the center like a figure from a painting, was Ursula Veramendi Bowie.

So, this is her. She took in the vision of the woman who had claimed Bowie's heart. Ursula radiated poise, her every detail a calculated perfection. The deep navy-blue of her dress shimmered, its rolling fabric draped over a golden blouse appearing to catch and hold any glimmer of light in the room. The red sash at her waist was bold, almost defiant, and her crisp white collar framed a face so beautiful it bordered on unfair.

"*Feliz año nuevo*, James." Ursula's words carried across the grand hall like the ringing of bells. The striking woman greeted Bowie with a kiss and an embrace—the kind of gesture that spoke of a love so familiar, so secure, it needed no explanation.

Isobel's chest swelled with an unexpected sense of joy, as if the celebration had found its way inside her. She came with no clear expectations, but the love of family and friends, the wonder, and the welcome of the place stirred something she'd nearly forgotten. Belonging.

"*Lo siento*, Ursula." He bowed his head for a moment. "I stayed in San Felipe a few more days than I planned." He stepped back, his hand arcing toward the small group. "May I present General Houston, Kelvin MacDonald, and his wife, Isobel."

Ursula moved with effortless grace, her navy dress flowing like water as she approached Sam. She extended her hand, poised yet inviting. He bent, pressing a polite kiss to her fingers. The gesture was formal, almost regal, as though she was the queen of the grand palace.

Ursula turned to Kelvin next, offering the same elegant motion. He followed Sam's example, his usual easy demeanor tempered by the weight of the moment.

Then it was her turn. Isobel's stomach fluttered, but she straightened her spine, determined to make a good impression. Ursula looked at her with curiosity and kindness, then raised a brow. "You have accompanied the men from Tennessee?"

Isobel met her question head-on. "Yes, ma'am." She extended her hand with a firm grip, despite the temptation to soften her hold. "I'm pleased to meet you, Mrs. Bowie."

For a heartbeat, Ursula searched Isobel's face. To Isobel's surprise, she stepped forward and wrapped her in a brief, gentle embrace. "Please call me Ursula."

The unexpected kindness caught Isobel off guard, her tension easing. "Thank you, Ursula." For the first time since stepping into the palace, she was less like a stranger and more like a member of a family.

Isobel saw Maria Josefa glide into the room and her heart beat a little faster. The matriarch, Ursula's mother, commanded attention with little effort, her every step exuding grace. As if summoned by some unspoken cue, Bowie straightened from his easy stance, dipping into a low bow before lifting Maria's hand to his lips. The gesture was gentlemanly, yet Bowie's rugged charm added a rough-hewn sincerity.

"*Bienvenido, Santiago.*" Maria spoke with a sweetness like honey. Her presence filled the space, soft yet undeniable, like the scent of gardenias on a summer night.

Isobel glanced at Bowie, searching his expression. His Spanish was competent but carried a twang. It stood out against Maria's natural cadence. "*Gracias, señora.* I'm mighty glad I made it in time for the New Year's celebration."

The faint lines at Maria's eyes crinkled with fondness. "Juan Martín is in his office completing the year end ledgers. He will join us soon."

Bowie replied, "I'm lookin' forward to meetin' up with him. I reckon he'd be keen to meet my friend Sam Houston. They got a lot in common, seein' as General Houston was the governor of Tennessee."

The low murmur of conversation shifted as Juan Martín Veramendi entered the room. He strode in with his characteristic presence, every step purposeful. "*Santiago,* James. Our New Year celebration is now complete."

Bowie straightened his posture into something more formal.

"Thank you, Governor. My friends and I rode into San Antonio from San Felipe this evening. Feels good to be home."

Home? Her brows knit closer. *Béxar* had embraced Bowie, yes, but it was now embracing her.

Veramendi inclined his head. "Did I hear you say General Houston is with you?"

Sam stepped forward, extending his hand. "I'm on a mission from my *presidente* to report on the Comanche. My two friends are also agents of *Presidente* Jackson."

Veramendi was as gracious as ever. "*Con much gusto, Don* Samuel. You're all welcome here, *por supuesto.*"

Ursula moved toward her husband, her skirts swishing over the tiled floor. "Let's go to the parlor for a drink and conversation."

"It's wonderful to meet your family, Jim." Isobel tried to match the spirit of the room while keeping her curiosity at bay. She looked up at the high ceilings and intricate tile work shimmering in the flickering candlelight. "I've never seen Spanish architecture and culture. It's delightful."

Before Bowie could respond, Veramendi stepped forward. "San Antonio de *Béxar* is much different than New York or New Orleans. We value our ancestry and try to keep it alive in a changing world."

Sam said, "This is the first Tejano town we've seen." He gestured to the walls of the room as if it encapsulated the city itself. "The adobe and stucco masonry, and the stonework are all exceptional. I noticed paintings on many buildings, but I'll have to wait until daylight to see how colorful they are. I can understand now why *El Camino Real* runs from Nacogdoches to San Antonio."

Veramendi gave a gracious response. "The Spaniards built settlements around their mission system. There are several large missions here like those in their other colonies."

Isobel wasn't sure what held her focus more. Was it the architecture humming with centuries of history, or the way this world drew her in, one piece at a time, like it was claiming her for itself?

Sam asked, "We rode by a complex I thought looked like ruins. How long ago did the Spanish come here?"

Isobel's attention drifted to Veramendi as he answered. "They came to this area in the late 1600's. They set up missions that did well for a time, but some of them deteriorated. The remains you traveled past this evening are from one such mission. The priest who started it named it *San Antonio de Valero*. It's where San Antonio received its name."

Her thoughts lingered on the crumbled ruins they had passed. There had been something haunting about them, as though they whispered secrets to the wind. She straightened and cut through the moment. "Immigration laws require us to convert to the Catholic Church, *Señor* Veramendi. I hope there'll be churches in other parts of *Tejas*."

"There are many." Veramendi continued, "Where there are no physical buildings, the priests ride out to celebrate the mass."

Kelvin coughed, earning a sharp glance from his wife. "I hope we won't have to worship in a dilapidated site like *San Antonio de Valero*."

Isobel clenched her hands in her lap. Kelvin's condescension grated against her nerves. *That's not like him.*

Veramendi's expression did not change. "It's no longer a church. The building is over one hundred years old, and the roof has caved in. Passing troops use it as a shelter from time to time."

Ursula faced Kelvin. "They call it the Alamo."

Isobel glanced toward Ursula, catching the faintest glimmer of pride in her words. *The Alamo.* The name hung heavy with a significance she couldn't quite grasp, but it lingered all the same, settling in her thoughts like the distant toll of a bell.

As they moved into the parlor, she trailed behind, scrutinizing the luxurious room. The heavy wooden furniture gleamed in the soft light of the candles, and the delicate patterns of the tiled floor whispered stories of another time. She settled into a chair, her hands resting in her lap, though her conceptions churned with questions she hadn't yet asked aloud.

Sam's presence commanded attention. "Governor Veramendi, President Jackson sent me here to gather information on the Comanche. May I ask your opinion on the matter?"

The governor's expression shifted, taking on the distinction of someone who had lived these tales rather than hearing them. "*Don* Samuel, they are fierce and unconquered. They're the chief reason *Tejas* is not populated in large numbers. Stephen Austin justified bringing in Anglos because of the threat the Comanche pose. The Mexican government approved the settlements so whites could create a buffer zone between them and Mexico. We call *Norte Tejas* 'Comancheria.' They kill or conquer neighboring tribes as well as Mexican and American settlers. No matter the agreements you reach with Coahuila or Mexico City, the Comanche rule *Norte Tejas*."

Isobel tried to imagine a wide, boundless landscape where every step could be a life and death gamble. The colonists' fragile hold on this land was tenuous, like a thread stretched taut over a yawning chasm.

Then a memory clawed its way to the surface. Peta Nocona. The mere recollection of his dark, piercing eyes sent a shiver rattling down her spine. They had passed each other in peace, the space between them heavy with unspoken tension. Her hand brushed her arm, as if the memory had left a physical mark. Something lingered. She didn't know what it was, but there was a possibility, a fiber left dangling in the stillness of the future.

She forced herself to refocus, tuning in to Veramendi's steady rhythm, but the truth persisted in the back of her mind, unspoken and undeniable. This land was far from tamed, and the people who ruled its wilderness were as unbroken and fierce as the storms that swept across its open skies.

Kelvin leaned back in his chair, crossing his arms in a casual way. "Will they negotiate as the eastern tribes of America do?"

Veramendi's words were measured and deliberate. "They have no central leader. Each warrior is his own authority, so they cannot powwow or treat for the entire tribe. When one of them makes his mark on a piece of paper, he signs for himself, not the tribe. So, to answer your question, they do not and cannot negotiate in ways which are familiar to you."

Isobel blinked in surprise. "They have no chief?"

He turned his attention to her. "No. If a group goes out on a raid, they choose a leader for the raid. Once it's over, the position is dissolved. Their world is built on the independence and strength of the individual."

The explanation stirred something in her, a mix of admiration and unease. A people without a ruler yet bound by an unwritten code. It was as foreign to her as the sprawling land itself, and yet, it was strangely captivating. It explained Peta Nocona riding through the woods alone. She looked at Sam, who sat stroking his chin in thought, and then at Jim, who was watching his father-in-law with an intensity she couldn't quite read.

Sam leaned forward with the sharp interest she had come to expect from him. "That's a critical observation. President Jackson needs to know this. Do you ever see Comanches in San Antonio?"

Veramendi replied, "Yes, they come through during the winter months. They trade like other tribes. They're excellent horsemen, even their boys can shoot from the back of a horse."

A faint chill crept up on Isobel despite the room's steady heat. The governor's words conjured images of shadowy figures galloping through the night, arrows flying swift and true.

Ursula's remarks held a peculiar sharpness. "They are the biggest threat to any settler. The Comanche will burn a farmhouse and kill or capture anyone inside. As my father said, they're the reason Mexicans couldn't settle *Tejas*."

Veramendi emphasized the point. "*Don* Samuel, don't underestimate them. They're the best fighters in *Tejas*."

Sam showed a glint of respect in his eyes. "Thank you, Governor. Those are wise words of counsel. President Jackson and I will never forget your warning."

Maria's assertion rose, clear and bright, cutting through the room like sunlight breaking a storm. "Let's talk about happier things.

El año nuevo brings fresh possibilities. We meet new friends, grow our families, and strengthen our bonds."

The shift in atmosphere was almost jarring, but Isobel clung to it, grateful for the reprieve. Maria's words were a reminder of what they were here for. She desired hope, connection, and the possibility of peace, even in a land ruled by uncertainty.

"I'll drink to that," Bowie's hearty toast rang out, drawing chuckles from the room.

Maria and Ursula exchanged knowing glances before gracefully ushering everyone into the dining room. The rich, inviting scent of roasted meats and spiced sauces mingled with the wood burning in the fireplace. Isobel looked to the table, a magnificent oak masterpiece, its surface gleaming under the light of an ornate chandelier. Around it, servants moved with ease, their happiness genuine, their demeanor content. It was a stark contrast to the plantations of the South, where such labor often carried the heavy shadow of chains.

"Sam, you've got to try this beverage the governor serves his guests," Bowie said.

"I'm always up for a new drinkin' experience." Isobel believed Sam carried an easy confidence that could charm or command as the moment required.

One of the servers stepped forward, presenting a small shot glass filled with a light-colored bronze liquid. Sam accepted it, holding it to the light before bringing it to his nose. Isobel caught the faintest whiff of something rich and earthy, the aroma unfamiliar yet intriguing.

Sam took a sip. He swirled the glass thoughtfully. "This is good. It doesn't taste like Kentucky bourbon or Tennessee whiskey. It's something different."

Isobel's lips twitched. "What do you think it is?"

Sam glanced at her with an amused expression. "Something worth another sip."

Bowie's guffaw boomed. "They call it *tequila*, Sam."

The conversation flowed with ease, the room buzzing with energy. Isobel allowed herself a moment of calm, soaking in the soft hush of the evening. Whatever lay beyond these walls faded into the background, its edges blurred by the comforting camaraderie around her.

Servants entered, carrying steaming bowls of vibrant red stew. A waitress placed one in front of her. The aroma was intoxicating and savory, with a hint of spice. Maria said, "This is *pozole rojo*. It's made with pork and hominy corn."

Isobel dipped her spoon into the broth, steam brushing her cheeks as she sampled it. The flavor exploded on her tongue, bold and hearty, followed by a creeping heat. Her eyes widened as she grabbed for her water. "It's delicious, but it has quite a kick. What makes it so hot, *Señora* Veramendi?"

Maria's eyes sparkled. "Chili peppers. They're essential in most Mexican dishes. *Pazole* is traditional for *Nochebuena* or Christmas Eve, but *Santiago* was away in San Felipe, so we're celebrating now."

Isobel took smaller bites as she adjusted to the spice. "It's unlike anything I had before."

The next course arrived: roasted turkey draped in a dark, glossy sauce. Maria introduced it with pride. "This is *mole poblano*."

She took a cautious bite. It was complex, blending earthy richness with a subtle sweetness. She paused, intrigued. "It's spicy, but there's something sweet I can't figure."

"Chocolate," Ursula said. "*Mole* includes cocoa."

"Chocolate in a sauce?" Isobel blinked, surprised. "Mexico's food is full of contradictions. I love sweet and heat in the same dish."

Kelvin chuckled. "Contradictions leave a lastin' mark. Just 'cause somethin' don't add up right away don't mean it ain't a trail worth followin'."

Bowie replied, "You'll fall in love with Mexico, Kelvin, the way I have."

Isobel glanced at him, seeing the fondness in his expression. He wasn't speaking about the food or culture alone. This place had become a part of him, woven into his being. It claimed something deep and quiet, something that didn't let go.

The servants moved through the room serving foreign food and drink with a practiced elegance. Isobel couldn't miss it. This home was civilized and tame, but the land outside stretched unconquered and wild under a vast sky. It wasn't Tennessee. It never would be. Maybe that was the point. Maybe home wasn't where you came from. Maybe it was where God was leading you, even if the road scraped your feet raw.

Could she love this land the way Bowie did? Could it reach inside her and stitch itself to her heart? She didn't know yet, but something in her stirred—a restless hope, the faint rustle of belonging not yet claimed. She wondered if it could be the same for her.

As the guests finished their main course, the clinking of cutlery faded, replaced by the soft murmuring of conversation. Isobel leaned back as the waitresses entered once more, carrying small plates. They placed an unfamiliar dessert before each guest. It was a round item resembling two pieces of flatbread with a dark, scorched pattern and a layer of something sandwiched between them. Isobel tilted her head, studying it with equal parts curiosity and confusion. Around the table, Kelvin and Sam exchanged puzzled looks with her.

Maria noticed the hesitation, gesturing toward the plates. "These are *quesadillas*. Tonight, our chef, Lorenzo, prepared them as dessert. Each *quesadilla* has a top and bottom flour *tortilla*. The filling is *queso asadero* and *el zapallo*." Maria paused, glancing at Ursula with a light chuckle. "Ursula, please translate. I can't think of the English words for those ingredients."

Before Ursula could respond, Sam spoke up, already halfway through his first bite. "I think I can help. Cheese and pumpkin."

Ursula's eyes twinkled as she turned to him. *"Es correcto, Comandante. ¡Muy bueno!"*

Isobel picked up her fork, cutting a small piece of the *quesadilla*. The first bite was sweet and comforting, the melted cheese blending unexpectedly well with the flavor of the pumpkin. She raised her brows in surprise, glancing toward Ursula. "What does *quesadilla* mean in English, Ursula?"

Ursula paused, her brow furrowing in thought before she shrugged mischievously. "Little cheesy things?"

The words lingered for only a beat before the entire room erupted.

Even the waitresses joined in, their soft giggles weaving through the guests' hearty guffaws. Isobel couldn't help but laugh too, the sound bubbling out of her as easily as the room's gentle ease seeped into her.

As the room settled, she glanced around the table, taking in the easy camaraderie between friends, the blending of cultures, and the shared joy over something as simple as dessert. She caught Kelvin's eye, and his small, contented smile mirrored her own.

If this was what living in Mexico would be like, Isobel thought, her heart swelling with a mix of hope and excitement, then she and Kelvin had indeed embarked on the happiest of all journeys.

CHAPTER THIRTY-NINE

March 29, 1833

The Peyton Tavern

San Felipe de Austin, *Coahuila y Tejas*

T he evening carried the tang of horses and dust as Isobel
stepped into the lamplight of the inn. Her pulse still
thrummed with the rhythm of their ride from East Texas.
She tugged at her coat, as much to steady herself as to shake off the
chill.

Angelina greeted them. "Evenin'. Y'all in town for the
convention?"

Before she could answer, Kelvin replied, "Yes, ma'am. We rode in
from Nacogdoches. Can we trouble ya for our usual rooms?"

Angelina replied, "I figured you'd be here and saved 'em for you.
Place is gonna fill up fast, though. People are comin' in from all over."

The creak of Isobel's boots brought her a small comfort as she
followed Kelvin inside. "Thanks for rememberin' us. Heard any news
from outside San Felipe?"

The innkeeper poked at the hearth, her expression tightening.

"Bustamante's out. Santa Anna's the president now. I'm thinkin' it'll make the convention easier to manage."

Relief rippled through Isobel. "We got ourselves a *federalista* at last. Maybe now we'll get closer to becomin' our own state."

Angelina nudged a log in the fireplace. "Wharton and the *War Party* ain't gonna sit still for Austin's *Peace Party*." She straightened, her expression keen and unflinching. "Where's your general? Ain't he with you?"

The question landed more like an accusation than curiosity. Kelvin stepped in. "He's tryin' to get more Tejanos involved. He's upset last year's convention excluded so many of 'em."

She sighed. "I hope he can convince 'em, but I doubt it. Miguel and some others told me they don't want trouble. These meetin's are illegal, and they don't wanna risk jail. Most of 'em can't understand English anyway."

Isobel's frustration simmered. "I hate to hear it. Every Texan deserves representation, no matter where they come from."

Angelina shook her head. "They don't see it that way. They're Catholics, and they don't mind the Church bein' the state religion. They're stickin' to their own interests, like land grants. I reckon they think it's safer to stay out of this fight."

The truth of it hit Isobel hard. *Of course, they wouldn't risk their lives and livelihoods for something they don't feel is theirs to claim.*

Kelvin folded his arms as if he could push the situation into neat order. "They ain't gonna make any headway if they don't represent themselves."

Angelina held him in a steady look. "You and I know it, but I'm afraid it'll be a tough lesson for 'em to learn."

Isobel's lips pressed into a thin line. "Somethin' tells me this'll be a long-term problem."

A familiar voice cut through the room. "It's a forever problem."

Her head snapped up. "Jim. We were hopin' to see you."

There he stood, covered in road dust and a relaxed look on his face. "General Sam asked me to recruit Tejanos from *Béxar*. No luck. Some might show at the final stretch."

She wanted to believe him. "Maybe so. How's Ursula?"

Bowie answered, "She's doin' well. Told me to say 'hello.' Her folks send their best."

Isobel replied softly, "I got a letter from her. She worries about your travels."

A faint shadow of guilt crossed his face. "I know she does, but I can't accomplish my tasks through the mail."

Kelvin cut in. "Isobel keeps up through letters. She writes her friends, Harriet and Josef. I expect our Cincinnati contacts will pay off one day."

Bowie let out a chuckle. "*Buena suerte, amigo*. Hope you do well."

Before the conversation could settle, Angelina brought up another subject. "Jim, I heard you and the pirate, Jean Lafitte, were partners. Is it true?"

Bowie erupted like a cannon blast. "The scoundrel's been dead over ten years, and I'm still hearin' about him."

Isobel crossed her arms, her brow arched as her lips tugged curving into a teasing curve. "Well. Mr. Bowie, we're waitin' for the rest of the story."

He sighed, shaking his head as though trying to shake loose the memories. "Yes, he was a pirate I knew from New Orleans. Me and him imported goods to Louisiana and Arkansas. He was clever, but he and his band of men lived for one object: profit."

Isobel's question came in quietness but cut through the room. "Did you import slaves?"

His expression darkened. "We did. He tried to go around U.S. law and bring in African born slaves by goin' into his port at Galveston."

Isobel didn't flinch. *The truth is a heavy thing, but better to face it head-on.*

"Did it work?" Kelvin asked, his words stripped of emotion.

Bowie's jaw tightened. "It did until the U.S. Navy ran him off. Importin' slaves from Africa is against the law most everywhere now. General Sam plans to bring such a resolution to the convention."

Isobel's mind raced ahead. "What about Galveston? It's got me thinkin'. Is it still a viable port?"

Bowie's eyes lit up. "Some say it'll be the New York City of the South."

Kelvin chuckled. "We went to New York with the general. It's somethin' to see."

He leaned in, a glint of conspiracy in his eye. "I'll connect y'all to my friend, Juan Seguin. He's got interests on the coast and can claim land as a Tejano."

The glimmer of excitement in Jim caught Isobel's attention. She didn't know if Galveston would be a gateway to the world or a powder keg waiting to ignite. But there was one thing she knew, Texas didn't wait for anyone to make up their mind. "Yes, please. We want to meet him, Jim."

The fire crackled, but Isobel's attention was fixed on Bowie.

He leaned back. "Sure. When it comes down to it, Juan'll fight. This is where Sam might underestimate the Tejanos. More of 'em will fight than attend conventions."

The tavern door groaned as it swung open, letting in an unseasonably cold gust that sent a shiver through Isobel. She turned, her look settling on the man stepping inside. He moved with a quiet purpose toward Angelina, his small stature offset by an undeniable presence. His delicate features, framed by thick brown hair and piercing brown eyes, held the room's attention without effort. There was a disciplined precision in his lean frame, and a quiet dignity that spoke louder than any introduction.

Isobel murmured just above a whisper. "Who is that gentleman?"

Bowie looked at her, a knowing expression spreading across his face. "That's your greatest benefactor, Isobel. Come with me, and I'll introduce you."

Her heart quickened as she followed, nerves and curiosity tangling in her mind.

Bowie stepped up to the man. "Evenin', Colonel. I'd like to introduce you to some friends of mine."

The man dipped his head with quiet approval, his eyes locking onto Isobel's. He extended his hand toward her, the movement delicate, like he was offering a fragile red rose to her. Isobel hesitated, caught by the contrast between his gentle demeanor and the tomahawk tucked securely into his belt. The weapon seemed so at odds with the measured grace of his actions that she found it hard to imagine him wielding it in violence.

She spoke softly, the words barely above a whisper as she stepped forward. "Sir, I'm Isobel MacDonald, and this is my husband, Kelvin." She kept her manner easy, careful not to flood him with too much enthusiasm. Something about him seemed sensitive, not weak, but intentionally restrained, like a river held back by a dam.

He met her look with steady eyes then shifted his focus to Kelvin. He took Kelvin's hand and offered a firm shake, his grip one of confidence but not dominance. He flicked his eyes between the two of them, an unreadable expression settling over his face, as if he were weighing them, testing their mettle against some unseen standard.

"Stephen Austin. Pleasure to meet you both. I've seen your names cross my desk at the land office. You come highly recommended. Now that I see you in person, I'm even more impressed."

Kelvin's eyes widened at the unexpected praise. "The pleasure's all ours, Colonel Austin. I'm glad my wife and I finally managed to connect with you after many attempts."

Austin inclined his head slightly. "I hope to see more of you during the convention, Mr. MacDonald. You're here with General Houston, if I have my facts straight."

Kelvin stood shoulder to shoulder with Isobel. "Your information's correct, sir. We came with General Houston from Washington City. President Jackson wants more information 'bout the Indians in the Indian Territory and in Texas."

Isobel observed Austin closely, noting the interest in his expression. *He's measuring every word, weighing its significance.*

"I'm sure he wants insight about any subject in Texas." There was a hint of dry humor threading through Austin's remarks. "We're making progress toward self-governance. I don't know what it'll look like, but I do know it takes patience and wisdom to follow the trail."

His words settled over her like a challenge, stirring a mixture of hope and curiosity. She tilted her head, asking, "Colonel, do you think we'll ever be independent?"

He paused, his expression guarded but thoughtful. "Well, I don't know. Right now, we're hopin' to become one state under Mexico's sovereignty. The Mexican government's goin' through some changes. They can be frustratin' to many, but I reckon I understand 'em better than most."

She caught the faint hint of weariness in his eyes, the kind coming from years of navigating fragile alliances and competing priorities. "You can't rush 'em into makin' decisions. Anglos tend to make that mistake too often. If we do end up bein' independent, it'll be 'cause we acted in good faith and with plenty of perseverance."

His words hung in the quiet. Something stirred—admiration for his steady hand. But doubt slipped in, cold and unwelcome. She checked Kelvin, catching signs of agreement, then turned back to Austin. "I reckon forbearance is somethin' we'll all need to learn."

Austin's contemplation met hers, and for a moment, she thought she saw a flash of approval. "It's gonna take all of us workin' together." The truth of his message hung between them like a fragile promise.

Angelina hooked her arm through his and guided him toward a table where eager delegates awaited him. Isobel studied the exchange, noting the ease with which he commanded attention without demanding it. His quiet charisma lingered, and she couldn't help but feel drawn to the paradox he embodied. He was a man of refinement and intellect, and here he was, shaping the future in this rugged, untamed wilderness.

He doesn't belong here, she thought, *and yet, no one belongs here more.*

Gathering herself, she hurried along as he was walking away. "It was a pleasure meetin' you, Colonel. We look forward to seein' you again."

He paused and gave her an easy look. "Likewise, Mrs. MacDonald. I'm sure our paths will cross many more times."

As he moved away with Angelina, a curious mix of admiration and apprehension settled over her. *Crossing paths? A man like him didn't just cross paths, he shaped them, altering the course of everyone who walked beside him.*

Kelvin turned to Bowie, careful at first, but with an edge of thoughtful observation. "He's not like others we've met. Men like Houston, Travis, and yourself are bound to clash with him. I'm not sure if it's your vision for Texas that's different or if the issue's your approach to achievin' it."

Bowie gave a little grin. "He's a sharp one, ain't he?"

Isobel folded her arms. "Yeah, he's a philosopher on a little higher plane than the rest of us. But he's also a cartographer and surveyor. A practical academic sort. I think he sees the whole map before anyone else knows there's a trail to follow."

Kelvin furrowed his brow as he continued. "Most men would've run outta patience dealin' with the Mexicans by now. His perseverance is enormous. He's not a big man with an imposing figure like you or the general, but he still commands awe and respect."

Bowie rubbed his chin, his expression darkening a bit. "We'll see how the convention plays out. Santa Anna takin' charge is a good sign for us. Austin's the one to talk to him in Mexico City. Everybody agrees on it."

Isobel tried to imagine a chess board with all the pieces moving about. Santa Anna, Austin, Houston, Travis, Bowie. They were all pieces on the board. She was on the board too. What would her God have her do? She didn't know. She prayed for clarity every night, but none came. *Patience. Patience is the key.*

Then Angelina gave a shout. "I got a skillet of hot fresh cornbread. Who wants some?"

All hands shot up.

The mirth of the moment settled over Isobel. She thanked God for small mercies that reminded her who the Chessmaster was.

CHAPTER FORTY

April 13, 1833
San Felipe de Austin, *Coahuila y Tejas*
Closing Day of the Convention of 1833

The atmosphere was heavy enough to choke on. Sweat, tobacco, and the sharp tang of something Angelina had simmering on her stove clung to every pant Isobel managed. She shifted on the hard seat, the wood creaking between her. Her dress stuck to her legs, the fabric bunched up no matter how she adjusted it. She wasn't a delegate, not even close, and the exclusion burned her more than any heat from the kitchen. She sat stiff-backed in the corner, her hands gripping the end of the bench as if she might bolt from it at any moment. Every fiber of her being hummed, while men, *only* men, decided the fate of Texas as she waited in another building, tension coiling tight as a rattlesnake ready to strike.

Thirteen days. Isobel ran her fingers along the smooth grain of the bench's arm, her nails catching on an uneven edge. Thirteen blistering, nerve-shredding days of waiting as the men behind closed doors argued themselves hoarse. Words flew fast, or so she heard, wild and sharp, like sparrows battered by a storm.

She had Bowie, her man on the inside. His drawl rumbled low and heavy. "Today's the last day. I hope somethin' good comes outta this meetin'. Last year was nothin' but a waste of time."

Isobel bristled, her pulse kicking against her ribs. "They better not leave us hangin' again." Her words were hushed but pointed. "Colonel Austin has to get our resolutions to the government."

Across the table, Kelvin chipped in. "More and more folks are rollin' into *Tejas* dreamin' 'bout revolution."

Isobel's lips pressed tight. "They don't get all he's done to raise up the colony. It's hard to understand patient men."

She wanted to add more, but Bowie cut her off. "Patience don't build nations. There's a time to act. I gotta go." He walked away.

The convention dragged on for most of the day.

"I'll be glad when Jim gets back," Isobel said. "It's been hours."

Kelvin called above the din, "Over here, Jim."

Isobel turned in time to see him stride in.

He slid into the chair across from her. Kelvin shoved a mug his way, and he took it. He dug into his pockets, pulling out a wad of crumpled papers like a man wrangling stray cattle. Isobel narrowed her eyes and crossed her arms over her chest.

He squinted at his own handwriting. "Chicken scratch."

She drummed the table with her fingers. "What'd you learn, Jim?"

He shot her a crooked glance. "If I can make sense of my own writin', I'll tell y'all everythin'."

"I'll wait." She held her arms tighter, a small act of restraint to keep from snatching the notes out of his hands.

He found what looked like a starting point. "First off, the main proposition is to be a separate state. It's the backbone of everything else."

Kelvin let out a low whistle. "We figured as much. A lone star, not two."

"Right. Second, the Mexican Congress must repeal the ban on American immigration and bring back the empresario system."

She clinched her jaw at the mention of the congress.

Bowie took on an edge of frustration. "No more special grants favorin' the Tejanos gettin' the best coastal land."

Isobel's heart twisted at his words. She didn't begrudge the Tejanos their due, but the playing field wasn't level.

He went on. "Third, they gotta revoke the custom taxes so we can put the money back in the colony."

Kelvin muttered his approval, but Isobel's scrutiny stayed on Bowie.

Bowie's face darkened. "Fourth, we requested more troops to protect us from Comanche raids. It's a shame how many settlers we've lost 'cause the army's stretched too thin."

Isobel remembered the nights she'd lain awake, listening for the slightest sound of danger.

Bowie continued. "Fifth, we need a mail system. Can't build a state if folks don't know what's happenin'."

She agreed. It was true enough. Half the colony ran on rumors and guesswork.

He looked up from the paper and met her stare before looking back down. "Last, number six, free public education for all children."

Kelvin gave his approval. "Looks like they've been busy."

Isobel's mind was spinning, wrapping itself around the possibilities Bowie's words had laid bare. A future that could be built, not just endured. But there was something missing. She tried to stay unruffled and hide her disappointment. "Was there anything else?"

He leaned back. "A committee drafted a constitution. Had a lot in it."

She cocked her head to the side. "Like what?"

Bowie replied, "Why don't you ask the man who wrote it?"

She blinked, thrown off balance. "Where do I find him?"

"Look behind you," Bowie said.

She stiffened, heat rising in her cheeks as she whipped around. She saw Sam there. Her mouth opened to speak, but the words stuck for an instant. "I'm sorry, General, I didn't see you. Please tell me what's in your draft."

Sam reached into his bookbag. "I got the original copy here." He tapped the pages for emphasis. "It covers the freedoms we all cherish under the United States Constitution. Things like free speech, free press, and the freedom to assemble. All stuff we don't have now."

Her fingers tightened. "And you think we can make them listen?"

Sam didn't answer right away. "We're not askin'. We're tellin'."

The room fell away. "I'm mindful of our past agreement, but can I ask if there's anythin' in today's resolutions bannin' slavery?"

He reached into his satchel. "Once again, I got the initial instrument. I know how you feel, so I held onto it for you."

Her heart skipped at the admission, but she said nothing. Instead, she took the paper and placed it on the table, positioning it under the lamplight.

She read it verbatim. *We do hold in utter abhorrence all participation, whether direct or indirect, in the African Slave Trade: that we do concur in the general indignation which has been manifested throughout the civilized world against that inhuman and unprincipled traffic; and we do therefore earnestly recommend to our constituents, the good people of Texas, that they will not only abstain from all concern in that abominable traffic, but that they will unite their efforts to prevent the evil from polluting our shores.*

Isobel straightened, her hand hovering on the edge of the document as its force pressed down on her, heavy and unrelenting, like an approaching storm. The firelight danced across the lines of text, but her mind was elsewhere, turning over every phrase and nuance.

"This..." She looked up at Sam, her reflections sharp, searching. "This is a start."

He put a reassuring hand on her shoulder. "A start, yes, but it's more than words on a page. It'll take people like you to make sure it doesn't sit here doin' nothin'."

Her fingers tightened on the edges of the draft. She knew he was right. Words could inspire, but action was what changed the world. "And you'll stand with me?"

He didn't flinch. "I already have."

Isobel handed the composition to Kelvin, gesturing for him to read it. She turned to Sam, her general, and embraced him, tears streaming down her cheeks.

"I told ya I wouldn't bawl," she whispered against his shoulder, tears slipping free. "But ya keep givin' me reasons to love Texas." She pulled back enough to meet his eyes, her eyes shimmering with gratitude and conviction. "Thank you. I hope this here finds its way into our laws. I know it doesn't do anythin' for slaves born here, but it's a start. To me, the words in the draft describe all slavery, not just African-born. The resolution makes Texas something I can fight for with my whole heart."

Kelvin spoke up, quieter than usual. "Thank you, General. This here means a lot to us."

He gestured at the papers. "We called for immediate enactments of everything." His cadence was deliberate. "But the majority voted to take the list to the Mexican Congress for approval."

Isobel frowned. "It'll take time we don't have."

Sam said, "Colonel Austin's takin' the documents to the capital in person."

The hope in her depths reignited. "So, somethin's gonna happen."

He placed his hand on her shoulder. "Yes, ma'am. But it won't happen overnight. It'll take grit, fight, and people willin' to see it through."

Isobel's eyes widened. "Anybody goin' with him?"

He placed his bag on the table. "We voted to send Dr. James Miller and Erasmo Seguin with him. It's a mighty long and risky journey."

The truth of Sam's statement settled on Isobel like a heavy stone. "When's he leavin'?"

He glanced toward the window. "Any minute now. He and Dr. Miller should be hittin' the trail any time."

Her heart leapt into her throat. "Any time?" The words were as sharp as Bowie's blade. "'Scuse me, General." She dashed for the door.

The door slammed shut behind her with a bang. Her eyes swept across the street until they landed on a familiar figure, busy tying supplies to a mule. The sight of him, mild and methodical as always, steadied her nerves. Squaring her shoulders, she strode with a purpose. "'Evenin', Colonel."

Stephen F. Austin turned, his face calm and composed despite the urgency of his preparations. "Good evening, Mrs. MacDonald."

She stood in front of him. "General Houston told me y'all are fixin' to head off to Mexico City. I come to bid ya farewell and safe travels."

His lips curved into a faint smile, though his eyes betrayed the responsibility he carried. "You're mighty thoughtful. Obliged. I don't look forward to the journey, but the colony always comes first."

Isobel said, "At least you'll have a physician with ya. Dr. Miller can tend to any health concerns along the way."

His expression changed. Something she couldn't read passed across his face. "Dr. Miller can't come with me. There's cholera outbreaks all 'round, and he figures he's needed more here."

The news hit her like a blow. "Cholera. Good Lord, such a terrible affliction."

He bowed, his thoughts distant as if recalling faces lost to the disease. "Yes, I've seen many good people taken by it."

She fidgeted with the fringes of her coat, a nervous habit she couldn't break. "Our folks always warned us 'bout watchin' our drinkin' water. They believed diseases like the bloody flux and cholera came from fouled wells. Doctors nowadays call it old wives' tales and superstition. Still, be mindful 'bout what ya drink."

Austin said, "I reckon it's good advice for anyone. Thanks for the warnin'."

He approached the mule, Isobel's brow furrowing when he began to mount it. "Colonel, you mean to say yer ridin' a mule?"

He glanced down at her from his seat atop the animal, his expression amused but unbothered. "Sure am. Me and my friend here been all over the colony. I ain't in no rush. Slow and steady suits me fine."

She let out a soft sigh, the tension in her shoulders easing for a moment. "I reckon you're right. Didn't our Lord ride into Jerusalem on such a creature?"

He let out a chuckle. "I've never pondered it that way, but it's true."

Something in his sincerity touched her deeply, and she stepped closer, reaching out her hand. "Take care, sir. I'll be prayin' for ya every night of your journey."

He took her hand, his grip firm. "Thank you for your prayers. I'll need 'em."

She swallowed hard, her heart heavy with unspoken words. Finally, she opened her mouth. "Colonel, will you say a prayer for me, too? Sometimes I don't know what God wants me to do. I hope you don't think me selfish, but somethin's happenin' here and I can't tell what my part is."

He tilted his head before looking into her eyes. "Texas is lucky to have you. We all have our parts to play. None are more important than any other. I've learned waiting, hoping, and praying will keep you grounded."

She put her face in her hands. "But it's all so overwhelmin' for me. Whatever it is, I don't got enough to keep goin'."

"His grace is sufficient. Whatever it is, you got enough."

She shook her head. "I ain't a knife fighter or saber rattler. I get discouraged and I'm weak."

He replied, "His power is made perfect in weakness. Take pleasure in your infirmities."

An apostle said all that. I remember Mama readin' it.

She kicked at the ground. "Findin' my way and my part is hard."

"I'll pray you find His will. It's all any of us can do." Then he froze, his brow furrowing as he searched her face, an unspoken question flickering in his eyes. His lips parted, a breath caught on the verge of forming words, but he let it hang in the silence, unspoken. Instead, his gaze held hers, unwavering, like he was trying to anchor her to something unseen. At last, his voice came low and certain, cutting into her heart. "It's alright if you're the only one who hears Him."

Isobel gasped. He'd knocked the wind out of her. An ache pulsed deep in the marrow of her soul. "I think I hear him… in a fiddle tune I keep hearin'." She trembled. "But I'm all torn up. It keeps pullin' me away from what I *want* to do and sends me down another path. Am I insane?"

"Were the apostles insane?" he asked.

She shook her head. "No. But they were special."

He leaned closer. "They didn't think so. They had doubts. They had fears. Just like you."

Tears spilled, silent and relentless, blurring everything in front of her. "But I don't know what to do."

"Yes, you do," he said. "Listen. Remember what the Master said—'My sheep hear my voice, and I know them, and they follow me.'"

Isobel closed her eyes. The fiddle's melody lingered. It was not loud, not forceful, but steady, like a thread pulling her forward. She didn't have all the answers, but she knew now where to place her feet. One step. Then another. Not toward certainty, but toward obedience.

She caught herself and managed a polite, "Thank you, Colonel." She stared into the dirt as hooves echoed in her ears. A storm of emotions churned inside her as the mule and its rider grew smaller in the fading light. She stood there a few moments longer, her hands folded together, clutching hope like a lifeline. "Goodbye," she whispered to the empty air.

Unease settled over her as she went back to the tavern. The image of Austin, small and weary, perched on a mule and setting off on a perilous journey of more than twelve hundred miles, stuck in her mind like a thorn. He carried more than supplies and papers. He bore the fragile dreams of Texas, and it gnawed at her. She got back to the table and eased into her seat beside Kelvin, Bowie, and Sam, her thoughts heavy.

Kelvin turned to her with genuine curiosity. "Did ya say goodbye to him, Belle?"

She folded her hands in her lap. "Yes, but he looks so frail sittin' on a mule, aimin' to ride over a thousand miles. I'm mighty worried about him." The words came out faster than she intended.

Bowie leaned forward. "Havin' Dr. Miller with him should be a comfort."

Her throat tightened. "Dr. Miller ain't goin'. He said there's cholera outbreaks here and he can't up and leave the colony now."

Sam shook his head. "Such distressin' news. Cholera's a dreadful thing. He's a brave soul. Some folks might reckon him unfit for such a perilous task, but he's got courage and competence in spades."

"I agree, Sam." Bowie's admiration was clear. "There're different kinds of bravery, and he's showin' us one kind. It takes guts to carry them documents, what some might call seditious, on a dangerous trek all by himself."

Isobel glanced at him, grateful for the acknowledgment of Austin's resolve but still uneasy. *It's alright if I'm the only one who hears Him?*

"He might convince Erasmo to go with him from *Béxar*." There was hope in the way Sam spoke.

Bowie shook his head. "Naw. Erasmo ain't goin'. He reckons it'll make him look bad 'mongst the other Tejanos. Austin might get him to sign them papers, but when it comes to sloggin' all the way to Mexico City, he's on his own."

The thought sent a chill through Isobel, and she couldn't stop her tremor. "All the more reason to pray for him every day. I'm downright fearful 'bout his long and hazardous route."

Sam softened as he looked at her. "True enough. We're expectin' him to keep us posted by mail. I'm hopin' to hear news from the trail."

She gripped the lip of the table. "I sure hope so, General. I can't help but feel like the future of Texas is ridin' on the back of a mule and headin' into an unknown province."

Sam looked distant, but resolute when he spoke. "Sometimes the mightiest dreams hang on the frailest reeds."

The weight of his words settled over the table, and a small release passed through her as the knot in her belly loosened. Dreams had always seemed fragile to her, and yet, here they were, daring to hope, even in the face of the impossible. *And God willing, this reed will hold.*

CHAPTER FORTY-ONE

October 14, 1833
The Sterne Residence
Nacogdoches, *Coahuila y Tejas*

Eva held the envelope aloft, her fingers brushing over the bold pigment of the postal service's seal as if it was more than simple paper and ink. "Got somethin' here from the postmaster." Her eyes widened with a hint of mystery. "It's for the MacDonalds."

Before the last syllable left her lips, Isobel shot up from her chair, almost knocking it over. Her eyes sparkled with a mix of hope and anxiety as she leaned forward, hands twitching as if ready to snatch the letter from Eva's grasp. *Finally. Please let it tell us where our trunks are.* "I've been lost without most of my things."

Kelvin shifted as he tugged at his collar. "I'm startin' to regret shippin' those chests all the way from Tennessee, but what else could we have done?"

Isobel ignored him, her fingers closing around the envelope Eva offered. The coarse edge of the paper scraped against her skin, and something inside her dropped as her eyes landed on the postmark.

New Salem, Illinois. Her brow furrowed, the words blurring for a moment before sinking in. A cold thread of unease wove through her thoughts. "Why would the postmaster of New Salem know anything about our crates?"

Sam cut through her contemplations, low and teasing, but edged with his own impatience. "Well, don't just stand there gawkin', Isobel. Open it up. I'm dyin' to know what it says."

She braced herself and broke the seal with trembling fingers. The paper crackled under her touch while the others stood by, their faces drawn tight with worry. No one said a word, the room's silence swelling as she unfolded the missive.

She skimmed the note, her lips moving with the words as she browsed. The scratchy ink carried the postmaster's message straight to her ears, dry humor dripping from every line. She read it aloud.

"Dear Mr. and Mrs. MacDonald. You have some attractive trunks. They appear serviceable by any measure. I'm quite sure the contents are intact and look forward to coming into your possession. The shipping and receiving arms of our postal service may not be as fast as you were expecting. It's like the old horse that's so slow, he can't get the family to his master's funeral on time. Yes, sir and madam, your shipments are on the way to Texas. I believe they will find their way to you, but I can't say how they ended up here in New Salem. Maybe I was lucky. I hope they won't be like the nascent nag and discover you have no more need of them when they make their long-awaited appearance."

Kelvin's chuckle broke the silence. "The postmaster's got a knack for words, don't he?"

Sam agreed, "Ain't it the truth. I bet he keeps the whole town in line with nothin' but stories and a good dose of patience. You can tell he's the type to settle a squabble with a tale rather than a fist."

Isobel's eyes sparkled. "He sounds like my kind of man."

Kelvin leaned forward, his curiosity sharpening the lines around his eyes. "Did he sign it?"

Isobel unfolded the paper and glanced at the bottom. She caught the signature written in a confident flourish. "Abraham Lincoln." She let the name float in the room before a giggle bubbled up. Folding the letter, she tapped it against her palm. "This one's goin' in my Bible, right next to the Psalms. Somethin' to remind me there's still a little wit left in the world when it feels too crushin' to move on."

SAM LEANED CLOSER to the dim candlelight, his brow furrowed in that way it always did when something refused to yield. The flicker lit the edges of the law books scattered across the table, titles Isobel couldn't pronounce and pages that smelled like dust and beeswax. He turned one over, slow and deliberate, like he meant to wring truth from it. Every few lines, the same name surfaced time and again: the Galveston Bay and Texas Land Company, a client too powerful to ignore.

But she'd seen it, how his jaw tightened after every hearing. The Spanish tangled on his tongue, and the courtroom went thick with things he couldn't quite say. Ambition was never his problem. The language was.

Isobel remembered the day he admitted it. Not in words, but in the way he closed the book and looked up at her and Kelvin like a man willing to be humbled. That's when they found Anna Raguet. Seventeen, clever as a whip, with a manner like cool water and a poise that didn't match her age. Her father's name opened doors, but it was Anna who held the key once they stepped inside.

As they stumbled through verbs and vocabulary, Anna's patient corrections and encouraging lessons became a beacon of hope in their quest for fluency. "No, Isobel, it's *aprender*, not *aprendar*. You're close, though."

Isobel brushed a stray curl from her face. "*Gracias*, Anna. We're learnin' more and more every day. You're a fine teacher."

Anna flashed a glint of pride in her eyes. "Thank you, Isobel. Some folks figure it won't be needed much once Texas gets its independence."

Isobel looked up from her notes. "I don't reckon there'll be a time when it becomes a useless skill. Businesspeople will need it to strike deals and understand each other. Languages don't die because borders shift."

Anna's eyes softened at her words, and Sam paused, his pen hovering over the paper. "Yes, Anna, anyone practicin' law or runnin' a big establishment will be in a fix if they don't know the language. I'll bet it'll still hold true a hundred years from now."

Anna said, "Y'all are so kind. Folks come by Daddy's house every day askin' for my help. I manage to make a little money while providin' a service."

Isobel tilted her head. "Are there many ladies requestin' your guidance? I can see readin' the Mexican almanacs and garden books needs more than English."

She shook her head with a puzzled expression. "No. Now that you mention it, it's men, not women, who seek my translations."

Isobel blinked, the realization hitting her like a bucket of cold water. *A beautiful girl with a skill.* She closed her eyes for a moment, willing away the sting of annoyance. When she reopened them, her look cut sharp and icy between her husband and Sam. *"Really?"* Her question was as brittle as frost.

Kelvin froze, his grin slipping as he exchanged a glance with Sam. The sheepish twist of their lips and the faint pink creeping up their necks told her all she needed to know. The door creaked open, and a servant stepped inside, shattering the silence like a dropped glass. "There's a rider with urgent news for General Houston."

Sam straightened. "Please show him in."

The man who entered wore the dust of long miles, his hat clutched in calloused hands. Shadows darkened his face, worry etched deep in every line. *"Me llamo* Jose Mendoza." His words were thick and heavy with the heartache of his message. "There's an outbreak of cholera in *Béxar* and Monclova. Ursula Bowie died. I'm trying to reach *Santiago,* but I don't know where he is."

The words hit Isobel like a gut punch, leaving her hollow and stunned. "Oh, no." The image of young Ursula's face flashed in her mind. "Oh, no."

Sam turned to the window, gripping the sill as though the solid wood could anchor him. His inquiry rattled through the room. "Do you know how her parents are, sir?"

Mendoza's head dipped, his grief plain. "Both died, I'm sorry to report."

Sam crumpled into a nearby chair and buried his face in his hands, the trauma of the statement pressing down on him. "This is a brutal dispatch. The family was honorable and invaluable to Texas. Their loss... beyond words."

Isobel's throat tightened. Cholera, the relentless foe, had taken more lives. She counted Ursula among her most cherished friends. A tear slipping down her cheek, she looked up. "She was only twenty-one."

Kelvin's mouth opened, but no sound came out. His eyes widened, and he stood motionless, as if the bitter remarks knocked the wind out of him.

Isobel looked at the rider, pitying the man with a dreadful duty. "Thank you for your service, *Señor* Mendoza. Breakin' this kind of news is heart-wrenchin', but necessary."

He wiped his eyes. "*Gracias, Señora.*"

She turned to Sam, trembling. "General, didn't you get a note from Jim not too long ago? Did it say where he was?"

He blinked as if pulled from a daze, a glimmer of gratitude in his eyes. "Yes, he left word he's over in Mississippi, near Natchez, I think. You oughtta find him along the river somewhere. He ain't the type to fade into the background. Folks might not know his name, but they sure remember that knife when they see it."

Mendoza tucked the information away. "Thank you, General. I'll be on my way."

Sam shook his head. "Sir, your horse is played out. Rest here and continue your mission tomorrow."

Kelvin stood up. "I'll get you squared away. Follow me."

The door clicked shut and the echo lingered in the stillness. Isobel stared at the faint scratches on the tabletop, her chest rising in shallow pulls, as if the atmosphere itself had thickened. Her hands tightened in her lap, knuckles white against the dim flicker of the lamp.

Isobel's cheeks bore the salty wetness of her grief. The memory of Mr. Lincoln's letter surfaced, his wry humor and easy wit whispering in her mind. She wondered if he had anything in his bag of stories for this. She doubted an Illinois postmaster could envision death on the scale she feared would visit Texas. She looked toward the window, the darkness outside pressing on the panes like a harbinger of what was to come. A thought coiled deep within her, sharp and unrelenting. *How many times will Texas break my heart before she claims us all?*

CHAPTER FORTY-TWO

April 18, 1835
The Sterne Residence
Paschal Vigil, Eve Before Easter Sunday
Nacogdoches, *Coahuila y Tejas*

The flames leaped and danced, hungry for the kindling piled high by the Sterne family and their neighbors in a fire pit behind the main house. Their crackling song filled the night, blending with the murmurs of gathered expressions, the scent of woodsmoke heavy. Shadows flickered across Isobel's face as she shifted closer to the fire's glow, wrapping her arms around herself, though it wasn't the chill of the night making her shiver. This was no ordinary gathering, it was a turning point, a step tying her faith and future to a foreign law and a church that wasn't truly hers.

The firelight caught Eva's face, serene and glowing, as she carried a quiet strength Isobel envied. "Thank you for bein' our godmother, Eva." The words settled into the space between them, as sacred as the vows she was about to take. "This is a night I'll never forget. I know Kelvin and Sam won't either."

Eva turned, her kind eyes meeting Isobel's, and for a moment, the gravity of the night turned lighter. "You're brave, Isobel. It's an honor to stand with you."

Kelvin stepped closer, a touch of awe in his words. "Your family has been so generous with your support. We appreciate it more than you'll ever know."

Generous. Yes, the Sternes were more than generous. Isobel knew this generosity came with a price. Immigrating here, owning a vast swath of Texas, it all hinged on tonight, on this baptism. On fulfilling a law written just for people like her. She tried to appear composed, but the baptism's representation pressed on her heart.

She glanced at the fire, the embers swirling skyward like prayers, and wondered if God could hear her doubts. She listened. Could He hear the fiddle music that wasn't playing tonight, the melody she heard deep in her heart, whispering something she didn't yet understand?

The box in Sam's hand seemed almost ordinary, but Isobel knew better. He pulled it from his leather travel bag and offered the little case to Eva on behalf of Isobel, Kelvin, and himself.

Eva's fingers hesitated on the lid for a heartbeat before lifting it. A diamond ring sparkled against the velvet lining like it had stolen a shard of sunlight. Her gasp filled the silence.

His words, gentle as the firelight, carried the familiar sentiment Isobel had come to know well. "This here's our christenin' gift to ya, to show how much we appreciate all you've done for us. Lifelong friendship's worth celebratin'."

Eva's hand trembled as she brushed her fingers over the ring. "Thank you, Sam. I'll cherish this ring forever."

They shifted then, turning to Adolfo. Isobel couldn't miss the emotion in everyone's faces. The weight of their gratitude seemed to press against Isobel's skin, tangible and heavy with unspoken words. Adolfo had been a rock in the chaos of Texas. He was steady and unyielding.

Adolfo's hand enveloped Sam's in a firm grip, his eyes gleaming with a quiet pride. "My wife will treasure her ring as a sacred gift. You honor her by making her your godmother. But as a Son of Abraham, I can't in good conscience act as your godfather. I may have converted on paper, but I'm still a Jew in spirit."

The words struck Isobel like a distant church bell. She glanced at Adolfo, her heart tugged by the quiet strength in his confession. He wasn't defiant, it was something deeper. Truth, maybe. Honor. In his way, Adolfo was as unshakable as the Texas soil beneath their feet.

Isobel straightened, the familiar pull of conviction tightening in her chest. Her reply came quiet but firm. "We understand, Adolfo. We're Protestant Christians, and our ways differ from the Catholics, but we stay true to our God, the Father, Son, and Holy Ghost. That truth doesn't change for us, same as it doesn't for them."

Sam stepped forward, his presence solid. "When Texas shakes loose from Mexican law, folks will worship how they're led, or not at all, if that's what they choose. Freedom's gonna spread across these forests and prairies like wildfire. But we gotta be ready. Showin' ourselves as baptized landowners before the break is what matters now. It's the law."

Sam's belief pressed in, heavy and certain. It wrapped around her, drawing her toward a future that didn't yet have a name. *Be ready.* The words rang clear. *It'll come like a thief in the night.*

The cool night carried Father Michael Muldoon's verses over the crackle of the fire. Flames danced, casting flickering shadows across the gathered faces. When he raised his hands, his method steady and commanding, the people mirrored his gesture, crossing themselves in unison. "In the name of the Father, Son, and Holy Ghost." Isobel's fingers brushed her forehead, chest, and shoulders in rhythm with the others. The air stirred around her, charged with something unnamed, something that hummed through her skin and settled deep.

The priest's words sliced through the cool night. "Bring forward the Paschal Candle."

The deacon stepped forward, the Paschal Candle a bright pillar in his hands. Isobel's eyes followed Father Muldoon's careful movements as he took up a stylus, the tip catching the firelight. Each stroke carved meaning into the candle wax. A cross, the alpha above it, the omega below, and the year 1835 set in place like an anchor. There was purpose in every motion, a solemn precision making her heart fill with reverence.

When he lit the wick from the flames, the words he spoke seemed to wrap themselves around her. "May the light of Christ, rising in glory, dispel the darkness of our hearts and minds." The scent of burning wax mingled with the sharp sweetness of incense as the deacon stepped forward, the censer swinging gently in his hand. Smoke curled upward, softening the edges of the night.

The procession began, Father Muldoon's lit candle leading the way. Isobel clutched her unlit taper, her grip firm, her steps careful as they followed him toward the Sterne residence and entered. The house, transformed into a sanctuary, carried a holiness that defied its ordinary walls. The flickering candlelight stretched across the room as if chasing away shadows which had no business there tonight.

Father Muldoon's tools, so plain in their practicality, held a quiet kind of holiness. He packed candles, vestments, and the small baptismal font and carried them for miles on the back of his mule. Isobel couldn't help but marvel at the man's devotion. His movements, even now, as he prepared for the baptisms and the Eucharist, were deliberate, each one steeped in a faith that seemed to fill the room as much as the scent of the incense.

She tightened her grip on the candle, appreciating the light of God's Word. Whatever challenges lay ahead, for now, they stood together in blessed illumination, bound by a faith that refused to waver. The priest poured a small stream of water on her head and anointed her with holy oil. He repeated the process for Sam and Kelvin.

Isobel stifled a yawn, her body heavy from the yoke of the night's reverence and effort. The Easter Vigil Mass had to end before dawn, Father Muldoon made that clear, and no one seemed eager to drag the ceremony out. The candlelight, the incense, the solemn prayers, the sacraments, all left her both awed and drained. She glanced around at the others, their faces softened by exhaustion, but they had been initiated into Holy Mother Church.

The merriment could wait for tomorrow, Easter Sunday. That was as it should be. A proper tribute belonged in the light, when hearts were rested and strength restored. For now, the quiet stillness of the moment carried its own holiness—soft, solemn, and near to God.

Kelvin stepped forward respectfully. "Thank you, Father Muldoon. We sure do appreciate your service." He handed an envelope to the priest. Isobel could guess what it held. "Hope this helps with your travelin' expenses. I hear you go all around Mexico ministerin' to folks."

"That's right, Kelvin." His affirmation carried both faith and purpose in equal measure. "I've been all over *Tejas*. Some of the conversions are political, sure, but folks' spiritual needs are real. I do the Lord's work from here to the Pacific Ocean."

Isobel leaned forward, her curiosity sparking. "You must know a lot of people, Father."

"I know many." There was a shadow of weariness in his eyes, though he held no complaint. "And I meet many more. I've served in grand palaces and cold prisons alike."

Kelvin said, "We're grateful for your service here in Nacogdoches."

"I'll have your baptismal certificates after Easter." He tucked the envelope into his bag. "You can pick 'em up at Judge John Dor's office next week."

"Thank you, Father. We'll try to be patient." Isobel's attempt at humor was thin but sincere. She was tired of waiting for so much these days.

"Patience is a virtue." The priest was instructive. "Last winter, around February, I ministered to a prisoner in Inquisition Prison. He told me the Mexicans had long since exhausted his patience. Years of dealin' with their government will do that. He was an Anglo political prisoner."

A streak of unease creeped up Isobel's spine. "Do you remember his name, Father?"

The priest tilted his head, thinking for a moment. "*Esteban.*"

The question clawed its way out of her throat. "Did you hear his last name?"

Father Muldoon's answer landed like a rock. "Austin."

Something shifted, the weight of his words pinning Isobel where she stood. Her knees gave, and she sank into a chair. "He left two years ago." Her words trembled in the space between them. "We haven't seen him since."

Isobel barely noticed Sam stepping closer, her thoughts caught on Father Muldoon's mention of Austin. Sam cut through her worry. "Padre, can you tell us anything else about Austin's situation?"

Father Muldoon adjusted his stance, his hands clasped loosely in front of him. "He went through a lot with cholera. After leavin' San Felipe, he made his way to *Béxar*, then down to Goliad tryin' to rally Tejano support. *Señor* Seguin backed the convention resolutions but couldn't go to Mexico City. Austin found no support in Goliad, so he rode his mule all the way to Matamoros. That's where he caught cholera the first time."

"The *first* time?" Isobel shook. The thought of such a lonely, grueling journey struck hard, her mind flashing to memories of Ursula and her family's battle with the illness. "Lord, I can't even imagine. Travelin' alone, no friends along the way, and then gettin' cholera…"

The priest's face turned grim. "After recoverin' in Matamoros, he made his way to the port and booked passage to Vera Cruz. What should've taken a week stretched into a whole month. He was seasick the entire way."

Sam let out a slow whistle. "Nobody can say he ain't persistent."

There was the briefest upward pull at Father Muldoon's lips. "Persistent, indeed. He reached Mexico City by July and waited there with a patience I'd call remarkable. But, as you'd expect, they move slower than molasses, and the delays wore him down."

Kelvin shook his head. "That man has the patience of Job."

The priest said, "True enough. While he was waitin' to see the officials, and tryin' to bring back somethin' for the folks, he got cholera again. This time, it was bad."

Isobel buried her face in her hands. "The poor man. How much can one person take?"

Father Muldoon softened a bit. "By the grace of God, our Lord delivered him, but that second bout changed him. His patience was gone, and he was feelin' mighty discouraged. He told me he wrote a letter in October to the *ayuntamiento* [council] in *Béxar*, a letter he said he'd never have written in normal times."

Sam lifted his head slowly. "Yes, we know 'bout the letter. He told 'em to set up their own government without waitin' for Mexican approval. The council members thought it was seditious and sent it straight to Mexico City. That's what got him thrown in the dungeon."

"It sure is," Father Muldoon agreed. "He might've been out of his mind when he wrote it, comin' right after his brush with death."

Kelvin stepped closer. "Have you heard anything 'bout him since he was in Inquisition Prison?"

Father Muldoon shook his head. "Not directly, but I know he managed to get a meetin' with Santa Anna after a lot of wranglin'. *El Presidente* moved him outta the dungeon and into another jail where he wasn't stuck in a tiny cell with just a few hours of light and a rat for company."

Isobel shuddered at the thought of a Mexican dungeon, where the silence pressed in and every scrape or drip reminded you of how far you were from mercy. "He's incredible. What else have you heard, Father?"

"Last I heard, they moved him to the Prison of Deputation on the Main Plaza in Mexico City."

Sam said, "I know that's where he was when we sent lawyers to Mexico City to make inquiries. They ended up bribin' the judge so he could make bail."

Father Muldoon gave a look edged in wryness. "He made bail, but he had to stay in the city. If my information's right, he's still in Mexico City under house arrest."

Sam crossed his arms, sharp with frustration. "No civilized country will ever respect Mexico with bribery and corruption as their main currency. Austin's case shows the world their crooked customs."

Kelvin shifted uneasily. "Is it true Santa Anna's flipped sides in their civil conflict?"

The priest sighed. "It's true. He was a *federalista*, but now he's a *centralista* to gain the support of the military. He's set up a larger standing army since."

Kelvin asked in disbelief, "Why do the people allow it?"

Sam's answer came fast, cutting through the question like a blade. "An illiterate people can't govern themselves. They'll always be under the heel of a tyrant."

Father Muldoon's expression was grim. "I'm afraid that's true."

Isobel stepped up, her eyes meeting the priest's. "Father, I'll be thankin' the Lord tonight for your service to the people of Mexico. I believe prayers work, and Stephen Austin's survival proves it. You, Father, are the hands and feet of our Lord in this world." Her words broke as she embraced him, the extent of her gratitude spilling over.

The priest pointed toward Heaven. "Esteban told me His grace was sufficient."

Isobel said, "His power is made perfect in weakness."

The priest tilted his head. "Yes," he said. "Saint Paul wrote those words from prison."

CHAPTER FORTY-THREE

September 8, 1835
Brazoria, *Coahuila y Tejas*

The midday sun bore down, turning the dirt road of the coastal town into shimmering waves of heat. Isobel smoothed her dress and wiped the sweat from her brow. *September, still refusing to surrender its summer fury.* She stepped forward, her heart beating quickly at the sight of him. Stephen F. Austin, back on Texas soil.

She dipped into a curtsy, the fabric whispering against her boots. "Welcome home, Colonel." She met his eyes, hoping he'd see how much his return meant. "We sure have missed ya."

Austin's fatigue was etched into his face. "It's mighty good to be home." His voice was lower and softer than she remembered. "Had a tough go of it in Mexico City." His sigh carried a burden she couldn't fathom, like he bore the dreams of every Texan on his shoulders.

Kelvin stepped up, pushing for more details. "Father Muldoon told us 'bout your time in the prisons and how you battled cholera."

Austin glanced at Isobel with a butterfly's gentleness. "He was an answer to your prayers. I couldn't have made it without his kindness."

Her eyes glistened at the memory of her appeals to Heaven. The mention of the ruthless disease sent a wave of distress through her body. "Cholera's horrible." The words burst out. "It took Jim Bowie's young wife and her folks. He's plum heartbroken."

The sorrow in Austin's eyes deepened as her meaning sank in. "The Veramendis?" The disbelief almost masked his heartbreak. "Oh my. We've lost a wonderful family. I'm crestfallen."

Crestfallen. Such a gentle word for a mournfulness so vast. She folded her hands together as she urged herself to hold steady. Yet there were so many more families in anguish. "Colonel, have you heard 'bout the atrocities in Zacatecas?"

A shadow passed over his grim features. "The dictator'll stop at nothin'. When he unleashed his forces on Zacatecas, his troops ravaged the city. He won't hesitate to torture and kill his own people."

Isobel shook her head in disgust. "You talked to him, didn't you?"

Austin replied, "Pleasant enough, agreed to our resolutions, or most of 'em, but turned right 'round and did the opposite. He's as two-faced as they come."

Kelvin's question suggested curiosity, not fear. "What do you reckon changed him?"

Austin's look shifted as if he saw something far off. "The *federalista* reforms riled up the army officers and the bishops. They wanted to keep the people uneducated, ignorant, and outta the government. Santa Anna learned there wasn't no advantage in helpin' the people, so he switched to the *centralistas*. The real power and money are there."

She gritted her teeth, the bitter taste of anger rising in her throat. "He has no scruples."

His eyes flicked back to her. "None."

She hesitated, then said, "General Houston thinks Santa Anna's comin' for us."

Austin's expression hardened, the lines on his face deepening. "I'm sure his plans to wipe us out are already in motion. Freedom can't coexist with a military dictatorship."

Kelvin broke the silence. "You were always the moderate and patient one, Colonel. Are you sayin' war's inevitable?"

He didn't waver. "We can either leave or fight. The time for workin' things out is long gone."

Isobel swallowed hard, her heart pounding. She thought of the families she'd seen loading wagons. She listened to many hushed conversations over whether to stay or flee. She fought to calm the trembling in her body and looked at him. "Most folks agree with you."

Kelvin broke the uneasy silence. "Do you know 'bout the disturbance in Anahuac?"

Austin glanced up, his expression unreadable. "Yes, it happened before I left."

He shook his head. "No. There was another one where a Texian ship captain refused to pay bribes, and he was arrested."

Isobel's stomach tightened.

A flash of concern crossed Austin's face. "I came to Brazoria from New Orleans on a schooner. It had a runnin' gun battle with a Mexican gunboat. I figured it would stir up Santa Anna, but there's *another* incident?"

Kelvin answered, "Yes. Some documents were captured that confirm your fears."

Austin was calm. "What did they say?"

Kelvin replied, "Santa Anna's marchin' on a punitive expedition like in Zacatecas. But before he comes, a general named Cos will take firm control of Texas."

Austin's brows drew together. "Martín Perfecto de Cos?"

Kelvin rubbed his chin. "Sounds familiar."

Austin exhaled. "Cos is the dictator's brother-in-law. This fight is gonna get personal."

Personal. Isobel's stomach clenched. The word carried more menace than any she'd heard so far.

Kelvin looked Austin in the eyes. "He put out an arrest warrant for Buck Travis. Accused him of bein' an 'ungrateful and bad citizen.' Buck's the one who led the expedition to free the ship captain."

"Naturally." Austin exhibited wry humor. "Where's Cos now?"

Kelvin shifted a bit. "He issued the warrant from Matamoros. I'm sure he's on the move north, but I couldn't tell you where he's at today."

Austin appeared distant. "Cos will blunder his way into a fight. He ain't ready to face a people who hold him and his brother-in-law in utter contempt."

The tension rose, but he pressed on. "Colonel, a call for delegates went out for a convention coming next month in Washington on the Brazos. You got home at the right time."

Austin said, "The revolution is in motion. There's no turnin' back."

Kelvin quickened his words. "General Houston called for armed men to report to him in Nacogdoches. The men there appointed him their general and commander in chief. He also put an ad in the New Orleans paper for able-bodied men to come here with their muskets and horses."

Austin fixed his eyes on something he alone could see. "All wise moves. The fight is upon us. Cos is the first wave. He won't be the last, nor will he be the most lethal."

Isobel couldn't stop the words. "It's frightenin'."

He focused on the horizon as if searching for a storm they all knew was coming. "Any man who ain't frightened now is a fool. I've seen the power and force these corrupt despots wield firsthand. They have no kindness to govern their behavior. Mercy is a weapon deployed and withdrawn in devastatin' fashion. Make no mistake, Santa Anna has already cried, 'Havoc!'"

The words hit Isobel like a blow and sent her heart racing. The fear coursed through her veins, but beneath it the seed of resolve stirred. This land was her home. Whatever came next, she wouldn't run from it.

CHAPTER FORTY-FOUR

November 14, 1835
San Felipe de Austin, *Coahuila y Tejas*
Final Day of Legislative Consultation of 1835

Isobel scanned the countryside, her chest tightening at the unease carried on the wind. She and Kelvin rounded up information from the colony for Sam. Stephen F. Austin's warnings, his fiery-eyed insistence trouble would come, had proven to be more than talk. She could see it now, painted plain on the horizon of their lives. On September 20th, General Cos landed at Copano Bay with five hundred *soldados*. The landing sent waves of alarm racing through the countryside, turning quiet evenings into anxious nights.

By the end of the month, another wave of fear rolled in. Another hundred *soldados* marched to Gonzales and demanded the return of cannons loaned to the colonists for defense against Indian attacks. But the settlers weren't about to bow their heads. Isobel had heard the mutterings of defiance and seen men's faces harden as she and Kelvin rode from settlement to settlement gathering information for Sam. When she arrived in Gonzales, the residents' determination simmered like a pot ready to boil over. She saw a banner there as it snapped in the wind. It was a white cloth painted with a lone star, a cannon, and four bold words. *Come And Take It.*

When Isobel and Kelvin entered San Felipe de Austin on November 14th, the village buzzed with the tension and urgency of impending war. They had met with Austin in *Béxar* and rode to deliver his message to Sam.

Tension hung as thick as a thundercloud in every hurried footstep as Isobel searched for Sam. She spoke over other clipped conversations that buzzed around her. She found him in the street in front of Angelina's place. "General, we have news from *Béxar*."

Sam stood still. "Let's hear it."

Isobel brushed the road dust from her face. "Colonel Austin has General Cos surrounded in *Béxar*. He said he can't leave there just yet, but he don't want anybody to think this meetin' here ain't important just 'cause he's not in San Felipe."

Sam rubbed his chin. "Austin decided to surround *Béxar* instead of attackin' it head-on. That's good thinkin'. Starvin' General Cos out of the town is much better than sacrificin' lives and ammunition. I sure hope the siege works."

Kelvin yanked off his hat, giving it a sharp slap against his thigh. A puff of dust rose from the brim and swirled in the sunlight. "Well, folks ain't talkin' 'bout much else these days. The men in Gonzales sure gave Cos's *soldados* somethin' to remember when they came sniffin' around for those cannons. Ran 'em clean off."

The corner of Sam's mouth twitched, and he shook his head like he could see the scene playing out. "Heard about their flag. Ain't no shortage of stories flyin' now."

Kelvin shook his head. "Congratulations, General. We heard you're now a major general in command of the regular army of Texas."

Sam drawled, "That army consists of you and me."

Kelvin laughed, and Isobel shot him a withering glance. "It's serious, Kelvin."

He shook his head. "Sometimes ya gotta laugh at your predicament, or it'll get the best of ya."

Sam kicked the dirt under his feet. "We all know it's only a matter of time before Santa Anna arrives with a real army and overwhelmin' numbers. We gotta raise and train an army. Austin's volunteers in *Béxar* will be there for a while. We need to get men and train 'em now."

Kelvin asked, "Are you gettin' any responses to your ad in the newspaper?"

Sam gestured toward the door of Angelina's tavern. "Let's get off the street."

The charged atmosphere emboldened Isobel. She walked to the tavern counter and brought a box that was under it back to their usual corner table. She reached in and pulled out a stack of letters, her fingers trembled as excitement tangled with unease.

Sam raised a brow and reached for the leather case beside him. He drew out several opened letters and handed them to her. "Got a fair few. I reckon we'll see volunteers streamin' in from the old states, but it's gonna take time."

Isobel unfolded the first letter and scanned the neat handwriting. "This one's from Felix Huston of Natchez, Mississippi." Her throat was dry, so Kelvin got up and got her a glass of water. "Mr. Huston writes that we'll have the whole Southern portion of the United States on our side. Here's another letter from Angus McNeill of Natchez sayin' we'll be overrun with volunteers. These gentlemen'll likely bring their planters' slaves and their economy to Texas to serve King Cotton. I hate that."

Sam glanced her way, his thoughts unreadable. "There's more letters from free soil places like Vermont. Keep lookin'. Volunteers'll come into Texas with all kinds of motives." Sam moved forward in his chair and the wood creaked under his weight. He locked his eyes onto Isobel with an intensity that filled the room. When he spoke, the words cut like Bowie's blade, the calm gone, replaced by a heated edge. "There was a time when Stephen Austin examined each newcomer and their fit in the colony, but those days are over. We need men with guns, and we need 'em now."

She swallowed hard and shifted to the next letter, but Kelvin broke the silence before she could read it. "I share Isobel's concern, General. If Texas becomes a slave state, it'll set back our chances of joinin' the Union."

The words landed heavily, and Isobel glanced up, meeting Sam's eyes. There was no surprise there, no sudden revelation, just a resigned understanding of the truth Kelvin laid bare.

Sam finally responded. "Every decision's a gamble. Right now, Texas don't have the luxury of choosing who fights. The only issue we have is whether we're still standin' when this war's over."

Isobel's grip tightened on the letter in her hand, and her heart beat against her ribs. She hated the tangled mess of slavery, survival, and sacrifice. Sam was right about one thing. This fight was bigger than any single issue. *But what was the right choice?*

The fire in the hearth crackled, but its heat didn't reach Isobel. Sam's words filled the room like a storm cloud, and the room had a chill in it. She gripped the arm of her chair, her knuckles white against the worn wood, and willed herself to stay calm.

Sam stood up and paced the room. Isobel thought he was a man burdened with too many truths. He stopped and looked into her eyes. "Santa Anna's on his way."

Isobel's stomach churned, the familiar nausea of raw emotions rising. She knew the consequences of what she was about to ask, but the words spilled out anyway. "General, you showed me the resolution against the slave trade in Texas. Did you mean it?"

Sam's shoulders sagged. When the firelight flashed across his face, he looked older than he was. "I meant it then, and I mean it now. But I won't turn a man away from this fight 'cause of what he thinks about slavery. Texas matters more than any single issue."

Isobel's throat burned, anger and sorrow mixed into something she couldn't contain. "What about the families, the fathers, mothers, and babies?" Her throat cracked, and tears streamed down her face. "What about the lives torn apart for the sake of cotton and profit? How can Texas matter more than that pain?"

Sam's face was somber. "I know what I'm sayin' is makin' light of the pain of those families. It's real, but before Texas can deal with it, we gotta have a Texas."

She brushed away the tears and grew whisper quiet. "If our forefathers had stopped slavery in its tracks, we wouldn't be havin' this conversation."

Sam's eyes were unyielding. "If they'd made a fuss about it back then, there'd be no United States. The southern states would've pulled out altogether."

The walls closed in on her. Oxygen barely reached her, like her own body had turned against her. "I understand what you're sayin', General. There's an urgency, and Texas is gonna be born outta violence and the ugliness of the slavery. I don't know how I can fight for such a state."

Sam stepped closer, sharp but not unkind. "Look at your husband, Isobel. I am commissioning him a captain in the army of Texas today. He and hundreds more are gonna fight or die. Santa Anna's gettin' ready, gatherin' his army. I reckon he's so enraged, he'll march 'em through the unforgivin' winter just to get 'em here faster. He don't care 'bout his troops. Most of 'em are Indian conscripts, and he don't give a care if they live or die."

Isobel froze as the truth of it hit her, lodged like a stone in her throat. Her husband and her general would fight for this land, this dream of Texas, no matter the cost. Even though she hated the compromises being made, the injustices tangled up in their struggle, she couldn't bear the thought of either of them fighting without her.

The fire crackled again, and she looked down into the flickering flames. Her thoughts churned as the room fell silent. She didn't know how to reconcile her beliefs with the bloody path ahead, but one thing was certain—there was no turning back.

The room was alive with tension, the kind that made every word searing, every inhalation sharper. Isobel stood still. Her fingers gripped the fabric of her skirt, and her heart pounded in rhythm with the passions of revolution.

Sam's pacing slowed, and he turned to look at her, his voice dropped to a simmer that burned even hotter. "Ask the folks in Zacatecas 'bout slavery. Ask 'em 'bout governin' themselves. Ask 'em 'bout their so-called benevolent leader. He ain't no leader. He's a master of slaves, and we ain't gonna be slaves to no man. Never! The fight for liberty's begun. The dawn of glory's upon us."

The meaning of his words settled in her chest, and she struggled to calm herself. "I understand what you're sayin', General. I know our lives are hangin' in a precarious balance, as if we're on the edge of a cliff and one wrong step will be the end of us. Despite the sufferin' of those in bondage, I know Texas must come to be. If she's born a slave state, we'll need a remedy for it. You were straight with us from the start, back when we crossed the Red River. I'm ready to risk everythin' so this baby can be born. You're my general now and always."

Sam's expression softened, the edges of his sternness gave way to something almost tender. "I appreciate y'all's support more than words can say. You're a sharp one, Isobel, with a keen eye for what's goin' on."

Kelvin spoke up. "She's as sharp as any man I know."

Sam looked at Kelvin and Isobel. "The Matagorda Militia captured the Presidio Bahia to stop General Cos in Goliad. Cos had already passed through, but the militia snagged a heap of weapons and supplies. There was a skirmish, and the Mexicans killed one Texian, Samuel McCullough."

Kelvin, who'd been leaning back with his arms crossed, straightened. "He sounds like a good Scotsman. It's too bad we lost such a man."

Sam shook his head. "He wasn't a Scotsman, Kelvin, even though he had the name and fought like one."

Isobel's curiosity flared and her eyes narrowed. "Who was he, General?"

"A free black man." Sam's words landed like a spark in the room. "History beckons her heroes to come, and she cares not their color or sex."

The fire crackled in the silence. Sam's words soared like a heaven-bound prayer.

A rush of conviction swelled in her heart, and she found herself speaking before she realized it. "Heroes will rise."

"Amen." Kelvin's single word response carried hope and power.

For a moment, the three of them stood in the charged stillness, bound by the magnitude of the fight ahead. Whatever came next, they would face it together.

CHAPTER FORTY-FIVE

Christmas Day, 1835
MacDonald/Houston Quarters
Washington on the Brazos, *Coahuila y Tejas*

Isobel nudged the door of the cabin open, the sharp December cold turning her breath to mist. The flicker of candlelight caught the outline of a man standing in the doorway, and her heart leapt. Jim Bowie. His broad shoulders sagged like a giant from another world had crushed him from the inside out.

Isobel stepped aside to let him in. "Jim." She whispered the name as Kelvin and Sam followed, their footsteps soft as if they were afraid to disturb their friend.

Bowie moved like a man in a dream, or a nightmare, each step slower than she remembered. As the light washed over him, Isobel could see the hollows in his cheeks, the lines carved deep around his mouth. This wasn't the Jim Bowie who had once puzzled over dominoes and whiskey, arguing politics with a fire that could light up the coldest night. That man was gone. What that Bowie left behind was a shadow that barely held itself together.

Isobel trembled as the words left her throat. "I'm so sorry about

Ursula, Jim." She reached for him, wrapping her arms around his rigid frame. He was thinner than he used to be, his strength worn down, like a razor gone dull. "I can't imagine what you're goin' through."

He hugged her back, briefly, and his hands fell away almost as soon as they'd landed. "Thank ya, Isobel." His reply was low and rough, like gravel underfoot. "I miss her somethin' fierce. I ain't never gonna be the same."

Sam wrung his hat in his hands. "Losin' family to cholera's a terrible shame." He wavered, the words too small to match the enormity of what they meant.

Kelvin cleared his throat, his usual easy confidence subdued. "We all felt it, Jim. Words can't describe how hard the news hit us. Hope ya know we're here, if ya need to lean on us."

Bowie lowered his head, slow and careful, like even that small motion took more strength than he could muster. "Appreciate it, I do. But..." He looked away. "Some burdens you gotta carry yourself."

The room fell silent except for the soft hiss of the candle's flame. Isobel's heart ached, the burden of his loss clamped down on her. She couldn't fix it. None of them could. As Jim stood there lost and broken, she vowed to herself they'd at least make this night a little less cold for him. "Kelvin's right. You can lean on us."

"I know." His smile was faint, like a sliver of light breaking through thick clouds. A flicker of softness reached his eyes. "It makes things a mite easier, knowin' y'all are still here for me. But I also know I ain't good company now."

Isobel thought of the Jim she'd known, the one who made any room brighter just by walking in. "New Year's Eve at your place was one of the happiest days of my life, Jim. That night showed what Texas and her people could truly be."

"That was a great night," Kelvin and Sam echoed in unison.

His expression didn't shift much, but there was a subtle light in his eyes, like a distant ember that still burned. "I reckon y'all know 'bout Ben Milam takin' a force into *Béxar* and fightin' General Cos. Did ya hear how Ben died?"

Sam shook his head as he spoke for all of them. "Not exactly. We just know he died and never knew about our victory there."

Bowie didn't flinch. "A sniper shot him while he was rallyin' his men. He yelled, 'Who'll follow Old Ben Milam,' then he fell dead at the entry door of Veramendi Palace."

Isobel gasped like she took a sharp jab to the ribs. Her mind flashed to that doorway, to the friendly glow of lamplight and the first time she'd met Ursula there. The memory hovered, delicate, as if even a sparrow's weight might break it. "I remember meetin' Ursula there for the first time. I know Milam's death hit all of us hard, but it must be the worst for you, Jim."

He didn't respond right away. The silence was broken only by the faint crackle of the fire. Then, he shifted and reached into the leather bag slung across his shoulder. "Since it's Christmas, I wanna give ya somethin', Isobel."

Her heart skipped and jumped as he handed her a small package, wrapped in oilcloth. The bundle rested heavily in her hands. Her fingers worked carefully, almost reverently, to peel back the layers, each movement deliberate, like she was unwrapping a relic from a saint. When the cloth fell away, she gasped, stunned by what she saw. "Jim, it's a knife like yours."

Bowie's face darkened, but it carried a hint of humor. For the first time in what felt like an eternity, Isobel saw a hint of the old Jim, the man who still had something to fight for. "It's a good bit smaller than mine. The fella who made my knife in Arkansas made this smaller one for Ursula. She passed before I could give it to her, but I know she'd want you to have it."

Her eyes lifted to meet his, the significance of the gift settling over her like a mantle of quiet grace. It wasn't just a knife, it was a piece of him, something he offered in a world where he had so little left to share. She swallowed hard, the words stuck in her throat. "I'm speechless, Jim." Hot tears traced her cheeks, but she didn't bother to brush them away. "I'll treasure it. Always."

Kelvin leaned in closer, his eyes wide as he took in the craftsmanship. "It's beautiful, Jim. Ursula would be so proud of you."

Isobel blinked hard against the sting in her eyes. "Jim..." She traced the delicate lines of the blade. Tears blurred the intricate Cherokee beadwork that decorated the scabbard, its colors vivid and alive in the firelight. She could no longer speak.

Sam shook his head as he marveled at Bowie himself. "Jim, you're a true friend of ours. Ain't nobody I hold in higher esteem."

Bowie cleared his throat and straightened his shoulders. "Lots of folks think we've won, and Mexican troops won't come back to Texas. Men left *Béxar* thinkin' the revolution's over."

Sam's jaw tightened. "Fools." The word charged through the room.

Kelvin crossed his arms. "Santa Anna's avengin' army is likely on its way to Texas right now."

Bowie agreed, his frame as steady as the blade he'd just handed over. "Of that, you can be sure."

Isobel eyed her small Bowie knife and brushed the smooth blade with her thumb. It was more than a weapon—more like a promise, or a warning. "What are we gonna do? The Texian government is power-less, or better said, nonexistent."

Sam stepped forward, determined. "Jim, I need ya to go to *Béxar*. Colonel Neill says he's got twenty-one artillery pieces there. Move 'em to Goliad after ya blow the place up."

Bowie replied, "Yes, sir, Sam. I'll go, but Colonel Neill's got orders from Governor Smith to fortify the place."

Sam sighed and ran a hand over his face. "I understand. The government's in total disarray now. Smith sent the delegates packin', but they turned 'round and impeached him."

Isobel shook her head as her thoughts churned. A governor who fought his own people while Santa Anna's army loomed over them. It was madness. She didn't say it aloud; she didn't have to. The grim looks on their faces told her they all felt the same.

She tightened her fingers around the knife's scabbard, and the intricate beadwork pressed against her palm. Whatever came next, she'd fight for Texas with everything she had. She looked at the weapon in her hands. *Can I kill?* She didn't know.

Kelvin's face was edged with doubt. "Will Colonel Neill follow your orders, General? Governor Smith ordered *Béxar's* defenses."

"Probably not." Sam's frustration dragged him down. "That's why we're countin' on Jim to carry out my orders."

Isobel couldn't bite her tongue any longer. "This tomfoolery of a government's gonna cost good men their lives 'cause of its ineptitude."

Sam said, "We gotta call a convention for independence. It'll set up a proper government, free of Mexico, to defend Texas and get folks ready for a bloody war."

Bowie leaned forward. "When can such a meetin' happen?"

Sam glanced around the room. "There's one set for March 1st right here."

"Too late," Isobel shot back. Her mind painted the grim picture of Santa Anna's army marching across her country, slashing and burning everything in its path. Her stomach churned. "That'll be too late."

Sam's face darkened, but he remained calm. "We'll have to make do with what we got."

Kelvin pressed him. "What's our move, then?"

Sam's gaze swept over them. "Am I still your general?"

"Yes," they all yelled. The word echoed through the room and accentuated their unity. A surge of loyalty swelled in Isobel's heart, a defiance against the chaos that closed in on all sides.

Sam turned almost contemplative as he laid out his scheme. "My plan's always been to block the *El Camino Real*." He searched their eyes for understanding. "*Béxar* first, then Goliad. We'll fight a defensive battle and pull back, like the old fellas did in the Revolution. The Mexicans can't handle us out in the open. Santa Anna must not catch us behind walls. General Cos proved an army can't move in a fort or city streets. Colonel Neill's gotta leave *Béxar* and head to Goliad with the artillery. He has all our artillery in one spot. I don't like it. We'll start our defense in Goliad, closer to our supplies and rein-forcements."

Kelvin said, "Jim, it's up to you to get this plan goin'."

Isobel stepped up before Bowie could respond. She drew her knife

from its scabbard, the blade glinted in the firelight. "Be careful, Jim."
She was firm, but soft around the edges. She searched for any trace of
hesitation in his eyes. "Listen to the general. Fightin' behind walls or
in the streets means certain death. Don't let it come to that." Her
fingers curled tighter around the handle of the knife. "Thank ya for
this weapon. It may be small, but its lethality looms large. Godspeed,
Jim."

Bowie agreed, his face hard with determination. "I'll see to it."
Then he coughed.

As he turned to leave, the room grew colder, emptier, like the
oxygen itself had slipped out with him. Something inside Isobel
tugged hard. It was an ache she couldn't name but couldn't ignore.
Suddenly, the future loomed uncertain and heavy. She didn't like the
cough. Now that she reflected on it, he had coughed a lot. It was
something that lingered with him like a shadow he couldn't shake.

She didn't like the city streets of *Béxar*. They pressed in, sharp-
edged and dangerous. There was no place to run. The Mexicans had
just proven it.

"Wait." She whispered it barely louder than a thought. Her friend
didn't hear her, or maybe he didn't want to. She wanted to run after
him, to shout for him to come back, to stay, to promise he wouldn't
disappear into the unknown future. But her feet stayed rooted, heavy
as stones.

And then a discordant fiddle note hit her, undeniable and unmistakable, but she didn't want to believe it. *This is the final farewell.*

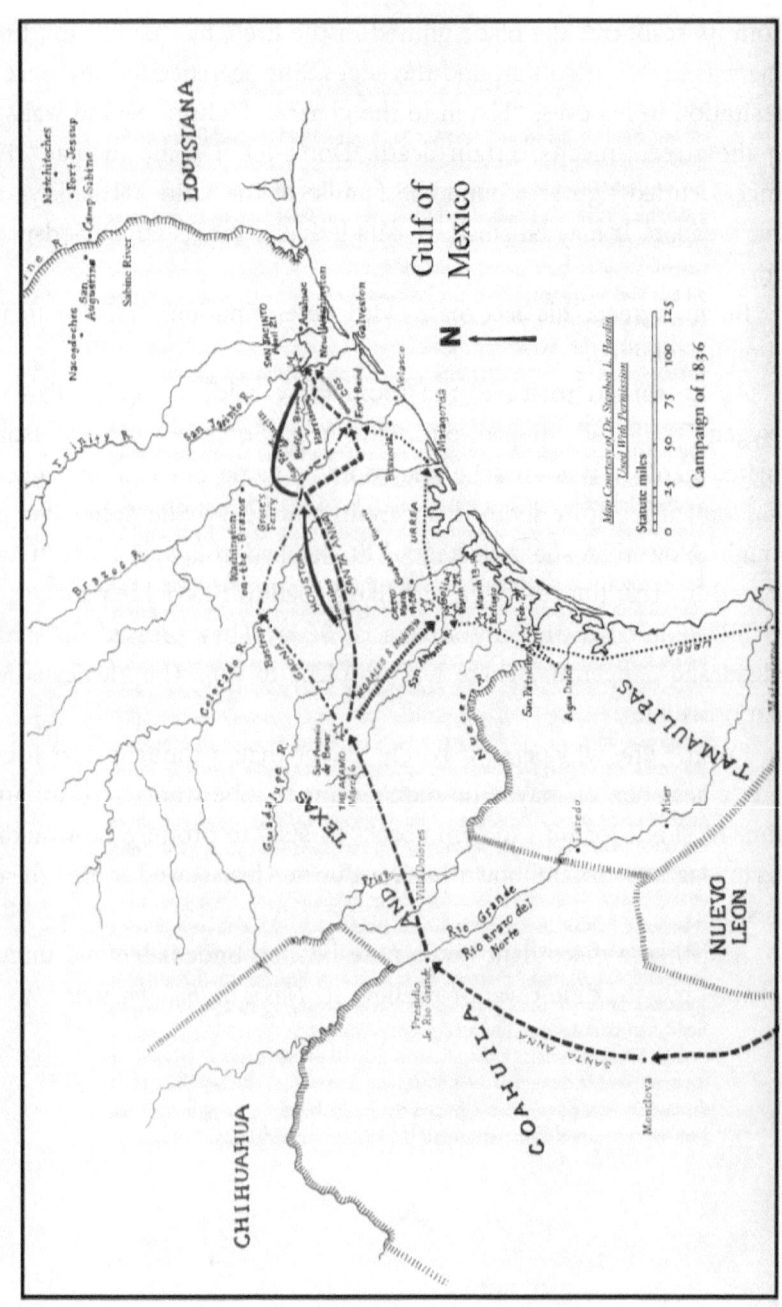

Map of the 1836 Texas Revolution Military Campaign

CHAPTER FORTY-SIX

March 2, 1836
Independence Hall
Convention of Delegates to Declare Independence
Washington on the Brazos, Republic of Texas

I sobel leaned forward as a convention delegate's announcement cut through the murmurs of the room. Her heart thudded. "We've got a message." The man's declaration drew every eye. "It's from Buck Travis in *Béxar*."

The room shifted, heavy with anticipation. She froze as the man raised a folded paper. His fingers lingered on the edges before he unfolded it. "I'll read it aloud." The words came slow, heavy with meaning.

Commandancy of The Alamo
Bejar, Feby 24th. 1836
To the People of Texas & All Americans in the World-
Fellow Citizens & compatriots-

I am besieged, by a thousand or more of the Mexicans under Santa Anna - I have sustained a continual Bombardment & cannonade for 24 hours & have not lost a man - The enemy has demanded a surrender at discretion, otherwise, the garrison are to be put to the sword, if the fort is taken - I have answered the demand with a cannon shot, & our flag still waves proudly from the walls - I shall never surrender or retreat. Then, I call on you in the name of Liberty, of patriotism & everything dear to the American character, to come to our aid, with all dispatch - The enemy is receiving reinforcements daily & will no doubt increase to three or four thousand in four or five days. If this call is neglected, I am determined to sustain myself as long as possible & die like a soldier who never forgets what is due to his own honor & that of his country - Victory or Death

William Barret Travis
Lt. Col. comdt

The final words of the letter rang out and echoed in the hall like the last notes of a great hymn. She caught herself, lungs aching with the stillness. Her hand gripped the corner of the table until her knuckles ached. She couldn't swallow. Her heart thundered. The force of the remarks lifted her higher than the stars and cast her into the depths of her own fears, all in the same moment.

Isobel wasn't the only one affected. The message ignited an overpowering sense of purpose. Murmurs of agreement and determined looks spread through the room as the sentiment hit home. The delegates, galvanized by Travis's plea, made a historic decision. Independence. They would vote on it at last. After years of sidestepping the issue, it was time.

Buck's letter changed everything. She had never heard anything like it. She stood at attention. Her pulse throbbed in her ears while the representatives rose, one by one, to cast their votes. Each aye struck like a trip-hammer driving a nail into the coffin of their ties to Mexico. Her hands stayed at her sides. She gripped the fabric of her dress.

"This is no easy thing," Kelvin murmured, as he stood next to her. "When it's done, there ain't no turnin' back."

"I know." The weight of the moment pressed down on her shoulders. It was like she was poised at the top of a cliff, staring into a great, dark abyss. "We can't go back. Not after Buck's message."

When the last vote was cast, the room exhaled all at once. The hum grew louder, and the delegates leaned into each other and exchanged handshakes and solemn words. Isobel didn't join the buzz of conversation. She couldn't. Her mind raced, desperate to find a way to reach her friends before it was too late.

Kelvin turned to her. "Finally. Independence. We're free."

Isobel squeezed his hand, though the word didn't feel real yet. *Free.* The cost of it loomed in her mind, but so did the vision of what it could mean for Texas where people could stand tall, where no one would bend to a dictator again. "I always reckoned this day'd be joyful, but I'm too worried 'bout Buck and Jim to celebrate."

She pictured them out there alone, surrounded by a storm of Mexican soldiers. She'd heard her father's friend, David Crockett, had also entered the Alamo. There was something about him that lingered in her memory. She couldn't quite place it, but it was there.

Too many sentiments swirled in her heart for her to feel only one. Pride. Fear. Courage. Dread. Admiration. She could almost see the price they would pay etched into the faces of the men who surrounded her. The ones who might not live to see the Texas they dreamed of; whose names would one day be carved in granite. And yet, admiration took hold and dulled the sharp edges of her swirling fears. These men, flawed and human as they were, had dared to stand. Their votes, united, carried something far greater than themselves.

Kelvin looked around the room. "Plenty of the delegates wanna head out and help 'em right now."

Sam shook his head. "That'd be foolish. We can't act out of panic."

"Even so, Buck's letter says he needs reinforcements now. We'll lose everything if we sit idle." The raw urgency in Kelvin's admonition cut through the silence.

"Those were the most beautiful words I've ever heard." Isobel's voice had a tremor of adoration. The simplicity of his plea had left her dazed. He didn't beg but demanded action with nothing but pure honesty. His meaning settled deep inside her, certain as sunrise. *Of course, we'll go to his aid.*

Sam looked Isobel in the eye and didn't flinch. "Buck sure has a way with words." His face hardened and the oppression of command settled over him like a familiar coat. "But his letter spelled it out plain. We can't go off half-cocked. Santa Anna's numbers are growing into the thousands. What can a mob of a hundred volunteers do? If they had listened to me, we'd have over a thousand troops and twenty-one artillery pieces ready to meet him in Goliad." His eyes darkened. "If Texas is to survive, we've got to gather men and train 'em on the march."

The words hit Isobel like a slap, but the fear that clawed inside her wouldn't let her hold still. *Buck. Jim.* The names filled her mind, each one a fresh spark to the fire already ablaze in her soul. Her blood burned for them. Her hands trembled as they curled into fists. She forced him to meet her question head on. "But what about Buck and Jim?"

He moved his head from side to side, tight-lipped, his expression as unreadable as stone.

Her voice cracked as she pressed on. "What about Mr. Crockett and the others? They're our friends."

He let out a sigh, his head shifted in a clear refusal.

The gathered delegates turned their attention to the fervent scene.

She couldn't hold back. She screamed. "We *must* help them!"

Again, he shook his head.

She stood on her toes and met him eye to eye. "We *have* to go to the Alamo! They need us!"

"They're dead already!" Sam's shout thundered through the room and silenced every murmured conversation in the room.

The words punched through her and hollowed her out. The ground beneath her tilted, and her chest heaved in ragged rhythm. *No. No, they can't be gone. Not Buck. Not Jim.*

Her knees buckled, and the world blurred as she hit the floor. A guttural cry tore loose from her chest. Her tears and wails sank through the cracks of the floorboards as if they could carry her grief somewhere far away.

Kelvin's impregnable arms wrapped around her and lifted her like she weighed nothing. Her head fell against his shoulders as her cries turned to muffled whimpers. His scent and soothing whispers grounded her just enough to breathe.

Sam stood with them, his hand smoothing her hair. His lips pressed on the crown of her head, gentle. He tried to soften the blow of the vicious statement he'd spoken.

"She's strong," someone said, low and distant.

"She'll have to be," came another reply, closer, sharper.

They talked about her like she wasn't even there, like her soul hadn't shattered at their feet. She wanted to speak, to scream again, but the millstones of grief and exhaustion crushed the words before they could rise. All she could do was cling to Kelvin and let her tears fall.

ISOBEL PACED and her boots scraped against the same wooden floor she cried on an hour earlier. The tension coiled tighter inside her. She froze mid-step and turned to Sam. "What *can* we do? If I sit here another minute, I'll die."

He didn't hesitate. "We head to Gonzales. Our forces need a rally point, and I've already ordered Fannin to move his men there." He advanced a step. "Neill's bringin' reinforcements. Left the Alamo to tend to his sick family, but he couldn't get back there in time."

Isobel pictured Colonel Neill, his shoulders weighed down as if by an invisible yoke, his eyes shadowed with regret. She could almost hear the words he might whisper to himself in the dead of night, the kind that claw at a good man's soul when duty and kin pull in opposite directions.

Sam turned to Kelvin, all business now. "I need you to ride to East

Texas and round up every man you can find and bring 'em to Gonzales. Speed's of the essence."

The obligation of his next statement landed right between her eyes. "Isobel will stay with me and act as my courier."

Her heart skipped, torn between the fear of what lay ahead and the fierce relief of not being left behind.

"Our horses are in good shape." His stance softened. "Faithful Saracen is on his way from President Jackson's stables. He'll be here soon, coming through Galveston on a ship."

Kelvin's spirit was electric, the fire in his eyes alight like kindling. "Let's ride!"

Isobel swallowed hard, the burn of horror still clawed at her, but as her pulse pounded, she heard it again. The faint, vaporous strain of the fiddle. The melody wove through her like a thread of heavenly light, which pulled her from the dark grip of panic and despair. She knew now it wasn't just music. It was a calling, a promise.

The bow rose and fell in steady strokes, each one sure and calm. With it came a quiet solace that pushed back the cold terror around her heart. The song whispered a truth—she wasn't powerless. Not anymore. Whatever lay ahead, she would meet it. She wouldn't stand idle. Not now. Not ever. Chaos, battle, and heartbreak were no match for the Harmony of Heaven only she could hear.

CHAPTER FORTY-SEVEN

March 13, 1836
Texian Army Rally Point
Gonzales, Republic of Texas

The late afternoon sun bled across the horizon, streaking the sky in burnt orange and crimson. Isobel stood at the camp's edge, arms wrapped tight around herself. A distant rumble of hooves on the road pricked her ears. Dust curled upward like a slow-moving ghost in the fading light.

She took a step forward and raised her hand to shield her eyes. Riders. Walkers. A handful of them.

Survivors.

The word landed in her gut before her mind could catch up.

She saw "Deaf" (Deef) Smith at the front. His weathered face gave nothing away, but she knew. Knew by the way he held his reins, the stiffness in his back. Knew by the woman who clung to a child like she could press life into the bones of the dead. Two Negro men trailed behind, their silence louder than any words.

The camp stilled. Conversations faded. People turned and watched.

Isobel's fingers curled, her lungs tightening with each shallow draw. Each step the refugees took appeared to darken the day and drag the burden of whatever hell they'd escaped.

Sam's broad frame filled her vision. His eyes met hers for a beat before shifting to a nearby soldier. "Fetch Isobel. We need her to talk to 'em."

She didn't wait. Her feet moved as dust rose in her wake.

Sam cut through the stillness. "Did ya make it to *Béxar*, Deef?"

His head tilted, a quiet no. "Found these folks headin' east, straight from the Alamo. Figured you'd wanna hear everything they seen."

"Good work." His face displayed no sign of relief. "Get some grub. We'll take it from here."

Isobel drew closer, she got more excited as the group came into clear focus. Her stomach jumped at the sight of one of them. Joe, Buck Travis's enslaved manservant, was one of the band. Retrospection slammed into her and knocked the wind from her lungs. She took a moment to gather her wits. "Hello, everyone. My name is Isobel. I already know Joe. Could I trouble you for your names?"

The woman at the center clutched a child close, her clothes torn, streaked with blood and dirt. The baby whimpered, and the woman tightened her arms as she shielded her.

"I'm Susannah Dickinson." She held the tot up. "This is my daughter Angelina." She motioned to the men. "Joe, you know, and this is Ben."

Isobel looked toward Sam. "Could we get some camp stools?"

Sam gestured for things to sit on. "Mrs. Dickinson." He crouched near her. "Isobel's gonna help us piece together what happened."

She looked at Isobel, her red-rimmed eyes brimmed with exhaustion. "I see." She sank onto the stool and shifted Angelina in her arms. Joe and Ben followed. They moved like men with no strength to spare.

Isobel reached out and squeezed Susannah's hand. The woman flinched as she let out a gasp.

"Y'all were at the Alamo?" Isobel asked.

"Yes, ma'am." Her grip on the little one looked almost desperate. "My husband, Almaron, he... he was with us."

The words cut like jagged glass, the gashes deep under her ribs.

"Where you from, Susannah?"

"Here. Gonzales." A flash of pride broke through her sorrow. "Almaron was the blacksmith. One of the 'Old Eighteen.' He was there at the start, when the first shots of the war were fired. Waved the *Come And Take It* flag hisself."

Isobel started to choke. She turned to Sam. "Can we get some water?"

Within moments, cups passed between them.

She knew the next question, dreaded it. Forced the words past a lump in her throat. "Did your husband...did he survive the battle?"

The misery in her eyes spilled over as sobs wracked her frame. "Nobody survived." Tears ran in blistering streams. "I saw him after the walls broke. He told me to save our child if I could. Then he disappeared. I never laid eyes on him again. I looked for his body but never found him."

Her broken words hit like a cannon blast, and Isobel sensed the sharp sting behind her own eyes. But she held firm. She tightened her hand around Susannah's shoulder. "You did what he asked." She stroked the baby's soft cheek. "You saved her."

Angelina stirred and let out a frail whimper. Isobel recognized the reality of it all. The sacrifice, the loss, and the unbearable cost of this war etched themselves deep in her soul. She also saw the spark of resilience in the woman before her, the will to survive despite the impossible.

Isobel blinked hard, trying to keep the tears at bay, but Susannah's grief wrapped around her like a vise. "Can you tell us what you saw?"

Susannah shifted the babe in her arms. Isobel thought of taking her, but she knew her mother would never let her go. "Every night, the Mexicans fired their cannons at us. Every single night." The heft of her recollection was thick with exhaustion. "My baby couldn't sleep, none of us could. But the last night..." She hesitated, her lips pressed into a thin line. "The last night, they didn't fire. Not one shot."

She could hear Susannah's unspoken dread.

"We finally got some rest," Susannah whispered. "After all those nights of not sleepin', we thought maybe..." She shook her head, as if the thought itself were too foolish to finish.

"What happened next?" Isobel spoke softly, though the question screamed inside her head.

"They came while we slept." Her eyes fell to the child. "They reached the walls before anyone knew. Screamin', shootin', men firin' as fast as they could load. It was so ... loud. It went on forever."

Isobel suffered the image of the young mother who clutched her little one while smoke thickened, explosions shook the ground, and agonizing screams rose from men on both sides as they fought and died. "And after the battle?" Her query was gentle. "Did they let y'all leave?"

Susannah hugged her daughter tighter while the lass squirmed in her grasp. "A Mexican officer found us in the sacristy. He saved us, told his *soldados* not to harm the women and children." She stammered. "But he couldn't save Angelina's daddy. Nobody could."

Sam stood behind them, silent, his face unreadable. Isobel didn't need to see him to know he'd carry this forward, turn it into a useful lesson. But right now, all that mattered was the shattered woman before her and the unbearable force of survival that pressed on them both.

Susannah's words rose above the wind. "A Mexican colonel, Almonte, I think, saved me, Joe, and a Tejana woman named Ana. Kept the *soldados'* bayonets off us. Said Santa Anna wanted to see us, so he took us to him the next day."

Isobel heard the words, but her eyes caught something glinting in the dusk. She took a step closer. Her pulse began to hammer. The light flashed on it again. There was a ring tied to a leather strand around Angelina's neck.

Cold recognition smashed her.

She knew the ring. Had seen it on the hand of a man who once sat in the corner of Peyton's Tavern and shuffled dominoes like he hadn't a care in the world. A man whose absence now cut deeper than she could bear.

"Mind if I ask where she got that?" Isobel motioned toward the jewelry.

A shadow passed over Susannah's face. "It belonged to the garrison commander, William Travis." She shuddered. "He took it off his finger, tied it 'round Angelina's neck. Said he didn't want no *soldado* wearin' it."

The words landed like a kick to the gut.

Buck was dead. Jim was dead. Every man from Gonzales was gone.

The ring struck like fresh trauma to her heart, showing there was no end to the madness.

She couldn't fall apart now. She swallowed the lump in her throat and forced herself to focus. "Santa Anna talked with y'all?"

Susannah gave a slight tilt of her head. The corner of her mouth twitched, but it was too bitter to be relieved. "Didn't speak English, but Colonel Almonte does. Santa Anna offered to take Angelina to Mexico City. Said he'd educate her in the best schools." Her jaw clenched. "I was too stunned to cuss him, but I turned him down. He gave me two *pesos*. Two *pesos* for killin' my husband. Like he could make it right." She paused and remembered something else. "Ana, the Tejana with me got the same. But he didn't offer to take her little boy, Enrique. Tossed her two *pesos* and an army blanket for her troubles."

Isobel bit the inside of her cheek. "Did you see her again?"

She shook her head. "No. He sent us away."

Isobel's heart ached at the thought of Ana, alone and forgotten. "Do you know her husband's name?"

Susannah replied, "Gregorio Esparza. Last Texian to enter the Alamo. He came in with her and the kids. Enrique is the boy I know."

Sam stirred beside them. "He was one of Juan Seguin's men. Fought Cos in the streets."

She took her hand. "So, y'all walked away?"

Susannah's shoulders sagged. "Yep. Colonel Almonte told his cook, Ben, to go with us. Him and Joe... they took care of us the whole way. Could've left us anytime, but they didn't. They stayed loyal." She paused. "I'll never forget them."

The gratitude softened her words, but it didn't erase the deeper hurt. Isobel glanced at the baby, her tiny fingers curled around the leather strand holding Buck's ring. The memory of it seared into her heart.

Isobel's hands clenched into fists again, and her resolve turned to iron. There would be no turning away from this war, no shrinking back. For Buck. For Jim. For Susannah and Angelina. For Ben and Joe. For all of them. There was tyranny *or* there was liberty. *Where the Spirit of the Lord is, there is liberty.*

Her throat burned as she leaned closer to Susannah. "I know it's hard, but what did Santa Anna do with the bodies?"

She shuddered like the memory had returned in full. "He made me... made me pick out Bowie, Crockett, and Travis." Her hands quivered. "He ordered all the Texians piled up and set 'em ablaze. Two hundred men, burnin' like a common brush pile." She shook her head. "Like they was trash." She stumbled over the words, but she pushed on. The horror poured out of her. "They started mixin' 'em together, Texians and Mexicans, 'cause they couldn't tell 'em apart. But the *soldados*, bein' Catholic, they wouldn't have it. Went to great pains to pull their own dead for proper burial."

Isobel's stomach churned, bile rose in as she imagined the macabre scene. The acrid smell of burnt flesh, the cries of the women and children, the sheer inhumanity of it all descended on her.

Sam's question broke through the haze of her imagination. "Anything else, Mrs. Dickinson?"

She dipped her head and closed her eyes, as if the images played on the folds of her mind. "Afterwards, he paraded his army 'round town, like he'd conquered the King of England. Pompous, vain man." She spat on the ground.

He lowered his chin, his face unreadable, but his eyes sharp. "Thank ya kindly for sharin' this with us, ma'am. We owe you a debt." He paused and observed her. "Somethin' more?"

She shifted her eyes to him. "You're General Houston?"

"I am."

Her expression changed from disgust to admiration, mixed with concern. "Santa Anna said to tell you he's gonna kill you and everyone else who stands in his way. He *hates* you, General Houston."

Sam declared grimly, "I can promise you, ma'am, the feelin's mutual. We will avenge your husband and all the heroes of the Alamo."

Susannah drifted into the arms of her Gonzales neighbors. The women clung to each other, bound by loss, their silent grief heavier than words. Thirty-two men had gone to the Alamo. None returned. Isobel stood nearby, the pain nearly crushing her.

Sam pulled her back. "Isobel." The word landed with quiet urgency, but no harshness. "Make sure our widows get somethin' to eat. Tell 'em to take whatever they can carry from their homes. We're burnin' the town. Can't leave a thing for the Mexicans. They'll cross the Colorado with us, and we'll set the ferry ablaze once we're over."

She bowed her head. Burning what little these women had left was cruelty atop sorrow. She answered, though her heart ached for them. "Yes, sir. I'll see to 'em."

She hesitated, a question pressed against her ribs. She looked into his eyes. "What kind of man kills two hundred men without a shred of mercy and hands widows two *pesos* for their loss?"

Sam's face darkened. He kicked at the dirt beneath him. "The kind who needs killin'."

The words lingered, cold and final, as Isobel stood rooted to the spot. She was awash in a sea of blood. She reached down and drew her knife. *The kind who needs killin'.*

CHAPTER FORTY-EIGHT

March 29, 1836
"The Runaway Scrape"
Gonzales to San Felipe de Austin, Republic of Texas

The din of the Colorado River filled Isobel's ears as she stood on the bank, smoke from the burning ferry thick around her. Sam's plan was working. It was a maddening, brilliant game of chase keeping Santa Anna's forces stumbling over their own frustration. She gripped the reins of her horse, Dream, fixing her eyes on the reflection of the flames as they danced in the current.

"Burned their path, didn't we, girl?" Isobel muttered. She cast a glance back at all the people huddled on the east side. Women, most widows, clutched their children tight, faces pale beneath soot-streaked brows. Soldiers adjusted their packs, muskets slung, weariness etched into every movement.

Sam thundered, his broad shoulders square, his command carrying over the people. "Keep movin'! We make Beason's by nightfall. Sherman's men'll meet us there."

Isobel pressed her lips thin. Another march. Another crossing. She'd heard whispers among the troops. Grumblings echoed, sounding an awful lot like mutiny. Nobody wanted to retreat. Sam's strategy didn't look anything like a charge at Santa Anna. It looked like something else, but she trusted him with her life and the life of Texas.

He rode up to her and took a long swig from his canteen. "Time for growth." He put the cork back in. "Every step east, we grow stronger. The enemy grows weaker."

"Men are belly-achin', General." She held the reins a little tighter.

He laughed. "A soldier's right."

She stroked Dream's neck. "We're countin' on you."

"You talkin' to me or the pony?"

She looked up at him, so tall in the saddle. "Both. All our dreams are teeterin' on the edge. I'm not countin' all the lives already lost." She patted her horse again. "We can't squander this."

Sam's eyes fixed on the flames. Of course, he was thinking about the Alamo—she could see it in the way his jaw tensed, in the silence that stretched too long. "I don't know what's keepin' Fannin. I have a bad feelin' about him." He shook his head. "We ain't gonna waste anything. I know these men want to turn and fight now. The hardest part of this whole strategy is controlling their passions. We gotta keep movin' east. We'll engage Santa Anna on ground of our own choosin'."

Dream's restless snort matched the tension around them. She patted the mare and looked back at Sam. "We're dependin' on you to get us to the enemy."

Her words filled the space between them. Sam's speech was low and firm as he delivered his orders. "I sent Moseley Baker to defend San Felipe." He shook his head. "It's a token defense, nothin' more. If the Mexicans come, he's gotta torch it, every inch of it. Ain't leavin' em anything they can use to get across the Brazos. Burn it all."

The finality of it struck her like a jab to the ribs. "Set the whole town alight?" The words came out sharper than she meant. "Includin' Mr. McFarland's ferry?"

"Yes, ma'am." He met her astonishment with steel in his stare. "Get everyone beyond the river. Touch off anything capable of floating.

Kelvin's headed to Groce's Ferry to meet us. He's bringin' two artillery pieces from Cincinnati. Your friends there came through for us."

"Well, it's somethin', at least." Her throat cracked. "I'll see you on the other side of the Brazos."

Sam leaned closer. "Be wary. Their army could be anywhere. They're marchin' in this direction."

Isobel gripped the reins tighter. "I'll be careful, General. You do the same."

Sam's eyes lingered on her for a moment. "You know what I want?"

"I know." She didn't wait for more. She gave Dream a quick slap on the flank. The horse lunged forward, hooves tearing into the earth as they raced toward San Felipe. The wind tore at her hair, but she hadn't noticed. The images of her San Felipe friends consumed her mind.

Her hand slid to the treasured Bowie knife at her belt, the cool metal grounding her. If she met Mexican troops before reaching the settlement, she'd handle it as her general trusted her to do.

San Felipe churned with chaos, the atmosphere choked with smoke and panic. She pressed her knees to Dream's flanks, urging the mare forward. She wove through clusters of people who scattered in all directions. Men shouted orders over the vibration of crashing timbers and hurried footsteps. The village had already begun to surrender to the flames.

Moseley Baker stood in the smoky street, a commanding figure amid the frenzy, his face grim and set.

She guided Dream closer. She remained steady, even as a knot formed in her stomach. "What's happenin', sir?"

He glanced at her, his focus locked on the destruction. "I'm puttin' it to the torch." He pointed to a building engulfed in fire. "Started with my own office. Santa Anna's approachin'."

She frowned and scanned the horizon as if enemy cavalry might emerge from the haze. "I didn't see any signs of the Mexican army, sir. Are you sure they're near?"

"Don't matter how close he is." His cadence was rough with frustration. "Orders are orders. General Houston wants the place burned, and we'll leave nothin' behind they can use. Now get to it if you're helpin'."

She clenched her jaw, looking past him at the collapsing buildings and scattered belongings that littered the streets. She swallowed, quieter now. "Stephen Austin would be heartbroken to see this." She shook her head. "His life's work, gone up in flames."

Baker's expression softened, but only for a beat. "Not only his." He gestured to the burning community. "This is everyone's life's work goin' under the torch. It's a hard night for all of us."

Hard wasn't the right word. The burden of what they were losing— what they were leaving behind—closed in like a noose pulling tighter around her neck. But there was no time to dwell. She dug her heels into the mustang, steering the mare toward Peyton's Tavern, where the ghosts of home still lingered—familiar, hollow, and aching to be mourned.

She reached it and dismounted in one fluid motion. She tied Dream to a post outside. Smoke stung her eyes and throat as she shoved the door open. She yelled through the roaring flames. "Angelina!"

"I'm here!" Isobel started to breathe again as she spotted her in the dim light. The woman clutched a bundle of salvaged items, her face streaked with tears and soot. "Tryin' to save some valuables, but it's no use."

Isobel stepped closer. "Let me help. I can take you and some of your things."

She shook her head, her eyes hollow with exhaustion. "I think I got all I can take." The fires came to life around them.

Isobel hesitated but gave a brisk order. "Stay here, I'll be right back."

Her boots pounded against the dirt as she sprinted toward Buck Travis's law office, her heart racing faster than her legs could carry her. Smoke clung to her throat, burning her lungs with every frantic gasp. She reached the door and pushed it, the light of the growing flames outside casting flickering shadows across the room.

The sight of Buck's desk was like a beacon. She darted to it, and her fingers flew over the cluttered surface. Stacks of paper drifted to the floor as she grabbed the bundle of land grant documents Buck had been working on. She yanked open a drawer and rifled through its contents until her fingers brushed against something familiar.

"The dominoes," she whispered, then louder, "The dominoes!" Her lungs burned, her hands trembling as she pulled out the worn pouch. She cradled it for a fleeting moment before she shoved it into the satchel with the papers. This was no time for sentiment. Not now. She bolted back to Dream, where Angelina stood, her face pale beneath the streaks of soot.

Angelina looked at the flames as they licked closer. "We gotta get to the ferry! The fires are everywhere." She coughed, struggling to get the smoke out of her lungs. "I didn't think this place could go up so fast."

Isobel lifted her chin and swung herself onto Dream's back. Angelina scrambled up behind her, grabbing hold of the saddle. Isobel urged the horse into a full gallop.

Buildings blurred past in a whirl of black clouds and flames. Empty streets stretched before them, abandoned by the inhabitants, claimed by the fire. Angelina craned her neck around Isobel and looked ahead. "We're almost out." San Felipe, the proud little outpost that had once bustled with life as the colonial capital of Texas, was now a hollow, burning shell.

At the riverbank, a long column of people crowded near the ferry. Their faces reflected the haunting glow of the flames. The heat pressed against their backs like a living thing and goaded them forward. Dream skidded to a halt when they reached the landing. Isobel jumped down, tugging the reins to steady the anxious horse. They got in line.

McFarland's throat was hoarse from all the yelling. He motioned to the women. "Get on, both of you!"

Angelina gripped his arm as she climbed aboard. "We're the last ones, John. Nobody's left." Her speech broke and tears flowed down her cheeks.

His face twisted with pain, but he gave a short dip of his head. When the craft reached the opposite bank, Isobel looked back. She scanned the blazing village one final time. The river mirrored the inferno, the flames dancing like specters across the water's surface. San Felipe was no more, swallowed whole by the firestorm.

Isobel turned to him. "You know what you have to do."

His eyes grew watery, his heart fixed on the vessel that had carried so many to their dreams. Now, he hoped it had conveyed them to safety. "I do." His words were heavy with resignation. "But it ain't easy."

"We stand together, John." Angelina used the kind of words that quieted storms. "The pain's not yours alone. We all bear it. Santa Anna will feel it soon enough."

McFarland inclined his head and struck the torch against the ferry's wooden frame. Fire burst to life, devouring the vessel with crackling ferocity. Flames lashed outward like ravenous wolves consuming their helpless prey. The people watched in solemn silence. Tears ran down their faces, the light of the burning ferry showing in their swollen eyes.

Isobel turned away, her chest tightening as she led Dream into the night. With each step, the conflagration's roar faded, the sounds of the people growing louder. She gritted her teeth. The bitter taste of loss filled her mouth and mingled with the steady resolve of her heart. Santa Anna would stumble. When he did, General Houston would strike like a lion.

"I aim to kill him with my own hands." Angelina's declaration was steady, the fire in her eyes hotter than San Felipe's inferno.

Isobel didn't reply right away. Instead, she reached for her belt and drew her Bowie knife. The steel caught the flicker of firelight and gleamed like a promise. She turned the blade over in her hand and ran her thumb along the edge to test its sharpness.

A faint pull tugged at her lips, cold and resolute. "Jim gave me this knife." Her murmur was quiet but unshakeable. "He meant to give it to Ursula. Now both of them are dead." The memory of her friends flashed through her mind. She tightened her grip. The leather-wrapped handle fit snug against her palm. "And I know exactly what I'm gonna do with it."

CHAPTER FORTY-NINE

April 14, 1836
East Bank Brazos River
Groce's Ferry, Republic of Texas

The sun beat down on Groce's, the river flashing each time a boat crossed. The scrape of poles against boat hulls rang in Isobel's ears as steady as a heartbeat. For two weeks, the land had hummed with the murmur of soldiers and the clang of steel. Men drilled. Their numbers rose like the tide.

She scanned the lines, but there was no sign of Kelvin.

The camp bustled, the march east imminent. The atmosphere tightened, like an arrow notched and ready to fly. A sharp jolt ran through her when she caught sight of him, flanked by S.F. Sparks and Howard Bailey. Her heart took a wild leap, but she stayed put, hands pressed firmly at her sides.

Kelvin cut through the camp's noise with the rich, easy pride of a man who had brought home a prize. He motioned toward the cannons his companions dragged behind them. The brilliant bronze barrels caught the light and gleamed like fire. "The general'll be mighty glad to see these here pieces." A grin tugged at his face the way it had when they were young, before war stretched the world much wider.

Sparks, speech thick with Texas grit, lifted his chin in sharp agreement. "We lost near all our artillery at the Alamo. Reckon these'll give us some teeth again."

Bailey slapped a cannon's side, the thump solid as his calloused hand. "The *Twin Sisters* pack a punch. Hauled 'em all the way from Galveston without a scratch."

Kelvin chuckled, the sound rolling over Isobel like the Brazos current. "My wife oughtta be 'round camp somewhere." His suggestion sent her stomach into a tumble. "Ain't seen her for a spell. Be nice to set eyes on her again."

The army surged to life. Excitement swept through it like a flame in dry grass. Soldiers waded in the river, their shouts rising above the steady murmur of the water. The cannons shone in the Texas sun, full of promise and vengeance.

But Isobel saw only him.

She stood beneath the shade of a pecan tree. The strong line of his shoulders held her attention as he spoke to the men near the crossing. Sunlight lit the top of his hair, and for a moment, the noise of the camp faded away. He stood strong and sure, as if the whole weight of Texas could rest on his back and he'd bear it without a complaint. Her chest tightened, not with fear, but with something fierce and quiet— love, full-grown and rooted deep.

Her heart pounded, loud enough she feared he'd hear it.

She smoothed her clothes out of habit, tension coiled tight. It wasn't the reunion she'd pictured, not the quiet moment by the river she'd dreamed of, but none of it mattered now. He was here. Safe.

She moved through the crowd, eyes locked on his broad shoulders.

Kelvin scanned the swelling ranks of troops, eyes searching. His face flickered with something. Doubt? Surprise? He looked at her. It was in his eyes. She knew he was still hers.

Men swarmed the cannons. They clapped and hooted.

"Calm down, boys." Bailey waved them off like a cowboy shooing restless colts. "Don't go breakin' 'em. They came all the way from Cincinnati with nary a scrape."

Isobel crossed her arms and lifting her exclamation above the noise. "Bout time y'all got back. I've been run ragged keepin' things together. The general's pullin' volunteers from all over."

Her words came out steady. Her hands, not so much.

Kelvin's face softened as his eyes met hers, the world around them faded. Without a word, he closed the distance. His eyes held something far deeper than any greeting.

She tensed for a moment as he embraced her and pulled her close. Their lips met in a kiss filled with weeks of longing, sleepless nights, and every danger war could muster. She melted into him, gripping his worn buckskin coat, afraid he might vanish if she released him.

The cheers broke over them. She heard the good-natured hollering, the mirth tinged with yearning, but it all drifted past, distant, like a dream she couldn't quite enter. The men might have cheered for the kiss, but Isobel knew better. They applauded for their own memories, for the wives and sweethearts they left behind, for a moment of hope amidst so much loss.

She didn't want to let him go, didn't want to break the fragile bubble of safety his embrace offered. She hungered for him more than she could ever say, more than even he could know.

When he pulled back, he was quiet, rough-edged. "I love you."

She managed a shaky response. "Oh, how I love you and missed you."

His expression faded into something more familiar. "I'm sorry, Isobel." He dropped his head. "The general's stallion slowed me down. Saracen made it from Galveston safe, though. And the *Twin Sisters* are here too."

She raised her eyebrows. "*Twin Sisters?*"

He motioned to the cannons. "Two six pounders. Gifts from our good friends in Cincinnati."

Relief swept through her like a summer storm, sudden and unstoppable. Tears she hadn't allowed herself to cry streamed down her cheeks. "You're here. I can't believe it."

He chuckled, his hand brushing a strand of her hair. "You act like I'd let something keep me away."

She loved his sincerity. She looked at the big guns as their polished bronze caught the sun. She tilted her head in wonder. "We gotta make a trip to Ohio when this is done." She moved her hands over the barrels. "Thank Josef and all the good folks there. These beauties might shift the balance in our favor."

Kelvin looked up and down the river. "Did Fannin get here yet?"

Isobel paused, gathering her thoughts before she spoke. The hardness of the news pressed on her. She hadn't wanted to say it. Not when his eyes held so much hope after weeks apart. "Kel... Colonel Fannin surrendered at Goliad."

His brow furrowed, his body going still as he braced for the rest. She couldn't look away, though she wished to. "Santa Anna ordered all the prisoners to be executed." Her throat tightened. "Without mercy. Over four hundred men... murdered."

His eyes darkened, the light in them extinguished in an instant. She saw the pain settle into his face like a shadow. "All of them?"

"Every last one." Her fingers trembled. "James Fannin, too. They made him watch, Kel."

The silence suffocated her. It was broken only by the faint sound he made as he tried to take it all in.

"Executions aren't war." His words were cold and sharp. "They're butchery."

She gave a small dip of her chin as tears stung her eyes. "It's why we can't lose. Not now. Not ever. There's no surrender. It's like Buck said, 'Victory or Death.'"

A familiar nicker sounded behind her, and she turned. Saracen nudged his way through the crowd, his dark eyes wide with recognition. Something passed between them—Maryland and Washington City, all of it still alive in that look. Isobel reached into her pouch and pulled out a handful of corn she'd meant for Dream.

The stallion lowered his head to accept her offering. His tongue tickled her palm as he ate, his gratitude almost human.

Kelvin's face softened. "Even Saracen missed you."

She wiped her tears on her sleeve, her heart lifting with a quiet but steady hope. For the first time in weeks, she thought the pieces were falling into place.

She rested her hand on Saracen's sleek neck. His coat shimmered like polished copper in the late afternoon sun. Her fingers brushed a lock of mane away from his brow. She squinted at Kelvin. "He's a beautiful steed, ain't he? No wonder the general prizes him so."

His expression was quick, full of light, carrying affection and pride as he stroked his own horse's muzzle. "He is, but my Skipper keeps up with him on the trail, no trouble at all."

Isobel giggled. "Skipper's a good boy, too." Her happiness faded as her mind turned to the darker moments of recent days. "Kel, I put Dream in harm's way."

His brows knitted closer, concern etched into his face. "What happened?"

"We went to San Felipe." She shuddered. "They needed help evacuatin'. The whole town was burnin', and Santa Anna's troops weren't far behind. Angelina rode with me to the landing. We were the last to leave."

He rubbed his eyes. "Did everyone get out?"

She lowered her chin. "We took Mr. McFarland's ferry to the other side." She shook her head as if the gesture would stop the destruction. "Then we burned it. It was horrible."

His jaw set in a hard line. "Did you save anything?"

"I managed to grab some of Buck's legal papers, things he was workin' on." Isobel continued with a bittersweet timbre. "And his dominoes." For a moment, she could almost hear the click of the tiles and Buck's deep laugh.

He fixed his eyes on her. "That's somethin'." His voice dropped, weighed down by the question he needed to ask. "I heard... Santa Anna killed everyone in *Béxar*. Is it true?"

She looked away. "Yes, to the last man."

His face darkened, and he clenched his hands. "Like Goliad."

She moved her head up and down in slow agreement.

He cast his look downward. "The general always said Fannin was ill-fated. Never went to Gonzales…What was the man thinkin'? Guess we'll never know." His words trailed off, heavy with regret for the lives lost.

"Ma'am," Bailey interrupted them. "Can you please take us to General Houston? We've got information he needs to hear."

She straightened and brushed the dirt from her dress. "Follow me."

She led them through the camp toward the Groce home. The house loomed ahead, a haven of activity as soldiers came and went with messages and supplies. Inside, Sam stood bent over the table, his tall frame hunched as he studied maps and notes scattered across its surface.

Isobel stepped forward. "Kelvin's back, General. He's with two other men who have urgent news."

His piercing eyes met hers. "Excellent. Show them in, please."

She moved aside and let Kelvin and the others pass, her pulse quickening as she lingered near the door. The room grew smaller as they gathered around the cluttered tabletop.

Kelvin didn't waste a second. "General, I have your horse, and these men have your six pounders. But most importantly, they have a crucial letter for you."

Sparks and Bailey came forward and shook Sam's hand with firm grips. They recounted their trek. They painted vivid scenes of the rugged journey from Galveston to Harrisburg. Sam listened, his eyes brightening at the mention of the cannons.

Sparks leaned in. "We came 'cross a free Negro ferry man. He gave us a note for you."

"Let's have it." His command was crisp.

Sparks fished into his coat and handed it over. Sam unfolded it and read it aloud. "Mr. Houston: I know you're up there hiding in the bushes. As soon as I catch the other land thieves, I'm coming up there to smoke you out."

The words hovered like a storm cloud. Sam's brow arched. "Did the man say who the message was from?"

Bailey replied roughly, "Santa Anna himself."

Sam's lips curled into something between a snarl and a smirk. "The arrogant maniac made his fatal mistake."

Isobel couldn't hold back. "Where did he cross the Brazos?"

Bailey didn't hesitate. "Fort Bend."

Sam rubbed his hands together. "Thanks to the folks who burned their homes and ferry at San Felipe, Santa Anna lost valuable time." He counted on his fingers. "Maybe four days. He had to split his army and follow the river all the way to Fort Bend and cross. The 'other land thieves' are the officers of the government meetin' in Harrisburg, I reckon. If we break camp now, we might catch him flat-footed."

Isobel's pulse raced. "You told us he'd make a mistake."

Sam turned to her, a fire burning behind his eyes. "He fancies bein' the 'Napoleon of the West'. That part of Texas is brimmin' with rivers, bayous, marshes, snakes, gators, and the biggest dang mosquitoes the Lord ever put on this earth. He's gonna find himself bound up with no place to turn." He noticed puzzled looks. "Remember Cornwallis at Yorktown? Washington won our independence 'cause Cornwallis got stuck on a peninsula. If we make our move, we can catch Santa Anna makin' the same mistake. This man's arrogance knows no bounds."

Isobel stepped closer. "May I see the message, General?"

He unfolded the paper and gave it to her. "Sure."

She examined the scrawled handwriting. Recognition prickled in her mind. "It matches the safe conduct note Ben, the Negro cook, had. It's in Colonel Almonte's hand."

He cocked his head. "Interesting."

She lifted her eyes to his. "I feel sorry for men like Almonte. I would bet he ain't too eager followin' Santa Anna's ways of murder and mayhem."

Sam said, "Perhaps, but his loyalty belongs to Mexico. Santa Anna uses all his subordinates like their lives don't count. It's where we'll find our edge."

Lines etched deep across his face. Isobel fingered the pommel of her knife. "He has no regard for anyone but himself. How can he trust anybody?"

Sam's remarks had a sharp rawness. "He trusts Almonte because he knows he's a good soldier who follows orders. The Mexican army's got officers who ain't happy with him turnin' 'em into executioners. General Castrillón, for one. He's a friend of our Vice President Lorenzo de Zavala's. It's a cryin' shame what Santa Anna's done to his own people."

Isobel's heart twisted at the thought of good men on both sides caught in the maniac's grasp. *A shame indeed. If there was only a way to reach* Castrillón *or Almonte.*

Before Isobel could say anything, Kelvin stepped forward. "Saracen's waitin' with your new artillery, General."

A faint gleam lit his eyes. "For the first time, it feels like we seized the advantage due to the madman's own arrogance. Saracen and those cannons comin' are sights worth cheerin'. No more wandering east without a plan." He paused, as his words landed with the prominence of prophecy. "We don't know the name of our battlefield yet. Santa Anna'll give it to us when we catch him. Make no mistake. We have a destination. We have a destiny."

The room vibrated with the impact of his declaration, and a spark ignited in Isobel's chest. She stepped forward, fists clenched, shouting with all the force she could muster. "Remember the Alamo! Remember Goliad!"

CHAPTER FIFTY

April 18, 1836
From the *Which Way Tree* to Harrisburg, Republic of Texas

The storm lashed Isobel's face with cold needles. Her soaked hair whipped in the wind, slapping her face. She gritted her teeth and led Dream through the mire. Her clothes hung heavy with water and mud, the soggy ground sucking her boots with every step. Her muscles burned after fifty-five miles in two days. The *Twin Sisters* rattled behind her with a constant grinding burden that never let up.

Ahead, voices rose through the downpour. Isobel blinked against the weather, swiping wet strands from her cheek. Mrs. Pamela Mann stood firm near the cannons, one hand gripping the yoke of her oxen, the other holding a knife.

"No, General." Her reply rang clear, sharp as a blade. "They're mine. My children need them more than your soldiers do."

Sam towered a few paces away. Rain dripped from his hat. "Pamela, the *Twin Sisters* are vital to the cause." He dragged a weary hand across his face. "We could sure use them."

She didn't flinch. With one quick motion, she sliced through the

286

traces that bound her animals to the artillery. The wet snap of leather sent a sick twist through Isobel's gut.

"Those cannons won't matter if my babies starve." She gripped the reins tighter. "You've used them up 'til now, but the women are turning north. You're goin' south. I've done my part. You'll have to find another way." Without a backward glance, she clicked her tongue and led the beasts away into the storm.

Her footsteps faded, and his shoulders sagged. Rain streaked his face like tears he'd never let fall. Something flickered in his eyes—frustration, maybe despair—but he didn't call her back. Didn't argue. His jaw tightened as he turned to the slog ahead.

Isobel clenched her fists. She wanted to say something, anything, to ease the sting of another loss, but what words could change the truth? Some of the women who turned north to Nacogdoches had already given their husbands and sons at the Alamo.

Mrs. Mann was right.

So, she said nothing. Instead, she stepped forward into the opposing wind. If Sam wouldn't beg, neither would she. They'd drag those cannons if they had to, one agonizing step after another. The army turned south.

The cannon's wheel sunk deep into the muck again. Sam swung down from his horse without hesitation. His boots sunk into the mud. He didn't clutch his injured shoulder, didn't flinch in front of the men. He braced his good arm against the wooden spoke and shoved as his muscles strained with effort.

Isobel looped a rope around her saddle horn and nudged Dream forward. Her pony was no ox, but every bit helped. Other horses strained and men heaved. The weight of the guns drug them down like anchors. The aches in her back and legs screamed, but she pushed it aside. Each time a wheel bogged down, it was another battle they couldn't afford to lose.

They'd drag the *Twin Sisters* to face Santa Anna's Legion, or the mud would swallow them whole.

By the time they stumbled into Harrisburg, the army was hollow-eyed and bone-weary. Isobel's feet throbbed inside her sodden boots.

Her stomach gnawed at itself. She reached for her swollen tongue. It was caked with dirt.

She lifted her face to the rain showers. She hoped and prayed for relief. Perhaps an inn remained. Maybe somewhere a fire still burned.

A jolt stopped her cold. Harrisburg wasn't abandoned. It was gone.

Charred beams jutted skyward like blackened ribs from a corpse. Smoke curled through the ruins, thick and bitter as it clung to the wreckage. Ash covered everything and smudged the world in gray. She couldn't move. Couldn't speak.

Around her, men stood frozen, their faces pale beneath the grime. Silence settled over them, heavier than the rain-soaked sky. It was broken only by the creak of wagon wheels and the slow shuffle of boots.

"Santa Anna," Sam said, cutting through the hush. He didn't have to explain. The dictator's cruelty clung to everything—the blackened ruins, the hollow faces...the hiss of the damp ash beneath her feet.

She swallowed hard. She'd seen the burned shells before, smelled the acrid smoke, but this was different. It wasn't like the people who burned their own homes. This was spiteful retribution.

Sam shook his head. "He's rushin' for the coast." He said it loud enough for the men to hear. "Thinks we're chasing our tails east. Let him run." His eyes raked across them, solid as iron. "We're not runnin' anymore."

Isobel's heart stuttered. The shift came certain and quiet as a prayer. A new purpose settled over her like a mantle. Santa Anna was no longer the hunter. He just didn't know it...yet.

She tore her eyes from the ruins and hitched her pack higher. Exhaustion clawed at her, but she wouldn't allow it to win. Not now.

Hoofbeats echoed through the incinerated town.

"Riders comin' in, General." Kelvin tipped his hat toward the figures as they emerged through the smoke. "Reckon it's Deef Smith and Henry Karnes. Looks like they mighta got themselves a prisoner."

Isobel's pulse quickened as she straightened. Her eyes focused on the trio. Between the scouts slumped a man, bound and hunched in the saddle. His fine uniform was smeared with dirt, and his face was pinched with fear and resentment.

Sam motioned to Lorenzo de Zavala, Jr., as he stood near a cannon. "Please." The young man wiped his hands on his trousers and readied himself to translate.

The captive rattled off rapid Spanish. His words tumbled over each other. Lorenzo listened with a furrowed brow. "'*El Presidente*' is leading one wing. They're at New Washington now but headin' south. He's separated from the other wings of the army."

A ripple of dread ran through Isobel.

Sam went still as his exhaustion sharpened into something fiercer. "We gotta cross the bayou tonight." He was a rock. "We're worn down, but I've saved my speech for the right time. The time is now."

He strode toward a clearing amid the ruins. His boots crunched over debris. Isobel followed. Her heart pounded in anticipation.

"Gather round!" The men stumbled closer, their faces etched with fatigue. "We're crossin' Buffalo Bayou and meetin' the enemy head on. All of us *might* get killed. Some of us *will* get killed. But we ain't retreatin' no more." He measured them with a steady look.

Tension snapped through the ranks. He ordered a call to battle. "Y'all are soldiers of Texas! Remember the Alamo! Remember Goliad!"

A murmur stirred, then grew. "Remember the Alamo!"

It rolled through the formation and swelled into a roar. "Remember the Alamo!"

The words echoed in Isobel's ears and reverberated through her bones. She clenched her fists, her weariness forgotten. This wasn't about survival anymore. It was about vengeance. It was about justice. "Remember the Alamo!" The shriek burst from her throat, raw and fierce. It mingled with the shouts of Kelvin and every soldier around her. Her hand dropped to her knife, a tangible symbol of the battle cry, a promise made, and a prayer. She fingered the pommel of her weapon, ready.

The men clapped each other on the back, their grins wide despite the exhaustion etched into the lines of their faces. Energy sparked among them, cutting through the trail-worn weariness. It stirred something in Isobel too, low and strong.

Kelvin slung his musket over his shoulder. "Where are we headin', General?"

Sam answered, "Lynch's Ferry. 'His Excellency' is makin' for it. Even that arrogant twit might realize he's painted himself into a corner. If we get there first, he's doomed."

Isobel looked at the prisoner. He stood stiff between the escorts. His face was unreadable, and his shoulders were tight. He was not some poor, conscripted Indian soldier thrown into battle as cannon fodder. No, this man was different. Sharper. A professional.

His blue uniform was in stark contrast to the mud, the red trim still vivid despite the grime. The brass buttons gleamed, each stamped with an eagle that clutched a snake. His frock was finer than anything her people wore.

Her eyes drifted to his horse. The saddlebags didn't match his uniform. They looked familiar, a detail tugged at the margins of her memory. Isobel stepped closer. She brushed her fingers across the worn leather.

Then she saw it.

A gasp caught in her lungs, and her hand froze over the etched words. Her lips moved, but no sound came out. *No. It couldn't be.*

"Kelvin!" Her call cracked. "Kelvin, come here!"

He was at her side in an instant as his boots kicked up mud. "What is it?"

Wordlessly, she pointed. Her hand hovered over the leather like it might burn her.

Kelvin squinted, tension flaring across his face. His throat bobbed as he swallowed hard.

"William Barret Travis."

CHAPTER FIFTY-ONE

April 20, 1836
First Day, Battle of San Jacinto
Lynch's Ferry, Republic of Texas

The rain-soaked earth squelched underfoot as the column halted, and Kelvin's triumphant shout pierced the dampness. "We made it. We beat Santa Anna to the landin'. We trapped the rabid dog!"

Isobel tightened her grip on Dream's reins, her boots sinking into the muck. "Should we attack now, General?" Her pulse drummed with the thrill of the chase.

He gave a faint shake of his head. "He ain't goin' nowhere. No need to rush in."

Kelvin paced a few steps. "We raced all night to get here. Now we're supposed to wait?"

"That don't sound right." The words tumbled out of Isobel's mouth. She hated waiting. Action was her answer to everything.

Sam took on a storytelling lilt. "Y'all 'member what our kin did in Scotland at Prestonpans?"

Isobel blinked. The name tugged at a dim memory. Scots against the English, a British defeat. But the details? Out of reach. She shook her head, frustrated.

Kelvin's face lit up. "Yeah. The British got stuck with a marsh at their backs, and a Highland charge routed 'em."

Sam touched the brim of his hat in agreement. "Right. They fired their muskets and cannons, covering the field in smoke. When they charged through it, the English broke. Took fifteen minutes."

Kelvin darkened. "But the English got wise when they tried it again at Culloden."

"Aye," Sam replied. "It only works once." He paused and asked, "Y'all know my father died young?"

She glanced at Kelvin. They both answered in unison. "We know."

Sam continued. "He was a major in Morgan's Sharpshooters in the Revolution. Told me about King's Mountain."

The name stirred a memory in her, a flicker of old tales.

"I've heard of it." Kelvin carried a quiet pride. "Our fathers and grandfathers fought there. It was a devastatin' defeat for the Crown."

Sam agreed. "Yes. We got the same kinda of force here. The volunteers from Kentucky under Sherman can shoot. My daddy said a sharpshooter with a Tennessee long rifle took out the British commander from three hundred yards."

Isobel visualized such a shot with wide eyes. She could tell Kelvin thought the same as the look in his eyes mirrored her own amazement.

Sam softened but he didn't lose the significance of the moment. "We Americans had a lot of Scotsmen in our ranks who remembered Prestonpans. They grouped up in squads of twelve, like the huntin' parties of the clans from the old country. Their simple orders said each man was his own officer. They didn't wait for orders to fight."

The mention of Prestonpans sparked Isobel's imagination. Sam's belief in drawing strength from the past resonated with her. History wasn't just stories. It was a map and a guide. She asked, "You see Prestonpans and King's Mountain here?"

Sam replied, "I do."

Before Isobel could process an answer, Kelvin spoke up. "But,

General, the courier said Santa Anna ordered General Cos to reinforce him here. If we wait, Cos'll bring more men than we got."

Sam's expression didn't waver. "Let him come." The hair on Isobel's arms stood up as she considered the quiet power in his words. "Let Cos come. It just shows Santa Anna ain't a man of his word. Cos comin' here breaks the terms of his surrender in the first battle for *Béxar*. He ain't supposed to be in Texas. We can kill a thousand *soldados* as dead as five hundred."

The gravity of his words settled over her like the enormity of a prairie cyclone. Sam wasn't just leading them into battle. He carried the burden of their survival, their future.

Death hung heavy in Isobel's mind, as vivid as the red streaks of dawn breaking over the horizon. Sam spoke of a slaughter like it was inevitable, and maybe it was. Her stomach twisted at the thought of a thousand men cut down. She bowed her head low and saw the blood-soaked Texas mud.

Behold a pale horse: and his name that sat upon him was Death. And Hell followed him.

Isobel glanced at the soldiers around her. Their eyes simmered with the kind of anger that could only be ignited by betrayal and apocalyptic loss.

The Alamo. Goliad.

Names that tasted of ash and massacre.

Her own fury burned just as fiercely. Santa Anna's mockery of their grief, a paltry two-*peso* consolation for the slaughtered, had struck her like a cold slap in the face. Buck's stolen saddlebags from the Alamo reeked of powder and despair, bringing his nightmare closer than she wanted to admit. Angelina Peyton's determined face as she torched her own business seared itself into her memory like a red-hot branding iron.

She fingered the pommel of the Bowie knife at her side. Jim's face flashed in her mind, hollowed with grief as he'd pressed the weapon into her hand. She could still hear him whisper. *Stay alive, Isobel.* The knife weighed more now, as if it carried his sorrow. She drew the blade, remembering what and for whom she fought. Her hatred for

Santa Anna smoldered hotter than the fires that tore through San Felipe, Gonzales, and Harrisburg. She wouldn't let him win.

Movement on the horizon snapped her out of her thoughts. Deef Smith. His wiry frame moved with the easy confidence of a man who always brought answers. If anyone had news worth hearing, it was him. She strode toward him, her heart beating faster, half in anticipation, half in dread.

Smith gave a raspy report. "General, we captured a flatboat full of supplies, courtesy of 'His Excellency'."

Isobel stopped a few steps away, straining to catch every word.

Sam beamed. Isobel hadn't seen him with a smile on his face in a long time. "Good work, Deef. What's the cargo?"

"Mostly flour." Smith was upbeat, as if it was more than a small victory.

Flour. Her mouth watered. It had been days since she had eaten anything more than cold corn dodgers.

Sam chuckled and rubbed his hands together. "The men butchered beeves earlier. Have 'em make dough cakes, and we'll have a fine breakfast of roasted steak and bread."

Isobel's stomach growled, but her thoughts stuck on Smith. Supplies were a blessing, but not enough. Not yet. The fight ahead demanded more than a good meal. For now, she'd take what strength she could.

The smoky aroma of charred beef lingered as she sank her teeth into the hot roll wrapped around seared meat. It wasn't perfect, but after days of cold cornmeal mush, it tasted like heaven.

Kelvin sat nearby and tore into his food with the same fervor. Sam took his time as he chewed every morsel. A rare stillness settled over the camp.

She tensed. *Quiet never lasted.*

Hoofbeats smashed the peace like gunshots. Her head snapped up. Scouts barreled in as mud sprayed her. Their faces were covered by expressions that shouted urgency.

The lead rider didn't dismount. "General, we skirmished with some Mexicans near New Washington. Not far."

Sam rose to his feet, the sandwich forgotten. "Alright, y'all, grab your eatin' gear and save your chow. Pull back to the trees on the bayou bank. Move!"

The calm shattered.

Isobel grabbed her knife and what was left of her bread, heart pounding. Kelvin was beside her in an instant, jaw tight.

They fell in step with Sam as the camp scrambled back. Three quarters of a mile later, the forest swallowed them. The woods offered cover, but Isobel shot a glance toward the open field. Too exposed, too wide. *Not enough.*

They still held Lynch's Ferry. Still blocked the road to Vince's Bridge.

But for how long?

Sam barked orders. "Colonel Neill, put the Sisters in the open. I want 'His Excellency' to feast his eyes on his demise."

The gunnery crew muscled the guns into place. The barrels gleamed in the dappled sunlight as vengeance reared in her heart.

Isobel leaned back against an oak trunk, half-eaten bread in her lap, rough bark pressing into her shoulders. Around her, the men did the same and waited.

Sam's voice carried. "*El Presidente* ain't gonna sit easy with two cannons pointed at him. We're gonna play him like a two-*peso* fiddle." He lifted his eyebrows slightly.

Her irritation flared. The two *pesos* had come to symbolize everything she loathed about Santa Anna's outrages.

"Let's see how quick he dances to our tune, General."

Sam tapped his saddle horn once but said nothing. He mounted Saracen and rode to the edge of the tree line. She wiped her hands on her skirt as she tracked him with her eyes. From there, they couldn't see the entire expanse, but she could see the slope where the *soldados* camped. The prairie grass was thick and waved in the wind.

The waiting gnawed at her.

A cannon blast.

She flinched as debris rained down from above. Branches crashed to the ground, her body going still. Santa Anna's twelve-pounder, *El Volcán*, had fired.

Kelvin brushed splinters from his clothes. "Too close."

She forced a smirk. "Looks like the two-*peso* fiddle played on time."

Kelvin chuckled, but his hand stayed on his musket. She tightened the grip on her knife. The dance had begun.

A deafening crash of trees sent Isobel to her knees. Her heart slammed against her ribs as shattered limbs thudded into the mud beside her. She ducked, gripping the Bowie knife.

She forced herself upright and peered through the branches to her right, lungs working in uneven wheezes.

She saw it.

El Volcán, a hulking monster of iron, flanked by two ancient live oaks, dwarfing the *Twin Sisters*. The sinister, dark barrel shone in the early morning light.

Too close. Far too close.

Sam called out, sharp and steady, "Colonel Neill, you may return fire."

Neill didn't hesitate. He moved like a man with something to prove. *Maybe it was so.* First commander at the Alamo—forced to leave, haunted ever since.

Isobel's pulse pounded as the gunnery crew sprang into motion. They had drilled without powder, firing nothing but empty practice rounds, yet they operated with seamless precision.

The first Sister roared.

Isobel flinched, and her arms flew up as the blast split the stillness. The sheer force of it rattled through her body. Her stomach churned, knowing what they'd crammed down those barrels. Gunners fed broken horseshoes, rusted door hinges, chains, and cannonballs to the Sisters. They shredded Saracen's blanket for cartridge packets.

The second Sister followed. The earth trembled.

Her ears rang, and the world became a haze of smoke and fury. She lowered her arm. Her vision cleared enough to see Neill and his men as they worked through the swirling gray.

The pride in her chest was almost unbearable.

For the *first* time, Texian firepower had answered in response to Santa Anna's atrocities.

Kelvin hollered through the echoes of artillery fire. "What a shot, Colonel!"

Isobel turned to see the enemy artillery position thrown into chaos. Gunners scattered like startled quail as the Sisters' shots struck home.

But the relief was short-lived. A low boom echoed, and Isobel's stomach sank. *El Volcán* roared to life as its ordinance carved a brutal path through the camp.

Her world shattered. A gusty blast whooshed past her. The force of something massive just missed her. She heard screams. Agonized. Distressed. Wounded.

She spun as her heart hammered. *Where had it hit?*

Blood sprayed in a crimson arc and painted the battlefield with its brutality. Her mind raced. *Who?*

At last, she saw him.

Sam was down.

But the blood wasn't his.

Saracen writhed on the ground and pinned Sam beneath his immense weight. The stallion's bellows ripped through the woods. The sound was so raw, so full of pain, it buckled her knees.

She stumbled forward as her hands trembled. *Calm him. Help him.* But the bridle was gone, shattered by the cannon blast. Blood gushed from the gaping wound. Saracen's mighty heart pumped his life away with every wretched beat.

Isobel spotted her husband as he sprinted past. "Kelvin!" she yelled.

He drew his flintlock, face set like stone.

She followed, unable to stop what she knew came next.

Kelvin crouched beside Saracen and murmured something she couldn't hear over the throb in her ears. The horse's wild eyes met his, and for a moment, the stallion stilled. Acceptance flickered there. A final dignity.

He raised the pistol.

A shot rang out.

Isobel screamed. "No! Please, no!" She clutched her head as she covered her ears, but nothing could block out the reverberation of death. The wails wouldn't cease. The cries of men, the shrieks of the dying.

A new note. A human moan, sharp and raw.

She turned toward the Sisters, and her heart lurched.

The cannons stood firm.

Isobel crawled through the wreckage, choking on the smoke. She followed the noise until she found him.

Colonel Neill.

He thrashed on the ground. Blood pooled beneath him. The same shot which felled Saracen had torn through him and left a mangled ruin of flesh and agony. His pain mirrored the stallion's acute and sorrowful anguish.

A crushing stillness settled over her, suffocating and complete.

"Colonel." She whispered to him as she reached out with trembling hands. *Do something.* But what? Smoke thickened, screams sliced through the chaos. Helplessness pressed down and nearly suffocated her.

She closed her eyes. *Please, Lord. Help. Help us.*

She listened with her heart and found it.

The melody. *Her* melody.

Soft and tranquil, like an old friend. *Mercy.*

She leaned in and placed a shaky hand on his shoulder. "I'm here."

His ragged gasps steadied her. His fingers twitched and weakly guided her hand toward his hip. She swallowed hard as her fingertips found the wound. The shot had slashed through him. He clenched his jaw, the anguish consuming him.

"We'll get you out. You're not alone."

She turned and scanned the trees for help. "Kelvin!"

No answer.

There he was, bent low, as he worked to free Sam.

"Come on, General," Kelvin urged. "Hold on."

With one last heave, he hauled their leader from beneath Saracen's lifeless form.

A big gun roared. The ground heaved.

The blast threw her backward. Her dress snagged on splintered branches. The fabric ripped as she hit a tree, pain lancing through her shoulder. She gritted her teeth and shoved herself up. She surveyed the field.

The prairie stretched before her, and its golden grass rippled under the brutal sun. Now, it was marred by war.

She tracked the Sisters' latest shot. Smoke curled around the Mexican cannon. The massive barrel sagged, its carriage ruined. One of the *soldados* lay motionless, the others scrambled in confusion.

They'd done it. They silenced the monster.

"Isobel!" Kelvin's shout yanked her back. He and Sam stood by the twin guns, Sam barked orders to steady the crew. She comforted Neill, though her lungs tightened with each passing moment.

"George." Sam yelled over the din. George Hockley, Neill's second in command, stepped forward. "You're in charge now. Keep 'em firing. We need the edge."

Hockley's face was grim. "They'll perform, General. You have my word."

Neill raised his head. "Take care of them," he rasped. "And yourself."

Hockley knelt beside him and gripped his hand. "You've done your part. We'll take it from here."

They lifted him as gentle as the chaos allowed. Each step toward the bayou was heavier than the last. Isobel glanced back as her heart swelled. The Sisters still stood. They discharged fire and lead across the prairie.

Sam's command rang out. "Get the wounded to the Zavala house." Lorenzo, Jr., would ferry them over the water.

Neill disappeared into the trees. *Please, Lord, let him live.*

The sudden stillness jarred her as the world froze. She heard hoofbeats.

Colonel Sidney Sherman galloped into the camp, urgency in his eyes. "General, the Mexicans are pullin' their twelve-pounder back. My boys can take it."

Sam's jaw tightened. "It's not a retreat. Their cavalry's coverin' the move. You charge now, you'll get cut down."

Sherman bristled. "My men smell a rout."

Sam turned sharp. "You charge, you own the consequences."

Sherman's face darkened, but he wheeled his horse and rode back.

The cry of his troopers erupted moments later. Isobel pressed a hand to her chest. *This is wrong.* A string pulled too tight, ready to snap.

From her vantage point, she saw it unfold. She heard the thunder of hooves as the Texians surged forward. For a heartbeat, it looked like victory. Then the Mexican cavalry descended, fast and brutal.

The militia faltered. Gunfire cracked and screams split the battlefield.

Isobel dug her nails into her palms. She turned to Sam. His face was a mask, but it was there in his eyes. *He knew.*

"They're fallin' apart," she murmured.

Sam didn't look at her. "He's repeatin' Goliad. Four hundred souls slaughtered because someone thought boldness alone was enough."

Smoke thickened and obscured the lines. Isobel strained to see as the noise pressed in. Shots, the clash of iron, and mournful cries assaulted her ears. She gripped her knife. The cold steel grounded her.

She saw a sudden shift and more riders.

M. B. Lamar and his squad barreled forward and drug Sherman's forces back from the brink. Through sheer grit, they disengaged and retreated into the trees.

Kelvin exhaled beside her. "I hope they know how lucky they are, General."

"They do *not*," Sam said, exasperated. "If those dragoons had pressed, they'd have wiped us out. I know what I'm doin' here, but the men..." His eyes lingered on the field. "They're too riled up. Nobody can calm 'em this close to their quarry."

Isobel followed his gaze, her eyes narrowing at the distant Mexican camp. The faint strains of music drifted across the field and chilled her to the core. It was coming from Santa Anna's band. She'd never encountered the tune before. It was the opposite of the fiddler's refrain she knew so well. This one was of death, the other of abundant life.

Sam hardened. "*Degüello*. It's the same song his troops played at the Alamo. He's mockin' us. He's sayin' he's fixin' to put us all to the sword. His arrogance is drippin' off every note."

Isobel said, "That arrogance could be his undoing. Pride goeth before destruction."

He turned to her, respect in his eyes. "If we meet him with clear heads and strategy, it could be our greatest weapon."

Isobel replied, "At this point, only *we* can defeat ourselves."

Kelvin's disgust showed. "And we saw how easy it could happen."

Sam let out a heavy sigh and ran a hand over his face. "I want y'all to get some shut-eye tonight. The *soldados* will spend the whole night buildin' up a breastwork, thinkin' we're fixin' to attack at first light. Tonight, our boys need to eat proper and rest." He rubbed his chin.

"We'll keep watch, post sentries, and stay sharp, but I reckon the Mexicans'll be busy buildin' their little fort to hide behind."

Kelvin eyed him. "So, we're charging them at sunrise?"

A wry twist played on Sam's mouth. "Maybe."

Isobel didn't miss the look in Sam's eyes. The wheels of strategy turned even as he spoke. Tonight might be quiet, but dawn would bring more than sunlight.

The fire crackled softly as the night deepened and shadows danced on the weary faces of the Texian camp. Isobel sat cross-legged on the ground, her back pressed against the rugged bark of a tree.

Sam stood nearby, his shoulders silhouetted against the dim light. He carried an edge of calm authority that belied the storm brewing in his mind. "We ain't attackin' at dawn. Most of us will still be asleep, gettin' some well-deserved rest. Come dawn, we'll rustle up a good breakfast of roast beef and biscuits again. While we're eatin' good, the *soldados* will be toilin' on their pitiful little fort, which any one of us could stroll across."

Isobel's eyes narrowed. "What'll we be doin'?"

He smirked. "Sittin' around. Swattin' skeeters. Not much."

Kelvin crossed his arms. "What's your plan, General?"

Sam pivoted to Isobel. "Remember what Mrs. Dickinson told us on the Gonzales road?"

A chill ran through her. "I could never forget it."

"Nor could I," Sam said. "Santa Anna kept 'em up all night with artillery fire until the last night."

Recognition flickered in her expression, subtle but certain. "He aimed to keep 'em disoriented, half asleep, tryin' to fight."

Sam's eyes gleamed with the sharp and calculated look she'd come to recognize. "Right. It's why we ain't hittin' 'em at dawn."

Kelvin frowned. "We're waitin'? Why?"

"*El Presidente* will reckon we're not ready to pounce. He'll let his troops rest after workin' all night and through the mornin'. When Cos drags his men here after marchin' all day and night, they'll walk right into our trap."

Isobel shot a glance at her husband, who looked skeptical. She spoke up, steady, despite the unease that twisted inside her. "The hardest part'll be keepin' our boys from jumpin' the gun."

Kelvin said, "Today showed us the difference between professional soldiers and volunteers. How do we rein 'em in?"

Sam exhaled, his face shadowed with the encumbrance of the coming battle. "I'm gonna need my friends' help. When I unleash 'em, the dogs o' war will charge without mercy. It'll be a day of retribution and carnage we'll look back on with terror in our old age."

Isobel's stomach churned. She could already picture the battle-ground and the horrors that waited. Her concern shifted to Sam. She said softly, "I'm sorry 'bout Saracen. He was a brave member of our band."

Pain flickered across his face. "First one we lost here. I'm grateful it was him instead of Colonel Neill."

Kelvin cleared his throat. "I had Apollo brought up. He'll carry you fine tomorrow."

Sam studied him. "I didn't get to thank you for your act of mercy." He turned quiet. "Saracen was in agony." He straightened. "Stick close to me tomorrow. It's gonna be a bloody day. You and Isobel split up. One shot could've taken you both out today. I can't afford to lose either of you."

Isobel laid her hand over her chest in quiet affirmation. "Thanks for not orderin' me to stay back."

He chuckled, low and humorless. "Would it have done any good?"

The stress of the coming dawn pushed on her heart.

"Good evenin', General."

CHAPTER FIFTY-TWO

April 21, 1836
Second Day, Battle of San Jacinto
Confluence of Buffalo Bayou and the San Jacinto River
Lynch's Ferry, Republic of Texas

9:00 AM

"General Cos is joinin' the party." Kelvin's observation reached Isobel over the thrum in her head. Over five hundred *soldados* spilled into the Mexican base, their dark uniforms pooling like a flood. Isobel pressed her hands against her ears, trying to focus on the rising strains of the fiddle only she could hear. It was her melody. Her warning.

Sam stepped out of his tent, looking almost rested. She struggled to recognize him without the weight of exhaustion pressing into his features, dull and shadowed. He turned his face to the sky and murmured, "The sun of Austerlitz has risen again."

Isobel frowned. Kelvin leaned close to her and whispered, "Napoleon's impossible victory." His meaning landed sharp as a blade. Today would change them all.

Colonel Wharton's boots thudded against the damp earth. "Senior officers want a word, General."

Sam tilted his head and fixed his eyes on Wharton as if the next steps had already taken shape. "At noon." His order was firm but wrapped in restraint.

The moment didn't last. Deef Smith appeared next, his presence as familiar as the sight of home after a long journey. Isobel exhaled slowly, tightening her fingers on the fringes of her sleeve.

Sam leaned toward Smith. "Deef, I know Cos rolled into the Mexican camp. Can you creep over and scout their positions? Just need a count of their tents."

Smith saluted and moved before Sam had finished speaking. "I'll take Lane with me. Won't take long." Something in his calm steadied her, quieted the tight coil in her chest. But the moment the scouts disappeared into the trees, that calm shattered. Her stomach clenched, every rustle in the underbrush sharp as a warning.

Time stretched. Each minute drew her nerves tighter. She paced the edge of the camp, fighting the itch of worry. When Smith and Lane reported back, Isobel's eyes widened. Lane looked pale, almost sickly. His hands shook so badly he had to grip his reins just to steady them.

Kelvin noticed too and stepped close. "What happened?"

"I was holdin' Deef's mount while he was countin' men and tents with my spy glass." Lane's words tumbled out in a rush. "Whole time, *soldados* were shootin' at us. Deef's a great scout and worth any ten *soldados* in a fight, but he never heard them shots."

Kelvin laughed. "So, what we took as bravery was only bein' hard of hearin'?"

The absurdity must've struck Lane, too, because a nervous chuckle slipped out. "He's brave, but bein' hard of hearin' sure helps out."

Isobel didn't laugh. She couldn't shake the image Lane painted. Shots rang out while Smith, unaware, carried on like nothing was amiss. Her stomach twisted at the thought of how close they must've come to death.

Smith turned to Sam. "We counted over three hundred *soldado* tents." His words were grave. "But our mission got cut short. Mounted dragoons spotted us and gave chase. We had to get out fast."

Sam didn't flinch. "Where'd Cos come from, Deef?"

"Lane heard some of the *soldados* complainin' they marched all night from Fort Bend." Smith counted on his fingers. "That's at least twenty-five miles on these muddy roads and trails."

Sam's eyes narrowed. "Are they tired?"

"You know they are, General." Smith shook his head. "Santa Anna don't care, he put 'em on the breastworks without no rest."

The words floated between them. Isobel could sense the currents shifting in Sam's mind. She could visualize the strategy forming like a storm on the horizon. She looked toward the enemy camp, imagining the exhausted *soldados* pressed into service. No rest. Sam would use that. She only hoped the cost wouldn't be too high.

Sam asked, "How many men you reckon he's got over there?"

Isobel didn't need to count them. The weight of the numbers pressed her hard and heavy.

Smith's calm caused Isobel to wonder if he knew his answer described an army that wanted to crush them. "Over a thousand. Maybe twelve hundred or so."

"All worked through the night, huh? Are they exhausted?" Sam's questions sharpened with each word.

Smith let out a low hum. "Yes, sir. They'll get more tired as the day drags on."

Isobel caught the flicker in Sam's eyes, a calculation, the kind that always made her wonder about him. He turned every word over, fitting it into a plan she couldn't yet see.

Sam lifted his head slowly and rubbed his chin. "Cos came by way of the road and Vince's Bridge. That road's the only way in and out now that the ferry's gone. What do you think of the bridge?"

Smith didn't hesitate. "General, me and my men think we oughtta burn the bridge."

The gravity of his words settled over them. Burn the bridge. Her heart quickened, and her hands trembled. She could feel the heat of the flames already, see the smoke rising like a signal of no quarter to either side.

Sam was careful. "I've been considerin' that, but it'd leave you exposed to enemy fire. I don't wanna lose you."

Smith didn't waver. "I think we can do it, General."

Sam's jaw tightened, and Isobel knew he weighed the risk, not just for Smith, but for every man left to face what would come after. "General Filisola might be on Cos's heels. I don't want him crossin' that bridge like Von Blucher did at Waterloo. Von Blucher turned the tide for the British just when Napoleon had it won. We can't let any more *soldados* on the field today."

Smith touched the brim of his hat. "I'll take some men and burn the bridge."

Sam explained his reasons. "It'll stop Mexican reinforcements and keep Santa Anna from retreating."

"Nobody can retreat without the bridge." Smith shifted in his saddle. "Not even us."

"That's right." Sam's words were the coldest Isobel had ever heard from him. "Nobody leaves the field. You gotta hurry, Deef. The green prairie'll turn blood-red if you don't get back quick."

As he rode off, her pulse hammered. Dust rose in their wake, a bitter trail stinging her eyes. She bowed her head and prayed.

Sam turned to Colonel Seguin. "Juan, I want your men protecting the camp and supplies."

The Tejano stiffened. "General, we've done all you asked." He steadied himself. "Santa Anna burned our homes. My parents are refugees in East Texas. We got nothin' left. This is our fight."

Sam hesitated and his face softened. "In battle, some Texians might shoot at all *Méxicanos*, includin' you. I don't want to lose you."

Seguin's shoulders squared. "We'll mark ourselves." He pulled a deck of cards from his coat. "Put these in our hatbands. Let us march to the sound of the guns."

A long moment passed. "As you wish, Colonel. Command your men as you see fit."

Seguin turned on his heel, determination in every step. Isobel whispered a prayer that his men would not fall to friendly fire.

Kelvin broke the silence. "General, need anything before the noon council?"

"A battle flag. And a fifer."

Kelvin scratched the back of his neck. "Sherman's unit has a flag. Said some ladies in Kentucky made it."

"What's on it?"

His mouth twitched. "Goddess of Liberty holdin' a sword, with a banner sayin', 'Liberty or Death.' There's a Phrygian cap on a pike in the background."

Isobel frowned. "Phrygian cap?"

A smile flashed across her husband's face. "Romans gave it to freed slaves. A sign of freedom."

She tilted her head, considering it. *A freed slave's hat on a battlefield in Texas.* Strange. Fitting.

Sam gave a slow dip of the head. "It's the only flag we've got. We'll march with it."

Kelvin's grin widened. "We got a fifer, but he only knows one tune: *Come to the Bower.*"

Isobel's lips curved despite herself. "So, we're marching under a Roman flag to an Irish saloon song?"

Sam's reply held no humor. "It will have to do."

12:00 NOON

THE SUN BLAZED OVERHEAD, bearing down on the camp like the drumbeat of war. Tension crackled through the Texian positions. Whispers slithered through the ranks. Murmurs of doubt, of impatience. Some said Sam Houston was wasting the day. Isobel knew better. He never wasted anything.

Inside the headquarters tent, men clashed. She couldn't catch every word, but the sharp edges told the story. Frustration. Pressure. Distrust.

Wharton's words sliced through the canvas walls. "We gotta act, General. Now."

Sam's reply was quiet but steely. "We're goin' to do somethin', sir."

The argument carried on, loud enough to draw wary glances. Isobel clenched her fists, her Bowie knife pressing her side. She needed oxygen. Space away from the storm of men who argued over a fight that hadn't yet begun.

She made her way toward the ferry landing, Dream's reins firm in her grip. The mare's steady presence comforted her, a tether against the tide of unease rising from the army. Across the bayou, the de Zavala home stood silent, the ghostly spirit of what had already been lost.

A familiar word broke through her thoughts. "Belle."

Kelvin. He wove through the camp, his tricorn tilted at its usual careless angle. His face softened when he saw her, and something in her heart loosened.

"I see you dressed for the occasion." His voice was light, but his eyes weren't. "I'd forgotten how fierce you look in your Comanche clothes. The raven feather fits you now more than ever."

Her expression lifted, just barely. "Thank you. You look nice in your battle outfit."

He smirked, but sobered. "The general's holdin' steady, but the officers..." He shook his head. "He sent 'em away. When you look for us later, he'll be wearin' his plain brown tricorn instead of his fancy white beaver hat."

Isobel's stomach knotted. A sign, subtle but deliberate. "I'm sure y'all are handsome enough to do Tennessee proud."

Her pulse quickened. She tightened her grip on Dream's reins. "I need to ask somethin' of you."

Kelvin dipped his head, studying her. "What is it, Belle?"

She swallowed hard and braced herself. "If anything happens to me today, I wanna be buried in my Comanche garments. They show the love of friends and my new country."

Something shifted in Kelvin's face. His easy attention on battle plans snapped into something deeper. "I'll do all I can."

She stepped closer. She needed him to *hear* her, to understand. "Please call to mind my request as long as you live."

He took her hand. "I'll remember your words all the days of my life." He kissed her.

It was too brief, too fragile. A threadbare promise against the force of what lay ahead.

She forced herself to focus. "I took the raft over to check on Colonel Neill earlier. He's still hurtin' bad."

Kelvin tightened his grip on her hand. "At least he fired the openin' salvo."

"True." She looked toward the tree line, the time of battle drawing closer. "All our hopes and dreams come down to this one day. I ain't afraid. I don't know why."

Kelvin winced. "The general says we're more angry than scared. 'His Excellency' stoked a fire only he could pull off."

She chuckled, the sound edged with something bittersweet. "Yesterday got my first-time jitters out, I reckon."

"It made an enemy out of Sherman." Kelvin's expression darkened. "The general dressed him down, put Lamar over the cavalry."

She sighed. "Houston and President Jackson both got loud enemies, but today, they all hate Santa Anna more. At least, I hope so."

Kelvin squeezed her hand. "Still hearin' the fiddle music?"

She met his eyes. "Sometimes sharp and strong. Other times…not at all. Gotta be a reason, but I don't have it figured yet."

He drew her closer. "Don't stop listenin' for it."

She had no time to respond before he kissed her again. Gentle. Lingering. When he pulled away, his eyes burned into hers. "Most folks wonder why I follow your lead. It ain't because I'm lazy or doubt myself. You discern God, Belle. The song only you can hear. I'm calling it *Isobel's Song*, but it guides us both. I have faith in Him. And I have faith in you."

Emotion swelled in her chest. "I love you."

He kissed her once more and glanced toward the camp. "I gotta go. The general's waitin' for *El Presidente* to drop his guard. When he figures it's too late in the day for an attack, he'll allow his *soldados* to sleep and unsaddle his cavalry's horses."

She said, "I figured as much."

Kelvin hesitated. "Mrs. Dickinson gave him the spark for the plan."

Isobel let the impact of it settle. "It's bold. Santa Anna's Alamo strategy in reverse."

Kelvin's jaw tightened. "I'll be right beside the general when the charge begins. I don't know how to help 'til the time comes." His eyes locked on hers. "Pray I don't falter."

She cupped his face. "You won't. Nor will you lose heart." She inhaled deeply. "Take care of our general. When this is over, all of Texas will rally to him under a new flag. Victory has a way of settlin' old disputes."

For a moment, there were no words. Without warning, he kissed her, fierce and consuming. The kind of kiss carrying everything they couldn't say and all they feared they wouldn't have time for.

When he pulled back, he said quietly, "I love you. Be careful. I know you got plans for your knife but wield it with great care."

"I love you too." She gave his hand a final squeeze before turning, stealing one last glance at the camp. "Let's get to it."

3:30 PM

THE HEAT PRESSED down like a heavy hand, thick with sweat and tension. Perched on Dream, Isobel tracked Deef Smith's approach, his face set, shoulders squared, as he strode toward Sam.

"No way out now," he said. "The bridge is gone. *Soldados* quit work on the breastworks, too tired to move. They're in their tents."

Sam's focus sharpened. "What about their cavalry?"

He shook his head. "Horses ain't saddled. No Mexican scouts watchin' us. They think it's too late for an attack."

A slow, knowing curve touched Sam's lips. "We'll put 'em straight soon enough. To your post, Deef."

Kelvin swung onto Skipper and Sam mounted Apollo. Isobel steadied herself, heart thrumming as the Texian force, less than nine hundred, moved from the trees to a nearby stand of timber, hidden by tall prairie grass. They formed ranks, quiet but eager.

From her place with the cavalry on the right, she fixed her eyes on her husband as he rode the line. He spoke with the troops, calm and direct. Not a rousing speech. Just the plan. Cross the narrow ridge. Charge. Her throat tightened. They all knew what waited on the other side. Dream shifted beneath her, hooves stamping as if her own tension had bled into the reins.

Lamar's cavalry shifted into place where Sherman's unit had clashed with the enemy the day before. Isobel glanced at the Mexican camp, relief washing over her. Santa Anna had moved *El Volcán*. The cannon no longer commanded the field.

The men didn't need rousing. They coiled tight, yearning for battle. The fight was coming.

And they wouldn't have to wait long.

She bowed her head, lips forming the words that steadied her soul. *Father, into thy hands, I commend my spirit.*

A red and white tent sat on the horizon. Santa Anna's headquarters. *The tyrant's throne.* Deef had pointed it out earlier, and now its bold stripes mocked her, a symbol of power, untouched and certain.

Isobel tightened her grip on Dream's reins, her free hand curling around the handle of her Bowie knife. While others fought, she would carve a path straight for the tent. The blade pulsed with the heat of her fury, ready. *I will not falter. Not today.*

A sharp yell split the air. *Sam.*

The Twin Sisters roared.

This is it.

"REMEMBER THE ALAMO! REMEMBER GOLIAD!"

The battle cries tore through the ranks, raw and furious, rattling through her body. Men surged forward, boots pounding the earth, horses galloping, the sound a relentless drumbeat of war.

The Mexican breastworks loomed ahead, dark and imposing, but the Texians never hesitated. No fear. No doubt. They charged, a force too savage to be stopped.

In the enemy camp, chaos erupted. *Soldados* stumbled from their tents, muskets grabbed in panic. *Like the Alamo.* The thought burned inside her. They awoke to the same terror they had inflicted.

The first musket fire cracked, hurried, desperate, wild. They weren't ready. The *soldados'* shots scattered, their line crumbling before it could form.

It happened in an instant.

A single shot rang true.

Apollo reared, his powerful figure jolting as he crumpled. Sam tumbled to the earth.

Isobel's pulse hammered in her ears.

Kelvin was already on the move. "Take Skipper, General!" He leapt off his horse, vanishing into the melee.

Sam swung onto the quarter horse, jaw tight, eyes locked ahead. A rifle ball struck his ankle. He gritted his teeth, flinching, and drove the charge forward.

She saw him take the hit. Her heart pounded. He had to be the first into the camp. He had to stop the madness.

This wasn't a mere battle. It was an ending. And a beginning.

She leaned low over Dream's neck, pushing the mustang faster. The field blurred as her focus narrowed to the red and white tent. The marrow of the enemy.

A Mexican rider darted into her path, panic wide in his eyes, fleeing. She ignored him. Cowards didn't matter.

Gunfire, shouts, the clash of steel. Chaos roared around her. The Texians had breached the breastworks. The camp erupted in violence, blades flashing, bayonets thrusting. *Soldados* fell like autumn leaves in a windstorm, their unprepared ranks crumbling beneath the relentless charge.

The red and white command center loomed at the fore.

Texians swarmed it. Bowie knives slashed through the canvas as swords ripped its proud stripes to ribbons. The fabric sagged, folding under the onslaught. *Sam planned this to perfection: fast, overwhelming. They never had a chance.*

The Mexican cavalry was in complete disarray. The unsaddled horses panicked, their would-be riders scrambling without boots.

Victory. Swift and brutal.

She slowed Dream, scanning the battlefield. The *soldados* broke and retreated in scattered clusters. She steadied. It was almost over.

Near the huge artillery piece responsible for Saracen's death, a lone figure caught her eye.

An older officer. Arms crossed, unmoved.

He did not run. He did not fight.

He stood still as the world he'd known collapsed around him.

Something about him stopped her there. She stared at the spectacle, unable to look away.

Santa Anna. She studied him. But no. He was too old, his frame too sturdy for the wiry *El Presidente.* Her mind rushed back to something Sam had mentioned, a conversation about a Mexican general who was a friend of the de Zavalas. *This must be him.*

The fighting raged on near the cannon. Texians pressed hard as *soldados* scattered, but the gentleman held his ground. His arms remained crossed, his expression defiant, though his men ran away behind him.

A fierce rhythm beat inside her chest. The fight was nigh over. But he abided unshaken, unafraid.

They swarmed him. Blows rained down. He crumpled.

A chill crept through her. They left his lifeless body in the dirt and turned to the panicked *soldados.*

Not like the coward I saw earlier. That man had bolted, fear wild in his eyes, a deserter running for his life.

Dread coiled in her gut. *I let him go.*

She could chase him, run him down before he vanished into the confusion. But something held her back.

The music.

Soldados still ran, but something was wrong. They didn't flee into the open prairie. They retreated *backward.*

Her pulse quickened. *What are they doing?*

Deef Smith's warning echoed in her mind. *Don't go behind the camp. The marsh will trap you.*

The clinging mire. The mosquitoes. The snakes. The gators. A deathtrap.

And Santa Anna had positioned his army right in front of it.

Isobel snapped her eyes to the withdrawing troops. Their panic drove them straight into the morass. *Madness.* Any schoolboy with toy soldiers knew better. But here they were, plunging into the swamp as if it could save them.

The battle shifted. Texians stood victorious, their shouts rising wild with triumph. They fired at their enemies as equipment lay shattered beneath booted feet. Santa Anna's headquarters was theirs. They captured horses, guns, powder, *El Volcán*. Everything was under Texian control.

Isobel sat motionless atop Dream, her purpose wavering. *What now? Capture prisoners? Secure the camp? Help the wounded?* The rush of battle faded into a strange fog. She whispered a prayer. *Lord, please... Please what?* She didn't know.

A flash of movement near the marsh caught her attention. A shock ran through her.

Dozens of *soldados*, waist-deep in muck, flapped about in the sucking mud. Trapped. More waded in, their panic spreading like wildfire.

She squinted, trying to understand.

At last, she saw the Texians.

It all made sense.

They closed in, muskets raised.

In the quagmire, young men flailed, their legs ensnared by the inundating ooze. Terror twisted their faces, hands clawing for anything solid. Swarms of mosquitoes descended, thick as smoke, their high-pitched hum adding to the cries. Isobel slapped at her face, shuddering. Her buckskin sleeve turned black with them.

A volley of shots tore into the swamp.

The Mexicans jerked, collapsing into the sludge. Others screamed, struggling to flee, but only sank deeper.

Her stomach lurched. *This isn't battle. This is something else.*

Her hands trembled against Dream's reins, frozen between the instinct to turn away and the awful certainty of having to see it.

"What are you doing?" The whisper bled from her throat, but no one heard.

The scene warped, drowned in the pounding of her heart.

This was neither victory nor justice.

It was pure slaughter.

Her breath came too fast, too shallow. She yanked Dream's reins, forcing her mare away. The horror of it clung to her skin.

The battle was over.

The nightmare had only begun.

The wind came heavy, but something was wrong. It choked her with smoke and blood, pressing down like an iron hand on the back of her neck. She slid from the saddle, legs barely holding. Then the stench slammed into her: scorched powder, rank sweat, and the sour rot of death already setting in. Her stomach lurched. She stumbled forward, slapping at mosquitoes clinging to her face like leeches. She gagged, spitting out their bitter taste as they swarmed into her mouth.

Her stomach rebelled. She doubled over, retching until nothing remained but a hollow ache.

Shouts rang out. "Remember the Alamo! Remember Goliad!"

She pressed a hand to her forehead, dizzy, her prayer a whisper. *Show me, Lord. Tell me what to do.*

A flash of red. Blood.

Sam.

He rode into view, his boot slick with blood. It stained the leather in dark streaks. He barked orders, voice edged with something raw. "Fall back! Cease fire! Return to camp!"

No one listened.

A rage had taken root, deeper than grief, hotter than the flames that had gutted their homes. It consumed them, blinded them.

Isobel clenched her fists.

Sam looked, *God help him*, defeated.

They had won, but he no longer led an army. He was trying to hold back a storm with his bare hands.

Kelvin walked up, calm as ever. He took Skipper's bridle, murmured something low, something Sam alone could hear.

With quiet precision, he turned the horse and led their general away.

She couldn't tear her eyes from the muddy pond, its surface churned with blood and bodies.

A single cry cut through the mayhem. *¡Me no Alamo!*

The words hit her like a slap. Her heart buffeted her ribs. She clasped the reins tighter. She couldn't just stand there. She couldn't.

The music pulled her forward.

Another scream, *"¡Mama!"*

Her song. Her harmony. The sound only she could hear. It drowned out every warning screaming at her to stay back.

She moved to the water's edge.

Young men thrashed in the muddy water, their faces streaked with gore, their cries like daggers in her chest. *Boys.* Only boys.

A lad clawed at the bank, his fingers red from his own blood. Others sank deeper, their bodies too battered to fight.

One of them, a child in all but name, lifted a trembling hand and made the sign of the cross.

A Texian leveled his musket.

Father Muldoon's message rang through the memory of her baptism. The thought and the music collided, igniting something inside her—raw, uncontrollable.

She moved before she could think.

The Bowie knife was in her hand.

She threw herself in front of the muskets, arms raised, blade flashing. "Stop it!"

The words flew from her mouth, ragged and desperate. "Stop it in the name of Jesus! Stop!"

The muskets nearest her fell silent.

Her chest heaved as her gaze swept over the pond. Bodies littered the ground, draped over tree roots, submerged in bloodied water. The cries of the wounded mingled with the eerie silence of the dead.

Amid the carnage, there was movement.

Young *soldados*, battered and shivering, rose from the brine like ghosts. Their hollow eyes locked on her. *Not an enemy. Not a threat. A refuge.*

In a slow, deliberate motion, she slid her knife back into its sheath and raised her hands. She opened her palms, a gesture of peace.

"Come," she whispered calmly, even as her soul trembled. "You're safe now."

One by one, they crept forward, their trembling fingers grasping at her sleeves. Their tear-streaked faces labored to meet hers.

"*Gracias, Madre de Dios, por tu ángel,*" they muttered. They sobbed, clutching at her as if she were the one solid thing left in the whole shattered world.

Her eyes swelled. *I'm no angel.*

Beyond the bloody pond, movement caught her swollen eyes.

A Mexican officer near the riverbank. Calm. Purposeful. He gestured to the scattered *soldados*, gathering them for capitulation.

He's trying to save them.

Isobel's mind raced. She needed her Spanish. Now.

"*Camine hacia su oficial. Él te reunirá para rendirte.*"

Some Texians recoiled at the sound of her words.

For their benefit, she lifted her chin firmly and commanded, "Walk over to your officer. He'll round y'all up for surrender."

And one by one, they did.

A Texian she didn't recognize stepped up beside her and motioned the prisoners toward the Mexican officer in the clearing. The defeated *soldados* obeyed, trudging away from the bog with heavy, mud-caked steps. Their muskets lay abandoned, either sunk into the mire or forgotten in their tents.

"*Gracias, señora.*"

Stunned *soldados* passed by. Some reached out to touch her sleeve as they went. The Texians at her side stood in a daze, taking in the ruin of a once-proud army reduced to lifeless bodies and tattered remnants. Santa Anna's Legion now took its orders from a Tennessee mountain girl armed only with a sheathed Bowie knife.

As the captives moved away from the fatal pond, Isobel kept her eyes on them as they approached their officer. He directed them to sit before offering her a brief wave as he turned to tend his anguished flock.

Secretary of War Thomas Rusk continued to round up prisoners. When he reached the bloodstained water, the gruesome scene stopped him cold. His face hardened with horror.

"I reckoned I'd be glad to see Santa Anna's army all bloody and battered," he murmured. "But this here's a sight I wouldn't wish on nobody."

"There's a Mexican officer organizin' them." Isobel pointed him out.

Rusk squinted into the clearing. "Yep, I see him. Was it your doin'? I heard as much."

"I think it was God grabbin' our boys' attention. I was only His instrument." She hung her head. "I'd been dreamin' of the day I could plunge my knife into the mad dog's heart. Hate pushed us eastward, leavin' behind the ashes of so many dreams. Ain't no surprise it showed itself as a roaring lion among sheep."

He exhaled, his shoulders sagging. "I'm sorry you had to see this, Isobel." His face was thick with sorrow. "But I thank the Lord you were here. Who knows? Maybe it was for such a time as this."

She gave a slow hum of agreement and turned back to her mustang. A tremor ran through her hands as she untied the mare. The leather straps slipped out of her fingers, but she caught them. She swung into the saddle, her legs still weak.

Nudging Dream, she guided her through the battlefield. Bodies lay everywhere, sprawled in grotesque stillness, their lives stamped out in moments of terror. Her breath grew shallow as she picked her way around them. She wouldn't let the horse stumble on anyone.

Her eyes darted across the field. *Only soldados*, she realized with a chill. She saw no Texian remains. The victory was undeniable, yet the sight of it made her gut churn.

She crossed the Mexican camp, the silence deafening in its force. She saw *El Volcán*. It gleamed dim in the fading sunlight, a terrible monument to death. Nearby, she recognized the corpse of the general who had stood his ground during the charge. His lifeless form lay crumpled, his dignity stripped by the brutality of war.

Her stomach twisted again, violent and unrelenting. She hunched over in the saddle, retching, though there was nothing left to vomit. Dry heaves wracked her body, her throat raw as she gagged against the bitterness rising inside her.

Triumph? The notion scorched its way through her mind as she clutched the reins, fingers locked tight, knuckles white. This wasn't triumph. This was sickness, sour and vile, spreading through her chest and staining everything it touched.

The field of glory stretched out before her, littered with the remnants of men's lives. The taste of victory was not sweet. It was acrid and bitter, choking her as she spewed the last of her strength into the dirt.

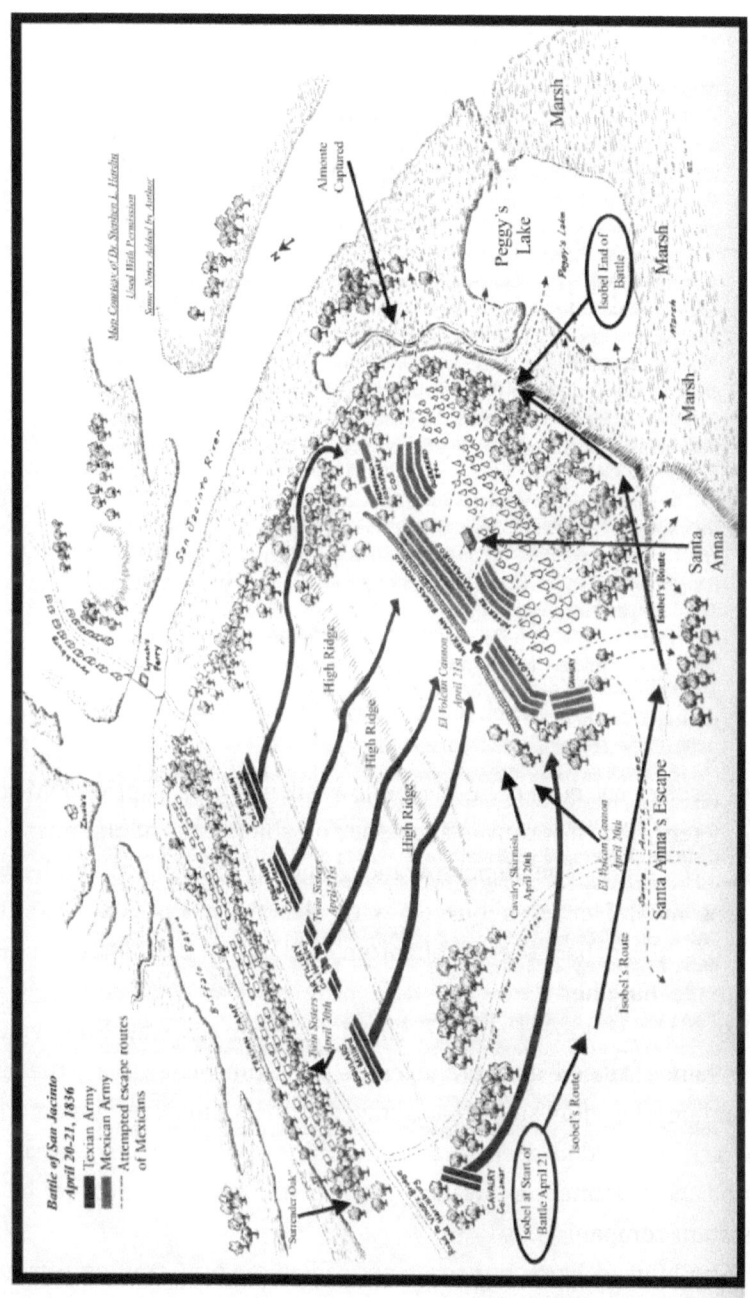

Map of the Battle of San Jacinto with Isobel's Route

CHAPTER FIFTY-THREE

April 22, 1836
East Bank of Buffalo Bayou, Rear of the Texian Army
Lynch's Ferry, Republic of Texas

I sobel lay curled in the hollow silence of a captured Mexican tent, the thin canvas above her no shield against the torment of the night. The stench of smoke and blood clung to her, heavy as a wet hide. Her eyes burned with the sharp light of yesterday's horrors. Sleep had been a phantom, lurking at the edges but never quite reaching her.

Beside her, Kelvin shifted. She didn't look his way. She couldn't. Her hands tugged at the fringes of her Comanche dress, the once-proud doeskin now stained and frayed at the seams. Her fingers traced the grit embedded deep in the grain. She could feel dirt, sweat, and blood. She grimaced, swallowing the bile that seemed to be her constant companion.

She blinked hard, but the tears spilled anyway, trailing warm and unbidden down her cheeks. "My dress." She thought of Tlahina and the day she gifted her the beautiful garment. She gripped the sleeves and held them like something fragile, something already dead.

Kelvin stirred, focusing his tired eyes on her. "What is it?"

Her nose wrinkled at the sour stench rising off her. Disgust bloomed as sorrow filled her heart. "My dress. It doesn't feel like mine anymore. I...I left something out there, Kel. On that field." Her throat tightened. "And I can't ..." A sob clawed its way free before she could hold it back.

Kelvin sat up, his silhouette outlined in the pale light of dawn as it filtered through the canvas. He said nothing. His eyes stayed on her. For once, she was grateful. Words wouldn't mend this jagged thing inside her.

She stared at her lap. "I thought a new day would feel like...something new." She gave a gradual shake of the head. "But it don't. It feels the same. Like I'm still there, stuck in the mud and the blood...and the smoke and the screaming."

He caressed her face, as if searching for something smooth and untainted beneath the grime. "You'll feel better when we have a chance to bathe and put on fresh clothes."

"What I'm wearin', Kel." She whispered it more to herself than to him. "It won't wash off."

The dawn pushed through the canvas walls, a stubborn gray light, but its promise didn't reach her. She stood, arms crossed, staring at the tent's sagging canvas as if it held answers. "Let's go check on the general. I'm mighty worried 'bout his wound. If it gets infected, they might have to take his leg."

Kelvin's brow tightened. "His shoulder's hurtin' bad enough, now the ankle's addin' to the pain. Seems like they're both aimin' to bring him down."

Isobel pressed her lips into a hard line. "His wounds tell the tale. He led from the front, Kel. Ain't a soul can call him a coward after the way he carried this army."

"They'll surely try." He stepped forward, holding the tent flap open for her.

"Thank you." Isobel ducked through and walked into the morning light.

The day had broken clear, golden rays filtered through the

sprawling branches of the oak that anchored the camp. Beneath its shade, Sam lay in an awkward position on a bed roll, propped on his left side. Around him, soldiers bustled or milled about. Others stalked the surrounding area as they beat the tall prairie grass with muskets slung over their shoulders. *Hunting,* she realized. Not for deer or birds. No, they scoured land and water for "His Excellency," the mad dog himself.

Isobel said softly, "I'm awful sorry, General. I let the monster slip away."

Sam shifted to her and waited.

"I was ridin' with our cavalry when a lone rider bolted from the Mexican camp." The memory flashed behind her eyes. "Didn't know it was him. But the way he rode off, bold as brass, leavin his men. Cowardice and arrogance like that. It *had* to be Santa Anna."

Sam's eyes held a faint glow, though whether it was approval or weariness, she couldn't tell. "It likely was him, but he can't have gone too far." He was in pain. "Deef Smith burned the bridge, and there ain't been any other reports of him." His words were low and rough. "Truth is, when he rode off, most of his army stopped fightin'."

Isobel swallowed and words clogged in her throat as she thought of the *soldados.*

His eyes met hers. "I know what you did at the swamp."

Her nails dug into her palms, and she forced herself to speak. "I heard the cries, General. I saw 'em."

"Thank you for tryin' to stop the slaughter." He shook his head.

"I tried." She stared at the bloodstains on her sleeve as her fingers traced the lurid marks. "But they wouldn't listen. I've never seen men so outta control. 'Twas..."

"Shameful." Sam finished her thought. "Without honor."

The memory tightened like a rope around her ribs.

"War'll do that to men." Sam looked into her eyes. "But it don't mean you stop tryin', Isobel."

She dipped her chin once, then again. *It don't mean you stop.*

Kelvin pulled her back to the present. "We gotta capture the man.

If he links up with General Filisola, them Mexicans'll outnumber us again."

Sam winced from the pain of his ankle. "Besides his lack of courage and honor, hookin' up with Filisola was likely his aim. If he reaches his army, we'll be back at the beginnin'."

Movement in the tall grass snagged her attention. A Texian boy, little more than a teenager, marched forward, his musket slung across his shoulder with an awkward sort of pride. Ahead of him trudged a captured *soldado*, his hands bound, head hung low. Even from where she stood, Isobel noted the uniform jacket. The buttons and blouse were dirty but unmistakable. *A private.*

Her brows furrowed as he drew closer. He wasn't like the other privates she'd seen. Older. Weary in a way that pulled his shoulders down. Her gut twisted. The ones she saw yesterday were only boys.

They passed near a guard fire where the other Mexican prisoners sat or lay, bruised and sunburned. At the sight of the captive, whispers trilled among them. The murmurs were soft at first, then louder, their cheers rising in an urgent chorus. *"¡El Presidente! ¡El Presidente!"*

The words clawed the stillness like a sudden wind. Isobel froze, and her heart thudded once—hard. The prisoners scrambled upright as some teetered from their injuries. They were determined, none-theless.

"Kel." She said it in a shocked whisper, though she wasn't sure he heard.

The boy leading the detainee looked just as startled. His hands flexed around the musket barrel with unease. He joined his officers, George Hockley and John Forbes, and said something Isobel couldn't hear. Together, they steered their man toward the sprawling oak where Sam leaned, propped on his left side, favoring his right ankle.

Isobel worried at the sight of Sam. He was wounded and worn down, but he still held himself with the authority that made men listen. He straightened as best he could, though the effort cost him.

The captive stopped in front of them, the same man who'd fled the field like a snake in the grass. *Santa Anna.* His dark eyes darted between their faces. His chin tilted upward as if the raggedness of his uniform couldn't strip away his arrogance. "*Soy Generalissimo* Antonio Lopez de Santa Anna. *Me gustaría entregarme a Don* Samuel Houston *como prisionero de guerra.*"

Isobel knew enough Spanish to understand the prisoner. *Generalissimo* struck like a hammer blow. She clenched her fists and cut her palms with her nails.

Sam's glare pinned Santa Anna like a spear. For a long moment, no one moved. Something cold and bitter settled over the group. Then Sam spoke, his command measured but edged with steel. "Find a translator, Kelvin. Fetch 'em back so we can parlay with this prisoner."

Kelvin turned on his heels, striding toward the guard fire. He addressed the ranking enemy officer. "Do you speak English, sir?"

The officer rose from the shadows, his expression calm but guarded. "*Sí.* I speak English."

Kelvin replied, "Come with me."

Kelvin and the man returned to the big oak without hesitation. He was tall, dark-haired, and poised despite the dirt and wear of battle. She wasn't sure, but this could be the same man the *soldados* walked to as they got out of the bog.

Sam pushed himself a little straighter against the tree. "What's your name, sir?"

He straightened his shoulders and lifted his chin. "Colonel Juan Almonte, General."

Isobel blinked several times. The name struck like a spark on flint, her surprise mirrored in Sam's and Kelvin's glances. *Colonel Almonte.* An honorable man and a rare light in a dark enemy.

Sam's look sharpened. "Can you identify this prisoner, Colonel?"

Almonte turned his head, his brown eyes falling on the man who stood rigid and unrepentant a few feet away. "Yes, General. He is the *Presidente de México, Generalissimo* Antonio Lopez de Santa Anna."

The words dropped like stones into a silent pond.

Isobel locked her eyes on the face of the man who had haunted them all. *Him. The tyrant.* The face they'd imagined every time they buried a friend, every time they mourned brave men left with no graves at the Alamo and Goliad. Buck Travis. Jim Bowie. James Fannin,

David Crockett. The names whispered through her mind, heavy and cold. *This man had killed them all.*

Her stomach twisted with a fury so deep it startled her. A hangman's noose? Too merciful.

Around her, the Texians stood stiff, eyes fixed and hard, their silence louder than any shout. Isobel couldn't tear her stare away, couldn't stop herself from memorizing every detail. His stained and wrinkled uniform, his face drawn but defiant, and his dark eyes that yielded nothing. He exhibited no shame. No remorse.

Sam broke the stillness. "Can you translate for us, Colonel?"

"Yes, General. I am at your service." Almonte gave a crisp salute.

Sam looked at Santa Anna and motioned him to repeat his earlier words.

The dictator squared his shoulders and repeated his earlier statement. He made Isobel's skin crawl.

Almonte gave a smooth translation, his manner neutral. "I am General Antonio Lopez de Santa Anna. I wish to surrender to *Don Samuel Houston* as a prisoner of war."

A prisoner of war? Unbelievable! Coward! Her friends' faces flashed in front of her, their laughter and light turned to ash.

Sam waved at Kelvin. "Someone get *El Presidente* a stool or somethin' to sit on. I'll not have him lookin' down on me."

Kelvin hurried over and got a wooden crate. The scrape of it against the dirt made Isobel flinch. He set it down within Sam's reach and the *generalissimo* settled onto the makeshift seat. He sat on it with a practiced ease, as though disgrace could not touch him.

For the first time, his scrutiny swept over Isobel and paused. His eyes narrowed as the recognition dawned slow but certain. *He remembers me.* Her heart thudded at the thought and her spine stiffened under the imposition of his stare. She'd ridden straight into his camp yesterday as her golden hair flew and her Comanche dress marked her like a flame in the dark. He'd seen her then; he saw her now.

But she didn't look away. She held his view, cold and unblinking, until he shifted, the lines of his face tight despite the golden sun. *Good. Let him remember.*

Wharton and a cluster of other officers gathered close. Tension thickened. The way they looked at the dictator sent a shiver up Isobel's back. She didn't need to hear their minds to know what they thought. The oak tree stretched wide and ancient overhead, and its branches reached out like arms. If ever a tree was made for hangin' men, this was it.

"Get a rope!"

The call set off a ripple through the crowd.

"No. Not today!" Sam cut through the noise like a blade.

"He's a murderer!" A man spat on the ground.

"Not today!" Sam repeated.

Isobel's head snapped toward Sam. He lay propped against the oak, his body too still, too worn. He struggled to lift himself, his face twisting in pain and frustration. Her heart ached. She saw him as an impotent invalid. *Lord, give him the strength and the words.*

Colonel Almonte stood apart, calm as stone. His expression revealed nothing. Not pity. Not disdain. Just quiet observation, as though he were watching a scene unfold that he'd expected all along.

Sam received strength and words. He roared, and the sound cracked like thunder across the restless camp. "Listen to me!"

The crowd stilled as all eyes turned toward him, their anger caught for just a moment.

"There's still a wing of the Mexican army out there somewhere." Sam was clear. "That wing's stronger than anything we got here. It ain't crippled by the directions of this incompetent buffoon." His eyes flicked to Santa Anna, full of fire. "Under its professional officers, it can hit us hard, and we'll lose all we've fought for."

Isobel's heart thumped as Sam spoke. His words dug deep into the gathered men like spikes.

"We gotta keep him alive." Sam's tone softened enough to pull them closer. "He's a hostage and head of state. Nobody detests this man more than I do." He paused. "Nobody wants to kill him more than I do. Nobody deserves the hangman more than this devil." Sam's face twisted, full of pain and fury. "But we gotta think of what's best for Texas."

The silence after was heavy, thick with unspoken arguments and smothered rage. Isobel's scowl swept the crowd, seeing the war in their faces. She saw the desire for vengeance as it wrestled with the hard truth Sam had laid bare.

Her frown flickered back to Santa Anna, who sat stiff and silent atop his crate, arrogance still clinging to him like a second skin. She hated him, hated everything he'd done, every soul he'd stolen. But Sam was right.

Texas comes first.

And if Sam Houston, broken and bloodied, could still see that truth, then so could she.

Murmurs rolled through the men like a restless tide as anger ebbed into a slow, grudging acceptance. Faces yielded, hard lines of fury softened as Sam's words sank in. The truth wasn't easy to swallow, but it was clear. Execution meant throwing away their only leverage, though the consequence of it burned bitter at her core.

Her angry stare slid back to Santa Anna. He perched on the crate like a crow on a fencepost. His smug indifference made her fists clench. She knew it wasn't luck that had dragged him back into their hands after his coward's escape. No, the hand of God had placed him here. The tyrant sat, a prisoner, vile and small, in the heart of the army he'd tried to destroy.

Santa Anna's lips moved, his words a quiet slither of sound that made Sam's brow furrow as he strained to catch the meaning.

"Please translate for me, Colonel." Sam's request was sharp with suspicion.

Almonte stood like a bridge between the men. "The conqueror of the Napoleon of the West is born to no common destiny, and he can afford to be generous to the vanquished."

The words ground like sandpaper against her skin. *Generous?*

Sam's face darkened. "You should've remembered that at the Alamo!"

"I was acting on the orders of my government, sir," Almonte translated evenly.

Sam's eyes blazed as he pointed and shook his finger at the dictator. "You *are* the government, sir!"

Santa Anna listened to Almonte's translation, then shrugged, his face indifferent. His casualness set Isobel's teeth on edge.

Sam pushed himself forward. "What of Goliad?" His accusation cut sharper now, like steel dragged across stone. "General Urrea accepted the surrender of Colonel Fannin and his four hundred men and then murdered them. On *your* orders."

Almonte hesitated a beat before he translated. "General Urrea had no authority to accept their surrender. I will execute him myself when I return to Mexico City."

The crowd rolled, curses low and furious spilled like sparks, but Sam gave a slow shake of his head. "This madman just don't quit."

Almonte remained still. With discretion, Sam's remarks went untranslated.

That was when Isobel's patience snapped. The fire in her belly leapt high and the flames licked at the edges of her self-control. She stalked forward. She kicked her boots through the dirt as her rage heightened with every step. The gathered men parted and allowed her to get through.

Santa Anna's lifeless stare found her, and for a moment, the camp fell away. It was just her and him. Her eyes met the fire-lit glower of the devil's own specter, the wicked demon who'd unleashed hellfire on Texas. Her chest heaved as she stopped a step away, close enough to see the faint sheen of sweat on his brow despite his defiant mask.

"You piece of filth!" she spat, her voice trembling with fury as it poured out of her. "Look out on that field!" Her arm shot out, pointing toward the brutal landscape of the battlefield, where men and boys still rotted beneath the sun. "Behold what you've done. Hundreds of sons, husbands, and fathers lay rottin' in the sun 'cause of you. You put Texas to the torch and launched a conflagration for the ages."

Santa Anna's mask held, but Isobel saw a flicker in his black eyes. He couldn't look at her wrath.

She pressed forward, and her words pounded him like a sledgehammer. "You turned us into murderers!" Her words cracked, but she didn't stop. "You put a rage in our hearts that spilled onto this field without mercy. *You* did that! And now? Now you sit there, smug and untouchable, because you're our ransom."

Her hands gripped the blood-stained sleeves of her dress, fingers curling into the leather like talons. "You might think you're the Napoleon of the West, but you ain't. You're nothin' but plain trash."

Almonte flinched as uncertainty cast a shadow over his once steady face. He looked from her to Sam, then fell back to the captive dictator, as though waiting for someone to tell him what to do.

"*Tell him!*" Isobel exploded and rounded on Almonte. Her voice rang out, fierce as a whip crack. "Tell that trash what we think of him."

The camp held its breath. Isobel didn't move, didn't blink, her eyes locked on Almonte, then back to Santa Anna. If her words were all she had to fight with, she'd let him choke on them.

And still, the dictator said nothing. His face carved of stone, revealed no cracks. But Isobel didn't care. She'd seen the truth. Her fury was a hot coal, and it had blistered him.

Almonte leaned in, his words a soft murmur against the stillness, their meaning reserved for Santa Anna alone. Isobel's sharp eyes didn't miss the change. The dictator's shoulders stiffened, his jaw went hard, and the smug mask slipped just enough to reveal the man beneath. He was the man who'd burned the bodies of heroes on a common brush pile. He was the man who'd buried souls and their dreams in unmarked graves.

His dark eyes narrowed and locked onto her like a predator, but she didn't draw back. Let him glare. *Let him know who stared back and didn't blink.*

He spoke low, a quiet hiss of Spanish, brimming with something spiny and venomous.

Isobel's pulse thrummed. Her fists curled at her sides. "What did he say?" she snapped.

Almonte straightened. His mouth opened to speak, but he faltered mid-sentence, caught off guard by the fire in her words. "He said he does not like—"

"I don't give a Tennessee mare's road apple 'bout what he likes!" Isobel's yell rang out like a shot, every syllable jagged and sharp. She took a step forward as her boots ground into the dirt, her eyes boring into Santa Anna's. "Nobody 'round here cares what he likes or don't like."

The space between them crackled with something raw, something dangerous, and it surged up in Isobel like a spark looking for flame. It was a fury so fierce it tore at her ribs, demanding to be unleashed. Her hand dropped to the worn leather handle of her knife. She ran her fingers over the hilt and lifted the knife in its sheath.

Santa Anna's gaze flickered to her hand, and his stare widened a fraction. She followed his eyes to her knife. *Good.* Satisfaction twisted sharp in her breast. For the first time, she saw it in his face. *Fear.*

Almonte stumbled through his translation as he faltered. Isobel could scarcely hear him. Her mind spun, racing over memories she'd shoved deep into the darkness of her heart. She could see Buck's saddlebags with the dominoes tucked inside, Jim's blade gleaming bright, and Angelina's tavern reduced to smoking embers. Faces, laughter, and lives lost or changed because of the man in front of her.

Her hand flew from her knife to the small leather pouch at her waist. Her fingers found the coins, cold and heavy against her palm. With a flick of her wrist, the two *pesos* spun through the air. Silver flashed in the morning light before striking the dictator's face with a metallic snap.

The sound echoed, and silence followed. Santa Anna jerked back and blinked as the mask of indifference broke for just an instant.

Isobel's voice rose, trembling with the raw edge of grief and delirium. "Susannah Dickinson told me to bring back your blood money." She took another step toward him with her hand on the knife. She was close enough to see the sweat gathered at his brow. "She knew I'd lay eyes on you. And she said...she *begged* me to throw those *pesos* in your face before I killed you." Her words came fast, then her hand tugged at the blade. She didn't look away from him. Didn't back down.

The camp was silent. No one moved. Isobel could feel every eye on her and her knife. She could sense the encumbrance of their grief and anger as it pressed against her back like a thousand hands. Her chest heaved as she stared the Mexican *generalissimo* down, and dared him to speak, to move, to answer for what he'd done.

But the tyrant said nothing. The coins lay at his feet where they'd fallen, two small tokens of the contempt everyone had for him.

Isobel held his glare a moment longer, then straightened, her grip loosening on her knife. The fire inside still burned hot, but she stepped back, shoulders squared, chin high.

For now, he would live. Texas needed him alive. But she wanted him to know, to feel, that the faces of every man, every woman, every child who'd suffered at his hands were still watching. And they would not forget.

Isobel spun on her heels, her steps firm and quick as she marched away from the camp and its wicked burden. Her vision blurred, feverish tears streaking down her cheeks like fire. The rage thundered deep within her, a pounding rhythm she couldn't silence. Santa Anna's face, his arrogance, and indifference burned into her mind, fueling the storm swirling inside her.

Her pace quickened as if she could outrun it, but the tears only came harder. They soaked into the neckline of her blood-stained dress. She didn't stop.

Then came the sound of footsteps behind her, light but deliberate. *Kelvin.* She gritted her teeth, ready to snap, ready to send him away and beg him to leave her be. *Just for a minute.*

She whirled around as her fury flared hot on her face. She froze.

It wasn't Kelvin.

Colonel Almonte stood a foot or two away, his dark features calm, his posture straight but softened. Not the rigid form of a professional soldier, but something closer to a man. "Pardon me, *señora*. May I have a word?"

Isobel blinked tears from her eyes. Her chest heaved as she swallowed the sobs that threatened to choke her. Every fiber of her being screamed for him to go away, to let her breathe. But her promise and

Susannah Dickinson's faint whisper shoved its way forward. *If you see Colonel Almonte, speak to him.* She bowed slightly and swiped at the tears on her cheeks.

He stepped closer, though he kept a respectful distance. "I saw what you did yesterday." He paused. "At the bog."

The words sent a jolt through her. She forced herself to meet his eyes. There was no mockery there, no smugness. She saw quiet sincerity.

"I wanted to thank you in person." He looked at the tears in her eyes and on her face. "And tell you how much you mean to the young men you saved." The significance of his message lingered between them. "I know it was difficult."

Isobel gasped as the memories surged. She saw mud-slicked bodies and heard screams of terror. "Colonel, we first noted your name while we were in Gonzales." Her eyes caught his, searching for something, but she didn't know what. "Mrs. Susannah Dickinson told us you saved her life and the lives of the other Alamo survivors."

Almonte gave a grave dip of his chin. "I took no pleasure in our victory at the Alamo. The Texians fought with distinction. They were fierce and brave to the last man." He looked past her, toward the horizon. "We lost many *soldados* there, too."

Her anger raged like wildfire, and sympathy was rain she couldn't let fall. "This whole mess was so unnecessary, Colonel." Her throat was still raw. "We were makin' good progress negotiatin' for self-governance in our own state under Mexican rule. But Santa Anna." Her outrage flared bright again. "Snake that he is, switched sides in the civil war and vowed death to anyone opposing him."

Almonte carried the burden of a man who had seen too much. "Civil war is terrible, *señora*. My country suffers every day because of it. Just because I wish for peace and prosperity does not make it so. Regardless of what happens, our countries will always be neighbors. Only a fool would make an enemy of his neighbor."

Isobel's heart still thundered from her outburst. *Only a fool.* "Santa Anna is that fool, Colonel. I recognized your handwriting on the note from the ferry man. That was the most arrogant and foolish thing I ever did see. When General Houston read it, we knew Santa Anna was all but defeated."

Almonte's brow lifted a touch. "As you can imagine, I lobbied for him to leave no message, but he would not hear of it." He looked at her then, his dark eyes unreadable. "General Houston is right to fear our troops in the field. They are not hobbled with such foolishness. They would never take up a position on a peninsula with that muddy lake behind them."

Isobel narrowed her eyes as her mind whirled with the implications of his words. "Would they obey an order to get outta Texas if Santa Anna issued it?"

Almonte hesitated for an instant. "I believe they would. The army did not want this fight in the first place."

The quiet truth of it settled like a stone on her chest. She blinked and stared past him for a moment as the fury inside her began to ebb. It left a strange hollowness in its wake. *Didn't want this fight?* And yet so many were dead. *Ours. Theirs. All the same in the end.*

A long silence stretched between them, broken by the wind in the bayou reeds and the distant shouts of men back in camp. Isobel rubbed her damp cheeks with the heel of her hand. The tears were gone now, but they left behind the sting of their passing. Her voice dropped softer and quieter. "Buck Travis, Jim Bowie, my husband, and I all enjoyed playin' dominoes and chattin' 'bout the goings-on and politics, Colonel. I reckon you would've had a fine time with us on those evenings."

For the first time, something flashed across his face. Regret, maybe, or something like it. "Thank you for that, *señora*. Under different circumstances, we could have been friends."

Isobel's heart was a strange tangle of anger, sorrow, and something she didn't quite know how to name. There were unspoken truths that lingered like smoke on the wind. "Colonel, would ya mind escortin' me back to General Houston? He's probably wonderin' where we got off to by now."

Almonte dipped his head in polite acknowledgement. "Of course, *señora.*" He extended his arm, an old-world gesture that surprised her in its gentility.

"My name is Isobel MacDonald."

"*Con mucho gusto, Señora* MacDonald." He spoke calmly and guided her over uneven earth back towards the oak tree.

An Anglo woman stood there and gestured with frantic motions as she talked to Sam. Their opinions rose and fell in a spirited exchange. They were haggling about something.

"Madam, please slow down and tell me about your business." Sam looked tired.

"My name's Peggy McCormick. This here's my land."

Sam tilted his head, an eyebrow raised as though he were trying to make sense of her attitude. "Good for you, ma'am. You're the owner of land now sacred to Texas. I reckon folks from all over will come to see where the 'Napoleon of the West' met his Waterloo."

Peggy was sharp. "I don't care about all that nonsense. There's hundreds of bodies litterin' my fields and my lake."

"Does the lake have a name?" Sam frowned, his face weary.

"*Peggy's Lake,* of course." Peggy threw up her hands like she couldn't fathom his ignorance.

Sam pulled her back with a shrug. "What am I supposed to do? As you can see, I ain't got much to work with. I dare say there's not a spade among us."

"General."

Isobel turned to see a tall figure step forward.

Secretary of War Rusk looked grim. "General, we got about four or five hundred prisoners. Only four men guardin' 'em. Their unburied dead *amigos* are rilin' 'em up."

"Colonel Rusk, you saw yesterday what untrained militia are capable of. We barely controlled the men durin' the battle and had no control at all at," he paused, glancing at the upset woman, "*Peggy's Lake.* If the prisoners get riled up, their tormentors will kill 'em and Mrs. McCormick here will have even more corpses on her land."

Peggy's face flushed redder. "What are you gonna to do about all these stinkin' bodies on my land?"

Sam didn't even blink. "Nothing whatsoever."

Everything went still as Sam pushed on.

"This maniac." Sam jabbed a finger toward Santa Anna without looking at him. "This maniac left four hundred good men in a field at Goliad where he murdered 'em. If we didn't return the favor, our own maniacs would kill the rest of the *Méxicanos*." He drew a slow, heavy breath. "Maybe sometime down the line, the Mexican government can come back and take care of their dead. But for now, I close the matter."

Isobel and Almonte exchanged glances. Unease rippled through her. *Do nothin'?* Maybe Sam was right, but the thought of those bodies, hundreds of them, left to rot churned her stomach.

"General, may I have a word?"

The soft inquiry broke through the tension, as she turned and saw Lieutenant Lorenzo de Zavala, Jr., step forward.

"Aye." Sam shifted his weight against the tree.

De Zavala cleared his throat. "My father wishes for you to release the remains of Mexican General Manuel Castrillón to us. Our plots are here, and he wants me to bury the general with our family."

Sam said, "See to it. General Castrillón served with honor."

Almonte stepped forward, his words softer than Isobel had heard yet. "General, with your approval, I will assist Lieutenant de Zavala."

Sam held Almonte's regard for a long moment, and something unspoken passed between them. Then he gave a tired salute. "You may assist. I gotta thank you for lettin' your servant escort the ladies and children from *Béxar*. I also appreciate the note that proved *El Presidente's* undoing. My compliments, Colonel."

Almonte inclined his head. "*Gracias*, sir, I remain at your service."

Isobel stood in silence as her glance bounced between the two men. She turned and gestured to Kelvin, who had lingered nearby. "Kel, come meet the colonel."

Kelvin strode over and wiped his hands on his pants before offering Almonte a respectful salute. Introductions were made as the small group, Isobel, Kelvin, Almonte, and de Zavala, headed toward the ruins of the Mexican camp.

As they walked, the crunch of grass and ash beneath their boots seemed too loud in the heavy silence. Isobel's thoughts drifted, unbidden, to General Castrillón. She could still see him as a distinguished gentleman, arms crossed, back straight, and he stood alone beside the cannon. The picture of defiance. Even with the odds stacked against him, he hadn't wavered, and somehow that had stayed with her. When she pictured dignity, she saw him.

In the doomed camp, the tart bite of smoke still held on. Together, the little group retrieved the remains, moving with care and silence as though the man's spirit still remained in the ruins. They loaded his body onto the wagon and made their way to the ferry for the general's last journey to the de Zavala home.

After the crossing, Isobel checked on the wounded in the makeshift hospital. She learned nine Texians died in the battle. Nine dreams, nine futures sacrificed on the altar of liberty. She bowed her head as the meager band passed the remains of the Texian dead. Her lips moved in silent prayer. *Lord, hold their families close. Hold their hearts close. And help me remember what my freedom cost, so I can be worthy of it.*

When she lifted her head again, the horizon stretched wide, gold, and green under the endless Texas sky. Despite the victory and the hope that rose like the dawn, Peggy's Lake wouldn't leave her. The murky water where blood mingled with mud was a scene she reckoned would always be in her mind.

Texas is born. What's been paid in blood will build somethin' new. Somethin' good.

Her view shifted to Almonte, who walked beside her with quiet respect, and the thought pushed to her lips before she could stop it. "Colonel, I sure hope we can be friends. I believe our countries will be inseparable as neighbors. If men like you come into power, I can see great partnerships ahead."

Almonte turned to look at her and his eyes softened. "*Sí, señora.*" He paused and considered his words. "I agree. I believe my country has not lost a state but has gained a partner."

"Well said, Colonel." Kelvin was brighter than he had been all week.

Almonte offered a slight smile before he tilted his head. There was something curious in his expression. "I have but one question."

Isobel arched an eyebrow, surprised. "What is it?"

"May I know." His way was as formal as ever. "What is a *road apple*?"

For a heartbeat, there was silence as his question floated through the air. Then it hit her.

She slapped her hand over her mouth, but a giggle burst free before she could catch it. Kelvin doubled over and shook with laughter. His shoulders unwound as he let go of all the burdens he'd carried for months.

Almonte blinked, but his confusion deepened the hilarity of it all.

Isobel wiped her eyes as she laughed, the sound was raw and bright like the first crack of sunlight after a storm. She peeked at Kelvin and their eyes met. Both their faces lit with something unspoken. Something hidden until now. *Hope.*

Maybe, just maybe, there was hope after all.

EPILOGUE

April 23, 1836
Remnants of Santa Anna's Legion Headquarters
Lynch's Ferry, Republic of Texas

"What exactly are we lookin' for?" Kelvin's question broke through the smoke as his eyes skimmed over shattered equipment left to ruin. He stepped around the bodies. *Soldados muertos.*

Isobel rubbed her eyes. Did she even know? The words came out soft, almost unsure. "I'll know it when I see it."

He stopped and turned toward her, his brow furrowing. "This about *Isobel's Song*? The one you keep hearin'?"

Her spirit sagged beneath a burden she couldn't name. "Stronger than it's ever been."

"Well, we oughtta retrace your footsteps if we wanna figure it out." He was steady, even as the macabre scene around them clawed at the edges of their sanity.

She let him lead for a while as her mind pulled back to the bloody scene. They reached the Mexican cannon, its muzzle darkened with the memories of the battle. Her heart softened as her thoughts turned to General Castrillón. He was so dignified, even in his final moments. They moved onward to Santa Anna's tent, now a pathetic heap of red and white shreds.

"I was headed there," Isobel murmured and stared at the remnants. "I saw him, Santa Anna, run right in front of me, but I didn't know it at the time. I let him go." Her jaw tightened at the memory as shame prickled her skin.

Kelvin carried a load of considerations. "I've been thinkin' about that, y'know. If one of us had caught him... it might've led to somethin' worse."

She turned to him confused. "Worse? How do you figure?"

He pointed to the pile of canvas rags. "Look at his tent. Look at General Castrillón. If we'd netted Santa Anna that day, they'd have done him the same way. And then what? No leverage. No surrender. Just more bloodshed."

Isobel lifted her eyebrows. "You think God spared him? Kept him alive for this moment?"

"Seems like it." Kelvin scanned the broken camp. "Any Mexican soldier still breathin' oughtta be countin' his blessin's. Maybe even a miracle."

The words stuck with her as they walked toward Peggy's Lake. Mosquitoes buzzed thick in the humidity, but neither of them cared. The pests didn't notice them. The brackish brine came into view, a grim reflection of that day's horrors. Isobel's steps slowed, and she closed her eyes. *Lord, I don't know why I'm here, but I'm listenin'.*

"This is where I stopped." She pointed to the water. "The music... The music pulled me here. To the edge."

Kelvin looked at her. "You heard the fiddle music? *Isobel's Song?*"

She inclined her head. "Same melody. During the battle, during the slaughter, it was so loud. Louder than the screams or the gunfire. It carried me here, and I...I told them to stop. I told them to stop in Jesus's name. I don't know why I said it. It just came out."

"Can you hum the tune?"

Her head moved from side to side, a quiet rejection. "I can't hum the tune alone. It fades when I try. I can't bring it to life by myself. I can only follow where it leads."

Kelvin scratched the back of his head and gazed into the pond. "Sounds to me like you were meant to stop it, Belle. Save lives. Show the mercy of God."

She scanned the water's edge. Her heart ached as her eye caught a lifeless form. He was a boy, just old enough to fight. His body was half-submerged. He clutched a worn sack beneath him. Grief rippled through her as she imagined a mother somewhere in Mexico, who waited for a son who would never return.

The image didn't rise from memory; it came from someplace outside herself. She saw the boy, running barefoot in the golden fields, laughter spilling from him as sunlight crowned his shoulders. And just beyond the edge of it, the faint strain of fiddle music moved through the wheat like breath from heaven. It shimmered with Truth, too vivid to be imagined. *Lord, is this a vision?* Was the Fiddler lifting the veil, letting her glimpse a land where there were no more tears and joy would rise like morning wheat?

Then she heard a melody. A tune, faint but distinct. Different this time. Not the haunting melody from the battle or the vision, but something...older. Familiar.

"I hear it." She trembled, managing a whisper. "Another tune. Not *Isobel's Song.* Do you hear it, Kel?"

He let out a sigh, his face clouding with concern. "No, Belle."

Her eyes locked on the sack beneath the boy's still form. "It's comin' from *there.*" She pointed. "That bag." There was something oddly familiar about the sack.

Kelvin moved with care and knelt beside the boy. His eyes softened. "He was so young."

She swallowed hard. The words scraped their way out. "They didn't have any choice. Santa Anna sent them here to die. He cared less for them than he did for us. At least... at least some of them made it."

With gentle hands, Kelvin slid the sack from under the lad's body. "This it?"

The moment cracked wide open.

The tune rose in her mind, not imagined, not conjured—it was *given*. Clear as day, the music swept through her like light through stained glass. Her heart skipped. Her eyes drifted closed.

And there he was.

Not Kelvin. Not a soldier.

A tall man stood in a patch of Tennessee clover, a fiddle in his hands, the long-ago melody pouring from the strings. The bow danced with joy. He turned toward her—*her*—with a booming laugh that scattered every shadow in her young heart.

I remember.

She wasn't dreaming. This *had* happened. Long ago. And now, somehow, God had opened His hand and placed the memory right in front of her like a gift pulled from eternity.

I remember.

She quivered with anticipation. "Open it."

Kelvin loosened the drawstring and peeked inside. His face lit with recognition.

The bygone tune wrapped itself around her heart. "Pull it out."

He lifted the fiddle with a steady hand and held it up to the light. She already knew what he'd find. "Turn it over." Her words were soft like a gentle rain. "There'll be two initials."

His fingers traced the back of the instrument. *"D. C."*

Tears welled in her eyes as the harmony filled her mind, stronger now. She saw him again, the tall man who'd played for her. She saw his old fiddle. *I remember. I remember him.*

Kelvin's eyes glistened as he held the instrument close. "It was meant for you, Belle. All of it."

She could see the tall man as he twirled her in his arms when she was just a little girl. She heard the old melody, a happy mountain tune. She heard his voice echo across the years. *How 'bout a big ole Tennessee squeeze that'll last 'til we meet again.*

ACKNOWLEDGMENTS

Novels do not have footnotes, but that doesn't mean scholars and authors should go unrecognized. The 1929 Pulitzer Prize winning book, *The Raven*, by Marquis James is always the go-to book for anyone interested in Texas history. James Haley's *Sam Houston* is an updated and scholarly version like *The Raven* that is a must for any student of Texas History. McMurry University in Abilene, Texas, is fortunate to possess the "Dean of Texas History": Dr. Stephen L. Hardin. Dr. Hardin approved my using his maps in the book.

The staff at the San Jacinto Battlefield State Park scheduled a lecturer from the Texas Supreme Court Historical Society, Mr. David Furlow, to speak about the Scottish/Celtic traditions that influenced Texas History. I came to a similar conclusion, and when I heard Mr. Furlow confirm everything I learned, it was very encouraging. The information about Cowpens, Culloden, King's Mountain, and San Jacinto comes from that lecture.

As Americans, we are fortunate to have an army of volunteers, museum attendants, librarians, guides, reenactors, researchers, clerks, and rangers to help any of us with a project. The people who spend their days scanning historical documents into our digital records are unsung heroes. The next time you want to find out the exact address of the Galveston Bay and Texas Land Company in New York, you can thank a digital archivist at Yale University Library. That person scanned a newspaper ad into the record. I found that anyone working at any museum or historical park was eager to help. Don't keep a question to yourself!

Not everyone is fortunate enough to be married to a retired 7th

Grade English teacher. My wife, Becky, brought her red pen out of retirement and bled on the book. That was time consuming on her part and I am very appreciative of it.

My sister and brother were the first beta readers. They suggested other changes after the English teacher's bloodwork. That was very nice of them.

The Blue Ridge Christian Writers Conference is the home of many friends and colleagues who weave tales and the Gospel together for a broken world. One of those friends is my editor, Alycia W. Morales. She mentored me in the art of writing Christian fiction. She marked passages for me to change or delete. Her contributions are far too numerous for me to detail here, but all of them are treasured by me.

The final editor is called a "line editor" or "proofreader." Ashley Johnson took the manuscript and found typographaical errors, misspellings, extra commas, wrong words, missing quotation marks, etc. Until one actually writes a 100,000 word manuscript, it is impossible to imagine all the ways there are to mess it up. Any mistakes in the manuscript are mine alone.

Finally, my grandson, Lincoln, assisted me in our research trips. We traveled from the Alamo and "Come and Take It" battle sites in South Texas to the Hermitage in Nashville. We saw Washington on the Brazos, Independence, Baylor University, and the Texas Ranger Museum. We learned many amazing things the staff of each stop was eager to share. It would have been a lonely ride without him.

ABOUT THE AUTHOR

Daryl Lott is a history geek. He studied Texas history at Texas Tech University and received his B.A. in Historical Studies from the University of Houston—Clear Lake. He earned his M.A. in Humanities at California State University—Dominguez Hills. He is certified by the State Board of Teacher Certification for the State of Texas to teach Texas, American, and World History in grades six through twelve. He served as a history and English teacher in the Pasadena Independent School District, Pasadena, Texas. He is honorably retired from the Houston Police Department, having served for thirty-three years.

Daryl is a graduate of Liberty University's Bible Institute and teaches Bible study at his local church.

The Christian worldview presented in this work is exceptional, but it's hoped that you saw your own spiritual struggles and rewards in it. The author makes no claim to speak for God. It is difficult to document a spiritual struggle like Isobel experiences without presenting some form of the Holy Trinity's representation. Angels, visions, dreams, and the like are mysterious. In the final analysis, all traditional Christians believe in the supernatural forces of God at work in the world and in our souls.

Daryl is also a proud member of the Sons of the Republic of Texas, a fraternal organization whose members can prove their lineal ancestry to the era of the Republic.

BE ON THE LOOKOUT

If you enjoyed this book, please go to the site where you purchased it and leave an honest review. Many people ask me what they can do to help, and leaving an honest review is the most beneficial thing you can do outside of spreading the word.

If you want to read more of the continuing adventures of Isobel and Kelvin, look out for the next volume in the series. Please go to my website: www.faithfultexasfootprints.com to connect with me and to stay informed about the release dates of the next books.

www.ingramcontent.com/pod-product-compliance
Lightning Source LLC
Chambersburg PA
CBHW021527250626
47154CB00006BA/2003